Will Amanda follow her heart...

or renew her vow to another?

Walker's Point

Walker's Point

MARILEE DUNKER

BETHANY HOUSE PUBLISHERS
MINNEAPOLIS, MINNESOTA 55438

Walker's Point
Copyright © 1997
Marilee Dunker

Cover illustration by William Graf

Published by Bethany House Publishers
A Ministry of Bethany Fellowship, Inc.
11300 Hampshire Avenue South
Minneapolis, Minnesota 55438

Printed in the United States of America.

Library of Congress Cataloging-in-Publication Data

CIP Data applied for

ISBN 1–55661–997–9   CIP

To Mama,

who taught me that God loves me
and has a special plan for my life.

🙐 🙐 🙐 🙐

To Bob,

who lovingly releases me to be all
God has called me to be.

🙐 🙐 🙐 🙐

To Michelle and Stacey,

my greatest blessings and joy!

Portraits

The Balcony

Blind Faith

Endangered

Entangled

Framed

Gentle Touch

Heaven's Song

Impasse

Masquerade

Montclair

Morningsong

Shroud of Silence

Stillpoint

Walker's Point

MARILEE DUNKER is the author of *A Braver Song to Sing* and *Man of Vision, Woman of Prayer*, which won an Angel Award for its warm, honest depiction of her family's trials and triumphs. Marilee is a frequent seminar speaker and has been featured on a number of popular Christian radio and television programs. She and her husband have two grown daughters and live in California.

One

*T*he first time Amanda ran away from home, she was five years old. She emptied her baby doll's suitcase, carefully hiding the doll clothes under her bed, and replaced them with two pairs of her own clean underpants, socks, her favorite shirt, and—because she was the "responsible" child in the family—a toothbrush. She emptied her piggy bank of its three-dollar-and-thirty-six-cent treasure and slipped out the back door while her mom was on the telephone with her aunt Marge.

Exactly why she had chosen that particular moment to step out of character and "pull a Lindsey," as her parents would later put it, in honor of her older sister who was constantly getting into trouble, Amanda never could quite remember. But she vividly recalled the way her heart pounded and her blood raced as she took off down the street, pigtails flying, nervously glancing over her shoulder to make sure no one was chasing after her. It was a heady feeling, all that freedom . . . knowing she could do what she wanted without having to ask permission. It was also deliciously scary, like going through a haunted house at Halloween.

Eventually, after three ice cream cones and a leisurely stroll through the park, where she fed the ducks and climbed to the very top of an old oak tree without "breaking her neck," as her mother always warned she would whenever she got too high, Amanda couldn't think of anything else to do with her newfound freedom. So, cold and hungry, she had gone home to face her mother's tearful relief and her father's stern lecture on the dangers that await foolish little girls who wander away from home. Her punishment had been bed without supper and no *Mickey Mouse Club* for one whole week! It had been a high price to pay, but for two and a half glorious hours one day in 1955, little Amanda Rose Mitchell had been the master of her fate!

Now, twenty-five years later, Amanda was feeling that same heady rush of adrenaline and sense of anticipation as she packed her suitcase, adding floss and toothpaste to the toothbrush she'd already laid out. Of course, she wasn't really running away from home. The trip to New York was strictly business. Her employer, Laura Stanley, had walked into the antique shop the week before and handed her a ticket, saying she needed her new assistant to go with her on her yearly buying trip. Nick hadn't been thrilled with the idea, but he had swallowed his objections when he saw the eager, pleading look in his wife's eyes. Maybe a few days away would be good for her and she'd come home cured of the moody restlessness that had been plaguing her for months now, often making him feel as though he were living with a stranger.

So Amanda Kelly was packing. And tomorrow morning she and Laura would catch a nine-thirty flight out of LAX, two business-women off to the big city to do what they do best: shop! It would be the first time in over ten years that Amanda would function not as a wife or a mother or a daughter but simply as a person, and the very idea sent icy fingers of anticipation down her spine once again.

"Mommy! Help! . . . Stop it, Casey! . . . Mommy, come quick! Casey keeps splashing me and squirting me with Blue Goo! . . . Stop!"

A huge crash followed by the sound of water splashing all over the bathroom floor brought Amanda firmly back to the present. Tomorrow she might be a sophisticated traveler off to exotic places and new adventures, but tonight she was simply Kimberly and Casey's mommy—a job that often took the patience of Job, the wisdom of Solomon, and the diplomacy of Henry Kissinger.

"Kim, quit yelling. I'm here." Amanda walked into the war zone and quickly appraised the damage. Two little girls sat in the oversized claw-footed bathtub. Daughter One looked pathetic, eyes watering, mouth puckered in outrage, hair hanging in her face dripping water and Blue Goo. Obviously the victim.

Daughter Two, back turned and head bowed, was industriously scrubbing the dirt from between her shriveled, waterlogged toes. Incriminating flecks of Blue Goo dotted her arms and hands. The per-petrator.

"Casey, look at me."

Innocence personified looked up with eyebrows arched and eyes widened in surprise to see her mother standing there. It was such a good performance that Amanda had to bite the inside of her mouth to keep from laughing.

"All right, look, you guys. This has got to stop. I don't know why you always beg to take baths together when you end up fighting every time." A duet of accusations and denials was quickly cut off. "I honestly don't care who did what to whom or who started it. All I know is I am tired of the constant fighting . . . and the constant cleanup."

Amanda looked around the bathroom she had scrubbed to a spotless sheen only hours before. The floor was nearly underwater, at least four clean towels now lay in sodden heaps, and the walls and mirrors were speckled with Blue Goo. In exasperation she turned first to her older daughter.

"Kimberly, you're a big girl now. You need to stop letting your little sister push your buttons so easily. She only does it because you make it so much fun for her with your screaming and yelling. And, Casey," she said, lifting her younger daughter's chin to make direct eye contact, "the next time you try to turn your sister into a giant Smurf, I will personally turn your bottom into a little red tomato. Do we understand each other?"

A solemn nod was followed by a relieved smile and a smacking kiss.

"Now, tell your sister you're sorry and help her get that goo out of her hair. Then the two of you get out of the tub, brush your teeth, and get into your nightgowns without any more trouble. And maybe, just maybe, I'll still read to you before you go to bed."

Amanda picked up the soggy towels and laid out dry ones for the girls to use. As she headed for the laundry room she could hear the girls laughing, their recent dispute already forgotten. After depositing the towels in the washing machine, she continued to the back of the house, where Nick had converted a service porch into a small office. She found him exactly where she knew he would be, sitting at his drafting desk, pencil in hand, lost in a paper mire of blueprints and sketches.

She stood for a moment watching him, knowing that behind the furrowed brow and darting eyes a whole building was being constructed, torn down, and redesigned as he studied the lines and angles that would someday be a five-story medical building on Lake Street in South Pasadena. His intensity was almost palpable as she watched him searching for possible problems or ways to improve or streamline his design. This was the biggest project he had been given since he became a junior partner with the architectural firm of Morris and Shea nearly four years ago, and it had to be better than good. It was his chance to finally prove himself and move ahead of the group of talented, hardworking hopefuls he competed with every day.

"If I pull this off I'm almost guaranteed a full partnership. After that, it won't be so hard," he would often reassure her when he had to work late or cancel a family outing so he could work on the weekend.

She understood that this was a pivotal time in his career and that by working hard now he was in fact loving her and the girls by insuring their future together. But lately it had been harder and harder for her to accept the trade-off. There had been a time when she could walk into a crowded room and know that, wherever Nick was, he would sense her presence within seconds and seek her out. Now she stood in the doorway, not four feet away, and he didn't even know she was there.

"Hi." Amanda knocked softly.

"Hi," Nick replied, giving Amanda a distracted half smile before continuing with what he was doing. "What was all the commotion?"

"Just the usual. Bath time."

"Ah. Any casualties?"

"Well, the white towels your cousin Augusta gave us for our tenth wedding anniversary are now a lovely shade of blue. The same color as your elder daughter's hair the last time I looked. But other than that, I think everything's okay."

Amanda thought the line about blue hair deserved at least a raised eyebrow, but all she got was an obligatory "That's good."

"Nick, we really need to talk and go over the schedule I made up for you. I'm worried that I may have left something out and—"

"Don't worry about it. Your mom's going to be here."

"Yes, but she's going to need your help. We can't expect her to handle the girls all on her own. And on Wednesday she has that doctor's appointment, so you're going to have to pick the girls up from school. And on Thursday you've *got* to be home early to take Kimberly to piano 'cause Mom will be at gymnastics with Casey."

"Amanda, we've been over this at least ten times. I'll cover it. Don't worry." The second "don't worry" was strongly punctuated, although he still hadn't turned to look at her.

"Okay," she responded, knowing it was time to back off but not able to. "I'm sorry. It's just that the last time you said you'd pick up the girls, you were nearly an hour late. I just don't want you to get busy and forget or something."

Now she had his attention. He turned to look at her with an exasperated expression. "Amanda, don't start with this. Yes, I messed up once and I felt terrible about it. I feel terrible about it *every* time you bring it up!"

Amanda's gaze faltered and she started to gnaw her lower lip, a habit she had when she was feeling angry, worried, or guilty. Right now she was all three.

"Look," Nick continued, "I'll do the very best I can, but your leaving right now is not exactly good timing. . . . You know that. And if you are worried that your mom and I can't handle things while you're gone, then maybe you just shouldn't go."

Amanda nearly bit through her lip to keep from answering back with the angry words that came to mind. Her eyes teared and her hands curled into tight fists. How had this happened? She hadn't come in here to fight. But it seemed that even the most simple conversations turned into arguments these days, and a good part of the time she knew it was her fault. Like Casey with Kimberly, she knew how to push Nick's buttons, and sometimes she just couldn't keep from saying too much or pushing too hard. At least when they argued she had his undivided attention.

"Look, sweetheart, I didn't mean that," Nick said, rubbing his hands over his face. "I'm just tired and under the gun right now. I know how much this trip means to you, and I want you to go. Everything will be fine here . . . I promise on me sainted Aunt Brigette." He finished the sentence in a thick Irish accent, giving Amanda an impish smile and wink that made her laugh and broke the tension.

"You don't have a sainted Aunt Brigette," Amanda teased back, moving to take his extended hand and sit on his lap.

"Don't be so sure, me girl," he continued, sounding as though he'd just stepped off the boat from County Clare. "In a family as long and illustrious as mine, there surely had to be a sainted Brigette some-where along the line!''

By this time Amanda was giggling like a young girl, and Nick was taking husbandly liberties, nuzzling her neck and running his hands over whatever soft bare skin he could find.

''How about an ice cream break later on? You get the girls to bed, I'll finish up here, and we'll rendezvous in the bedroom.''

Early in their marriage they had gotten into the habit of taking huge bowls of ice cream to bed. While they ate they would talk . . . dreaming, planning, laughing, and eventually making love. They al-ways claimed that Kimberly was their chocolate chip baby, but on the night Casey was conceived they had been crazy enough to mix mocha almond fudge with pistachio rum. ''We should have known we were playing with fire!'' Nick would joke with friends, referring to his par-ticularly fiery-tempered and precocious younger daughter.

Of course, all this talk was not lost on the little ears that heard it. Once, when Kimberly was about five, Amanda had overheard her talk-ing with a friend about how babies are born. ''Well,'' she had confided knowingly, ''first you eat ice cream.''

Amanda took extra time tucking her daughters into bed. She had agreed to read one bedtime story for every night she was going to miss during the coming week, and now she sat on Kim's bed watching patiently as the girls pored over the neatly arranged bookshelves, con-ferring, arguing, removing one book only to put it back when another favorite caught their eye, trying to come up with the ultimate six books. Their attention momentarily diverted, she was free to feast her eyes on the amazing creatures she had given birth to.

Dressed in matching lace-trimmed granny gowns, faces scrubbed, their long hair brushed and free from any signs of Blue Goo, they looked like escaped angels. Amanda felt her heart fill with such love and tenderness, she had to literally squeeze herself in a tight hug to keep it from bursting. She noted with some surprise how much taller Kim was than her younger sister. At eight she was already starting to shoot up, her baby fat nearly gone, replaced by the long, slender arms and legs that meant she would take after her mother.

Casey, who was counting the days until her sixth birthday, was still all softness and ''pudge,'' as Nick used to call it when he would throw her on the bed and blow bubbles into her tummy, filling the house with her squeals of delight. It was too early to tell if she would take after her mom or be lucky enough to inherit the more voluptuous curves that ran in her father's family. But either way, Nick never had to worry that his girls would ever be mistaken for someone else's. They both had been blessed with the Kelly hair . . . Kimberly's dancing on the edge of strawberry blond and Casey's as fiery as a new copper penny.

Finally satisfied with their book selections, the girls scrambled up on either side of their mother, snuggling as close as flesh and bone would allow, and for the next hour the three were carried away to a world of magical cats in hats, flying horses, and poky little puppies. When the last story had ended "happily ever after," the girls knelt by the bed to say their prayers.

"Now I lay me down to sleep, I pray the Lord my soul to keep. If I should die before I wake, I pray the Lord my soul to take. God bless Mommy, Daddy, Kimmy, Grammy, Grampa . . ." Casey whizzed through the prayer like a pro, barely stopping to take a breath before ending with a grandly flourished "Amen!"

Then it was Kimberly's turn. Amanda hadn't realized how worried Kim was about her trip until she heard the slight tremble in her daughter's voice as she finished her usual "Now I lay me" prayer and started improvising.

"Please, dear Lord, keep my mommy safe. Don't let her get sick or hurt or hit by a car or anything. And please send angels . . . big ones . . . to hold up the plane all the way there. And please, please, bring her home safely! In Jesus' name, amen."

The last came out rushed and self-conscious, as if she suddenly realized how transparent she was being. As the "responsible" child in her family, she wasn't used to letting her own fears or needs take center stage.

Amanda told Casey to get into her own bed while she took a moment to talk with Kim. Taking the soft little body into her arms to give her some extra loving, Amanda was struck by how fragile the child was. As she felt her daughter's arms wrap around her neck, she knew if she hugged her back with the full force of all the love she was feeling, she would squeeze the life right out of her. How hard it was to know how to hold on to your children and yet let go at the same time. It was a constant challenge, one that Amanda took very seriously, praying every day that God would give her strength and wisdom. But lately He seemed as distant as her husband, and she constantly struggled with a growing sense of inadequacy.

By eleven-thirty Amanda's bags stood packed and ready to go by the front door, the bathroom was once more in perfect order, and Amanda was settled in bed savoring the peace and quiet as she waited for Nick to join her. She had called to him as she scooped out two generous helpings of rocky road, their current favorite, and he had called back, "Be right there. Just let me finish this one thing."

That had been nearly a half hour ago. Amanda watched the ice cream start to melt, determined not to eat hers until he came. It had been months since they had indulged themselves this way, maybe longer, and she was surprised at how much she wanted and needed him right now. She considered getting up and going to him, but that would mean leaving her warm bed and walking the entire length of the cold, dark house. The thought of it was just too much.

She snuggled down under the covers and felt her body collapse in exhaustion, literally deflating like an old balloon. Suddenly she had to sleep. It had always been this way. She would go and go, seemingly inexhaustible, and then suddenly she was done. She closed her eyes and was fast asleep within minutes.

She felt him slip into bed sometime after one. She knew he would reach for her, and she turned to him, still half asleep, needing to be needed. His body was cold and he wrapped himself in her warmth. They fit together comfortably, following some ancient ritual that had been born out of time and practice. Sweetly, gently, almost mindlessly, they came together. "I love you," she heard Nick whisper in her ear.

"I love you, too," she automatically responded.

Turning her head, she could see the bowls of ice cream still sitting on the nightstand, melted into soup.

Two

*I*n the morning Nick carried Amanda's suitcases out to the waiting airport limo. It was early and the girls were still asleep. She and Nick embraced, and she was surprised by the urgency she felt in his touch, as though he was suddenly fearful to let her go.

"Don't forget to miss me," he whispered in her ear before giving her one final kiss and releasing her to join Laura in the limousine.

The limo wound its way slowly down the tree-lined streets of Sierra Madre, a sleepy bedroom community nestled in the foothills of the rugged San Gabriel Mountains about thirty minutes southeast of Los Angeles. For once the mountains stood clearly defined against a crystalline blue sky, looking as fresh and new as the day God created them. No smog today!

Amanda stared at the mountains, their rocky grandeur bringing to mind a Scripture her grandfather often quoted: *"I will lift up mine eyes unto the hills, from whence cometh my help."* Then the limousine made a sudden left-hand turn, speeding away from the mountains toward the labyrinth of freeways that would zigzag across the face of Los Angeles and deposit them at the airport.

Eight hours later nature's skyscrapers had been replaced by a forest of glass and steel. New York City! Looking out the window of the speeding taxi as it careened drunkenly in and out of the bumper-to-bumper Manhattan traffic, Amanda felt her pulse quicken with the accelerated heartbeat of the city. The memory of that five-year-old girl came flooding back. She *was* that little girl again . . . excited, expectant, and for some inexplicable reason, slightly apprehensive. She linked arms with the stylishly dressed woman sitting beside her and gave her an affectionate squeeze.

"Laura, I can't believe I'm really here. Yesterday I was knee-deep in Play-Doh and Blue Goo, and today I'm in New York . . . free!" The last word was exhaled in a long, cleansing breath. "I can't remember the last time I went anywhere for more than a night without Nick and the girls . . . not that I won't miss them," she added, needing to balance the intoxicating sense of freedom with a little dutiful guilt. "I just didn't realize how much I needed a break until I felt the plane leave the ground. It was like a dozen strings of tension snapped and I just floated away! Thank you so much for bringing me with you!"

"You're welcome. I'm glad Nick let you come."

Laura Stanley patted Amanda's hand with the sympathetic understanding of a woman who had raised three boys and still remembered what a demanding job it had been. Then she gently but firmly disengaged herself. Outside, the air was crisp and biting, but the taxi they rode in from the airport was like a hothouse, and Laura could hardly wait to reach the hotel and escape its steamy warmth. Rolling down the window a crack, she gazed out at the passing street scene as if noticing it for the first time.

"This city *is* like an elixir," she affirmed, catching some of Amanda's enthusiasm.

"And we're going to drink every drop!" Amanda laughed in anticipation. "I promised my girls I'd go skating at Rockefeller Center, and there are at least two Broadway shows I want to see. And Mom wants a picture of me on the top of the Empire State Building, 'standing right where Cary Grant waited for Deborah Kerr in *An Affair to Remember*,' " she repeated in a perfect imitation of her mother's soft, lilting voice. "Oh, and I promised myself a new outfit from Saks and a sinfully expensive dinner at Tavern on the Green."

"Hold on," Laura laughed, delighted by Amanda's unbridled enthusiasm. "I'm exhausted already and we've only just arrived! We'll certainly try to see as much as we can in the next week, but I hope you won't mind if we do a little business while we're here . . . in between sightseeing and shopping, of course!"

"Just as long as it doesn't interfere with my primary objective!" Amanda teased, turning once again to take in the hustle and bustle outside the window.

"And just what is that?" Laura asked.

"To relax and reacquaint myself with Amanda Rose Kelly . . .

whoever she is," she added a little wistfully.

Laura leaned back and observed the young woman next to her with an affectionate smile. She had been right to bring her. The strained, exhausted look that so often shadowed her face was gone, replaced by a lively eagerness Laura had never seen before.

Amanda had wandered into her shop, Treasures of the Sierra Madre, eight months ago. Just two weeks earlier Laura had moved her small but flourishing antique and decorating business out of its cramped birthplace on a narrow side street into a large, eye-catching storefront right on the old town square. The much-needed room and added exposure gave Laura a chance to expand her business, which had grown gradually by word of mouth over the past ten years, bringing her clients from wealthy areas such as Arcadia, San Marino, and even Beverly Hills.

Laura and Amanda's first meeting had been less than promising. Laura had been busy trying to talk a regular client out of using a pretty but totally impractical white linen on her family room sofa when her ears perked up at the sound of a high-pitched wail. If there was one thing that terrified her, it was a small, unruly child running amuck in her shop, and her eyes searched the store to spot the pint-sized intruder. She found the three-foot culprit backed against a George the Fifth writing table, clinging possessively to a blue glass duck she had decided to take home. Her mother was on her haunches trying to reason with the copper-haired moppet, while a second little girl, who appeared a couple of years older, stood by nervously biting her nails.

"Please, Casey. The duck isn't yours. Mommy told you when we came in that you could look but not touch. Let's put the duck back, and I'll take you for ice cream."

"I don't want ice cream. I want my duck!" the child demanded, stamping her foot and tightening her hold.

"Give me that duck or I'll tell Daddy tonight—and you know what that means!" the young mother threatened, abandoning her attempts to negotiate and pulling out the big guns.

The child's big green eyes brimmed with unspilt tears and her lower lip trembled, but there was still a defiant look on her face as she grudgingly handed her mother the duck. Taking it with an exhausted sigh, it was obvious that while the young woman had won the battle, she had not won the war. The child would live to fight another day!

Standing, she turned to face Laura with a pitiful look of embarrassment. Laura was immediately struck by the woman's fragility. She would have been pretty, even beautiful, if it were not for the dark circles ringing her eyes and the gaunt thinness that robbed her tall frame of any curves or softness.

"I am so sorry! I knew I was taking a chance bringing them in here, but your shop looked so intriguing, I thought I'd risk it." She handed Laura the duck, pausing first to hold it admiringly in her hand. "Steuben glass. At least she has good taste."

With a rueful smile she left, herding the children before her. Laura was relieved to see them go, but her heart went out to the young woman as she remembered her own struggles to raise three active boys in the years when her husband, Howard, was too caught up in his own career to be much help.

A couple of days later, Laura was surprised to see the same young woman back again.

"I'm alone!" she immediately announced, seeing Laura's wary look of recognition. "The girls have Vacation Bible School this week, so I have three glorious hours of freedom every morning and I wanted very much to come back and have a good browse. Your things are so beautiful!"

"Thank you. You know antiques?"

"Actually, I used to work in my grandparents' shop. They didn't have an inventory as elegant as this, but being here sure takes me back. I'm Amanda Kelly," she said, extending her hand with a warm smile that lit up her face, giving Laura a glimpse of the spark hidden under the exhaustion.

The two women began talking, and Amanda proved herself far more knowledgeable than her modest credentials implied. Laura ended up making a pot of coffee, and before they knew it, it was time for Amanda to pick up the girls at church.

These morning visits became part of the summer routine. Even after Vacation Bible School ended, Amanda managed to stop in every few days to talk a few minutes, and Laura learned that she had been married for ten years to her college sweetheart. Nick Kelly was an up-and-coming architect with a prestigious firm in Pasadena, and Amanda always spoke of him in the highest terms, praising his devotion to her and their two young daughters. She would go on and on about how hard her husband worked to provide for them, proudly recounting how he had moved them into a historic old home on one of Sierra Madre's tree-lined streets when Casey was only two. But there was a lingering sadness behind her bright smiles and a slight defensiveness in all her praise that made Laura suspect all was not perfect in paradise.

The new location brought in all kinds of walk-in business, and Amanda soon found herself helping out by answering the phone or wrapping a gift if Laura was busy. Laura had started her business the year after her husband died, and she had always been able to handle the small shop on her own. But as the summer ended and the business grew, it became evident that those days were over.

Laura had actually been hesitant when Amanda offered to come in a few days a week to help her out. It had been a long time since she had found someone she liked as well, and she was afraid that becoming employer and employee might disrupt the budding friendship. But Amanda explained how eager she was to find something to do now that both of her girls were in school full time. For the past eight years she had given herself wholeheartedly to the demands of motherhood, pouring every ounce of creativity, energy, and love into her home and family. Now she was feeling a need for something that would balance the scales and feed her own personhood. Being with Laura at the store reminded her that she had once had a life apart from Dr. Seuss and Kermit the Frog . . . and could again.

That had been six months ago, and Amanda had proven herself indispensable. Not only did she have a natural talent for creating fabulous displays, but she brought a younger, more contemporary perspective to the shop that had broadened its appeal and increased sales. While she only worked three or four days a week during school hours, Laura had come to depend on her, releasing more and more responsibility into her capable hands and trusting her to make decisions when she wasn't there. Taking her to New York for the February buying trip seemed like the next logical step in what was rapidly becoming a true partnership.

❧ ❧ ❧ ❧

"We're here . . . at last! I swear the drive from the airport gets longer every year!" Laura declared, opening the door and stepping onto the sidewalk in front of the flag-bedecked hotel.

"The Plaza! I can't believe you booked us at the Plaza!" Amanda gasped, taking a moment to enjoy the surprise.

As a bellboy in a brass-buttoned uniform piled their luggage on a cart, Laura paid the cab driver. Then the two women walked into the world-famous lobby, turning heads as they passed.

"Reservation for Stanley," announced Laura, the seasoned traveler.

The hotel clerk sized up the two women as he registered them with a practiced air of polite aloofness. It was a game he liked to play . . . trying to guess who people were and rate them on a scale of importance so he could decide how much to ingratiate himself. The two women before him were both well dressed and striking in their appearance.

The older of the two, Mrs. Stanley was somewhere around fifty and just starting to lose the battle of the bulge around her thickening middle. Dressed for business in a gray pinstripe suit, she carried herself with an air of authority, and her upswept salt-and-pepper hair gave her a classic, dignified look.

Her younger companion could be anywhere from twenty-five to thirty-five; it was getting harder and harder to tell these days. Tall and model thin, she was pretty in a fresh, unpretentious way, her makeup understated, her red wool coatdress simple but well cut. In fact, everything about her seemed fresh and unpretentious as she gazed around the lobby with undisguised delight.

"It's smaller than I thought," he heard her whisper to her friend. "But so elegant," she added when she caught his quick glance, as though she were afraid she had hurt his feelings. "And that flower arrangement is stunning," she went on, pointing to a huge urn filled with a variety of expensive imported blooms.

"Thank you, madam. We do our best." He couldn't help smiling. "Enjoy your stay, ladies," he intoned as he handed them their keys, "and if there is anything I can do to make your stay more comfortable, please don't hesitate to call." He handed Amanda his personal card.

"How nice of him," Amanda remarked to Laura as they headed for the elevator.

Laura just laughed and said, "Remind me to take you with me more often!"

The next few days were a whirlwind of activity that started early each morning and went nonstop until they collapsed exhausted into bed late each night. The mornings were reserved for business as they visited every antique and home accessory showroom in town. More than once Laura congratulated herself on having the good sense to bring Amanda. Time and again her young assistant pulled her in a new direction or pointed out a look she would never have considered. Not that they always agreed, but the two worked well together, discussing new concepts and finding ways to integrate the gracious traditional look that Laura was known for with the more contemporary look Amanda liked.

At lunchtime the women would return to the hotel, change into comfortable clothes and walking shoes, and exchange Laura's briefcase for Amanda's camera. Laura admitted she had never taken the time to see half the sights of Manhattan, and Amanda had to tutor her in the finer points of being a tourist. For instance, the first time Amanda approached a passing stranger to ask if they would mind taking a picture of the two women together in front of the Rockefeller ice rink, Laura had nearly died of embarrassment.

"It's all right," Amanda had reassured her. "People don't mind. Besides, what good are pictures if we aren't in them? We might as well buy postcards!"

Laura proved herself a good student when on their third day of sight-seeing she surprised Amanda by grabbing a passing businessman on the sidewalk in front of Tiffany's and thrusting the camera into his hands.

"I know you won't mind taking a picture," she declared in an officious tone that left no room for argument.

Seeing the gentleman was in a hurry and not pleased by this sudden imposition, Amanda intervened, giving him her most winning smile. "We would really appreciate it . . . if you wouldn't mind."

The man, who was in his mid-forties and not beyond appreciating the attention of a pretty girl, immediately softened. In fact, the closer he looked, the more convinced he became that he had seen this girl before. Tall and slender, dressed in slacks and a turtleneck sweater with an oversized trench coat and a soft broad-rimmed hat pulled low over her eyes, she looked mysterious enough to be one of the high-fashion models who were always trying to blend anonymously into the city crowds, usually without success.

Certain he was capturing a celebrity, but unsure of which one, he took the picture and then startled Amanda and Laura by handing them his card and requesting they send him a copy. "Autographed, please."

As their taxi pulled up to the Plaza late that afternoon the women were still laughing over the man's strange behavior.

"I simply can't figure out who he thought we were," Amanda said, shaking her head with amusement.

"Me either, but he must have spread the word! Look at this!" The front of the Plaza was ablaze with lights. News photographers and TV cameras lined both sides of the entrance. At least a hundred people were milling about, jockeying for the best spots behind the thick black ropes that cordoned off a pathway from the curb to the hotel entrance.

"Who do you think is coming? The president?" Amanda asked as they left the safety of their cab and started trying to make their way into the hotel.

"I doubt he's all that popular with the bubble-gum crowd," Laura observed dryly, pointing to the teenage girls who dominated the first few rows behind the ropes. "My guess would be Christopher Davies. He's doing a concert at Carnegie Hall tomorrow night, and it wouldn't surprise me if he's staying here."

Christopher Davies and his band Out Cry! had taken the musical world by storm about eight years ago with a string of hits that were immediately labeled "America's answer to the British invasion." Written with the unflinching honesty of a workingman's son, the music captured the heart and soul of the average man and woman with a kind of passion and respect that raised it above the norm. Sometimes his music was dark and haunting, expressing the pain and frustration of lives lived paycheck to paycheck. But the next cut on an album could be as delightful and infectious as children's laughter, filled with joy and innocence and love of life.

Christopher had a gift for breaking the rules. Like an artist with a palate that included all the colors of the rainbow, he furiously painted the world as he saw it, oblivious as to whether the colors he mixed clashed or blended. He continually stepped over the boundaries of tradition, using jazz and blues alongside western and pop to come up with a sound that was usually dismissed by the purists as mongrel, but which was unerringly embraced by his audience.

The critics loved him because he always came up with something new for them to discuss and analyze, and because he was the real thing, a musical genius with the look of a rock star and the stage presence of a born performer.

At the mention of his name, Amanda felt her heart start to race. She turned to fight her way through the crowd, but a wall of human bodies closed in behind her and began steadily propelling her to the edge of the street just as a shiny black limousine pulled up to the curb. All around her, young girls started screaming, waving autograph books and record albums as the television cameras zoomed in and photographers' cameras flashed all around.

The roar of the crowd was deafening as the limo driver raced around to open the back door and the first passenger stepped out. One by one the band members were recognized and cheered as they walked the gauntlet of hysterical fans, stopping to sign a few autographs and kiss a few tearstained cheeks.

Then the crowd quieted as a soft chant began. "Chris! Chris! Chris!"

With natural dramatic timing, Christopher Davies emerged from the car, standing for a moment as though genuinely surprised and a little embarrassed by the emotional reaction of the crowd. Dressed in his signature cowboy boots, jeans, and black leather jacket, he made a striking figure, his dark hair falling just below his collar and his tanned face accenting the blazing blue eyes that now swept the crowd with a sincerely friendly and appreciative look.

Amanda felt herself being pushed even closer. If she reached out her hand she could touch him. For a moment she panicked that he would sense she was there . . . that he would turn and see her. She held her breath, pulling her hat down even lower, trying to make herself very small. The emotions she felt were overwhelming, a tearing inside that had nothing to do with the adulation felt by his fans.

The moment passed and he moved away. She watched as he slowly made his way into the hotel, his slight swagger achingly familiar. The smile she remembered so well flashed across his face as time and again he stopped to shake a hand or sign an autograph, greeting everyone like an old friend. Finally bodyguards appeared out of nowhere, whisking him up the stairs and into the sanctuary of the lobby.

Amanda stood rooted to the spot, her arms wrapped tightly around her, unaware of the tears streaming down her face. This is where Laura found her a few minutes later.

"Good grief, Amanda! What's wrong? Did you get hurt? Did you get crushed in the crowd? I tried to stay close but it was impossible! There were so many people and they just carried you away! Come on, dear girl, let's get you inside. You're shaking like a leaf!"

"No! I can't go in there, not now." Amanda took a deep breath and then smiled reassuringly at her friend. "I am sorry. I know I'm acting strangely. Could we walk down to Rumplemeir's and get some hot chocolate? I'll explain everything, I promise."

"Of course."

Amanda and Laura walked in silence down Park Avenue to the famous old restaurant. Laura had brought Amanda there their first day in New York, explaining that they had the best hot chocolate and homemade ice cream in town. They settled at a table by the window looking out at the fading twilight.

"Okay, let me guess," Laura finally teased to break the silence. "You and Christopher Davies are secretly lovers, but you're dumping him for Robert Redford and you don't know how to break it to him." Laura waited for Amanda to laugh at her outrageous scenario, but instead she looked up to find Amanda staring at her with a stricken expression. "Oh, Amanda . . . you *do* know him, don't you?"

Not answering her friend, Amanda turned to gaze fixedly out the window. But she wasn't seeing the blustery New York street or the wind-whipped trees of Central Park beyond. She was seeing instead her grandparents' beach house in Walker's Point the summer she graduated from high school . . . the summer she fell in love.

Three

Walker's Point, 1968

*A*manda, be back by four!"
The banging of the screened porch door put an exclamation point on her grandmother's words as the girl flew down the wooden stairs, past the wild confection of flowers, fruit trees, and ankle-high grass her grandparents called a backyard, and out the back gate. Ignoring the pain of feet made sensitive by a winter of shoes, she hurried barefoot down the pebbly dirt road that wound behind the collection of old houses and summer cottages that made up the bulk of Walker's Point.

A small dot on the Pacific Coast north of Santa Barbara, Walker's Point was largely ignored by the outside world nine months out of the year. This suited the three thousand year-rounders just fine. An eclectic group of ranchers, retirees, artists, and merchants, they lived their lives with a marked sense of peace and harmony, seemingly immune to the chaos of the outside world, up until sometime in mid-May when a subtle change could be felt in the air. One could best explain it as a sudden alertness, like a dog sniffing the air to pick up a scent. The otherwise unhurried pulse of the town began to quicken as people readied themselves for the inevitable invasion of summer residents and tourists. New coats of paint replaced the homey, weathered look of winter. Storm windows gave way to screens, and the smell of Windex, soap, and ammonia permeated the air. Window boxes and huge wooden tubs of wild flowers appeared magically overnight on every storefront and street corner. And what was once a sleepy, drab little town was transformed into what the tourist brochures described as "The perfect seaside getaway . . . quaint, charming, and friendly."

The girl hurried down the rutted road, through a grove of hundred-year-old cypress and past what was left of Cottinger's pasture, until she finally reached the sand dunes that stood sentry before the empty, windswept beach. In another week Walker's Point would officially open its doors for the summer season, and the beach would be invaded by the first wave of vacationers. Before that happened the girl meant to spend as much time as possible enjoying the unspoiled serenity of the place that had meant summer to her since her earliest memories.

Hiking over the sandy mounds like a conquering general, she hit the beach with the glorious abandon of a lost soul coming home. Her arms spread wide, she flew down the shore toward an outcropping of rock, feeling the salty wind in her face and relishing the feel of the cool, gritty sand between her toes. She drank in the heady fragrance of ocean air so pure and unpolluted it made her feel light-headed.

Out of breath, she stopped before tackling the fortress of rocks that surrounded the small cove she had come to consider her own private beach. Standing still, she closed her eyes and lifted her face to the gentle rays of early summer sun, listening. At first all she heard was what her grandfather called the "symphony of the sea," that ceaseless crescendo of waves rolling toward and finally crashing on the shore. Then the high, shrill call of the sea gulls joined in, seeming to welcome her back. Amanda felt a sense of peace and relief wrap around her like a soft, warm comforter. She had made it! The long, hectic school year was over and she had finally graduated. Her folks had watched proudly as she walked across the football field of Pasadena High School, one of nearly seven hundred energetic, fresh-faced hopefuls all looking forward to becoming real people in a real world.

Amanda had graduated 143rd in her class. She was bright but not brilliant. When she looked in the mirror she saw a girl pretty enough to always have a date for truly important occasions, but she baby-sat a fair number of Saturday nights, explaining that she needed the money more than she needed to spend time with some immature boy who didn't really interest her. She sang in the church choir—she had to . . . her father was the Reverend Warren Mitchell, pastor of the Allen Avenue Congregational Church—and usually had a small solo in the Christmas musical. But she was sure that had more to do with her last name than the quality of her voice.

She was the second of three children, the middle child lost between an overachieving older sister, Lindsey—homecoming queen, valedictorian, junior at USC—and a precocious twelve-year-old brother, Nathan, who caught everyone by surprise when he was born and had been unwilling to relinquish the spotlight ever since.

Yet if the truth were known, Amanda didn't resent the anonymous place life had handed her; rather, she appreciated the privacy and freedom it gave her. Raised in a home where Christian love and principles were not only preached but practiced, Amanda had grown up with a deep faith in God and in her own value as a person. This allowed her to take genuine pride in Lindsey's accomplishments, but she did feel an occasional stab of jealousy that her sister had inherited her mother's thick honey blond hair and blue eyes, while she was stuck with her father's fine brown hair and hazel eyes. And while Lindsey was a petite five feet four with curves in all the right places, Amanda just "grew like a weed," as Grams would say every time she saw her. At nearly five feet nine, she had nightmares that one final growth spurt would put her head through the roof, like Alice in Wonderland after she ate the mushroom. And of course those greatly-to-be-desired curves her mother reassured her would "come in time" never did, leaving her self-conscious about her slender, boyish figure.

Climbing the rocks with the surefootedness of a natural athlete, she willed her tender feet to callus up quickly, determined to have a head start on the small group of friends who would drift in from all over California in the next few weeks to occupy the summer cottages their families owned. It was considered something of a badge of honor to be able to go shoeless on the roughest rocks and hottest blacktop—a true sign that you belonged to the summer regulars and weren't a "tenderfoot" like the kids who came with their parents for only a few days or a week at the beach.

She would have seen him if she hadn't stepped on a small jagged stone and almost fell as she rounded the last wall of rock guarding the path down to "her beach." As it was, she was hopping on one foot, trying to keep her balance while examining the bottom of the offended foot, when she came down hard on another sharp edge. With a small cry she flailed her arms, beating the air in a desperate and comic attempt to keep herself from falling headfirst down the rocky cliff. For one heart-stopping moment she seemed to hang suspended in the air before feeling her body pitch forward toward certain doom.

She closed her eyes, not wanting to see the earth rise up to meet her when a pair of strong arms reached out of nowhere and pulled her back, slamming her up against the hard body of her rescuer.

The girl had appeared on the cliff without warning, shattering the tranquility Chris had been enjoying from his perch on a rocky ledge overlooking the water. He had discovered the small hidden cove a few days after arriving in Walker's Point and had made it a habit to seek a few minutes of solitude there whenever there was a break in the rehearsal schedule. Even after two weeks, the ocean still held him spellbound. Coming from a small town just outside of Lubbock, Texas, the only ocean he had ever known was the sea of endless prairie and sky that went on as far as the eye could see in any direction. Pictures and movies hadn't prepared him for the magnificence of the Pacific, nor for its humbling displays of unrestrained power. The sounds, the smells, the endless wrestling of the waves with their explosions of light and color struck a chord deep in his soul, the place where his music came from. And for the first time in many years, he felt a kind of kinship with whoever or whatever had created this incredible display.

At first glance all he had felt was irritation at the intrusion the girl represented, but his irritation had been quickly replaced by heartstopping panic as he watched her dance precariously on one bare foot, lose her balance, and begin to fall. It was pure spontaneous reaction that had made him leap from the rocky ledge where he sat to pull her back to safety.

Shaky and light-headed, Amanda allowed the faceless arms to hold her, keeping her from collapsing until her legs stopped shaking and the blood had once again returned to her brain. Her head clearing, she opened her eyes and became immediately aware of a black T-shirt stretched across the broad, well-muscled chest against which her face was pressed. The sound of a fast-pounding heartbeat told her that her guardian angel was also still recovering from the sudden exertion. She could literally see the blood pumping through the extended veins of the well-formed biceps and forearm that held her.

"That's quite an act you have there, ma'am," a deep voice drawled in an amused half whisper. "Put a little music to it and you might have something."

Embarrassed and laughing uncomfortably, Amanda started to pull away. "Boy, can you believe me? You'd think I never—"

Her voice broke off as her eyes traveled up the face of the young man who still lightly held her—the chin, slightly cleft; the mouth, full and curved in a half smile; the nose, medium sized and just slightly crooked, denoting it had been broken a time or two and not set with great care. But it was his eyes that robbed her of speech. A deep aquamarine blue—the color of the ocean on a bright sunny day when the water is crystal clear and you can see the sun reflected on the sand below—set in lashes so dark and thick it seemed frivolous of God to waste them on a man. These were crowned by equally thick, dark brows that were now arched in amused contemplation of her.

A bolt of electricity went through her as their eyes connected, and Amanda felt her knees give way once again.

"Whoa, there. Hold on to me," the young man commanded. "That was quite a scare you had. Why don't you sit over here for a spell until you get your breath back."

With the help of the adrenaline still pumping through his body, the stranger lifted Amanda as easily as if she were a small child onto the ledge where he had been sitting. Then grabbing a toehold, he swung himself up beside her.

"I'm Chris . . . Chris Davies."

She sat silent, stiffly staring out to sea.

"You got a name?" he asked when she didn't respond.

Amanda turned to speak and found herself staring directly into those amazing blue eyes. "I'm . . ." For one terrifying moment her mind went blank and she could think of absolutely nothing to reply. The eyes locked her in an unfaltering gaze, observing her dilemma with undisguised amusement. "Amanda. Amanda Mitchell," she finally managed to whisper.

He was used to the effect he had on women. Young, old, in between. It didn't really matter. Christopher Brian Davies was every young girl's dream and every grown woman's fantasy. Not that he'd ever taken much advantage of his appeal. In high school he'd dated Becky Thomason his junior and senior years more out of self-defense than any heartfelt attraction. Becky had been a pretty, sweet-tempered girl who was willing to trade him the freedom he needed to pursue his first loves, music and baseball, for the prestige of being "Chris Davies' girl." After high school Chris had gone on to the local college. His old man was determined to give his son the education that he had never had, and Chris had done his best to let his father know he appreciated the opportunity, sticking it out until he had received his degree. But his real education had taken place after school at Lucy B's, the local bar and grill where he'd alternated as a cook, busboy, and occasional bouncer. On weekends, traveling bands would come in and fill the creaky old roadhouse with some of the best western, jazz, and R&B music for fifty miles.

The first time Chris asked to sit in on a late-night jam session with a black R&B group out of Memphis, he was met with amused condescension. What could this back-country cowboy, still wet behind the ears, know about real blues? That kind of music couldn't be learned out of a book. It was birthed deep in the soul, out of pain and struggle and the very currents of life itself. It wasn't played by the notes, but by the heart. Chris knew what they were thinking. It was the need to answer that question for himself that had given him the courage to ask.

As he sat at the old piano, his fingers felt stiff and his palms were sweaty. What if they were right? What if the music that welled up inside him like a deep-river spring was nothing more than vapor . . . insubstantial and meaningless to anyone but him? For a moment he felt empty, suspended in a void. Nothing came. No feeling, no inspiration, no music. Then, as if of their own accord, his fingers began to move, caressing the keys with the intimate touch of an old lover.

The sound was tentative at first, shy and searching, but from the very first note it was obvious that the boy and the piano were acquainted. Smug expressions were replaced by exchanged glances of surprise and growing interest as the boy warmed up to his job and the piano began to sing. One by one the band members picked up their instruments and began filling in the background. They had no way of knowing exactly what the boy was playing. This was a new song, flowing freely straight out of an old soul. But it was a soul they recognized, and somehow they sensed where it was going. After a while someone else took the lead, and then someone else. The others followed with seamless transitions. The boy stayed with them, never losing the connection as the outpouring of music swelled and dipped, building to a frenzied peak before winding down to a satisfied moan.

In the quiet that followed, the men slumped, exhausted and in awe, knowing they had just had an experience that one would later describe "as close to heaven as this sinner's ever gonna get!" The boy had brought the best out in each of them, causing them to reach deeper than they had in years and reawakening the old passions so easily lost in the mundane, smoke-filled world of one-night stands and forgotten dreams.

After that night the word spread. "Let the kid play. He's one of us." Even groups that had never been to Lucy B's before would invite him to sit in on a set or jam with them late into the night. They all wanted to know if the kid was really as good as they said.

Chris took full advantage of this musical education, listening, watching, asking questions, and taking every opportunity to learn something new. It was in the smoky after-hours that he got his graduate courses in guitar and sax, mastering each sufficiently to occasionally fill in when a band member was sidelined by a hangover or irresistible groupie. It was through one such grateful musician that Chris had gotten the gig with the Walker's Point Summer Musical Theater. The guy had worked there several summers in a row and had committed to the 1968 season. But at the last minute he had been offered a chance to tour in the British Isles. Remembering Chris, he had given the producers his number, assuring them they wouldn't be disappointed. Three days later Chris was on a plane headed for California.

Four

Now Chris found himself seated on a cliff overlooking the Pacific Ocean next to the young woman whose life he'd just saved as they both tried to catch their breaths.

"Nice to meet you, Amanda . . . Mitchell?" The Mitchell came out with a question mark, since Chris had barely been able to hear her soft reply. *Pretty but shy*, he thought to himself as he studied the profile she once again turned to him. *Probably younger than she looks. Certainly shouldn't be wandering around these steep rocks on her own.* "Listen, next time you decide to climb these cliffs, you might consider having someone follow you with a safety net. I might not be around next time you take a header."

There was just enough condescension in his tone to bring Amanda fully back to herself. "Look," she snapped, indignant at being labeled a helpless female. "I just stepped on a rock and lost my balance. It could have happened to anybody. I've been climbing these rocks since I was old enough to walk, and I certainly don't need some smart-alecky stranger telling me what I can or cannot do. I know these rocks like the back of my hand and—"

"Whoa! Hey, take it easy. I'm sorry!" There was surprised laughter in his voice as he pulled back, raising his hands against the sudden fiery explosion of words. "I didn't mean to make it sound like I thought you needed a keeper. I'd just hate to see that pretty face get all messed up. That's a long drop down there and those rocks could do some damage!"

The two looked down silently for a few moments at the jagged rocks that guarded the small, hidden beach below. When the tide came in, the half-moon of sand would disappear completely and only the highest peaks would remain uncovered to endure the relentless pounding of the surf. But now they were fully exposed, like bony fingers with scales of razor-sharp barnacles and coral.

"You're right. Next time I'll use a net," Amanda deadpanned.

Giving each other a sideways glance, they both burst out laughing. The laughter built to near hysteria, fueled by the fear, shock, and relief of the close call they'd just experienced. Helplessly they grabbed on to one another while tears streamed down their cheeks.

"I can't laugh anymore," Amanda finally managed to gasp. "It hurts . . . my stomach hurts." Gulping in huge breaths of air, they both leaned back, resting their heads against the wall of stone behind them.

"I don't remember ever laughing so hard. I've heard people say they laughed until they cried, but I didn't think they meant it literally." Chris wiped his eyes with the back of his hand. The two lay in companionable silence while they let their stomach muscles relax. "So you've lived here all your life, have you?" Chris finally asked.

"No, I live in Pasadena—you know, the Rose Bowl and all that. But my grandparents own a summer cottage here, and about five years ago they started living here year-round when my grandpa retired. We've been coming here during the summer ever since I can remember. What about you? You certainly didn't grow up around here."

"No, ma'am. I'm from Texas." Chris tipped an imaginary Stetson as he deliberately deepened his accent, making Amanda smile. "I'm just here for the summer, working at the theater."

"Really? Are you an actor?" Amanda asked, thinking that explained his extraordinary good looks.

"No, nothing so exalted. I'm a mere musician. I play the piano, guitar, sax . . . whatever they need. Seems like a pretty good gig. It doesn't pay all that much, but it got me from Texas to California, and when the summer's over, I'll head on down to L.A. and check things out."

"So how'd you find my beach?"

"*Your* beach?"

Acknowledging his question with a royal nod, Amanda continued. "Not even many locals know about this place. It's underwater most of the time, and as you noted, the climb is pretty extreme, so most people don't bother coming here even if they do know about it. I, however, have been coming here since I was big enough to pull myself up on that first outcropping of rock. When I was about ten, I even planted a flag right down there in the sand.''

"You know how to get all the way down? I've been up here nearly every day for two weeks, and I still haven't been able to figure out how to get down to the beach. It's sheer rock!''

Amanda searched his face, trying to discern if he could be trusted with her secret. Finally she nodded slowly. "Okay . . . on one condition. I'll show you how to get down, but you've got to promise me you won't show anyone else. I'm serious when I say this place is special to me, and it will be spoiled if a lot of people find it.''

"It will be our secret. Scout's honor.'' Chris lifted three fingers in the Scout salute.

"Somehow I can't see you as a Boy Scout. Were you?''

Amanda jumped down from the ledge and began carefully navigating the narrowing path that ran across the face of the cliff. It finally appeared to dead-end into a solid wall of stone, which dropped off suddenly to the beach below.

Looking down nervously, Chris inched behind her. "Since it appears we are going to die any minute now, I'd better tell the truth. . . . No. And what's more, I never wanted to be. I don't even like Boy Scout cookies.''

"That's Girl Scouts, cowboy. Boy Scouts don't sell cookies.''

Chris looked up to reply and found he was alone. Amanda was gone! For one horrifying moment he was afraid to look down. How could she have fallen so quickly, so silently? Before real panic could set in, a hand reached around the edge of the rock and he heard her voice.

"Take my hand. Edge as close to the end of the rock as possible, then take one foot and step around the end of the rock.''

"You've got to be kidding!''

"You'll be all right. There's a wide ledge just inches from where you're standing. Once you've done it, you'll see how easy it is. Remember, I've been doing this—''

"Since you were just out of diapers. I know, I know.'' He took her hand and started to reach around with his foot, feeling nothing but air. "Are you sure. . . ?''

"I'm sure. Trust me. Call it a leap of faith. You know what faith is, don't you?''

"An act of stupidity!'' he yelled as he launched himself around the corner onto the broad, sandy ledge. For the second time that day he found himself holding on to Amanda Mitchell, only this time it was he who needed to catch his breath.

The ledge was actually the mouth of a cave that tunneled down through the mountain of rock, ending just three or four feet above the white sand of the beach. Leading the way, Amanda nearly danced with excitement, proudly pointing out unusual rock formations, occasionally warning him to duck when the ceiling would dip below six feet, and making sure he fully appreciated what an incredible example of "God's handiwork" this natural sea cave was. The floor of the cave was covered with a thick carpet of sand, which grew cold and damp as they approached the opening.

"At high tide the ocean rushes in and fills the cave nearly halfway up. And when the big winter storms come, Grams says the water pushes all the way up, spurting out of the rock wall like a giant waterspout. I've never been here in the winter to see it, but now that I'm out of school, it's definitely on my list of things to do! I bet it's amazing to see."

They stepped out of the dark coolness of the cave and gave their eyes a moment to adjust to the bright sun. Before them the water sparkled like a Vegas show girl, the waves rising in three- to four-foot swells of bluish green, then curling over to rush to the shore.

"This is incredible," Chris announced as he jumped down, creating the first footprints in the pristine sand. He turned and raised a hand up to help Amanda. Suddenly shy, she hesitated. "I took yours when you offered it," he teased, smiling for the first time directly into her eyes.

Smiling in return, Amanda grabbed his hand as though accepting a challenge and jumped to the sand, racing full speed toward the water. Her laughter floated behind her, inviting Chris to follow. He ran after her, allowing himself the joy of holding nothing back as his muscles pumped and his lungs began to labor. He still had his tennis shoes on, and soon his legs began to weary as his feet became weighted with wet sand. Slowing, he fell to the sand, lying flat on his back with his arms stretched out wide. He could feel his body downshift as his heart slowed and the blood stopped pounding in his ears.

Finally he had enough energy to sit up. He searched the beach with his eyes, seeing that Amanda had already run the entire length and was now at the water's edge, fully engrossed in a game of tag with a small flock of sandpipers. He watched her, as free and unselfconscious as a small child, and he realized that, unlike him, she was not an intruder on this beach but a prodigal come home.

After a time she seemed to suddenly remember him. With a small wave she made her way back, nestling into the sand beside him. "So you like my beach?" she smiled, smugly sure of the answer.

"Yes, ma'am. This is just about the best beach I've ever been to. 'Course, it's the *only* beach I've ever been to." He laughed and ducked as she picked up a handful of sand to throw at him. "But I'm sure it wouldn't matter how many beaches I'd seen. This one is real special, that's for sure." He was looking directly at her as he spoke those last words.

Leaning back on her elbows, she turned her face up to the sun and quickly changed the subject. "You still haven't told me how you found my beach."

He didn't answer immediately. Stretching out on his side with his head propped up on one hand, he contemplated the foam-tipped waves that rolled lazily to the shore and back out again, trimming the sand with bits of white lace, which evaporated in the sun as quickly as they came. He liked the fact that she didn't press him. She was comfortable with the silence.

"Just lucky, I guess," he finally replied. "I like to find out-of-the-way places. Places where I can be alone. Places where I can be quiet and just listen. So much of the time I'm surrounded by noise that I have to get away where I can just . . . hear . . . what's inside, you know?"

Chris couldn't believe he was talking like this. He rarely tried to explain himself to others. The closest he came to letting people see inside was through the songs he wrote. He could always find the right words to say what he felt when he could set them to music . . . maybe because it was safe that way. The music itself became a buffer. After all, it was just a song! But now he was sitting on a beach with a girl he'd just met and he was talking. . . . No defenses, no fear. It was easy, and somehow he wanted her to know him.

"That's so amazing." Her voice had a dreamy quality. "I remember when I was little I used to sneak down to the beach after I was supposed to be in bed. I don't know why, but I just loved to sit on the sand after everyone else had gone home, all alone. It would be dark and sometimes it was cold, but I'd just roll myself up in a blanket and sit looking at the stars and watching the night-lights in the waves.''

"The what?" he had to ask.

"You know, that phosphorous stuff that kind of twinkles in the water some nights . . . like fireflies caught in the waves.''

"I've never heard of that," he replied, shaking his head in wonder. "I'd like to see that.''

"It's beautiful, and when I was a little kid it seemed sort of magical. Anyway, usually I got back to bed before anyone knew I was gone, but this one night I fell asleep, and my grandpa came to find me. I thought he'd be real mad, but he carried me back to the house without saying a word. And after he tucked me in, he sat on my bed and asked, 'Amanda Rose, what were you doing out there on the beach all alone?' He always calls me Amanda Rose because the Rose is after his mother. 'I was listening,' I said. 'Oh,' he said, and he sounded almost pleased. 'That's all right, then. But next time you go "listening," you let me and your grandma know, okay?'

"He kissed me and asked God to give me sweet dreams and started to go out. Then he turned and asked me what I'd heard while I was listening. It was a difficult question for a five- or six-year-old. I remember thinking real hard to come up with an answer that felt right. 'Happy' was all I could think to say.''

They sat quietly for several long minutes, uncertain how they had jumped from being perfect strangers to such intimacy. Chris was the first to finally break the silence.

"Your grandfather sounds great. What about your folks? Are they here for the summer, too?''

"No, not this year. My sister, Lindsey, has a job in L.A. She thinks she wants to be a lawyer, so a friend of my dad's is letting her work at his law firm as some sort of glorified gofer so she can see what it's really like. And my little brother, Nathan, is really into sports, so he's doing all these camps and summer leagues, which means my mom can't get away 'cause he's only twelve and, of course, she has to drive him and be at every game. . . .''

Chris found himself only half listening as he took this chance to study the young woman lying beside him. He decided she must be around twenty. After all, she had said something about being out of school. Her voice had a musical quality, low and a little husky but full of resonance. Her hair was brown and fell just above her shoulders.

He guessed it would be several shades lighter by the end of the sum- mer and streaked with gold. With her eyes closed and her face lifted to the sun, he could see the faint sprinkling of freckles across the bridge of her nose and the copper lashes that fluttered lightly on her cheeks, hiding eyes he had at first dismissed as simply hazel. But they had blazed with shards of gold and amber when she got angry, like a stained-glass window when the sun suddenly hits it.

His gaze traveled down to her mouth, too wide to be fashionable, with full, pouty lips she moistened frequently as she talked. A slight dimple played peekaboo, appearing and disappearing as different ex- pressions drifted across her face. Her cutoff jeans revealed legs that were long and slender, her skin smooth and already slightly golden. In a few weeks she would have one of those deep Coppertone tans that would be the envy of the beach.

His eyes drifted back up to her mouth, and he found himself won- dering what it would be like to kiss her, to feel her arms around him, to run his hands over that soft, smooth skin.

". . . and my dad never takes more than a week's vacation"—the music of her voice played on—"because he doesn't like to be away from his pulpit more than one Sunday at a time. So that leaves me to carry on the family tradition."

A warning bell went off in Chris's head. *Pulpit . . . what'd she say about a pulpit?*

". . . I could have gone to Hawaii with some friends for high school graduation, but I couldn't wait to get here. For me, summer doesn't begin until I hit this beach. And, besides, I usually work in my grandparents' shop, and they need me to help them get ready for the season."

She'd just graduated from high school? That made her only, what? Seventeen? Eighteen? And to top it off, her dad was a holier-than- thou preacher! That explained all the God talk. "Boy, can I pick 'em," he groaned as he pulled himself up to a sitting position.

"'Scuse me? You say something?"

"Just that I gotta get back. I never intended to stay so late." He stood up, stretching muscles cramped from sitting too long.

"Okay, I'll walk up with you."

"No, you stay!" He responded more adamantly than he had in- tended and made an effort to soften his tone. "I don't want you to cut your time short on my account. Look, this has been real nice, and

I thank you for sharing your beach with me. I promise I will guard its secret well."

Amanda watched in disbelief as the young man abruptly turned and started back toward the cave. What had she said? What had she done? She watched as he reached the low wall of stone and stopped. He stood for several moments, his hands on his hips, his head swiveling from side to side as if he were having a good argument with someone. Finally he turned and marched back across the sand like an angry little boy sent by his mother to apologize. Evidently, whatever the argument had been, he had lost!

"Look, I'm sorry, Amanda," he said, sounding a bit guilty. "I really did enjoy being with you this afternoon. You're a nice girl."

The way he said "nice" made Amanda want to cringe. Suddenly she understood. He wasn't interested in wasting his time on a "nice" girl. Tears stung her eyes as she fought bravely to hide the hurt and embarrassment she suddenly felt. Whatever the unspoken test was, she'd obviously failed it.

"You . . . uh . . . should come sometime . . . to the theater," he managed, glancing uncomfortably at her eyes. "I get free passes. I think the shows are going to be . . . okay."

The words came out haltingly, pushing through his better judgment. This girl was young and obviously inexperienced. Not that at twenty-two he was any Don Juan himself. But working at Lucy B's had given him plenty of opportunities for brief, uncomplicated encounters that had met his natural needs without demanding much in return and that's how he liked it. Looking at Amanda he saw beauty, sweetness, and vulnerability. In other words, Trouble with a capital "T," and even as he heard the invitation come out of his mouth, he knew it was a mistake.

"That would be great. Thanks," she replied, obviously sharing his discomfort.

Her humiliation stabbed at him, and he found himself feeling both guilty for hurting her and angry that he felt guilty. "Well, I've really gotta go. I'm probably late for rehearsal as it is. . . . You need me to see you up these rocks?" he teased, trying to recapture some of the afternoon's lightheartedness.

"You just be careful yourself," Amanda gamely teased back. "You're the tenderfoot around here, not me."

"What's a tenderfoot?" he asked, taking the bait.

"Take your shoes off and climb back up in your bare feet. Then you tell me."

"You'd better watch it, Amanda Rose. That sassy mouth of yours just may get you in trouble one of these days," he threatened over his shoulder as he started back across the sand.

"Forget her, Chris," he muttered to himself as he walked back toward the cave. "She's not for you. Too young, too sweet, too . . . good. She'll only get in the way this summer. She is definitely a complication you don't need!" He repeated this under his breath like a mantra, forbidding himself to look back at her. "Break it clean. When she comes to the theater, give her the tickets, pat her on the head, and send her on her way. It's best for you and it's best for her."

As he reached the cave entrance, Amanda yelled after him, "Sassy? Did you say sassy? Nobody says sassy anymore, Chris Davies! Hope you write songs better than you talk!" He could see her laughing as he jumped up on the rock ledge and turned to give her an exaggerated bow. Then he quickly stepped into the mouth of the cave.

Amanda expectantly watched the ledge in front of the upper cave opening. When she saw him emerge she waved, but he didn't look down, swinging easily around the corner onto the path that wound up the face of the cliff. Several times he disappeared from view, to emerge at a spot closer to the top. Each time she waited expectantly for him to turn and wave, and each time he resolutely climbed on without so much as a backward glance.

By the time he had reached the last stretch of path she could see before the top, Amanda had accepted the truth. Boys like Chris Davies weren't interested in girls like her. She'd seen it before. She was "nice." Oh, she was pretty enough to get their attention, but the minute they found out her dad was a preacher, forget it. Usually she was glad for the safeguard. Boys who were only interested in seeing how far they could get didn't interest her, no matter how good-looking they were. But there was something different about Chris Davies. While he was definitely the most dangerous young man she had ever met, he was also the most gentle and the most vulnerable. Sweet, sexy, scary, safe. A study in contrasts.

Forget it, Amanda, she silently ordered herself. *He isn't interested. He was just being polite. He thinks you're a kid. He thinks you're "nice." Look at him climbing those rocks. He's already forgotten you! He doesn't even care enough to look back. Oh, please, God, let him look back. Just one quick glance.*

But the trim figure just kept going, carefully negotiating the tricky ups and downs of the path nature had gouged out of stone. *Of course he isn't going to look, so just grow up and get real. What did you think . . . that he fell in love with you at the first sight of your clown act on the cliffs?* She sighed, feeling a ridiculous sense of loss. *Well, at least something happened today . . . something different . . . maybe not wonderful but interesting. I'll have something to write in my diary.*

Searching the cliffs one last time, Amanda spotted him just as he was about to disappear over the final crest.

"Good-bye, Chris Davies. Have a nice life."

No sooner had Amanda whispered those words than the figure stopped, almost as though he had heard her. She saw him turn and scan the rocks below. She stood very still, afraid to wave in case he was just taking one final look at the sea and not looking for her at all. Then she saw his hand come up and reach toward her. Her own came up in reply, and for an instant she almost felt she could feel their fingers touch. Then he was gone and a rush of pure happiness flooded through her whole being.

"Dear Diary," she would write tonight. "Something happened today . . . something wonderful!"

Five

*A*manda awoke slowly the next morning, stretching like a sleepy kitten under the patchwork quilt her grandmother had made. She was filled with a mixture of joy and melancholy as she looked around the bedroom she and Lindsey had shared for so many summers. So many memories! It seemed strange not to have her sister there. She lay quietly, letting her eyes take in every detail. The room sat in the upstairs back corner of the old house with windows on two sides. A window seat, covered with an assortment of flowery chintz pillows, overlooked the wild tangle of the backyard. The side window came to a high peak and was covered by crisscrossed cream-colored sheers, which were now softly billowing like sails in the brisk sea air.

She was still getting used to the wallpaper, which Grams had proudly announced she'd "put up herself" to freshen the room for her darling granddaughter. At first Amanda had a hard time hiding her dismay. The pink rosebuds that had danced across those walls since she could remember had always been there to welcome her back, and somehow the change made her feel sad, as though she had lost something. But the new paper was an old-fashioned stripe of dusty rose and cream, trimmed at the top with a border of rose vines and yellow ribbon, and it really did make the room feel fresh without losing any of its charm.

The bed she lay snuggled in was an antique four-poster with a lacy canopy overhead. "Our first double bed," Grams had once confided with a girlish grin.

Amanda glanced at the clock and was surprised to see that it wasn't even eight. When she was in school, having to get up before nine had seemed a terrible hardship, but now that she could sleep as late as she wanted, some inner alarm had gone off and she was wide awake. As she rolled over on her side and closed her eyes, determined to go back to sleep, memories of the day before came flooding back. The beach, the boy, the stupid things she had said. The fun and excitement, the strange feelings, the uncertainty . . . all churned inside of her, making her feel almost sick with excitement and dread.

"Amanda, you up?" Her grandmother stuck her head in the door. "Good morning, sweetheart. Sleep good?"

"Great! Thanks, Grams."

"Well, you've got a visitor."

Amanda's heart leaped into her throat. It couldn't be him. He didn't know where she lived.

"Hi, Manda! I'm here. Let the games begin!" A small bundle of energy with blond hair and enormous blue eyes burst into the room and threw herself on the bed, wrapping Amanda in a huge bear hug.

Amanda squealed in delight, hugging back with all her might. "Stace! I can't believe you're here. I thought you were going to Europe for graduation. I didn't even think I was going to see you this summer. Oh, I'm so glad you're here!"

Stacy Chamberlain had been Amanda's best "summer friend" since an afternoon in 1956 when she had looked up from the moat of the sand castle she and her dad were building to see a golden-haired little girl about her own age watching with undisguised interest. With her big blue eyes, turned-up nose, and dimpled cheeks, Amanda had thought she was the prettiest little girl she had ever seen, like a Madame Alexander doll come to life. Her father watched the girls eye each other, curious to see what his daughter would do. It certainly would have been understandable for Amanda to ignore this intruder and protect her territory. But she simply said, "Hi. You want to help?"

"Sure!" The little girl jumped into the moat and proceeded to dig as though her life depended on it. Within minutes the girls were laughing and talking like old friends. It was a friendship that was still going strong twelve summers later.

Disentangling themselves, the girls propped pillows behind them and settled in against the headboard.

"So answer my question! Why aren't you in Europe?"

"I decided not to go. I couldn't. Not when I could spend the summer working in a real theater instead. I have been *discovered*!"

Stacy announced in her broadest theatrical voice.

"Really?" Amanda exclaimed, thrilled for her friend.

"Well, not 'Discovered' with a capital *D*," Stacy laughed, "but I have been cast in a couple small roles at the Walker's Point Theater this summer. They're doing *Oklahoma!* again, to commemorate their tenth anniversary, and *The Unsinkable Molly Brown*. And I have speaking parts in both, as well as getting to sing and dance in the chorus! I know it's not much. No one could believe I gave up London and Rome and Paris to come back to good ol' Walker's Point. But you know it's always been my dream to appear on that stage. And when Mrs. Albricht told my aunt they were having open auditions last month, I just jumped in my trusty Volkswagen and beetled my way here from Ventura."

"I can't believe it! I'm so happy for you! Of course, I've always known you were going to make it. When we had slumber parties and you would tell me about how you were going to grow up to become a great actress, I knew it would happen, just the way you said. I just can't believe you didn't tell me! Why didn't you call or write?"

"I wanted to surprise you! Besides, there just wasn't time. I actually had to take my finals early and skip graduation to be here for rehearsals. It's so weird, Manda. You dream and hope and pray that someday you'll get to do this great thing or be this great person. But because you're just a kid, no one expects you to do more than hope and dream. Then one day you wake up and 'someday' is here, and you realize you either get busy doing that great thing or all you'll ever have is the dream. Kinda scary, huh?"

"Yeah. . . . It's even scarier when you don't really *have* a dream. At least you know what you want to be when you grow up. Me, I still don't have a clue. It's like being all dressed up with nowhere to go."

"Hey, of all the people I know, you are the most likely to do something wonderful with your life. I've never known anyone more intelligent, more sweet, more unselfish—"

"If you say 'nice,' I'll hit you!" Amanda threatened, raising her fist to her face.

"Oh, I've missed you!" Stacy grabbed Amanda in another bear hug, and the two girls rolled across the bed in a tangle of arms and legs, ending in a laughing heap on the floor.

Lying on their backs with their heads together on the colorful hand-braided rug, Stacy picked up the conversation. "Seriously,

Manda, there's nothing that says you have to have your whole life mapped out. That's what college is for, to figure it out. It will all come, just as it's supposed to. Isn't that what you always used to tell me? 'Don't worry, Stace,' you'd say when I was freaking out because I was sure all the good movies would already have been made before I got to Hollywood. 'God's got a plan.' "

Stacy paused and took a breath. "But just in case He forgot to think one up for the summer, I've got one!"

"What are you talking about?" Amanda rolled onto her stomach to look at her friend.

Sitting up with excitement, Stacy grabbed Amanda's hand. "Come work at the theater with me. They're hiring people to work out front, you know, seating people, selling tickets, manning the refreshment stand . . ."

"You want me to work as an usher? That's your great plan for my life? Wonderful! I can see it now! You on stage taking all the bows and me *under* the stage scraping off the gum and sweeping up the popcorn. Oh, that sounds like fun!"

"Stop it," Stacy pleaded, laughing at the picture Amanda had painted. "It wouldn't be like that. You don't have any idea how much fun it is. Even the 'ushers,' as you call them, get dressed up in costumes, and you don't just seat people. You sing songs and tell jokes. It's corny but fun! You'll have a blast. Besides, with me busy every night, what are you going do with yourself? You'll be bored stiff!"

"You've got a point there. I'd probably just end up hanging around there most nights anyway. I might as well get paid for it. But what about the Shoppe?" Amanda's grandparents had opened a small antique and souvenir store shortly after they moved to Walker's Point, and Amanda had worked there the past few summers. "Grandpa and Grams are counting on me."

"This is only in the evenings. You can help them out in the mornings, and we'll still have our afternoons for serious beach time."

"Okay, I'm starting to like this plan. But what if they don't hire me?" Amanda asked, suddenly alarmed at the thought.

"They already did," Stacy replied with a sheepish grin. "You start in"—she looked at her watch, noting it was eight-forty-five—"one hour and fifteen minutes. I told Ana we'd be there by ten. Welcome to show biz!"

🍃 🍃 🍃 🍃

It wasn't that she had forgotten he would be there. But the excitement of seeing Stacy so unexpectedly had chased him just beyond the edge of her conscious thought, and it wasn't until she and Stacy were on their way to the theater that it actually hit her. Would he think she had orchestrated this to chase after him? Waves of dread began to roll across her stomach as she tried to imagine what he would say when he saw her.

"You're going to love the Albrichts!" Stacy enthused as they walked the tree-shaded streets toward the theater. "At first I was afraid of Mack. He used to be a teacher, you know, and he still has a little of that 'Behave yourself or I'll send you to the principal' air about him. But underneath he's a pussycat. And Ana is so much fun! She has this great sense of humor, and you can tell that she loves what she's doing!"

Mack and Ana Albricht had come to Walker's Point eleven years ago on vacation and fallen in love with the place. Schoolteachers in their early thirties, they knew they would never be able to save enough money to buy a summer beach house, nor would they be able to afford to spend more than a week or two without summer jobs. Mack taught vocal music at a small private college, and Ana taught high school drama. So it wasn't long before their fertile minds came up with the idea for a summer theater that would present family-oriented musicals to appeal to the swell of summer tourists. In the summer of 1958 they had presented their first production, an abridged version of *Oklahoma!* The show was presented in the Walker's Point High School auditorium, and from the beginning it was obvious the Albrichts had a hit!

Within four seasons they were able to transform an old stable on the edge of town into their own theater. With a full proscenium stage draped in rich wine-colored velvet, twenty rows of neatly spaced theater seats, an orchestra pit big enough to accommodate a piano, drum set, and two or three various other instruments, and a lobby complete with a ticket window and a small refreshment stand, the theater gave promise of someday being one of the finest summer theaters in the country. Each year their reputation grew and so did their audience, and each year they tried to add to or improve their facilities.

"You won't believe all they have done to the theater this past year!" Stacy continued, gesturing dramatically with her hands as she spoke. "The lobby has been expanded and totally redone. And the dressing rooms now have lighted makeup tables and costume racks! There's even a 'green room' where we can relax when we're not on stage!"

Amanda tried to pay attention, but her thoughts kept coming back to what it would be like to see Chris again. Would he be glad to see her or totally ignore her? Should she say hello first or wait for him to make the first move? The butterflies in her stomach grew more frantic as the theater came into view.

The first thing Amanda noticed was the new marquee. Centered over the covered entry, it ran nearly half the length of the front of the wooden clapboard building. "Walker's Point Musical Theater" was outlined in white lights across the top. Beneath that, *Oklahoma!* and *The Unsinkable Molly Brown* were announced in replaceable black letters. At the bottom in red letters was written, "Come help us celebrate our tenth anniversary!"

As they entered the lobby Amanda could see that everything had indeed been renovated. Red flocked wallpaper now covered the upper half of the walls, ending at a chair rail, which separated it from the dark wood paneling below. A beautiful new chandelier hung from the ceiling, casting rainbows on the walls and floor. The snack bar ran the full length of one side of the room and was fashioned after an 1800s soda fountain, with shelves on the wall behind for apothecary jars of licorice sticks, sour balls, and rock candy. Old-fashioned sofas and chairs covered in red velvet were placed appropriately around the room, and framed posters from previous shows covered the walls.

Stacy led the way through one of the two curtained doorways into the theater, and Amanda was immediately impressed by the silence. They appeared to be the first ones there, and the theater seemed to be holding its breath, waiting. It reminded Amanda of her father's church when there was no service.

"We were all up so late last night, Mack gave everyone a late call this morning," Stacy explained, unconsciously lowering her voice to a respectful whisper. "I'll go see where Ana is."

She walked to the front of the stage and disappeared through a door on the side. Amanda walked halfway down and sat in one of the seats to wait. Slowly she became aware of doors slamming and muffled voices behind the curtain as the theater came to life. She felt nervous and on edge as she strained to distinguish if one of the voices was his. She was so intent she didn't hear Stacy walk up behind her, and she jumped when she felt a hand on her shoulder.

"Easy, Manda. The only ghosts in this theater are friendly!" Stacy laughed, turning to introduce the woman beside her. "Ana, this is my friend Amanda Mitchell. Manda, this is Ana Albricht, my esteemed director and your new boss. I'll leave you two to get acquainted."

"Hello, Amanda. We're very glad you agreed to help us out this summer." Ana reached out and gave Amanda's hand a warm squeeze. Then she sat down in the chair directly in front of her, turning to face her over the back of the seat.

At first glance Amanda would have thought her to be in her mid-twenties. Dressed in jeans and a work shirt with the sleeves rolled just above the elbow, she was small-framed, with long sandy-colored hair worn in one thick braid that she absently flicked over her shoulder as she settled to talk. Her face was heart-shaped and her green eyes sparkled with life and good humor. It was only after you looked closer that you saw the faint laugh lines around her eyes and mouth that marked her age. Amanda liked her immediately.

"I think Stacy explained to you that what we need is someone to help seat people and work the snack bar at intermission. If you've been here before, you know that we believe the audience should be entertained from the moment they step through the doors, so we'll all be in costume. I think we'll put you in a saloon girl costume," she said, giving Amanda an appraising look, "something fun, with feathers. And we'll give you a short script to learn so that you'll have something clever to say when you greet people."

Seeing Amanda's sudden look of skepticism, Ana hastened to reassure her. "Trust me. You'll be great! After a while you'll really get into the spirit of things and you won't even need the script. You'll be making up your own lines and having the time of your life. Now, let me show you where everything is and then we'll get you measured for your costume. You can start on Monday."

The two got up and started up the aisle. Amanda was a little dazed at how easily she had gotten the job.

"I hope your grandparents can spare you during the afternoons next week to help get things set up before opening," Ana added.

Amanda stopped, looking at Ana in surprise. She hadn't mentioned her other job or her grandparents.

"When Stacy told me about you," Ana explained, "she said that you are Kevin and Emma Mitchell's granddaughter, a high recommendation around these parts, and that you work for them at the Shoppe. She also told me you were hardworking, trustworthy, and faithful. I wasn't sure if I was hiring a girl or a St. Bernard! But she also said you were pretty, fun, and great with people."

Amanda smiled, able to picture Stacy's dramatic sales pitch as she followed Ana up the aisle. Then thinking of the one question that hadn't been addressed she said, "I forgot to ask what I'll be making?"

Ana stopped so abruptly that Amanda nearly ran into her. Then she turned in amazement. "You expect to be paid for all this fun?" For a moment Amanda was at a loss, thinking she was serious. Then Ana's face broke into a mischievous smile as she put her arm around Amanda's shoulders and continued toward the lobby. "How's three dollars an hour to start, with a raise to three-fifty in a month if all goes well?"

"Sounds great." Amanda laughed and took a deep breath. *Stay on your toes, Amanda Rose*, she thought to herself. *You aren't in Kansas anymore!*

Six

*A*manda, be sure you unpack that box of greeting cards before you go."

Amanda groaned at her grandmother's reminder as she stood up from the crouch she had been in while counting the gift boxes stacked under the front counter of her grandparents' store. She stretched and rolled her shoulders while glancing anxiously at the grandfather clock that stood in the middle of the room ponderously ticking away the hours of the day.

It was nearly twelve. If she didn't hurry she would be late for her first day of work at the theater. She had explained to her grandparents that she would only need to be there during the afternoons leading up to Friday night's Grand Opening. After that she'd strictly be working at night, arriving at six to change into her costume and make sure the refreshment stand was set up. The doors would open at seven, and the curtain would go up at seven-thirty sharp. The show would be over by ten-thirty, and she should be home by eleven. This left her mornings free to work at her grandparents' store.

"Grams, I've really got to go. I'll get to them tomorrow. I promise!" Amanda walked to the back of the store and found her grandmother unpacking a straw-filled crate of beautiful hand-blown glass.

"These are Sara Reynolds' work. Aren't they fabulous?" Her grandmother held up a fiery red bowl and plate veined with swirling gold and silver. Besides the antiques her grandfather so lovingly restored, the Shoppe provided a showcase for local artisans like Sara. Beautiful handmade quilts shared the walls with original watercolors and oils. The tables were set with hand-kilned pottery, and the back wall displayed the driftwood artistry of a young man who had gone on to national prominence.

"But I always save my best pieces for you," he'd once told Grandpa Mitchell. "You were the first ones to believe in me and display my work."

Grams gently placed her treasure in a glass display case, then turned to look at her impatient grandchild. "Be off with you, then. I certainly wouldn't want to be accused of impeding my granddaughter's budding career in show business!"

"Thanks, Grams." Amanda planted a big kiss on her grandmother's cheek, turning to search frantically for her purse. Finally finding it on the chair where she had left it, she raced out the door already five minutes late.

She bounded up the front steps of the theater, through the deserted lobby, and into the auditorium, where she was greeted by organized chaos. Different cast members rushed around in various degrees of panic or sat huddled together feeding each other lines. The sound of hammers and power tools, accented by an occasional crash or shouted curse, could be heard coming from backstage where the crew was busy putting final touches on the sets. And in a side room, singers were warming up with scales and vocal exercises, while some of the dancers were on stage running the "Kansas City" dance number from *Oklahoma!*

"No! No! No!" The choreographer, a small man dressed all in black, stepped from the wings. Pounding the stage with a large stick, he raged, "Count it out. It's one, two, three *and* turn, not one, two, three, turn! We're not doing it with music till you can dance this thing in your sleep without it!"

Amanda cast a fleeting glance toward the orchestra pit, but it was empty. The musicians, she was told, would be back at one for a run-through. Finding Stacy in the dressing room having her final fitting, Amanda rolled her eyes and collapsed in a chair.

"Is it always like this?"

"Like what?" Stacy asked, not catching on at first. "Oh, you mean like nobody knows their lines and the set's never going to be finished and the dancers all have two left feet and Rodgers and Hammerstein are going to sue if we dare open? Yep, it's always like this. And if you think *this* is bad, just wait until the final dress rehearsals! Everything will go wrong! But somehow on opening night it all comes together.

You'll see." She smiled radiantly at her friend. "Don't you just love it?"

The next few days continued at a frenzied pace as Amanda worked at the Shoppe each morning and helped at the theater during the afternoon. On several occasions she saw Chris at a distance, usually seated at the piano during rehearsals, but he would always disappear right after. Once she walked into the green room just as he turned to walk out the door. She thought for a moment he had seen her and deliberately left, but she decided that didn't make sense. Why would he run away from her? What could he be afraid of? No. Either he just hadn't seen her or he had already forgotten their day on the beach.

Actually, Chris *had* seen her the first day she came to the theater. Her friend, the pretty blonde, had come backstage looking for Ana, announcing she wanted to introduce her to her friend Amanda. He hadn't been able to resist looking through a peephole in the curtain to see if it was her. After all, how many Amandas could there be in Walker's Point?

The sight of her sitting in the darkened theater filled him with a strange sense of longing, as though they had shared much more than a few hours one sunny afternoon. He'd never felt so immediately connected. Attracted, yes . . . even infatuated. But there was something about this girl that spoke to him in a way so fundamental he could only relate it to the feeling he got when a storm comes rolling across the Texas plain. You can see it in the distance, the lightning flashing in the black clouds as they rumble toward you, the thunder growing louder and louder, and the air heavy with the smell of rain. You know the violence that's coming and the beauty, and your stomach knots with expectation and fear . . . and joy.

The next few days he systematically avoided her, making sure that where she was, he wasn't. He had to think this thing through and come to peace with it before he faced her.

అ   అ   అ   అ

"Amanda Rose."

Amanda froze at the sound of the deep Texas drawl, her heart pounding wildly. He had surprised her, catching her in one of the rare moments when she was not on the alert for his presence. When he found her she was on a ladder arranging the highest display shelves behind the snack bar. Her years working at the Shoppe had taught her how to display things attractively to promote sales, and Ana had put her in charge of organizing the candy and souvenirs.

"Hello, cowboy." She kept her tone casual, trying to hide the fact that her stomach had just dropped to her knees. "Can you hand me those bears over there," she continued, pointing to several stuffed bears dressed in a variety of Western costumes.

Silently he handed her one bear after another as she studiously arranged them in different poses along the top of the shelf. She was careful not to actually look at him, keeping her eyes on the bears, arranging and rearranging until she had just the right look. But the whole time she was well aware of the fact that he never took his eyes off her face. She could feel his look, and finally she ran out of bears and had to turn to face him.

"How's that?" she asked, looking for a way to postpone the inevitable questions about why she was working there.

"Fine. . . ." Drawing the word out, he looked at her knowingly as he offered his hand to help her down. The gesture brought their day on the beach back in vivid detail, and she felt herself blush as she stepped off the ladder and found herself cornered between the wall and his body.

"You didn't even look. How do you know it's fine? Step back and take a good look," she insisted, all business as she squeezed past him and out to the safety on the other side of the snack bar. She stood with her hands on her hips, surveying her handiwork, and he moved to stand beside her. This time he really studied what she had done.

The bears sat or stood in different action poses, arms lifted, legs crossed, heads turned, as if caught in a freeze frame, creating the illusion that they were all relating to one another and having a grand time.

"It really *is* good," he said, unable to keep the surprise out of his voice. "You have a good eye. Do you paint or sketch?"

"I was considered something of a genius during my coloring-book period," Amanda replied, "but once I graduated to sketch pads and paints, I discovered I had absolutely no talent for putting what I see in my head down on paper. The best my freshman art teacher could ever say was 'Interesting concept.' So here I am, playing with teddy bears."

"Yes, *here* you are."

Amanda felt her neck and cheeks go from pink to scarlet as Chris nailed her with an appraising look.

"Okay," she said, taking a deep breath before launching into an explanation. "I know how this looks, but I really am not chasing you. My best friend, Stacy, surprised me by not going to Europe this summer and instead she turns up in my bedroom and says she's been 'discovered' and why don't I go with her and I said maybe they won't hire me and she says they already have and Ana is so nice and she said they could really use me and I can still work for my grandparents during the day . . . so you see, I really didn't have anything to do with it. It was all Stacy's idea."

Amanda listened helplessly as the words poured nonsensically out of her mouth. She realized how stupid she sounded, and by the time she breathlessly ran out of words, she knew Chris Davies thought she was an idiot.

Oh please, God, just let me die, or at the very least lapse into a five-year coma! she inwardly groaned, staring fixedly at her toes.

"Remind me to thank her."

"What?" Amanda glanced up in amazement to find him smiling at her with an amused but gentle look.

"Meet me for coffee at May's. I'll be finished by five."

Stacy walked up as this order was issued. Her eyes grew big as she looked with new respect at her childhood friend. Of course, she and every other girl working at the theater had a huge crush on the dark-haired, blue-eyed Texan. But so far he had kept to himself, always polite but not overly friendly, willing to pitch in and work as hard as the next guy but rarely entering into the social activities with the rest of the cast when the day was done. Usually he'd go off on his own, disappearing for hours with his old guitar in tow.

"Chris, this is my friend Stacy. But then you probably already know each other." Amanda was barely aware of what she was saying. She was still reeling from Chris's sudden invitation.

"Well, I've seen you, of course," Stacy stammered, "but we've never really talked."

"Nice to meet you," Chris replied, glancing at his watch. "Break's over. I've gotta get back in there. See you at five," he reminded Amanda. "And see *you* on stage," he added to Stacy, flashing her a devastating smile that made Amanda's heart clench with jealousy. "Oh, and by the way, Stacy, thanks." He threw that last remark over his shoulder as he disappeared through the curtains into the theater.

"Thanks? Thanks for what?" Stacy called after him, not understanding. "What did he mean by that?" she asked her friend, who stood staring after him.

"Beats me," Amanda replied, turning to hide the Cheshire-cat smile that spread across her face. By the end of the day her cheeks ached from smiling.

ॐ ॐ ॐ ॐ

Amanda walked into May's Diner on the stroke of five. She had managed to leave the theater early and race home for a quick shower, assuring Ana she had everything under control and that all would be ready by opening night that Friday. Her hair was still slightly damp, and she had purposely worn very little makeup, simply brushing her lashes with mascara and applying the merest touch of color to her lips. She still was uncertain how he felt about her, and she wasn't about to pull out the war paint to impress him. Still, she had lightly sprayed her neck with "Heaven Sent" just in case he got close enough to notice.

She took one of the half dozen booths that ran down the side of the small cafe. May's had been a part of Walker's Point as long as Amanda could remember. It was one of the few restaurants that stayed open year-round, providing the locals with a homey place to congregate over good coffee and homemade muffins, soups, and pastries. May had actually passed away several years before, but her daughter, Mary, had taken over, keeping the quality of the food up and improving the atmosphere with lots of hanging plants and multicolored tablecloths.

"Hi, Amanda. Glad to see you back. What can I get you?" a young girl with dark hair and friendly brown eyes called from behind the counter. It was Mary's daughter, Nancy.

"Hey, Nancy. Just coffee for now, thanks. I see your mom's got you working again this summer," Amanda commented as the waitress filled an oversized blue mug and brought it to the table.

"You know how it is. I would have rather stayed in my apartment in L.A. and worked close to school. But Mom just can't seem to understand that now that I'm in college I don't want to come home every chance I get." She gave a resigned shrug. "But she pays me well, and I actually make pretty good tips once the season gets under way. And, of course, there's the beach. . . . I would miss the beach if I weren't here. So I said I'd come back for one last summer, but this is absolutely the very last.''

"What did your mother say?"

"Oh, you know Mom. She said yes and nodded no."

The girls were laughing when Chris walked in and slid into the seat across from Amanda.

"Hi. Sorry I'm late. I had to go over some musical changes with Mack. I'll have coffee, too," he said, smiling up at Nancy. Then he turned his full attention on Amanda. "So . . ." He smiled at her and for a moment he seemed to lose his train of thought, his eyes locked on hers. "I felt we needed to get a few things straight."

Amanda felt her heart stop as she waited to hear what he was going to say.

"I'm twenty-two years old. You are what? . . . Eighteen?"

Amanda barely nodded, uncertain where he was going with this.

"I've basically lived on my own since I was sixteen, and I probably haven't been in a church since the year my mother made me sing in the Christmas musical at the First Baptist when I was eleven."

"You too, huh?" Amanda softly interjected.

He went on as if he hadn't heard her. "I used to smoke like a chimney, but I'm trying to stop . . . no good for the voice. But occasionally I still light up, particularly if I'm feeling stressed."

Amanda noted the outline of a half-empty Marlboro package through his T-shirt pocket as Nancy arrived with the second mug of coffee. "You need more cream?" she asked but made a quick retreat when she realized her two customers were too intent on each other to answer.

"I do drink beer . . . nothing better than an icy beer on a hot day," he continued, determined to complete his confession. "And if you get me riled, there's no telling what could come out of my mouth. The crowd I hang out with have very colorful ways of expressin' themselves."

He picked up his coffee and took several cautious sips of the rich black brew. He then stared into the cup like a seer trying to discern some hidden message in its depths. Finally he looked up, locking Amanda in his straightforward gaze.

"I'll be honest with you. I saw you the first day you came to the theater, and it didn't exactly thrill me. I had pretty much decided to give you a wide berth. It just didn't seem to me to be very wise to get involved with a girl . . . like you. Then all of a sudden you're there, right under my nose, and I'm trying like crazy to pretend I don't see you or hear you or smell you. . . ."

Amanda touched the back of her neck where she had sprayed the Heaven Sent and smiled.

"Then yesterday I went to our beach, trying to think things through, and I realized I was waiting for you, like somehow you'd just know and come. Crazy, huh?" He looked away, embarrassed. "Crazier still . . . I was disappointed when you didn't show." This was spoken into the coffee cup, and he raised it to his lips to drink.

"Well, I guess I must be crazy, too," Amanda confessed, touched by his honesty. "I read some eternal sign into the fact that you turned and looked back at me the other day." His look asked her to explain. "You were climbing back up the cliffs, and I knew you had decided not to see me again—that you thought I was too young or too nice or something. But I also knew that I'd never met anyone like you and that something had happened between us. So I prayed and asked God to make you look back, like some kind of sign."

Amanda paused, remembering the way her eyes had searched the cliffs for the solitary climber. "And then you did," she said simply, smiling into his eyes.

"Boy, you are . . . crazy," he spoke the last word softly, smiling back.

They sat talking for the next several hours, ordering hamburgers they hardly touched and a chocolate malt with two straws. Bumping heads as they both tried to drink, they laughed like children and began the intimate task of sharing their lives with each other.

When they finally walked out of May's, the streetlights had come on, casting the quiet streets in pools of misty light and shadow. Soon these streets would teem with tourists, and even late into the night Walker's Point would pulse with summer energy and life. But this night, the air was still slightly cool and damp, and the few people they passed walked with purpose, eager to get on with the business of the night.

There didn't seem to be any question that he would walk her home. They had walked several blocks before she even thought to politely object. "You don't have to walk me all the way home if you don't want to. I'll be fine."

"Your friend Stacy is a good actress," he said, walking on as though he hadn't heard her. "I paid special attention this afternoon. She's not real polished, but she has good instincts and she loves the spotlight! I've always thought that the most important thing is loving what you do. It's like me and my music. When I was young I didn't always understand what I was doing or why, but I always knew when it was right. . . ."

They talked as they walked, their steps unhurried, their shoulders touching from time to time. Finally their hands brushed together and Amanda felt her heart beat double time as he curled his fingers around hers. There was a moment, just a second, when she thought to pull away. Then the moment passed and she felt him squeeze ever so gently. They walked the last couple of blocks in silence, listening.

Seven

On opening night Amanda nervously donned her costume for the first time. The gold-embroidered dress was strapless, with a tightly cinched waist and full skirt that came just above her knees. At her first costume fitting Amanda had despaired that she wouldn't have enough to hold it up, but the costume lady had simply shrugged and handed her a padded merry widow, murmuring something about "the tricks of the trade." Black net stockings and high heels showed Amanda's long legs off to perfection, and Stacy had shown her how to do her makeup, adorning her eyes with several shades of eye shadow, eye liner, and mascara, and accenting her high cheekbones with two shades of blush. Her lips shimmered with a deep copper lipstick and her hair was swept up into a pile of soft curls on top of her head. The full effect was startling as she and Stacy studied the results in the dressing room mirror.

"I think I've created a monster!" Stacy declared in mock horror. "When your grandparents see you, they're going to want to lock you up and shoot me! Seriously, Manda, I've always known you were pretty, but I had no idea. . . . I mean, girl, you're gorgeous!"

Amanda blushed and pulled self-consciously at her top where a slight uncharacteristic swell could be seen.

"Here, wear this," Stacy directed, draping a long black feather boa around her neck. "With any luck no one will even notice you're a girl!"

Laughing, Amanda turned to give her friend a swat. "Just give me a minute to get used to the new me," she said, turning to take one last appraising look in the mirror. "You may be used to jumping from one personality to another, but I'm not."

"Are you implying I'm schizophrenic?" Stacy asked, feigning outrage as she linked her arm through Amanda's and pulled her unceremoniously toward the lobby.

"If the shoe fits . . ." Amanda laughed, stumbling slightly on her new spiked heels.

Stationing herself at her assigned spot at one of the curtained theater entrances, Amanda felt a rush of nervousness as she went over her few lines of greeting. "Evenin', folks, I'm Slue-Foot Sue . . ."

"You really gonna say that to folks?" a teasing voice interrupted, startling her and sending a shiver down her back.

She whirled around and found Chris lounging against the doorjamb, watching her with obvious amusement. But as he got a better look his expression quickly changed to appreciation, and he let out a low whistle of approval. "You look . . . nice."

This time when he used the "n" word it had an entirely different meaning, and Amanda felt herself blush as she stammered, "You look . . . nice, too."

Standing there in tailored black pants and a white shirt open at the collar, freshly shaven with his hair combed, he looked like an ad out of a magazine, and Amanda felt more intimidated than ever by the raw power of his masculinity. Maybe he was right. Maybe she wasn't ready for a relationship with someone so much older and more experienced.

As though reading her confusion, he took his finger and ran it lightly down the side of her face, then caught her under the chin, forcing her to look him in the eyes.

"You're beautiful," he said with a look that told her he really meant it. Then he carefully rearranged the black boa that had fallen off her shoulders to cover her bodice and kissed her on the forehead. "Meet me at May's. I'll walk you home."

Amanda stood staring at the place where he had disappeared through the curtains, completely mesmerized by what had just happened. It wasn't until she heard her name called and looked up to see her grandparents walking toward her that she realized the doors had been opened and the lobby was already filling up.

"Good evening, folks," she said with a slightly shaky smile. "I'm Slue-Foot Sue. Welcome to the Walker's Point Musical Theater!"

She stood uncertainly, waiting to see what her grandparents' reaction would be. They were understandably taken aback, not because there was anything wrong with the way Amanda was dressed, but because she shone with the radiant beauty of a woman, and they still saw her as a little girl with skinned knees and pigtails. Amanda was disconcerted to see her grandmother's eyes mist with tears, and she immediately pulled the boa more modestly around her. "It's just a costume, Grams," she said, torn between embarrassment and disappointment. "I'll ask Martha to change with me tomorrow night. She's dressed like Calamity Jane."

"You'll do no such thing," her grandfather immediately spoke up. "You look beautiful, sweetheart! So much like your grandma when she was young. I remember now why she stole my heart the first time I saw her," he said, giving his wife a look that belied his nearly seventy years.

"You've taken us by surprise, that's all," her grandmother added, dabbing at her eyes. "I guess we just hadn't noticed how much you've grown up this past year. Your grandfather's right. You *are* almost as pretty as I was." Grams threw her husband a coquettish look as she reached to give Amanda a hug. "Now, you'd better get to work, and we'd better start mingling. There are people here I haven't seen since last year!"

The opening-night crowd was more like a family reunion than a theater audience. It was a "by invitation only" event and nearly all the local merchants and year-rounders showed up for either Friday's or Saturday's performance.

Amanda felt her stomach knot with nervous anticipation as she stood in the back of the theater listening to the orchestra begin the overture. Stacy had been right. During final dress rehearsals the scenery had fallen, cues had been missed, and just about everything that could go wrong did! But when the lights went down, hushing the opening-night audiences, the curtain rose on two supremely professional and nearly flawless productions. The consensus on Sunday morning was that *Oklahoma!* and *The Unsinkable Molly Brown* were the best productions yet!

Amanda found life in the theater immensely entertaining. She loved the eccentricities of the people, the way she would ask someone a question and find herself listening to a five-minute standup routine in reply, or how she would look up from counting the money in the cash register to find a whole chorus line passing through the lobby doing perfectly synchronized leg kicks. And, of course, being with

Stacy was a special treat. This was the first time Amanda had seen her perform anywhere other than her backyard, and watching her shine on the stage night after night was a real joy.

And then there was Chris. Always. In everything she did, like a song she couldn't get out of her head. In the beginning they kept their relationship secret. He seemed to want it that way and Amanda took her cue from him, not even telling Stacy about them. She did mention once that he should come by the Shoppe and meet her grandparents. But he hadn't responded and he never came.

Every night after work they would meet in front of May's and walk the quiet, summer-scented streets of Walker's Point hand in hand. They'd talk about whatever came to mind: music, favorite movies, what had happened at the theater that day.

Amanda talked a lot about her growing-up years and the summers she had spent in Walker's Point. She had a personal story for just about every place they passed, and the telling helped her realize how rich and blessed her life had been. It was only when she made reference to God or her faith that she could sense any tension between them, as though she'd touched a sensitive spot buried deep in his soul.

Chris didn't talk much about his childhood, but he did talk about his love of baseball. "I struggled for years trying to decide whether I wanted to be a musician or a pitcher for the Dodgers," he confided one night as they approached Amanda's street.

"What finally made up your mind?"

"I was on the mound one day getting ready to pitch an inside curve to this yahoo from Brownsville, and I realized that every time I wound up to throw I was hearing Little Richard singing 'Good Golly, Miss Molly.' In fact, I had a different song for every pitch. Even on the mound the music had hold of me, but when I was in my music, I never thought of baseball. That's when I realized that there is a difference between what you want and what you need. I'll always have a love for the game, but music is what I am."

The first few nights he took her directly home, stopping at the whitewashed picket fence as though it represented a border he dared not cross. Swinging the gate open for her, he would decline her invitation to come in for coffee, and she would hear the gate click behind her as she walked to the front door. By the time she turned to wave good-bye, he would already be at the corner, but he would always stop and turn to raise his hand and take one final look.

The fourth night when they reached the corner of Beach and Main, he turned the opposite direction, leading her silently toward the sound of the pounding surf. When they reached the sand, they took their shoes off and walked down the moon-washed beach until they came to a large dune. Pulling her up in front of him, Chris sat down on the small mountain of cool sand, and Amanda found herself seated between his legs, using his chest as a backrest. It was the most intimate she had ever been with a boy, and she knew she should feel awkward or self-conscious, but all she felt was safe and content.

"Tell me about your family," she said. "You've talked about your music and your hometown and how you came to Walker's Point, but you've said very little about your childhood. You know just about everything about me. . . ."

"Not really. I'm still a little fuzzy about the third grade. Who was your teacher again and what was the name of the boy who sat behind you and sucked on your pigtail? I want to be sure I know all the answers in case there's a test."

Giving him an elbow in the ribs, Amanda continued. "As I was saying, I think this relationship should be based on trust and mutual blackmail material. So start talking! Tell me about your parents. What are they like?"

Chris was silent a moment, as if weighing just how much to say. When he finally spoke, his words were soft and halting, as though he were sifting through memories that had been filed and locked away long ago.

"She was a gypsy, my mom . . . at least that's how I always picture her. Beautiful, with long dark hair and flashing black eyes full of laughter and life. She came here from Italy with her parents when she was twelve. Why they chose to settle in Lubbock I'll never understand, but that's where they came to open a little restaurant . . . Italian, of course. I don't remember my grandparents. They didn't approve of my folks getting married . . . my dad wasn't Catholic. So they sort of disowned my mom and moved away shortly after. There was always a sadness in her when she spoke of them. But then she'd look at me and my dad, and her face would light up with such love. I don't think she ever regretted it. . . ."

Amanda sat perfectly still, not speaking, barely breathing, waiting for the flow of words to continue.

"My father was born and still lives on a ranch about twenty miles north of Lubbock, and I don't think he's ever been farther than Amarillo in all his life. He is a quiet man, more comfortable with animals than people. Good with his hands and generous to a fault, but the only time I ever saw him really laugh or talk more than absolutely necessary was when he was with her. How the two of them ever got together, God only knows. My dad was warm milk with a beer chaser. And my mom was fire and red wine and music!''

Another silence fell as the memories came flooding back. "She used to sing. My earliest memories are of her sitting on the edge of my bed at night singing me to sleep. And there was always music in the house, everything from Ezio Pinza—she loved him . . . it was her only fault—to Ella Fitzgerald and Elvis. I guess that's where I come by it. She told me once that my grandfather was a master violinist and that every generation of Bruzzis produced at least one great musician.''

He stopped to think about this, shaking his head as though the idea still amazed him.

"And could Mama cook!'' he finally went on. "I remember walking into my house late one afternoon after baseball practice. I was about ten, and Tim Rossler, who was fourteen and sort of my hero, had just shown me how to throw a wicked slider. There was a storm coming and the sky was all dark and cloudy. I hadn't taken my heavy coat like Mom had said, and the wind cut through my jacket like frozen razor blades. I walked into my house, cold and hungry and hoping my dad was home so I could tell him about the slider, and the first thing to hit me was the smell of garlic and tomatoes and basil. She always made her own spaghetti sauce from scratch. And homemade bread . . . I walked into the kitchen, and she was standing at the sink singing along with Hank Williams on the radio, a sure sign my dad was home.

"I remember just standing there, feeling the warmth of the house, looking at my mom, smelling those smells, hearing the music, knowing I'd accomplished something great that day, feeling safe and complete. It was perfect. . . . For just that one moment life was perfect.''

After another extended silence he finally spoke again, as if the words were physically painful for him. "Then when I was thirteen my mom was driving home from a church bazaar, and a drunk driver ran a red light and hit her broadside. She died instantly.

"My dad never really got over it. The life just went out of him.

She had been his life, and once she was gone, he just started going through the motions. The only thing that keeps him going today is the ranch . . . knowing that the stock needs to be fed and the fences mended. It's something he understands, something that makes sense. He used to play her old records late at night and cry. I tried to get him to talk to me once, to let some of the pain out, but it just isn't in him. He doesn't have the words."

"And what about you? How did you let the pain out?" Amanda asked.

He was quiet for so long she didn't think he was going to answer. Then finally he spoke. "I wrote a song about it. It was the first song I ever wrote, and I called it 'God Blinked.' See, my mom really believed in all that church stuff, just like you. Even though she had left the Catholic church, she still prayed all the time and always talked about how God loved us and was always lookin' out for us. At night, when she tucked me in bed she'd always pray, 'God bless my boy and watch over him as he sleeps.' And I asked her once when I was little if God didn't get tired staying up all night like that. And she said God never needs to sleep. That He's always watching over us, keeping us safe. That He never even blinks, so we never have to worry or be afraid. And I believed her, right up until we got the phone call saying she was dead.

"I kept thinking there was some huge mistake, that God would never let that happen to my mom. But He did. That's when I knew it was all a lie, like Santa Claus and the Tooth Fairy. I mean, maybe there is a God—certainly you can't look at this world and believe it all happened by accident—but whoever thought it all up and put it together is certainly too busy keepin' it all goin' to be concerned with me or my mom or *any* one person!"

Amanda felt tears well in her eyes as she pictured a young dark-haired boy standing by his mother's grave, looking up to heaven and seeing not a God who loved him or cared about him but only an empty expanse of sky, offering no comfort or hope. She knew he'd lost much more that day than his mother, and now he faced the world believing in nothing but his own strength and talent.

The two sat sharing the silence. Finally Chris kissed the back of her hair and whispered, "Thanks."

"For what?"

"For listening. For not trying to make it all better."

Eight

*I*t was two weeks since the shows had opened, and Amanda and Stacy were determined to spend some quality time together. Stacy had begun dating Ben Stewart, the actor who played Will Parker in *Oklahoma!*, so her afternoons and evenings had been as busy as Amanda's. Monday the theater was dark and Amanda didn't work at the Shoppe, so the girls were spending their day off catching up and giving each other manicures. They lay with their heads at opposite ends of Amanda's bed, having just finished painting each other's toenails. Their toes had cotton balls stuffed between them, and they each wore green face masks that smelled strongly of mint. Stacy spoke without moving her lips, trying hard not to crack her mask.

"Okay, start talking. Just what's going on with you and ol' blue eyes? I want to hear everything—every teeny-weeny little detail. And don't even try holding out on me. I always know when you're hiding something."

"How do you know?" Amanda asked, doing her best to keep from laughing.

"Your eye twitches."

"It does not."

"It certainly does. Just ask anybody. You haven't been able to keep a secret or tell a lie successfully since I met you. Remember the time we snuck into Mrs. Castle's garden and picked all her agapanthas and day lilies and then tried to sell them door-to-door? It was the first summer we met and people weren't wise yet to what little terrors we could be. I'll never forget your father confronting us. I swear he looked ten feet tall!"

"We were raising money for the little orphans I'd heard about in

Sunday school. It was a noble cause and I'm still not sorry!" Amanda declared with as much passion as her face mask would allow.

"Yeah? Well, you sure didn't sound so brave back then. I remember looking at your dad, innocent as can be, and saying, 'No, Reverend Mitchell, it wasn't us. We'd never do anything like that!' It was my first great performance. Then I heard him say, 'Look at me, Amanda. Did you take Mrs. Castle's flowers?' All you had to do was say no and we were home free. But all of a sudden your eye started twitching. I'd never seen anything like it, like a built-in lie detector. Your dad got that look on his face—you know, the one that says how hurt and disappointed he is—and you burst into tears and started sobbing how sorry you were, and all I could think of was how boring life was going to be from now on, knowing we were eternally doomed to be good! And all because of that blasted eye!"

The girls were laughing so hard they didn't hear the phone ring, and they were surprised when Grams knocked on the door to announce, "You have a phone call, Amanda. A Chris Davies?"

Amanda's breath caught as she looked at Stacy in disbelief. Chris had never called her at home before. Then with a delighted whoop she raced down the stairs to the phone in the hall.

"Chris? Hi!"

"Hi. Whatcha doin'?"

"Nothing," she answered, looking up to see Stacy sticking her tongue out from the landing above her.

"Well, I thought maybe we could hit the beach this afternoon. Meet me at May's at one?" he asked in the slow drawl she'd come to love.

"Sure. That'd be great," she said, rolling her eyes at Stacy in excitement.

They discussed a few more details and then hung up.

"Just let a man call and everyone else becomes chopped liver!" Stacy moaned, giving her friend a pitiful look of dejection. Then her eyes lit up as she asked, "What are you going to wear?"

The girls raced up the stairs, and while Stacy busied herself choosing the perfect outfit, Amanda washed the green off her face and brushed her hair into a ponytail. Then, ignoring Stacy's more glamorous suggestions, she slipped into an old swimsuit, cutoffs, and a T-shirt.

"Boy, things must be more serious than I thought!" Stacy observed as she watched Amanda dress. "If you're comfortable enough to let him see you like this, then you're way beyond the 'I hope he likes me' stage and well into the 'I can relax—he adores me!' stage. How long have you two been seeing each other?"

"I met him on the beach the day before I knew you were here. I know—I should have told you," Amanda hurriedly confessed, seeing her friend's surprised look, "but I honestly didn't think anything was going to come of it. And you always make such a big deal out of things! Then he came up to me at the theater—well, you know . . . you were there—and we spent the evening together and I've seen him every day since."

"Amanda Rose Mitchell, I am shocked! You mean all those times these past weeks when you told me you had to get right home after work or needed to help your grandma, you were really meeting him? Well, I stand corrected. I never saw your eye twitch once!"

"Oh, Stace, he's so wonderful, so sweet, so real . . ."

"So gorgeous!"

"That too," Amanda blushed in agreement. "But it's not like that with us. I mean, I break out in goose bumps every time he touches me, but that isn't the most important part. He talks to me and he listens, and sometimes we can go for hours without saying a word and it's all right. I've never had that with a boy, you know? Usually you feel like you have to fill up every minute with words, like it's your responsibility to entertain him. But with Chris the silence is as comfortable as the talking."

"And just what are you two doing during those 'comfortable silences'?" Stacy asked with her typical candor.

"A lot of the time we're just . . . listening." Amanda ignored her friend's arched eyebrows and continued. "But sometimes he sings to me. I swear, you've never heard anything like it. And he writes music, all the time. It just flows out of him. I can see it playing behind his eyes. His fingers will be tapping and he'll get this intense faraway look, like he's hearing something off in the distance. And sometimes we go down to the beach late at night after a show, and he plays his guitar and he writes something right there while I'm listening. It's the most amazing thing—like watching someone give birth."

"Whoa, you're really gone, aren't you?" Stacy laughed, giving her friend an assessing look. "You sure you're not doing more than 'listening'?"

"He hasn't even kissed me yet," Amanda reluctantly confided. As wonderful as their relationship was, this was the one thing that was starting to bother her. Ever since the night on the beach when he had told her about his mom, Chris seemed to be wrestling with something. It was as though he'd let her get too close, and now he was trying to decide whether to pull back or let her in all the way.

There were times when he would come up behind her, standing so near she could feel his body heat through her clothes, and he would touch her arm, lightly running his fingers down her skin, as though the feel of her was some new and wondrous sensation. A few days ago he had wrapped his arms around her and pulled her to him as though he wanted to meld them together. She had been sure he was going to kiss her and had raised her face and closed her eyes in anticipation. Instead, she felt him brush his lips across her forehead as he pulled away with a small groan. Ever since then he had barely touched her, acting as though her presence had no effect on him at all.

"Well, that's a new one" was all Stacy could think to say.

        ক ক ক ক

The day was warm and the beach was crowded as Amanda and Chris made their way to the cliffs that protected "their beach" from the masses. Glancing over their shoulders to make sure they weren't being followed, they quickly scurried over the rocks with the sure feet of those well acquainted with the path.

As they reached the ridge where they had met that very first day, Amanda couldn't help glancing down and shuddering at the thought of what might have happened. "Got that net handy?" she asked as she always did when they reached that spot. It was a standing joke between them.

Usually Chris had a humorous comeback, but today he responded with uncharacteristic seriousness. "I'm right here, babe. I won't let you fall . . . ever."

The look in his eyes made a chill run down Amanda's spine as he reached for her hand and pulled her along behind him. Something was different. She didn't know what, but she began to feel giddy with anticipation.

They didn't speak again until they reached the beach, exiting the tunnel to find the sand deserted and unblemished by previous visitors.

"Someday they're going to discover this place and it will kill me . . . simply kill me!" Amanda declared, choosing a partially shaded patch of sand on which to spread out her towel.

Chris just grinned at her as he carefully placed his guitar on his towel and then stripped off his T-shirt. "Last one into the water's a rotten egg," he challenged, taking off for the water in a full-out sprint.

"Cheater! That's not fair," Amanda yelled after him, throwing off her shirt and stumbling as she tried to step out of her cutoffs. "You have a head start!"

It was the beginning of a perfect day. They swam like children, splashing and dunking each other, making bets on who could float the longest and who could catch the longest ride on a wave. Of course, Amanda had a decided advantage. She swam like a porpoise and had an instinctive feel for the waves. Try as he might, Chris could never quite get the timing right as time and again the waves either left him behind or caught him off guard, crashing on top of him in a violent explosion that filled his ears with water and his shorts with sand. Finally exhausted, the two staggered to their towels and lay down to bake in the sun.

"Just wait till I get you on a horse!" Chris muttered, shaking his head to clear his ears of water.

"What was that? I didn't quite hear you," Amanda chuckled as she pulled out her bottle of baby oil mixed with iodine and started slathering the lotion over her arms and legs. Chris just watched her with an appalled look.

"Do you have any idea how bad that is for you? You're going to sizzle like a piece of bacon in this sun."

"Exactly the point," Amanda replied, settling herself spread-eagle on her towel, her chin slightly lifted to the sun so as not to cast a shadow on her neck and her eyes closed against the brilliant glare. She heard him sigh, then dig in the bag for his sun block. Then he lay down beside her, and all she could hear was the water rushing to the sand and the occasional cry of a gull.

They lay like that, not touching, not moving, not speaking, for so long that Amanda thought he must have fallen asleep. She herself had been lulled into a kind of half consciousness, so she was startled when she opened her eyes and found him bending over her, gently dabbing zinc oxide across the bridge of her nose. Squinting up at him she saw that the white cream covered his nose and coated his lips.

"Sorry. I didn't mean to wake you. I just couldn't stand to watch you fry any longer. Your nose is going to look like a cherry. They say this stuff really protects."

Amanda found herself deeply touched. "Like you . . . protector of falling girls and frying noses."

She looked up at him with eyes still blurred with sleep and sun. He loomed over her, his features lost in shadow except for the brilliant blue of his eyes and the clown white of his nose and mouth. Her eyes fixed on his lips.

"What about my lips? Aren't they burning?" she asked, her heart beating so hard she was sure he could see it.

"I was just getting to that."

Lowering himself down as though doing a partial push-up, he gently pressed his lips to hers, being careful not to touch her anywhere else. Moving his lips back and forth, he lightly brushed the cream from his lips to hers. The kiss was long and sweet and innocent . . . and incredibly exciting. Then he simply pulled back and lay down beside her again.

It was Amanda's turn to groan. A few minutes later she felt his hand reach across the sand to hers, his fingers lightly running the length of each of her fingers. Each stroke sent a ripple through her body, and Amanda was amazed at how sensuous touching hands could be.

Finally he said, "Amanda, I think it's time we—"

"We what?" Amanda interrupted, nervously pulling her hand away and sitting up.

"Eat. I'm starved!" he said with an innocent grin that belied the teasing look in his eyes.

"Right," she replied, giving him a sideways glance and busying herself with digging out the lunch she had packed earlier. As she handed him a sandwich, they both saw her hand was shaking, but for once he kindly refrained from comment.

After their late lunch they took one final swim, then walked down the beach as far as they could go, climbing the rocks at the end of the cove and looking for sea urchins and starfish in the tide pools. Amanda was having so much fun introducing Chris to this strange new world that she lost track of time. The unexpected splash of a large wave breaking over the rocks told them the tide was coming in and it was time to go. Hurrying back, they made it just in time to rescue their towels from the encroaching waves.

"Boy, the tide comes in fast!" Chris commented as they stood on the ledge outside of the cave and watched the sea reclaim the small beach.

"Yeah, it's easy to get caught if you're not careful. A fisherman got swept off the rocks not far from here and nearly drowned a couple years ago. A small boat just happened to be passing by and pulled him out. Everyone said it was a miracle."

Amanda turned to look at Chris and saw him gazing at the water with a mournful look. She knew what he was thinking. Why hadn't there been a miracle for his mother? Why did God come through for some people and not for others? It was a question Amanda had never had to grapple with. She had never lost someone she loved or felt that God had let her down. Standing with Chris and feeling his pain, she realized how easy her faith had always been . . . how childlike. And she couldn't help wondering how she would stand the test of real disappointment or loss.

"Brrr. It's getting chilly. We'd better start up." Amanda suddenly felt cold and tired.

"Here, put my sweat shirt on," Chris offered, handing her the shirt he had tied around his waist. "You really got burned today," he added, poking her arm with his finger and watching the white mark blush scarlet.

"That's not burn. It's tan . . . reddish tan," Amanda argued, gratefully pulling the sweat shirt over her head.

"You're gonna peel. I told you not to use that oil stuff."

"I will not peel. I never peel!"

"Like a ripe banana. Tomorrow morning your grandma's goin' to walk into your room and find an entire skin, just like a snake when it sheds."

The two happily bantered back and forth as they made their way through the tunnel and up the rocky cliff. When they reached the spot where they had met, they stopped to take in the view. The sun was getting low in the sky, and the sand and the cliffs were beginning to reflect the light, turning all shades of shell pink and blue.

"In the movies they call this magic time," Amanda said. "Everything gets all hazy and muted like a watercolor . . . so beautiful it's hard to believe it's real."

"You're right. If I saw this in a movie, I'd never believe it wasn't a painted backdrop."

"It only gets better," Amanda enthused. "Haven't you come out here and watched a sunset before?"

Looking at his watch, Chris replied, "It's a little after seven. I'm usually working or in rehearsal at this time. The few days I've had off, I guess I've been busy."

"Well, have a seat, Mr. Davies, and prepare yourself for the show of a lifetime!" Amanda pulled herself up on the ledge where they had sat the first day they met and patted the rock beside her. Seeing Chris's hesitation, she added, "Come on. We'll wrap the towels around us and be snug as a bug . . . and you can sing to me while the sun goes down."

Chris jumped up beside her and tucked one towel around their legs. The other he gave to Amanda to wrap around her like a shawl. Then he took his guitar and started strumming, letting the beauty before him write the music. Every once in a while Amanda would recognize a melody and hum along, then the tune would turn in a different direction and she knew he was improvising. Finally the chords fell into a pattern she immediately liked but didn't know, and he began to sing. It was a song about a gypsy woman, born in fire and carried away by the wind. It was about love and laughter and the giving of life. It spoke more eloquently about his mother and the way he remembered her than anything he could have said, and Amanda understood as never before the incredible loss he had suffered.

The song built to a frenzied celebration so full of emotion and life she couldn't decide if she wanted to laugh or cry. Then it was over. Chris carefully lifted the guitar over his head and leaned it against the rocks below. Amanda turned to say something—how much she'd liked it . . . how moved she was—but words wouldn't come. She just sat there looking at him, her eyes filled with light, her lips parted to speak. She saw him looking back, searching her eyes for something. Needing . . . wanting . . . The two came closer and closer, never taking their eyes from each other until their lips met. Gentle and self-conscious at first, the kiss soon took on a life of its own . . . hungry, eager, searching.

Amanda had been kissed before but never like this. Always before she had been very aware of noses and hands and lips. "Keep your lips soft," Stacy had once advised her. "That's the secret of a good kisser."

But Stacy's advice was the last thing on her mind as she was breathlessly lost in the moment. Finally pulling apart, the two sat looking out to sea, letting their emotions settle.

"Well," Amanda managed to say, her voice unusually low and husky.

"Well, well," Chris responded, equally shaken.

Chancing a sideways glance, Amanda couldn't help smiling at the bemused look on Chris's face. Feeling her eyes on him, he returned the glance and for the next few seconds they played eye tag, looking away and back again until they both sat staring straight ahead with silly grins on their faces. Then Chris put his arm around her, shifting around until she sat nestled in his arms.

As they watched, the sun became a blazing ball racing to cool itself in the waters of the Pacific, and the clouds caught fire in its glow. The sand reflected the copper light, and the waves sparkled as if dusted with silver confetti. As the sun touched the edge of the horizon, the wind grew still, paying homage to the ending day. At first the orange ball seemed to sit on the water, but within seconds a flat line cut across its bottom. Soon the circle was cut in half as the sun began to slip away. Chris was amazed at how fast it sank, as though someone had sped up the film and everything was happening in double time. Finally nothing was left but an orange glow.

Looking up, Amanda could see the first faint stars in the deepening blue sky, and she felt a supreme contentment. "Listen!" she whispered, leaning her head on Chris's shoulder.

"What?" he asked, not hearing anything.

"Happy," she replied, raising her face to receive his kiss.

Nine

*L*ooking back, Amanda always pictured that summer as an emotional roller coaster. The first few weeks were slow and labored as she and Chris inched their way cautiously to the top. But once at the summit, they plummeted into their relationship with breathtaking speed, taking the twists and turns of the summer with wild abandon.

Amanda felt the change immediately. Chris was no longer reticent to let people know about their relationship, practically making a public announcement the following night when he came into the girls' dressing room and in front of everyone asked her to wait for him in the lobby after the show. No more secret rendezvous at May's. The next evening he caught her at intermission, saying some of the gang were going out for pizza after the show and they had been invited. It was amazing to Amanda how quickly it was understood that she and Chris were now a "they."

On Thursday she was working at the Shoppe when she heard the tinkle of the bell that welcomed everyone who walked through the front door. She barely looked up, since the bell had been ringing all morning and she was intent on wrapping a small glass vase she had just sold to a visitor from Atlanta. She practically dropped the box when it belatedly registered that the newcomer was a tall, dark-haired Texan. Dressed in clean jeans and an ironed work shirt with his hair slicked back, it was clear he had finally come to meet her grandparents.

"Thought it was about time I saw where you spend your mornings," he greeted her, obviously enjoying her surprise. "This is a great place. Is it okay if I just look around?"

"Of course," she replied, unable to hide her delight. "If you give me a minute, I'll take you on a guided tour."

"Take your time. I'll go feed the fish," he said, nodding in the direction of a display of porpoises and whales carved out of soapstone.

Amanda watched him out of the corner of her eye as he studied the carvings with genuine admiration. He then moved on, unhurried, taking time to really look and appreciate, running his hands over the polished woods of the antiques her grandfather had so lovingly restored, even stopping to closely inspect the fine needlework on a particularly intricate quilt. *A lover of beauty,* she thought as she walked up to join him in front of the driftwood display.

"These are amazing!" he proclaimed, gingerly reaching out to touch one of the highly varnished works of art. "I see pieces of wood like this on the beach all the time. How incredible that a man can look at something so ordinary and see such beauty."

He casually put his arm around her shoulder as they turned away, nearly colliding head on with Amanda's grandmother.

"Grams!" Amanda gasped, wishing she had had a chance to prepare her grandparents for Chris's visit. It wasn't that they were unaware she was seeing someone. She had mentioned that a young man from the theater was walking her home each night, and when he called on Monday to ask her to the beach, she had confirmed that they were dating. But she knew her grandparents' idea of a suitable boy for their granddaughter was far removed from the rugged, worldly young man who now stood with his arm possessively around her shoulders.

"Grams, this is . . . my friend . . . Chris Davies," Amanda nervously stuttered.

Releasing Amanda, Chris held out his hand. "Happy to make your acquaintance, ma'am. Amanda has told me so much about you, I feel like I already know you."

Amanda could see her grandmother struggling to hide her surprise as she took his hand and nervously shook it.

"Well, I wish I could say the same. . . . Chris, is it? I'm afraid my granddaughter has kept you quite a mystery. But now that the mystery is solved, I'm happy to meet you, too." Emma Mitchell spoke haltingly, obviously flustered and uncertain what to feel about the young man who stood before her. "Please, come in the back and meet Amanda's grandfather," she invited, leading the way through a door hidden behind an antique Oriental screen.

Here was the room where Kevin Mitchell spent his time rescuing fine old furniture from the ravages of time and overenthusiastic do-it-yourselfers. As they entered the cluttered workshop, the pungent smell of turpentine and varnish assailed their nostrils. They found the silver-haired old gentleman painstakingly scraping off the last remnants of blue paint some misguided soul had used to "update" a nineteenth-century golden oak chest.

"Em, it never ceases to amaze me what fools people can be," he grunted, not bothering to look up. "Can you imagine painting over this wood?"

"But look at it now, Grandpa! It's going to be absolutely beautiful when you get finished with it!" Amanda stooped down, surprising the old man with a kiss. "He always complains," she explained, looking up at Chris. "But the truth is, nothing gives him more pleasure than uncovering a hidden treasure like this one." She traced the grain admiringly with her finger as she spoke.

"Kevin," Grams spoke up, "Amanda's brought her young man to meet us."

The old man stood slowly, removing his work gloves. Then he turned with a friendly, appraising look as his wife went on.

"This is Chris. . . ?"

"Davies," Chris finished, offering the older man his hand. "Nice to meet you."

"Is that an accent I hear?" Grandpa Mitchell asked, taking the offered hand in a firm grip. "Sounds like Texas."

"Yes, sir. Lubbock."

"You don't say. I spent some time there . . . years ago."

Amanda watched as the two men talked, grateful for Chris's efforts to ingratiate himself, even though she knew he had been extremely nervous and hesitant to meet her grandparents. Far more than she, he never lost sight of the differences between them, such as the inequities in their family backgrounds and financial situations, and most important, their differing views of God.

Chris had made it clear to Amanda that he saw God as some sort of aloof ultimate Being, capable of great creativity and superior intellect but uninvolved and cold. To Chris, God was this cosmic scientist who had put us on earth like rats in a maze and then dispassionately sat back to see how we were going to survive. He found Amanda's concept of a loving, caring heavenly Father naive and incompatible with his life experience. She sensed his discomfort whenever she talked about God, as though he found even the mention of God somehow threatening. It was a subject she felt she needed to approach carefully.

While Amanda finished her shift in the shop, Chris kept her grandfather company, offering to help sand an old armoire in the meantime. When Amanda came to get him an hour later, she was dismayed to find her perfectly groomed "gentleman caller" covered from head to toe with fine wood dust and sweat.

"Always did like a man who knew how to pitch in and be useful," Grandpa said, patting Chris on the back and giving Amanda a wink in reply to her look of outrage.

"I think you made a hit," Amanda laughed a few minutes later, trying to brush some of the dust off Chris's shirt as they stood on the sidewalk under the hand-carved sign that marked the entrance to the Shoppe.

"Believe it or not, I wasn't trying to make points . . . well, maybe a little. But I really enjoy working with my hands. And your grandfather is a great old guy. I enjoyed talking with him. Now, your grandmother is another story."

"What does that mean?" Amanda demanded, ready to fly to her grandmother's defense.

"Just that she's not so certain about me."

Amanda would have liked to deny it, but she knew it was true. After she and Grams had gone back out front, she had asked her grandmother what she thought. The older woman had hesitated, choosing her words carefully so as not to sound hard or judgmental. "He seems very nice. And he is certainly good-looking! I understand perfectly why you're attracted to him. But remember, Amanda, we are different. He comes from a world that doesn't understand many of the things we believe and . . . well, I just don't want to see you get hurt."

❧ ❧ ❧ ❧

On Sunday Grams insisted they both come for one of her famous fried-chicken dinners after the matinee. The chicken lived up to its reputation, crispy on the outside, tender and juicy on the inside. The conversation also lived up to their expectations . . . pleasant on the outside, probing and concerned on the inside.

At first Grandpa kept them in stitches with stories of his early days in the military and later as a stunt pilot traveling the circuit after World War One. He spoke honestly about what a rabble-rouser he had been until the day he'd lost control of his plane and stared eternity in the face. Amanda had never heard the story of her grandfather's dramatic conversion to Christianity. In fact, she had never heard half the stories he was sharing with them, and she was as fascinated as Chris to know that her dear, godly grandfather had once been a reckless, irreverent "sinner."

Her grandmother picked up the story, telling how the two of them had met. "I was nineteen and practically engaged to a boy named Bobby Watson. His family went to my father's church, and we had grown up together. Bobby was everything my parents thought I needed . . . stable, trustworthy, and the heir apparent to his father's nursery business. Boring!

"Then one Sunday I looked down from the choir loft and saw this tall, good-looking stranger sitting in the front row. In his leather flight jacket and dungarees, he stuck out like a sore thumb among all the proper suits and ties, but he drank in every word of my father's sermon like a man who'd just wandered out of the desert into an oasis. The more I watched him, the more I liked what I saw. And Lord knows he was cute! Still is," Grams added, giving Grandpa one of those looks that used to make Amanda feel uncomfortable when she was younger. Now she simply felt in awe of the love and passion her grandparents still obviously felt for each other. "By the end of the service I'd decided to marry him. . . ."

"And six months later, she did. I never had a chance!" Grandpa finished, giving Chris a wink as he reached to cover his wife's hand with his own. They sat holding hands like young lovers, and Amanda felt Chris take her hand under the table.

"Sometimes that's how it happens," Chris commented, "like a bolt of lightning. Someone comes into your life and you just know they're the one."

Amanda caught a worried look pass between her grandparents, and she was sure Chris saw it, too, because he tightened the grip on her hand.

"Lightning can be deceptive," Emma Mitchell softly replied. "It's beautiful to look at, but it can also be very destructive." For a moment the air was charged with tension, and Amanda breathed a sigh of relief as she heard Grams say, "But enough about us. We want to hear about you, Chris. Tell us about your family."

"There's nothing much to tell, really," he began in response. "I was born and raised on a ranch outside of Lubbock, as was my dad and his dad before him—"

"And his mother was a gypsy," Amanda gaily interrupted, relieved to be back on safe ground.

Her announcement succeeded in getting a surprised "Really?" out of her grandmother, and Chris gave her a nudge as he replied, "No, not really. That's just the way I always think of her. Actually, she was Italian, and she and my dad couldn't have been more different. But they loved each other." He paused. "She died when I was thirteen."

"Oh, Chris, we're so sorry!" Grams said, her eyes filled with compassion. "That must have been very hard for you."

"Yeah, well . . . stuff happens. Anyway, I played a little baseball in high school, but music is my first love. I graduated from college this year with a degree in music. I came to California hoping to eventually get to L.A. and find work as a studio musician or something. Who knows what will happen? Amanda's always telling me that God has a plan, but whatever it is, He hasn't let me in on it yet. If worse comes to worse, I can always teach."

His reference to God gave Amanda's grandmother the opening she'd apparently been waiting for and she jumped right in. "And do you believe that? That God has a plan?" Gram's look was direct and searching, but it was also kind and genuinely curious, and Chris answered her directly.

"Well, ma'am, I've never felt much need to go askin' anyone else's permission to do what I think is right. I think everyone's gotta take responsibility for their own life, whether they choose to do something with it or just fritter it away. Now, don't get me wrong. I've got great respect for God. He showed me a long time ago that He is bigger and stronger than I am, and I'm certainly not lookin' to get Him riled up at me."

Amanda was fascinated by what she was hearing. She was amazed that Chris was being so transparent. She also noticed with some amusement that his accent had deepened in direct proportion to the intensity of what he was saying.

"So you *do* believe in God?" Grams asked, sounding uncertain about Chris's explanation.

"Oh yes, ma'am, I do. I'm just not so sure He believes in me."

Chris and Amanda left the Mitchells' shortly after, explaining that they needed to walk off some of the potatoes and gravy and apple pie they had stuffed themselves with. Emma and Kevin Mitchell stood at the door and waved, watching until they disappeared around the corner as they headed toward the beach.

As they walked on the beach in the glow of the setting sun, Chris confessed that he had not wanted to go to Amanda's grandparents' for dinner that day, fearing he would have to listen to three hours of sermonizing. Instead, he had found them to be warm, real, and very down-to-earth.

"Yeah, *I* had no idea how down-to-earth they are," Amanda agreed, still reeling from her grandfather's revelation of his wild youth.

They both fell into thoughtful silence as they walked at the water's edge, allowing the waves to nip at their feet and chase them higher and higher until they were forced to find refuge on the jutting rock by the entrance to the sea tunnel.

Amanda found herself replaying the day, relieved that her grandparents had seemed to like Chris, even if they still had their doubts about how right he was for her. She had been proud of the way he had looked and talked and behaved, even offering to help with the dishes after dinner. And after hearing the story of how her grandparents met, she understood with far greater clarity why her grandmother was so concerned. Grams knew it was possible for a young woman Amanda's age to fall head-over-heels in love at a moment's notice, because that was how it had happened to her, and she was fearful that Amanda was following in her footsteps. For the first time Amanda wondered herself if what she and Chris felt for each other was more than a summer infatuation.

Silently they watched the remnants of the day fade to darkness and a full moon emerge above the Pacific.

"Penny for your thoughts."

Chris's soft drawl made Amanda smile as she realized she'd been lost in her reflections.

"You'd be paying far too much," she replied with a small laugh. She felt him put his arm around her, drawing her close to his side. She

instinctively knew that they had reached a new plateau in their relationship, having survived the treacherous ordeal of dinner with the
family, and there was a new intensity in the way Chris was holding her
that told her he felt the same.

She felt his lips on her ear, nibbling in a playful, intimate way. He
had never taken this kind of liberty before, limiting his displays of
affection to relatively chaste hugs and kisses. She knew he had kept
things deliberately low-key for her sake, not wanting to offend or
scare her. He saw her as very young and innocent when it came to sex,
and he was right. She had shyly admitted to him after their first real
kiss that she had never been kissed like that before.

Now as Chris turned her face and captured her mouth with his
own, Amanda found herself responding with an uninhibited passion
she thought only existed in books, which is why it took her several
moments to realize that Chris's hands had wandered out of the des-
ignated safety zones and into dangerous, uncharted territory. Suddenly she understood for the first time why parents always warned of
how easy it is to lose control and go too far.

Having never felt a strong physical attraction to any of the nice
but unexciting boys she had dated back home, Amanda had always
felt totally in control and even worried at times that she might be
frigid, as one rebuffed young man had once suggested when she had
refused to make out at a party. But she was suddenly quite sure that
the accusation had no foundation in fact, and it took every ounce of
self-control she had left to pull away.

Shaking and gasping for air, Amanda felt as though she had just
been in a train wreck. Her head spun, her heart raced, and every single
nerve in her body was buzzing. She knew Chris was watching her in
the moonlight, trying to read her expression, which she kept carefully
turned away until she felt at least halfway normal again. When she
finally had the nerve to look at him, she expected to find the same
amused look she'd seen so often when he knew he had succeeded in
flustering her.

Instead, his look was uncertain and confused, still smoldering with
the desire he obviously felt for her but questioning and even a little
fearful. Amanda wasn't used to seeing such vulnerability reflected in
those confident blue eyes, and her first instinct was to reassure him.
She smiled, laughing a shaky little laugh.

"It's okay, I just . . . I mean, I never . . ." Her words trailed off as she saw a slow smile spread across his face and he leaned in to kiss her again. "No, I mean—" But her weak protest was cut off and once again she felt herself lifted up and carried away on a deliciously unfamiliar wave of passion.

Chris had felt tremendous relief when Amanda had turned and smiled at him. He had feared he'd gone too far when he felt her pull away from him and saw how upset she was. The last thing he wanted to do was scare her or push her too fast. But God knew he had been careful, showing the restraint and patience of one of Amanda's saints until five minutes ago. And the way she responded to him told him she was every bit as ready as he was to take their relationship beyond the junior high level he had purposely kept it at.

Today had been a breakthrough. Today he had gone right into the lions' den and faced his worst enemy: Amanda's family. And not only had he come out in one piece but he'd emerged with Amanda still firmly at his side.

He knew that the Mitchells still weren't thrilled that Amanda was seeing a "heathen," but he felt they had been fair with him, acknowledging that he was a real person with worthwhile qualities and honorable intentions. As he was leaving, Emma Mitchell had surprised him by putting her arms around him and giving him a hug—not one of those quick, phony Hollywood hugs, but a real bone crusher. Then she had looked him straight in the eyes and said, "We trust you not to hurt her."

"I'd cut off my right arm first, ma'am," he had replied with all the sincerity he could muster, and the smile she gave him said she believed him.

This exchange had been whispered while Amanda was kissing her grandfather good-bye, and Chris knew she would have been furious to know that they had discussed her as if she were a child that needed special looking after. But in many ways, that was exactly what she was . . . and that was why he had been hesitant to get involved with her in the first place. Now he was in too far to get out if he wanted to. There was a good chance he was in love with this girl, and while the idea should have scared him to death, it didn't. But it *would* frustrate him to death if he couldn't start showing her how much she meant to him.

Holding her in his arms and feeling her return his kisses with such sweet abandon, he realized what a gift he'd been given. He would be the one to awaken Sleeping Beauty and introduce her to all the exciting pleasures a man and woman can give each other. Not that he would ever try to go all the way. He understood that there was still a line she wouldn't cross, and he would never want her to do anything she'd regret later . . . but it would be fun to see just how close to that line they could get.

Even as he was warning himself to take it slow, his hand slipped under her shirt, stroking her silky smooth back in lazy circles that gradually reached higher and higher. He was totally lost in the feel and the smell of her when suddenly she was gone, jumping up like a scared rabbit and disappearing into the dark of the sea tunnel.

This time Chris didn't bother to censor the colorful expletives that came out of his mouth. He had deliberately made an effort to clean up his language when he was around Amanda, seeing how uncomfortable she got when he peppered sentences with four-letter words. But she wasn't there to hear him now anyway, was she? She'd run away. Rejected him. Made him feel like a fool! A wave of anger washed over him. All he wanted to do was show her how much he cared for her in a normal, healthy way. It wasn't his fault that she had a case of arrested development when it came to men. Every girl he knew had made out in the backseat by the time they'd reached their sixteenth birthday—and that was in Lubbock! California girls were supposed to be even more experienced. It was just his luck to fall in love with the last remaining virgin on the entire West Coast!

He was well into working himself up into an indignant lather when it hit him. *In love* . . . There it was. He'd said it, if only to himself. He loved this girl, in spite of, or maybe—perish the thought—*because* of all the differences between them. She saw life in a clean, idealistic way he had forfeited long ago, and her simple optimism made him see possibilities far beyond the limits of his own timid dreams. He needed her, something he had never let himself admit before, and if he had to play by her rules in order to be what she needed in return, he would do it!

All of this soul-searching had taken no more than a few minutes, and Chris jumped up to follow Amanda. If he hurried he should be able to catch up with her before she reached the top. Making his way through the tunnel at night was more difficult than he'd expected.

The moonlight only managed to infiltrate a few feet, and Chris felt he was navigating a "black hole" as he groped his way through the cold, damp tube of stone.

He had stubbed his toe and nearly knocked himself out on a jagged outcropping by the time he came limping out on the other side. All hope of catching Amanda was gone. It had taken him far too long to navigate the short distance, and he was mumbling under his breath as he swung around the corner onto the path leading to the top. At least it was a clear night and the moon was bright. He would have no trouble seeing his way home.

"What took you so long?"

She was sitting on the familiar shelf of stone waiting for him. She had regained her composure, and her face was incredibly beautiful in the moonlight.

"Amanda!" He was so glad to see her that he immediately started toward her.

"Stay right there, cowboy!"

He hesitated, then started to move in, just wanting to hold her and reassure her.

"I mean it, Chris. One more step and you'll wish you'd brought a net!" she warned, casting a significant look over the edge.

"It's okay, Amanda. I promise I'm not going to attack you. It won't be easy," Chris said, looking at the way her hair shone in the moonlight and wanting to bury his face in it, "but I have myself under control . . . Scout's honor," he added, lifting three fingers with a mischievous grin.

Amanda laughed, then got serious again. "It isn't *you* I'm worried about. It's me. I've gotten a glimpse of what I'm capable of and it isn't pretty," she said, sadly shaking her head like a naughty little girl. "You see, I've never felt like this with anyone. I know you think that's crazy, but it takes two, you know, and I just never met anyone who really . . . got to me . . . until now."

She glanced up at him, her look shy and embarrassed. He knew how hard it was for her to be this honest with him, and he longed to make it easier for her, but he didn't know how. All he could do was smile at her encouragingly.

"You see," she went on, taking a deep breath, "being with you is the most exciting and wonderful thing that's ever happened to me and I really . . . care about you."

She hesitated, as if trying to think just how to explain her feelings. "But I also care about myself and I don't want to lose 'me' trying to be what you want me to be. I know you think I'm young and naive, and I know there is an awful lot about life that I don't understand, but I do know one thing. The things I believe are the foundation of my life, and if I start chipping away at that foundation, throwing out the parts that are suddenly hard or inconvenient, that foundation will eventually crumble and I'll go right down with it! So as much as I care about you and want you in my life, you're just going to have to understand . . ."

She finally ran out of words, looking embarrassed and uncertain how to finish.

"You're not going to sleep with me. I know," he finished for her.

Amanda looked at him, surprise written all over her face.

"Amanda," he continued gently, "I understand everything that you have just said to me. I've known it all along! Why do you think it took me so long to decide to get involved with you? I know who you are and what you believe, and while I may not totally agree, I certainly respect your right to live your life according to your own rules. I was just hoping we could bend them a little," he added, giving her a playful look that made her giggle. "Is it safe? May I approach now?" he asked, inching his way toward her, but her look was still uncertain.

"So you'll wait?" she asked in a small voice.

"*We'll* wait until the time is right for *both* of us," he reassured her.

"And you really won't mind?" she asked, finally looking at him with eyes so full of gratitude and joy he thought he'd have to kiss her soon or die.

"I said we'd wait. I didn't say I'd like it. I'm disciplined, not dead! Now, come here, woman, and remind me of all I'm going to miss!" He reached up and lifted her off the ledge, sliding her body slowly down his. "Oh yeah," he said as he bent his head to kiss her, "it's coming back to me."

Ten

C"old?" Chris asked, seeing Amanda shiver and rub her arms.

"A little," Amanda admitted, turning to look for her sweater.

"Come here. I'll warm you up," Chris offered, giving her a look that set her blood racing.

"I know. That's what I'm afraid of," Amanda laughed. "I think I'd better just put on my sweater."

They were sitting on a blanket watching the sun go down, only this time they were sharing the spectacular scenery with most of the cast and crew from the theater. Ana and Mack had arranged a beach party to celebrate the halfway mark of the summer, and everyone had spent this Monday off in late July swimming, playing volleyball, and lazing in the sun. A big bonfire had been started, and people were already gathering around it to cook hot dogs stuck on straightened wire hangers. Later there would be fireworks to make up for the ones they had all missed working on the Fourth of July.

Stacy and her boyfriend, Ben, came over and plopped down on the blanket.

"Mack and Ana sure do know how to throw a party," Stacy exclaimed, resting her head companionably on Amanda's shoulder. "I don't think I've ever been so worn out from having fun!"

She yawned big and let her full weight relax against her friend. Then suddenly she sat upright, as though she had just remembered something important. "Guess what I heard?" She looked around at her audience, making sure everyone was giving her their undivided attention. "There's going to be an open mike night at the Seventh Wave in Santa Barbara next Sunday."

"What's the Seventh Wave?" Chris asked, his curiosity piqued.

"Just the hottest club this side of L.A. All the big-name jazz and rock groups play there. But once or twice a year they have this open mike night and new talent can take the stage. Agents come up from L.A. and if they like you, you can walk away with a contract in your pocket, just like that!"

Amanda looked at Chris, knowing by the way he was intently studying his feet that he was trying hard not to show his excitement.

Stacy went on. "Now, I figure that if we get everyone to speed up the matinee on Sunday, we can be out of there by five-fifteen . . . five-thirty at the latest. It's an hour-and-a-half drive to Santa Barbara, which means, barring any unforeseeable problems—" she paused for dramatic effect—"we should have Chris there in plenty of time to make the eight o'clock deadline."

Chris looked up, unable to hide his surprise. He found all three young people grinning at him with expectancy. Of course, they all knew he was a great pianist. He managed to make the old upright he played at the theater sound like a whole orchestra every night. And he had occasionally fooled around backstage with his guitar, but he had never actually sung any of his own songs for anyone other than Amanda.

"I don't understand. Why me?" He looked at Amanda's twitching eye and suddenly understood.

"You never said your music was a secret!" she immediately defended. "It's so wonderful, how could I not brag a little to my best friend? Besides, you're never going to become famous if no one ever hears it!"

Chris looked at her with a mixture of affection and exasperation. His music was so personal, so much an expression of who he was, that he only felt free to share it in situations where he was safe. The way he saw it, at home everyone knew him. He was "Chris Davies, Boy Wonder," and everything he did was wonderful. At Lucy B's he only played late at night, surrounded by musicians who instinctively understood what he was trying to do and weren't there to judge. And then there was Amanda, who would think anything he did was great just because it was his. It never seriously occurred to him that what he wrote was so real and honest and uncompromising that one day the whole world would sit up and listen.

"Come on, Chris. You'll never know how good you are until you put it out there. Besides, what have you got to lose?"

This was Ben speaking. An intense young man with sandy blond hair and an infectious smile, Ben was a study in contradictions. Usually quiet and reserved in real life, he came to life on stage with an uninhibited charm that made Will Parker and his *Molly Brown* characters nightly favorites. Tall and lanky, he had seemed destined for the basketball court, giving his father visions of NBA glory in the future. But Ben had chosen instead to put his moves to music, and every night he amazed the audience with his ability to defy gravity with some of his jumps and turns.

"I don't believe my father ever forgave me for becoming a dancer," he had once confided to Chris. Here was a man who had paid a price to follow his dream. Now he was challenging Chris to do the same.

"I guess . . . nothing," Chris replied to Ben's question, allowing a smile to finally express his excitement. "I just don't know what I'll sing. How many songs do I do?" he asked Stacy, his mind suddenly racing.

"You should have two ready to go, but the second one is only used if the audience really likes you and wants more. So your first song should be your best. . . . I know! Why don't you sing us some and we can help you decide?"

Chris looked immediately uncomfortable, and Amanda was shocked to realize he was feeling shy. "I don't have my guitar," he mumbled.

"No problem." Ben jumped up and carefully stepped over Stacy as he explained. "Jake Peterson brought his. I'll just ask to borrow it."

Within minutes he was back and handing Chris the guitar. Chris self-consciously strummed a few chords, testing to see if it was in tune. Then thinking for a few moments, he chose a song he'd written about a year ago. It talked about the restlessness of a young man trapped in a nowhere town and how the love of a young girl finally gave him the courage to leave and pursue his dreams, even though it meant he would leave her behind. It was a soulful tune full of bittersweet refrains, and the images it evoked stayed with the listener long after the music faded.

After a moment of thoughtful silence, Chris then launched into a rib-tickling tune that described in vivid colors the regulars who occupied the barstools at a raucous old roadhouse like Lucy B's. And after that he sang a lively rendition of a song he had written in tribute to an old jazzman he'd met when he was just seventeen, who had taken great pleasure in describing to him the connection between playing his sax and making love to his woman.

By the time he finished that song nearly everyone on the beach was gathered around listening with rapt attention. Their enthusiastic applause and cries for more filled the air, and Chris could have gone on and on, oblivious of the fact that night was fully upon them.

But suddenly there was an explosion of colored lights as fireworks lit up the sky, creating a burst of falling stars that left fiery trails as they fell to the ocean. Then a large red carnation bloomed overhead, followed by a series of smaller green and blue bursts.

As quickly as the crowd had gathered it dispersed, breaking into smaller clusters to enjoy the spectacular display. Stacy and Ben snuggled, oohing and aahing over every new design. Amanda turned to Chris to comment, but he was staring out to sea, unaware of the explosions of light all around him. Reaching out, she took his hand.

"Hey, where are you?"

He slowly came back from wherever he had gone and squeezed her hand. "They liked it. They really liked my music." He looked at her with an expression of wonder and pure joy.

"Yes, they did." Amanda smiled in return. "Did you really think they wouldn't?"

"I didn't know . . . I wasn't sure."

Pulling her into his arms, he held her as the fireworks burst overhead, but close as they were, Amanda was aware she had lost him again to his own world. Every once in a while he would pat her arm, but it was an unconscious act rather than an acknowledgment of her presence. And when she tried to draw him into conversation, his answers were short and distracted.

He had once said that there was a difference between what he wanted and what he needed. For the first time Amanda wondered into which category she fell.

છે   છે   છે   છે

The drive to Santa Barbara that next Sunday made Mr. Toad's Crazy Ride at Disneyland look tame. True to Murphy's Law, everything that could go wrong did. The matinee started nearly fifteen minutes late due to the late arrival of a bus from the local retirement home. Since it carried nearly a fourth of the audience, there was nothing to do but wait. The show ran longer than it ever had, despite Stacy's constant admonitions to the cast to "Speed it up!" and by the time the four young people were ready to climb into the little red Volkswagen, it was already after six o'clock.

It was decided that Ben would drive and Chris would occupy the copilot's seat, since there was no way either man could comfortably fold his legs into the backseat. Stacy became the navigator, since she knew the route best. This cast Amanda in the role of the nervous backseat driver, alternating between urging Ben to drive faster and screaming for him to slow down as they wove in and out of traffic and careened around the hairpin turns of the Pacific Coast Highway.

It was seven-forty-five when they saw the exit signs for Goleta, home of the University of California at Santa Barbara. The Seventh Wave was located just off campus. Pulling into the parking lot of the renovated warehouse, Amanda was relieved to see that the parking lot was only about a third full.

"Looks like we made it in time," she said. "We're practically the first ones here!"

"The show doesn't start until nine and the audience won't fill up until after ten, but Chris has to be registered before eight!" Stacy explained as she was pushing Chris out the door and squeezing out of the backseat. "Ben, you park the car! Then you and Manda find us a table," she barked as she and Chris headed for the entrance marked "Artists."

A few minutes later Ben and Amanda walked into the Seventh Wave, presenting their driver's licenses to prove they were over eighteen. The large, high-ceilinged room could easily accommodate five hundred people if the tables were removed and the dance floor used for seating. But tonight tables had been set up in front of the stage and the back half of the auditorium had been closed off with portable screens. The effect was one of a small, intimate night club. The stage was bare except for a number of microphones, several stools, and a piano. Each performer or group would be given a few minutes to rearrange the stage to their liking.

Finding a table about halfway back and slightly left of center, Amanda and Ben settled in, waiting nervously for Stacy and Chris to join them. After twenty minutes passed and they hadn't returned,

Amanda started to worry that something had gone wrong. She was just about to go looking for them when she saw them enter through a side door. Waving, she caught their attention and they quickly made their way to the table.

"You won't believe it! They almost didn't let him play!" Stacy exclaimed, rolling her big blue eyes in disgust.

"Why not?" Ben asked.

"It seems I was supposed to send in a tape and preregister," Chris drawled dryly, giving Stacy one of his don't-mess-with-me-I'm-dangerous looks.

"You're not playing?!" Amanda gasped.

"Of course he's playing!" Stacy snapped. "I simply told them there had to be a mix-up. Mr. Davies sent in a tape, was accepted, and had flown all the way from Lubbock, Texas, to be here!"

"You lied?" Amanda said weakly, suddenly feeling sick.

"Not exactly. Chris did fly in from Texas . . . two months ago," Stacy muttered, refusing to look Amanda in the eye.

"And they believed you?" Ben added, unable to keep the admiration out of his voice.

Stacy flashed him a triumphant smile.

"Bravo!" he replied, giving her a three-clap salute. Then he turned to Chris. "When do you go on?"

"I'll be lucky to get on before midnight. I have to go last."

The room had filled considerably by the time the first musical group took the stage. Looking around, Amanda noted that it was a mixed crowd. Half were college age, dressed in the official uniform of jeans and T-shirts. The other half were older and more stylishly dressed, obviously friends and relatives of the performers, come to cheer them on.

And then there were the agents.

"There's one!" Stacy whispered excitedly, pointing to a fortyish man with thinning hair dressed in designer jeans. An open-collared shirt revealed a heavy gold chain around his neck, and he wore Gucci loafers without socks. "I wonder what label he's with?" This set the others on a visual scavenger hunt, and within minutes they had spotted half a dozen likely candidates.

For the most part the amateurs who performed that night were talented and polished. It was obvious that the Seventh Wave didn't allow just anyone to take their stage, and it was easy to see why so many successful singers got their first break on nights like this. Even so, the discerning audience only demanded encores about a third of the time, and even that was too often as far as the small group from Walker's Point was concerned. There were nearly twenty different acts waiting to go on, and every encore meant a later showtime for Chris.

During the early part of the evening, Chris managed to stay relaxed, listening to the music with an objective ear. There was one group called Eagle's Cry that particularly impressed him. Their music was crisp and clean, showing great originality and heart, and the audience loved them, enthusiastically demanding a second helping. The agent in the Gucci loafers also seemed impressed, jotting down about a half page of notes. Chris wasn't surprised. The four backup musicians were exceptional, and if it were not for the lackluster performance of the lead singer, he would have been surprised to see them walk away without a contract.

As the evening wore on, Amanda could sense a subtle change in Chris. Gradually he pulled away, separating himself from the table conversation to prepare himself for his time on stage. Around eleven-thirty he kissed her and excused himself, explaining that he needed time to change and prepare.

By midnight there were still three acts before Chris and Amanda nervously noted that people were starting to leave. Most of the "agents" they had spotted earlier had already left and Mr. Gucci, as they had taken to calling him, was definitely looking tired. A young woman dressed in a sequined pantsuit stepped to the microphone and began singing an overly dramatic version of an old Carpenters song. By the second note Amanda could tell the agent had had enough. Gathering his things, he didn't even wait until the song was finished before walking out.

The next two acts were just okay, and the audience was growing more and more restless. A number of them were standing to leave when the emcee stepped to the mike and announced, "Hold on, folks! We have just one more act, and I think this is one you're gonna want to stay for!" Since the man had never heard Chris's music, Amanda could only surmise that he was trying to pique their interest so Chris wouldn't come out to an empty house.

A few people still left, but most sat down, deciding somewhat grudgingly to stick it out. As his name was announced Chris walked out on stage, and Amanda was immediately struck by how compelling he was. He had changed into fresh jeans and a crisp white shirt, leaving the starched collar open and rolling up the sleeves a couple of turns. The cowboy boots he now wore made his legs appear even longer, and his dark hair hung loose and wild. The audience settled, fascinated by his presence on stage before he'd even sung a note.

It had been decided that Chris would open with "The Gypsy" and then follow it, if given the opportunity, with a more contemporary rock tune that would show his versatility. Both would be done with guitar, so it was a surprise to them all when he set his guitar down and sat at the piano. Taking a moment to adjust the mike, Chris looked out at the audience, locking those magnificent blues on as many individuals as possible. A slight smile played around his mouth, and his expression said, "Have I got somethin' good for you!" By the time he struck the first chord, everyone was leaning forward in their seats, waiting.

What happened next would always give Amanda chills when she thought of it. Chris's head went back and out of the depths of his being a note came out of such pure joy and power that the entire audience jumped as he launched into a jazz-inspired celebration of life. His fingers flew over the keys and his whole body rocked as the music exploded like a flame. His voice was both husky and clear with the rich timbre of a white man with a black soul. The words had to do with the good feelings a man has when he works hard all day and goes home to find his wife and children waiting . . . and for just that one moment, life is perfect. Amanda couldn't help remembering the story Chris had told her, and she was struck again with how closely Chris's music reflected his life.

When the song ended, the crowd clapped and hooted, stamping their feet for more. The emcee walked out visibly impressed to give Chris the go-ahead to do another. Picking up his guitar, Chris seated himself on a stool and then paused, his head lowered until it was so quiet you could hear a pin drop. Amanda was amazed at the natural stage presence he demonstrated. He seemed to know instinctively just how to take control and make the most of every moment.

When his head came up, his eyes were closed as his fingers deftly picked the strings in an opening refrain Amanda had never heard before. She threw a questioning look at Stacy and Ben, but they shrugged their ignorance, and together they waited to hear just what he was going to do.

Amanda Rose walks by the sea,
Her hair, gold streaks of sunlight,
Her eyes look to my very soul,
Her words of love can make me whole
And chase away the night.

Amanda gasped, unable to believe what she was hearing. Her hand flew to cover her open mouth, and her eyes shone with tears as the song went on to chronicle their relationship—not literally, but in sweet metaphors that captured the essence of what they felt for each other. The melody grabbed at the heartstrings, providing the perfect background for Chris's love letter to her.

When it was over, a dreamy silence hovered over the place, as though no one wanted to interrupt the last echoes of music that still reverberated in the air. Then the applause erupted, swelling to thunderous proportions as the audience rose to its feet.

"Gee, the most any boy ever did for me was spray paint 'Buzz and Stacy Forever' on a freeway overpass," Stacy declared, looking at Amanda in awe.

But Amanda was too overwhelmed to reply as she stared at the amazing young man who now stood on the stage bathed in light, accepting the roaring approval of the crowd as though he were born to it. Suddenly she saw his eyes begin to search the audience. He was shading his eyes looking for her, but the spotlight made it hard to see beyond the first few rows. She waited until she figured he was looking at her, then raised her hand, willing it to break through the blinding light. His eyes went past her and then returned as a brilliant smile lit his face and his hand reached out to her in response.

Eleven

*C*hris sang two more songs before the audience would let him go. "A new club record," the emcee announced when he finally shook Chris's hand and declared the evening officially over. It was nearly two in the morning by the time the star of the evening was able to extricate himself from the congratulatory crowd and the weary foursome could climb into the car to start the long drive home.

Chris had not walked away with a contract in his pocket because all of the major players had left by the time he took the stage.

"If only Mr. Gucci had waited just a few minutes longer!" Stacy bemoaned for the third time. "I could just strangle that sequined alley cat! I'm surprised *anyone* was left by the time she finished!"

"Don't be mean, Stace," Amanda chastised, fighting to keep from laughing. "I'm sure she's a . . . very . . . nice lady," she finished lamely. "Besides, we have to believe that what was supposed to happen, happened. Remember . . ."

". . . God has a plan," Stacy and Ben finished for her, in a tired duet.

"Well, He does," Amanda muttered, slightly wounded. "And besides, even though Chris didn't exactly get 'Discovered,' a lot of other nice things happened!"

"You're right, babe. The evening was exactly what it was supposed to be," Chris agreed, still trying to take in the amazing things that had just happened to him. The owner of the club had invited him back in the fall, promising to give him a prime spot on the program. And the drummer from Eagle's Cry had introduced himself, explaining that he was dating one of the waitresses and had been waiting around for her to get off when he heard Chris sing.

"Man, you really had 'em!" he praised. "I'd be real interested in hearing more. Let's get together sometime."

They talked a few minutes more, perhaps sensing that their chance encounter held more meaning than either could fathom at that time, and exchanged addresses, promising to keep in touch.

And just as they were piling into the car, a man appeared out of nowhere and handed Chris a card with his name, Myron Cole, and a phone number printed on it . . . nothing else.

"Nice work. If you're ever in L.A., give me a call" was all he said. Standing no more than five feet two, with a baby face, owl-like glasses, and a thick thatch of reddish brown hair, Myron Cole didn't look old enough to be out of high school, much less be a talent agent, and Chris couldn't help thinking that if they ever did the *Mickey Rooney Story*, he would be perfect for the part. He put the card in his pocket and promptly forgot about it.

Of course, the most startling and profound revelation had been Chris's magical connection with the audience. Something had happened when he walked out on that stage that even he was helpless to explain. A current seemed to flow out of him that filled the air with an electricity so intense one could almost feel the static. That same power had swept him up and carried him along as he had known, without even thinking, just what to do and when to do it. It was this natural instinct that had told him to change the songs.

"It was like I could hear what they were thinking," Chris explained when asked why he hadn't sung "The Gypsy." "The audience was tired and a little bored and ready to call it a night. 'The Gypsy' would have demanded something from them. You have to really listen to it for it to grab you. They didn't want to work that hard. They needed something unexpected and full of energy to pick them up and recharge their batteries. After that, they were ready to meet my Amanda Rose."

Amanda and Chris were cuddled in the backseat, and his arms tightened around her as he spoke. After the performance, the two had not wanted to be separated, so Stacy had put the front passenger seat up as far as it would go, and Chris and Amanda had managed to cram into the backseat for the ride home. They sat slightly sideways so Chris could stretch out his long legs, with Amanda practically sitting on his lap.

As he said this, Amanda turned her head, having to look up to meet his eyes. She still didn't know how to tell him what she felt. The song had been such a surprise, saying far more than he had ever dared to say in person, yet she knew he meant every word. She understood that music gave Chris a way to sort out his feelings and figure out how he really felt about things . . . the way writing in her diary gave her a chance to lay out her life so she could look at it and see what was really going on. The fact that he had decided to share his feelings with the whole world humbled her and filled her with . . . what? Joy, excitement . . . love? She didn't know. All she did know was right now she felt more intensely than ever before in her life, and the man beside her seemed essential to her very being. She wanted to touch him, hold him, feel his breath on her face. Looking up into his eyes, she saw the same need and desire looking back.

They hadn't gone far when the car suddenly swerved violently to the right. The excitement of the evening had finally worn off and they were all drained and exhausted. The three passengers had closed their eyes and promptly gone to sleep. Ben fought valiantly to stay alert, but he was quickly losing the battle, and the little car had drifted over the center line without his noticing. His quick reflexes were all that saved them from a head-on collision. Pulling over to the side, he apologized repeatedly as the reality of how close the call had been sank in.

"It's not your fault, man. You're worn out . . . we all are. I don't think any one of us is up to driving," Chris declared, looking at Amanda's and Stacy's pale faces and cringing again at the thought of what might have happened. "I say we find a cheap motel and get some sleep. We'll get up early and be home for breakfast."

None of the weary travelers were up to arguing. The idea of a soft bed and clean sheets was just too irresistible. At the next exit they saw a weather-beaten sign for a motel that none of them would have even considered staying in at any other time, but tonight the old row of chalet-styled rooms looked like heaven. By pooling their money they were able to come up with just enough to pay for one room with two double beds.

They parked the car and Ben went to open the door, his fatigue so great that it took him three tries to get the key in the lock. Stacy stumbled in after him and Amanda was right behind. But Chris pulled her back, wanting to say good night in private. She leaned back against the wall, too tired to stand on her own, and Chris faced her, propping himself with his hands on either side of her. "I guess I should thank you. Tonight would never have happened if it hadn't been for you."

· "Tonight would have happened, Chris . . . with or without me. You laugh when I talk about a divine destiny, but you have a gift, and someone would have seen it eventually. I'm just glad I was there when it happened. Someday, when you're big and famous, I'll be able to say I knew you when."

"Oh no, you won't, 'cause you're goin' to be right there with me, all the way."

Amanda smiled as she heard his accent thicken. She knew he was waiting for her to respond, but she was so tired her brain just couldn't keep up.

"Chris, honey, there are so many things I want to say to you, about tonight, about the song . . ." She felt her eyes fill with weary tears at the memory of that incredible song, and she wanted to tell him how much it had meant to her. She needed to tell him how much *he* meant to her! It was just that this big yawn kept getting in the way.

Watching her struggle to stay awake, Chris couldn't help feeling a little peeved. Here he was practically proposing, and she couldn't even stay awake. He leaned forward to kiss her and was greeted by another yawn. "Okay, sweet girl, off to bed," he finally gave up.

"But I want to tell you . . ." she protested sleepily as he opened the door and steered her into the room.

"You can tell me tomorrow. It will sound better coming from a person who isn't semicomatose."

It only took Chris a moment to assess the situation and see he was in trouble. Stacy and Ben were curled up together on one of the beds fast asleep. That left the other bed for him and Amanda. Personally he found nothing wrong with this arrangement, but he knew Amanda might not like it if she were in any shape to argue, and he knew for certain that Grandma and Grandpa Mitchell would not be a bit pleased. However, with Amanda practically asleep, he didn't seem to have much choice.

Leading her to one side of the bed, he balanced her against him in just the right position. Then he snatched the covers off just as she tumbled into bed. Removing her shoes, he covered her and then went around to the other side, where he proceeded to remove his boots and shirt.

Amanda snuggled under the covers, the feel of the cool, smooth sheets reminding her of the many times her father had carried her to bed after a particularly late church service when she was little. Her muscles would be screaming for sleep as she hit the bed, and a giant smile would spread through her body as she finally relaxed into peaceful slumber. She was almost there again when for no reason she opened one eye and saw Chris sitting on the other side of the bed calmly removing his pants. Her eyes flew open and she was suddenly wide awake.

"Christopher Brian Davies, what do you think you're doing?" she whispered furiously, trying not to awaken Stacy and Ben, who she just now realized were in the other bed together.

"I'm getting ready to go to bed," Chris replied in a tired voice.

"Which bed? *This* bed?" Amanda squeaked, knowing she was sounding slightly hysterical but not caring.

"Do you have any other suggestions?" Chris asked, turning to look at her with an expression of pure exhaustion. "I don't think there's room in *that* bed, do you?" He pointed his thumb at Stacy and Ben.

"Well, at least leave your jeans on," Amanda pleaded, somehow feeling that that would make it all right.

"I can't sleep in jeans—they're too tight, too stiff."

His back was still to her as he finished pulling off the second leg, so she couldn't see the smile playing around his eyes. He turned off the light and lay down on top of the covers, pulling the bedspread up over him.

"Go to sleep, Amanda Rose. You're safe with me. . . . And when you say your prayers tonight," he couldn't help adding, "be sure and thank that God of yours that I decided to dress up tonight and wear some skivvies."

He smiled into the dark, waiting for her response. Her outraged jab came two seconds later as what he'd said sank in. Then he felt her relax as she turned on her side.

"Good night, cowboy. You were wonderful tonight . . . truly wonderful! Oh, and if you ever breathe a word of this, I'll kill you."

Within minutes he could tell by her even breathing that she was fast asleep, but it was a good hour before sleep finally turned off the instant replay that kept going through his head. Over and over he experienced the thrill of walking out on that stage and feeling the

Twelve

*I*t was after nine o'clock in the morning by the time the little red bug pulled up in front of the Mitchells'. The young people had intended to sleep only a few hours, setting the alarm clock for six. Amanda had hoped to be back in her room before her grandparents even got up, but the alarm hadn't worked and the exhausted travelers had all slept until after eight.

Jumping out of the car, Amanda barely took time to wave as she hurried up the front walk. Chris had wanted to come in with her to explain, but she felt it would be better for her to face her grandparents alone. After all, they hadn't done anything wrong, and as soon as she explained what happened, she was sure the whole incident would be forgotten.

Emma and Kevin Mitchell listened to their granddaughter's apologetic explanation with mixed emotions. Amanda didn't understand that while her grandparents were always in bed by eleven, Grams never settled into a deep sleep until the creak on the stairs told her that Amanda was home safe and sound. She had expected Amanda to be late, but when she hadn't gotten home by two in the morning, Emma had gotten up to keep a nervous vigil by the front window. Within minutes her husband had joined her, his sleep disturbed by her absence. They had been seriously considering calling the police when Amanda had finally walked through the door. Amanda's explanation was simple and sensible, and the Mitchells had no doubt that all had been innocent. But the fact that Chris had not been man enough to face them after keeping their granddaughter out all night was a strike against him. Amanda never thought to explain that she was the one who had kept him from doing just that.

A few days later Amanda woke up to the sound of voices laughing outside her window. Grams often got up early to work in the garden before the sun got hot, and Grandpa would sit on the back steps drinking coffee and keeping her company. But the voices today were different, familiar but out of place. Suddenly Amanda jumped out of bed and raced to the open window.

"Mom! Dad!"

Amanda had expected her parents to bring Nathan up to Walker's Point for a family vacation the last week in August. They would see Amanda's shows, enjoy the beach, and spend time with the elder Mitchells. Then they would take Amanda back with them to get ready for college. A worried phone call had made them decide to rearrange their schedule.

Amanda threw on a robe and hurried down the stairs and out into the warm summer sun. Laughing and talking all at once, she hugged and kissed her parents, realizing how much she had missed her family the last couple of months. Obviously the feeling was mutual. Even Nathan gave her a hug, lifting her off the ground.

"Hey, little brother, what's Mom been feeding you? I swear you've grown four inches since I saw you last!"

It was true. Nathan was almost thirteen and was experiencing an amazing growth spurt. When Amanda left home two months before, they had been about the same height. Now he was at least two inches taller and would soon tower over her.

Karen and Warren Mitchell watched their children with affection and pride. Over the years their house had been jarred with the usual number of fights and complaints, but they were blessed to have children who loved and, more important, liked each other. Their kids had never given them any major problems, which was why they were so surprised and concerned when Warren's mother had called to say she thought there might be a problem with Amanda.

Of all their children, Amanda had been the most trustworthy and level-headed. Karen had sometimes worried that her younger daughter was too conservative, living her life with a quiet resolve that rarely left room for experimentation or spontaneity. She had dated sporadically by choice, turning down more invitations than she accepted and had never seemed overly interested in boys, unlike Lindsey, who had had a new crush every other week.

Warren Mitchell had been more than fine with this arrangement, often boasting that his Amanda was too grown-up to play silly high school dating games. But Karen had seen things a little differently, wondering if Amanda wasn't missing out on an important part of her education. Her daughter had such a simple, straightforward way of approaching things. There was right and there was wrong, and while Karen applauded Amanda's convictions, she knew they had never really been tested, and she wondered if her younger daughter understood her own vulnerability. This was one of the reasons she was happy Amanda had chosen to attend a small Christian liberal arts college located less than a half hour away from home. There she would meet young men of similar backgrounds and convictions who would be less likely to take advantage of her naiveté.

Of course, neither of the Mitchells had foreseen the sudden impact of Chris Davies on their daughter's life.

Amanda knew why her parents had suddenly decided to come to Walker's Point, and so did Chris when she called to tell him that she could not see him that day because her family had arrived. The next couple of days had a surrealistic feel as Amanda went back to being her parents' little girl, building sand castles with her father and brother at the beach in the afternoons, and sitting on her bed late at night catching up with her mother on all the news from home.

She found out that Lindsey was loving her internship with the Los Angeles law firm and would most probably work part time for them after she went back to school to complete her senior year. Of course, there was a certain young lawyer who had taken a special interest in her and in whom she had taken an interest in return. In Lindsey's case there was always a boy, although Amanda was quick to point out that you could hardly call a twenty-six-year-old lawyer a "boy."

"Maybe this will be the one," Amanda had said, finding it hard to imagine her flirtatious, pretty sister actually settling down. "It's got to happen sometime," she added.

"And when it does, I hope and pray that he will be right for her, just as I pray that you will find God's best . . . and Nate." Amanda knew her mother was trying to work up to asking about Chris, and she was relieved that they were finally going to talk about him, while at the same time she feared what her mom would say.

"So tell me about this young man you've been seeing."

Amanda's face lit up as she told her mother the story of how they had met and how slowly and carefully they had taken it at first.

"Amanda, you've been here less than eight weeks. It couldn't have been all that slow," her mother observed dryly.

"Well, it certainly felt like it! At first I didn't think he liked me at all. Then I realized he was actually afraid of me! It was so crazy . . . this gorgeous, talented man afraid of letting me get too close! Then one day, he just let me in. It was like he decided I was worth the risk."

Amanda went on to talk a little about Chris's music and his hopes and dreams. The more her daughter talked, the more alarmed and concerned Karen got. This was no adolescent crush. The young woman before her was no gushing girl, caught up in the throes of a summer fling. In her typical fashion, Amanda had entered this relationship with thought and care and frightening resolve. The fact that this was the first Karen was hearing about it was even more ominous.

"Are you in love with this young man?" she finally asked, dreading the answer.

"I don't know," Amanda said. "Maybe. I'm not sure I know what real love is. All I know is that I have never felt this way with anyone before. He makes me feel things. Magical things . . . like a character in a book. When I wake up, he's the first thing I think of, and when I go to sleep, he's the last. I know how corny it sounds, but I also know I've never been happier."

Karen looked at her daughter's shining eyes and remembered how she had felt the first time she thought she was in love. Fortunately, she had realized in time that he wasn't "the one," but it had been lovely and the memory had always stayed with her. From everything Amanda's grandparents had told them, Chris wasn't "the one" for Amanda, either, but if he gave her a memory to cherish . . . well, every girl should have a first love. Besides, if they made an issue of it and forbade Amanda to see him, they would only succeed in making him more irresistible to her.

"I think we need to meet this young man . . . the sooner the better," Karen suddenly announced, as though she had resolved a nagging question. "Why don't you see if he can have dinner with us tomorrow night?"

"Oh, Mom, thank you!" Amanda threw her arms around her mother.

On Saturday night, Amanda's parents took them out to dinner. She and Chris had to be at the theater before seven, so the Mitchells made an early reservation at the Cove, a Walker's Point landmark. Located in a renovated beach house overlooking a rocky inlet, the Cove was famous for fabulous seafood and two-inch-thick prime rib. The Mitchells were old friends with the owners, and a private screened-in porch with one large round table was reserved for the party of seven.

The porch was built out over a narrow open passage that ran along the side of the old house. Not much more than a wide crack in the rocky cliffs, the rushing waves were funneled through it with increasing speed and power to finally crash with breathtaking force on the rocks below. The resulting spray created natural "dancing fountains" that seemed to jump and sway in time to the classical piano music piped throughout the restaurant.

As they all filed in, Chris couldn't help commenting on the magnificent view. "This was worth coming all the way from Texas to see!" he said, sincerely in awe of the display before him.

"We agree with you, Chris," Warren Mitchell said, pulling out a chair to seat his wife. "We always make sure to eat here at least once during our vacation. The food and the scenery are worth the price!"

"Tell us about your ranch in Texas," Amanda's mom asked, immediately directing the dinner conversation in Chris's direction. The rest of the meal was a thinly disguised interrogation, with the Mitchells asking the questions and Chris doing the answering. Amanda was impressed with how willing he was to talk, showing both humor and intelligence as he hopped from one personal topic to another. By the time dessert was served, her parents seemed to have relaxed a little, and she knew they had been impressed, if not completely won over, by the young man in their daughter's life.

On Sunday night Chris came to the house for the traditional chicken dinner, and afterward Amanda imposed on him to sing some of his songs for her family. He carefully chose a number of fun tunes that had nothing to do with wine or women, finishing with "The Gypsy." Everyone was overwhelmed by what they heard. Her parents, her grandparents, even Nate, couldn't find enough nice things to say. So Amanda was feeling pretty cocky and optimistic as she and Chris finally slipped away for a walk on the beach.

"I think they love you! I can't believe how impressed my parents were. And Grams . . . did you see the tears in her eyes when you finished 'The Gypsy'?" She was dancing along beside him, her face flushed with relief and joy.

Chris watched her in the moonlight, like some mystical creature out of a fairy tale—so young, so beautiful, so hopelessly childlike in her belief that all stories end "happily ever after." How could he tell her it wasn't that easy? Yes, they had liked the music. And yes, they were being nice to him, tolerating him for her sake. After all, the summer was almost over. Three more weeks and they could whisk her off to school and out of harm's way.

But he had seen the fear in Karen Mitchell's eyes as she watched the two of them interact. And he had felt Warren Mitchell stiffen whenever Chris touched his daughter. He sensed now more strongly than ever that Amanda's family saw him as a threat precisely *because* he was presentable and talented with a promising future, not some awkward, pimple-faced kid whom Amanda would easily forget once she was away at college.

෨ ෨ ෨ ෨

The following Friday, Amanda and Chris waved her parents off on their way back to Pasadena. Nate was staying for another week, since a good friend of his had just arrived for a week's vacation and he could get a ride home with him. Amanda saw it as a great opportunity for her little brother to get to know Chris better. Only God knew what the future held, and it wouldn't hurt to have at least one family member in their corner. As soon as Nate found out that Chris had been a baseball pitcher, the two had started spending time together, throwing the ball and having long discussions on who the all-time best players were. Discovering they were both Dodgers fans had cemented the friendship.

After Nate left, the rest of the summer flew by. Amanda and Chris spent every possible moment together. In the mornings when Amanda was working at the Shoppe, you could usually find Chris in the back room, helping Grandpa Mitchell sand and refinish. Then the young couple would take off for the beach, occasionally meeting up with Stacy and Ben or a group from the theater. But more often than not, they would escape through the sea tunnel to their beach, where they could enjoy each other without the distraction of other people.

On the last Monday before the theater season ended, they planned to spend the whole day together. Amanda packed a picnic lunch, and Chris surprised her by picking her up in Stacy's car. "I had to promise her our first child if anything happens to it," he grinned, seeing Amanda's look of amazement.

She almost believed him. Stacy's little red bug was her pride and joy and she rarely let anyone else drive it. She had worked after school and on weekends to buy it, and Amanda was sure that as far as Stacy was concerned, it would be a fair exchange—their baby for her "baby"!

They drove up the coast, exultant in their sense of freedom. Amanda had seen this coastline dozens of times over the years, but seeing it now with Chris made everything look new and somehow more beautiful. They stopped at all the scenic turnouts, taking pictures like tourists and asking perfect strangers to snap pictures of them together.

The coastal highway finally wound its way into the towering evergreens outside of Carmel. Here the coast has a unique beauty, offering high, sheer cliffs decorated with patches of scrub brush and Monterey pines that fall away to rocky, inhospitable beaches. Chris began to slow down and seemed to be looking for something. He finally pulled off at a small rest stop hidden in the trees that boasted a number of old picnic tables along with primitive rest rooms. He got out of the car and opened the trunk to remove the picnic basket in the trunk. Then he came to Amanda's side and opened the door.

"Your table awaits, madam," he announced with a formal little bow.

Amanda got out, looking around at the dilapidated outhouses and lopsided tables. "After all the beautiful picnic areas we passed, we're going to eat here?" she laughed, disbelieving.

Chris just took her hand and started walking through the trees. Amanda saw that there was a path of sorts leading to the edge of the cliffs, where a rough staircase had been cut into the steep slope. Chris went ahead, turning to give her his hand as they cautiously descended. Every ten or twelve steps the path would smooth out for a short distance before a new set of stairs began. About a third of the way down the cliff they reached a broad plateau shaded by a half dozen pine trees. An old picnic table sat under their branches, its benches weathered but sturdy.

"How did you ever find out about this place?" Amanda breathed, looking out at the picture-postcard view.

"Remember I told you about the guy, Adam, who got me this gig?" Chris explained, setting the basket on a bench and pulling out a yellow tablecloth to cover the table. "He's worked at the theater for the last four or five summers, and he told me exactly how to get here. I guess he used to come here a lot to entertain his many 'fans.' He thought I should carry on the tradition," Chris added with a wicked gleam in his eye.

"And have you? Carried on the tradition?" Amanda asked, her mouth suddenly dry. She knew that Chris hadn't dated anyone else since the night of their first kiss, but he had been in Walker's Point nearly a month before they became serious and he attracted girls like bees to honey. And he *had* known exactly where to come.

"In my own modest fashion," Chris replied casually, refusing to look at her as he smoothed the tablecloth one last time and then started to empty the basket of its feast of cold chicken, potato salad, and homemade brownies. "Of course, I was only able to add a few notches to the ones he put in that tree over there," he said, pointing in the direction of a magnificent old Monterey pine standing guard at the edge of the cliff. "Go look. It's really amazing. He has them all dated and rated with one, two, or three stars."

Chris didn't have to look to know that by this time Amanda was practically gnawing through her lower lip, her eyes flaming slits of green and amber. He could hear the angry crunch of her shoes as she stalked over to the majestic old tree, and he could hear her thoughts as clearly as if she were screaming at him. How could he bring her here, to a place where he had been with other girls? How could he be so insensitive, so thoughtless, so. . . ?

The sound of her indignant march stopped abruptly, and he heard the small gasp and the catch in her voice as she called his name. He walked over slowly, feeling like a little boy, eager yet shy, hoping that his gift was wanted.

The tree stood as time and nature had sculpted it, its aged branches gnarled and twisted and its thick trunk swaybacked as if braced against the wind. The bark of the old tree was indeed scarred by the hands of men, but it had not been used as a scorecard for some vain young lothario. Instead, the fragile etchings paid tribute to the generations of lovers who had come before them.

"Tom loves Martha, 1956." "Ken and Lisa, 1948." "Lawrence and Grace, Forever, 1943." The oldest heart was nearly erased. Only the date, 1939, could still be read.

He found her tracing her finger lovingly over the newest carving . . . a small heart with "Chris and Amanda" written inside. Her eyes shimmered with tears, and her voice was particularly low and husky when she spoke.

"How did you . . . I mean, when did you. . . ?" She finally tore her eyes away from the heart, and her look told him everything he needed to know.

"I came up here with Ben and Stacy a couple weeks ago when you were with your folks. Adam really did tell me about this place, and I knew I wanted to bring you, but I wanted to check it out first . . . you know, see if it was as special as he said." Chris paused, suddenly feeling embarrassed. Pointing to the slightly crooked heart, he smiled apologetically. "I know it's a little hokey, but it seemed like something you'd like."

"Hokey?" Amanda started to giggle as tears streamed down her cheeks. "Did you say hokey? First it's sassy. Now it's hokey. Good grief, cowboy, we really are going to have to get you a dictionary! I can't have you running all over California sounding like some escapee from Hickville! Someone will throw a net over you and you'll end up on *Hee Haw* for the next twenty years!"

By the time she finished speaking the laughter had turned to little sobs and Amanda felt completely out of control. She turned and walked away along the edge of the cliff. She was just so overwhelmed. The summer had been so perfect. This day, the tree, the heart . . . Chris . . . was perfect. And soon it would all be over. Five more days and the theater would close its doors. Saturday would be their last performance. Some of the cast and crew would head out that very night. The rest would pack up and be gone on Sunday. Her father would be there bright and early Monday morning to collect his daughter and take her back to reality.

Chris watched her for a few moments, understanding exactly what she was feeling. She stood with her back to him, the wind whipping her hair about her face and billowing out her long peasant skirt. Her arms were wrapped around her thin frame as she braced herself against the fierce crosswinds, yet her face was lifted as though seeking its stinging assault. He knew she was crying. He could see the slight shaking of her shoulders, but he wasn't conscious of his own tears until the wind hit him full force as he walked toward her and he could feel the cool rivulets running down his cheeks.

As he came up behind her and enfolded her in his arms, he felt her sag against him, resting her head on his shoulder.

"It's going to be all right, Amanda Rose. I promise," he whispered almost fiercely in her ear.

The two of them stood for a long, long time just holding each other. Then they walked back to the picnic table, stopping to look at the old tree one more time.

"I wonder where all these people are now?" Amanda asked, reaching out to touch the little heart encircling their names one more time.

"Living happily ever after, of course," Chris replied softly. Amanda smiled up at him, so trusting and childlike, and then headed for the table. He watched her walk away with a thoughtful expression. She was so young and innocent. How could he expect her to understand what they were up against? There was so much she didn't know about him, things he had been careful to hide . . . things he'd been afraid to let her see.

They were surprised to discover that despite all the emotion of the afternoon they had not lost their appetites. The chicken and potato salad were soon nothing more than a pile of bones and an empty container, and they were starting on the brownies when a gust of wind burst through the protective screen of trees. The wind was definitely picking up.

"Let's go someplace and warm up," Chris suggested, helping Amanda quickly gather their things.

"Hot coffee would be great with these brownies," Amanda agreed, suddenly chilled to the bone.

"I know just the place," Chris announced, attacking the climb up with a sudden new resolve.

They headed the little beetle down the highway toward home. Chris pulled into the parking lot of a small bar and grill about twenty minutes from town, and Amanda was surprised to hear several people greet him by name as they walked in. The place was dark and rustic, a hangout for truckers and locals during the week and a raucous pickup bar on the weekends. It smelled of beer and old cigarettes, and Amanda felt uncomfortable as she made her way to the ladies' room. When she came out, Chris was seated at a table by the window, laughing with a blond waitress whom he introduced as Shelby.

"So you come here often?" Amanda asked after they had ordered two Irish coffees, one with and one without the Irish.

"I've been here a few times," he admitted, leaning back in his chair with studied nonchalance. "Ben and I discovered it with some of the other guys at the beginning of the summer. It's a good place to unwind after a show. Most everything else closes by midnight."

"So you come here . . . when? After you drop me off at home?" Amanda asked, uncertain whether to be upset or not.

Chris sat forward looking serious and intent. "Look, Amanda, when I'm with you I try my best to be what you want me to be. But I never said I had stopped being what I am. Sometimes I just need to kick back with a pitcher of beer and chew the fat. I feel comfortable in a place like this. The smells, the sounds, the people . . . they're what I'm used to. Some of the best music I ever wrote came from working in a place just like this, and from the struggles and hopes and dreams of people like this."

Amanda looked around the room at the few undistinguished customers and tired-looking waitresses and felt nothing but confusion. "I don't understand. Why did you bring me here?"

Chris was silent for a moment, searching to find just the right words.

"Standing on that cliff today," he began cautiously, "I realized how much I care about you. This is new for me, Amanda. I'm not used to thinkin' about other people as though I owe 'em somethin'. As though I need to give and take care of and be there. . . ."

He combed his hair with his fingers, uncomfortable but determined to go on. "I'm not sure just what I want to say or how to say it, but lately I've started thinkin' about what it would be like to have somebody in my life. To have a family, kids, a future with someone. I don't know if you and I are part of that 'plan' you're always talkin' about. God and I don't usually see eye to eye on such things . . . but if we're goin' to have a fightin' chance, we've got to see things the way they really are, not the way we want them to be."

He took a deep breath, and Amanda simply squeezed his hand and waited for him to go on, aware that his accent was stronger than she'd ever heard it before.

"You once told me that you weren't willin' to lose yourself trying to be what I wanted you to be, remember?"

Amanda nodded.

"Well, I reckon I need you to understand that the same is true for me. I brought you here so you would see me for what I really am—a good ol' boy with a taste for the simple things in life. Amanda, I'm never gonna be some knight in shinin' armor, and I'm never goin' to care about ownin' things or impressin' people. The most important things in my life right now are you and my music. And I think if I could have those, I'd never ask God for another thing. . . . But I'm not so sure that you'd be happy with that bargain."

Amanda was smart enough not to try to answer the question he'd been wise enough not to ask. They both knew they were in deep water emotionally and it was best to just drift for a while until they could touch bottom once again. There was much to think about and time was short.

They drove back to Walker's Point in thoughtful silence, and as the last few days slipped by, they spent a lot of time talking about the future and discussing what was and what wasn't important to them. They basically agreed about most things. About other things they were worlds apart. But when they were in each other's arms, they were in total agreement.

Thirteen

Saturday dawned bright and clear, free from the coastal fog that often blanketed the small beach community until late morning. Amanda stretched, squinting as a ray of sunlight fell across her pillow. She opened her eyes cautiously, vaguely aware that the dazzling sunshine was not the only reason she felt hesitant to leave the pleasant world of dreams and face the light of day. Tonight was closing, and tomorrow meant saying good-bye to Stacy and Ben and Ana and Mack and all the crazy, wonderful people who had come to mean so much to her. This was a thought she was not yet prepared to face.

A glance at the clock told her it was still early, not even seven. Amanda groaned and rolled over. Last night had been the cast party. Normally it was held on closing night, but too many people planned to take off right after the curtain came down tonight, so Ana and Mack had planned it for Friday. It had been a noisy, uninhibited, and emotional time with everyone laughing and crying and exchanging addresses. In a very real sense a small family was breaking up, and there were lots of hugs and kisses and promises to keep in touch. By two in the morning Amanda was thoroughly wrung out and ready to go home, but the party wasn't showing any signs of slowing down when she and Chris left.

Grams, God bless her, had given Amanda the day off, and she was free to sleep in as late as she liked. She closed her eyes again, snuggling down into the soft sheets, determined to doze back off, when she heard someone quietly open her door.

"Hey, Stace," she mumbled sleepily, without opening her eyes. "Come on in but keep it down. I'm still asleep." She felt the weight of someone slipping into bed beside her and soon the room was filled with their gentle snores.

When Amanda woke up again, it was nearly ten. Stacy was curled in a ball, still fast asleep. "Rise and shine, sleepyhead," Amanda said, giving her friend a little shake. Stacy whimpered and pulled a pillow over her head. "Stace, wake up. Half the day is gone. Come on, we've places to go and people to see!"

Stacy groaned again, pushing herself up into a sitting position against the headboard, and looked at Amanda with eyes at half-mast.

"Good grief, Stace! You look like one of those cartoons where Tweety Bird has to prop open his eyes with toothpicks. What time did you finally get to bed last night?"

Stacy glanced at the clock and answered, "About seven . . . I think."

"You stayed up all night? How late did that party go?" Amanda asked.

Stacy just gave her a stupid grin and slipped back down under the covers. Amanda got out of bed and grabbed her robe. She could smell the coffee all the way down the stairs, and the tantalizing aroma drew her to the cheerful kitchen, where she found a yellow mug and a sweet roll set out by the freshly brewed pot. A short note simply said, "Gone to shop. Enjoy your day. See you tonight. Love, Grams."

Amanda carried her coffee and the sweet roll out onto the back porch, where she sat enjoying the carefully landscaped chaos of her grandmother's garden. The flowers were in full bloom, filling the air with a mixture of sweet perfumes and drawing countless bees that buzzed busily from blossom to blossom. Closing her eyes, Amanda let the sun bathe her in its warming light as she tried to commit everything she saw, smelled, tasted, and heard to memory. This was one of Chris's perfect moments and she never wanted to forget it.

"Penny for your thoughts."

She smiled at the familiar words, not surprised that he had come. "I was thinking how incredibly perfect the moment was, but I was wrong. *Now* it's perfect."

She opened her eyes to see him standing at the bottom of the stairs, one foot balanced on the first step, looking up at her. His hair was still slightly damp, curling around his ears and falling well past the top of his shirt collar. Dressed in his traditional T-shirt and jeans, his blue eyes looked bluer than ever, and she thought no one had ever been more beautiful. He came up the stairs and gave her a kiss, then asked, "Is there more where that came from?" referring to her coffee.

"Help yourself," she told him, handing him her own cup for a refill. As she listened to him puttering in the kitchen, she couldn't help smiling. They had come so far since the first time they met. It was all so comfortable now . . . so easy . . . so right.

He came back out and handed her her coffee, fixed just right with milk and two spoonfuls of sugar. Then he sat beside her on the old porch swing, and for a minute they sipped and swayed in companionable silence. Finally he reached in his pocket and pulled out what appeared to be a letter.

"I wanted to show you this. I guess it came a couple days ago. Ana said she put it in my box on Thursday, but I didn't check my mail until this morning."

Amanda felt the weight and fine texture of the paper when he handed it to her, and she read the embossed heading: CTI. She looked at Chris questioningly.

"Read it," he said, excitement bubbling beneath his surface calm.

Dear Mr. Davies, Amanda read. *We met a few weeks ago at the Seventh Wave. I would like to express again how impressed I was with both your music and your stage presence. I would like to meet with you to explore the possibility of CTI representing you. I wait to hear from you. Sincerely, Myron Cole, Vice President of Talent Development, CTI, Music Division.*

Amanda read the letter three times before its meaning sank in. "Do you think it's for real?" she asked, looking at Chris, her eyes wide with wonder. "I mean, everyone's heard of Creative Talent International. They handle some of the biggest stars in the world!"

"I know. I couldn't believe it was real, either." Chris stood and paced excitedly as he talked. "So I called the number and sure enough, it was CTI. I talked with Mr. Cole, and I have an appointment to see him next Wednesday."

"Oh, Chris!"

Amanda flew out of the swing and threw her arms around his neck, kissing him so hard he almost lost his balance. He lifted her off her feet and carried her down the stairs, where he proceeded to swing her around and around as the two of them whooped and hollered like wild Indians.

"What in the name of heaven is going on down there?" Stacy

yelled, leaning dangerously far out of Amanda's window and shaking her fist at the two lunatics who had so rudely awakened her. "How do you expect me to get my beauty sleep with all this racket going on?"

"Stace!" Amanda cried out gleefully. "Come down and celebrate with us! Chris has been discovered . . . with a capital *D*!"

🐝 🐝 🐝 🐝

Saturday's performance played to standing room only as friends and relatives crowded in to bring down the final curtain with a standing ovation. Ana and Mack were called to the stage and presented with flowers and gifts of appreciation. Then Mack introduced the orchestra and stage crew. Even Amanda and the other two ushers were called out to take a bow. Then it was over. Amanda took off the strapless gold dress and hung it up with special care. Backstage was a beehive of activity as everyone checked in their costumes and packed up their things.

As Chris walked Amanda home one last time, they were both filled with a sweet sense of melancholy.

"It seems like just yesterday that we walked like this the first time," Amanda commented. "The summer went by so fast. I can't believe that in another week I'll be at school and all of this will seem like some wonderful dream."

"Or your worst nightmare," Chris said cryptically. Amanda gave him a puzzled look. "I plan to still be there when you wake up, my dear," he warned in a pretty fair imitation of Bela Lugosi as Count Dracula.

"You'd better be," she laughed, stopping to wrap her arms around his neck and bring her face up to his, "or I'll just refuse to wake up."

Amanda finished speaking just as their lips met. It took them a little longer than usual to walk the familiar streets to the Mitchells', and when they got there, they lingered at the front gate, holding hands and looking deep into each other's eyes as though trying to memorize every detail of the face before them. Finally Amanda started to laugh.

"Good grief, you'd think we were saying good-bye forever! We have all day tomorrow to be together, and you're riding down to L.A.

with me and Dad on Monday. And now that you've been 'Discovered,' you'll be staying in L.A. and we'll see each other all the time! We're going to have all the time in the world to figure out the answers to those question marks that keep popping up between us." Amanda finished this last bit through a stifled yawn, and Chris couldn't help thinking how much fun it would be to tuck her into bed. Instead, he kissed her chastely on the forehead and opened the gate for her to walk through.

"Oh, we're back to that again, are we?" Amanda grumbled sleepily, giving Chris a grimace as she passed through the gate. His response was a sharp slap on her backside, which drew a startled, "Oh!"

"Meet me at May's for breakfast at ten," he called after her.

He could hear her muttering to herself as she walked up the path, and he couldn't help smiling as he turned to walk away. No one had ever made him laugh or think or dream like Amanda did. She challenged him, like one of those old Chinese puzzles. Every time he thought he had her figured out, she did something surprising that made him think again. And perhaps most important, she had given him back his hope. Lately when he was with her he had actually started thinking that God might have a plan for his good, and this time it might be safe to believe.

He stopped at the corner to look back. She was standing by the front door, just as he knew she would be, waiting. He raised his hand and she answered in kind. Then he watched her open the door and disappear into the house.

"Please, God," he whispered under his breath. It was the closest he'd come to praying since his mother died.

❦ ❦ ❦ ❦

Amanda arrived at May's a few minutes after ten. The place was crowded with Sunday brunchers, and it took her a few minutes to discern that Chris wasn't there yet.

"Hey, Nancy! You seen Chris?" she asked, catching the busy waitress on a coffee run.

"No, he hasn't been in yet. If you want some coffee, help yourself. This place is crazy today, and two of the summer help have already left for school."

Amanda walked behind the counter and poured herself a cup,

stopping to fill a half dozen other empty mugs before she finally slipped out the front door to watch for Chris. The day was beautiful, and the street was alive with happy, tanned faces. Amanda loved to "people watch," and before she knew it, she had finished her coffee and a half hour had passed. Walking back into the restaurant, she searched out Nancy in the back.

"I'm really worried. Chris isn't here yet, and I know he would call if he were going to be this late."

"Well, he could try, but he wouldn't have much success," Nancy said, loading a tray with plates of eggs and bacon and crispy hash browns. "The phone's been out of order since last night. We've called the phone company, but so far no one's been out to fix it!" She picked up the heavy tray and yelled, "Comin' through!"

Amanda went back outside and was trying to decide whether she should walk over to the boardinghouse where Chris was staying when a car came screeching to a halt at the curb before her. She recognized the car as belonging to Ray Philips, one of the stage crew. The door flew open and Chris stepped out. One look and Amanda knew something was terribly wrong.

"Sorry, babe. I tried to call but the phone wasn't working," Chris hurriedly explained, taking her in his arms and holding her tight for a few moments. Then he pulled back so he could see her face.

"What's wrong, Chris? What's happened?" Amanda asked, suddenly shaking.

"It's my dad. I got a call about an hour ago from my aunt in Lubbock. My dad had a stroke last night. He's in the hospital. I guess it's pretty bad. I have to catch a flight out of LAX at five this afternoon. Ray, here, has offered to drive me."

Amanda listened, feeling as though she were in a dream, only this time it *was* a nightmare. "Oh, Chris, I am so sorry. What can I do?"

"Nothing . . . just maybe put in a good word with the Big Guy," Chris replied awkwardly. "Look, there are a million and one things I wish I had time to say, but I don't. If I miss this plane, there isn't another one until nine, and from what they told me, every minute counts."

"I understand. Don't worry about it. Just go!"

They came together for one desperate, searching kiss, and then Chris jumped back into the car.

"Wait!" Amanda screamed, suddenly remembering. "You don't

even have my phone number and I don't know how to contact you!"
She ran into May's and grabbed a napkin. "Anyone have a pen I can
borrow?" she cried out, and three startled hands reached out with
pens. She took one and ran back outside. Using the hood of the car
as a table, she hastily wrote her home phone number on half of the
napkin and Chris's rural box number on the other. Tearing it in half,
she thrust her number into his hand.

"Call me! I'll be home by tomorrow night."
One more quick kiss and the car sped away.

Fourteen

New York, 1980

It was dark outside by the time Amanda finally stopped speaking. The lights of passing cars sent searchlights into the trees across the street, revealing stark bare branches lifted to heaven like arms raised in outrage. Amanda stared out the window, hypnotized by the strobe-light effect. She had been talking for over two hours and felt utterly exhausted.

"Then what happened?" Laura reached out and touched Amanda's hand, bringing her out of her momentary trance.

"What?"

"Don't leave me hanging like this! What happened next?" Laura demanded, her eyes as bright as a five-year-old's listening to some wonderful fairy tale. "When did you see him again?"

"About two and a half hours ago, outside the Plaza Hotel."

"What!"

Laura's outburst rang through the now crowded restaurant, turning heads and causing the waiter to come by to see if everything was all right.

"I don't know. I haven't heard the whole story yet!" Laura replied, shooing the perplexed young man away. Then she leaned toward Amanda as if she needed to be very close in order to believe what she was hearing. "Would you mind repeating what you just said? I know I didn't hear you right."

"I said I never saw Chris again after we said good-bye in Walker's Point. Not in person, that is . . . until today."

"But how can that be? You were so much in love. Everything was so good between you. What happened?"

"Life," Amanda replied softly. "It has a funny way of throwing up roadblocks that you have no way of anticipating." She took a deep breath and began kneading the back of her neck as she continued in an emotionless monotone.

"After Chris left, I could hardly wait to get home. I made my dad turn right around and drive straight back to Pasadena the moment he arrived Monday morning so I would be there in case Chris called. And he did. He called that night to let me know that things were still bad with his father and that he didn't have any idea how long he was going to have to stay. He gave me the number of the motel where he was staying, and we talked almost every night until I had to leave for school.

"The last time we spoke he told me his father was improving, but it was still going to be a while before they would release him. And even after he was released, he was going to need lots of care for a long time. Chris was going to find an apartment close to the hospital where he could take his dad when he got out. He said he probably wouldn't call again until he was settled. That was fine with me because I was leaving for school the next day and would be busy myself for a while. So I told him to call my mom when he had a new address or phone number. We said good-bye . . . and that was the last time I ever talked to him."

"But that doesn't make sense. It sounds like he had every intention of staying in touch. Are you saying he never called or wrote or anything?"

Amanda just stared out the window. Laura could see her look of despair reflected in the glass.

The waiter came over for the third time to collect the check. The women had been ignoring subtle and then not-so-subtle looks from the staff for over an hour. It was the height of the dinner rush, and they had occupied a prime table for nearly two and a half hours over three pots of hot chocolate and one slice of apple pie they had ordered solely to keep from being asked to leave.

"Let's get out of here. I need to walk!" Laura said, covering the check with a ten, then adding a twenty-dollar bill to the pot. "Rent," she explained to the waiter, who wished them a good evening with a considerably friendlier expression.

The two women walked out onto the sidewalk and were imme-

diately assaulted by the bitter cold. Neither of them was dressed properly to be out at night and they linked arms, walking together like two
orphans in the storm huddled against the wind. Even as they walked,
Laura had to have some answers.

"I just don't understand," she started in again, as though their
conversation had never been interrupted. "Didn't you try to reach
him? Didn't you write?"

"I lost the address," Amanda answered in a voice muffled by her
upturned collar. "I don't know how it happened. I knew exactly
where I had put it . . . in the pages of my diary. But when I looked
for it, it was gone. I called the post office in Lubbock, information,
everyone I could think of, but no one could help me."

"What about the hospital? Wasn't he there every day with his
dad?"

"You don't understand. He didn't call!"

Amanda's words were an anguished wail as she suddenly pulled
away, stunning her friend with her vehemence. She turned into the
protection of a shop doorway, doubling over with a spasm of pain so
overwhelming it took her breath away. It had been years since she had
allowed herself to think about any of this. She had told herself it was
all healed and forgotten with no power to hurt her anymore. But seeing Chris again had brought back all the old memories, and the pain
had resurfaced, as cutting as ever. For a moment she thought she
wasn't going to be able to stand up. She felt Laura's arms come
around her and knew the release of tears. The words came with them
in sobs and gasps.

"Every time I'd call home and ask my mother if she had heard
from him, she'd say no. She kept insinuating it was for the best . . .
saying we'd had a great summer but now it was time to get on with
'real life.' She said she was sure that's what he was doing and if I
chased after him, I'd only be hurt. . . . I didn't want to believe her. I
didn't want to think that I hadn't really meant anything to him, but
as the days passed without word, I got scared. I wasn't the kind of
girl who chased after boys. I didn't have that kind of self-confidence.
So I just kept waiting. By the time I was desperate enough to call the
hospital, it was too late. His dad was gone, and they wouldn't give
me any other information."

Amanda let Laura hold her for a few moments until the tears had
stopped and she felt in control. Then she straightened up and blew

her nose on the handkerchief Laura offered her.

"I can't believe I just fell apart in the middle of Park Avenue. I must look a sight!" she laughed shakily, uncertain how to start acting normal again after such a complete breakdown.

"Sweetie, it's my fault. I shouldn't have pushed you. I was so fascinated by your story, I didn't stop to think how hard all of this must be for you. I mean, seeing him like this after all these years!"

The two finished the short distance to the Plaza in silence, slipping in a side entrance. They made it to the elevators without drawing attention, even though Amanda was sure she must look like a plane-crash survivor. Safe in their room, Laura drew her a hot bath, insisting she soak for as long as she wanted. They had made a nine o'clock reservation at the Tavern on the Green earlier that day, "But I'll call and cancel it," Laura said, reaching for the phone.

"Don't you dare!" Amanda called from the bathroom. "Just give me fifteen minutes in this tub and I'll be 'right as rain,' whatever that means."

"Are you sure?" Laura asked, still tempted to make the call. "We can always have room service and watch some TV."

"Oh, goody! Dinner on TV trays, just like at home. That's what I came to New York for!"

"Okay," Laura laughed. "I get your point. Let me at least call and tell them we'll be a little late."

At nine-thirty Amanda and Linda stepped out of a cab in front of the world-famous restaurant. The trees were strung with white lights and the park setting was just as Amanda had pictured it would be . . . charming.

Many eyes followed the attractive pair as they were led to their table by a window looking out on the courtyard. As though to prove the evening hadn't been ruined, the women had taken special care with their hair and makeup. Amanda wore an emerald green dinner suit with a short fitted jacket and a slim skirt that showed off her figure to perfection. She had let Laura pin up her hair in a French twist that accentuated her high cheekbones and long, slender neck. A gold and rhinestone pin and small matching earrings were all the jewelry she wore other than her wedding rings. The overall effect was almost regal, and Laura was well aware that even in her mink coat and diamonds, she didn't hold a candle to Amanda.

Even though it was late, they went all out, ordering appetizers and salad before their main course. They were both too full for dessert, but they let the waiter suggest a special after-dinner coffee. They were sipping the relaxing brew, quietly relishing their surroundings, when a particularly lovely tune came over the music system. It started with the cries of sea gulls, which were softly overwhelmed by a hauntingly beautiful piano solo, with strings and wind instruments eventually joining in. The song was a favorite of Laura's, and she was quietly humming along when it hit her that it was a Christopher Davies song. It had come out on his second album and was now a contemporary classic.

"Good grief! You're Amanda Rose!" Laura gasped as the name of the song dawned on her.

Amanda smiled and nodded, a sad look flickering across her face again.

"Oh, I'm sorry, Amanda. It seems you can't get away from Christopher Davies wherever you go, and I'm not helping much. But I have to say, it's a little overwhelming. You hear a song a hundred times—sing along with it in the car or while you're cooking dinner . . . dream about someone loving you like that—and then one day you find out that one of your best friends was the inspiration for it! Even at my age that's . . . surprising," she finished, unable to find a better word.

"I know. I was completely overwhelmed the first time I heard it. When it came out Chris was already a big star, and I was used to hearing his voice on the radio and seeing his picture in the paper or on TV. It felt weird but . . . I don't know. The Christopher Davies they showed was so different . . . a stranger all glitzed up and bigger than life. And by that time I had Nick, and Kim had been born. My life was full and happy, thank God."

Amanda was quiet for a moment, thoughtful. "But the song was mine. It was like he'd snuck into my room and stolen back a gift he'd given me. I never thought he'd use it. At the time, it felt like one more betrayal."

"Amanda, we don't have to talk about this if you don't want to," Laura said, not wanting to see her get upset again.

"No, it's all right," Amanda said, smiling reassuringly. "Actually it feels kind of good. I've never really talked about this with anyone."

"You mean Nick doesn't know?"

"Of course he knows. He's the one who got me through my heartbreak. In fact, I guess you could say Chris brought us together."

Amanda smiled as the memories came back.

"When I didn't hear from Chris, I sort of fell apart. Somehow I made it to my classes, but the rest of the time I spent in my room looking at old pictures and crying. I didn't go anywhere or even try to meet people. My roommate, Michelle, was a saint! If I had been her, I would have strangled me! But instead, she gave me my space and tried to be sympathetic.

"Finally, a few weeks after Christmas break, her patience gave out. She came charging into the room one night and said we were going out. There was a party at a friend's house and I was going, even if she had to drag me there. Truth was, I was ready. The jilted-lover routine had really gotten old, and a big part of me wanted to be happy again.

"When we got to the party one of the first people I saw was this tall, red-haired Irishman. You couldn't miss him. He was the one in the center of the room telling funny stories and singing little tunes in this horrible off-key voice! I remember thinking how wonderful it must be to enjoy life like that.

"I planted myself on a sofa and watched everyone else having fun. . . . Having fun isn't easy, you know," she observed as an aside. "If you don't practice, you lose your touch and you have to work back up to it. Anyway, there were lots of people there, but somehow my eyes kept going back to Nick. His face was so animated. He just oozed life, and when he smiled his whole face lit up. And he looked . . . kind."

Amanda paused to take a sip of water. Her long fingers played with the glass as she spoke.

"Michelle introduced us about halfway through the evening. Nick told me later he'd seen me watching him from my safe seat in the corner and he'd known right away I was a princess who needed to be rescued and he was the one to do it. Crazy Irishman!"

"So it was love at first sight . . . again?" Laura asked, somewhat taken aback.

Amanda laughed. "For him, maybe. Not for me. I didn't see Nick as my Prince Charming. He was just your standard-grade friendly frog as far as I was concerned. Someone to laugh with and talk to . . . someone to hold me while I cried and tell me Chris was a jerk and a fool and I was wonderful and worth caring about. Back then, I could talk to him about anything and he'd just listen and empathize. He had this incredible way of making me laugh. One minute I'd be ranting and raving, tears pouring down my face, and the next I'd be laughing so hard I could barely stand it! I look back on that year and am amazed at his patience. He was always there for me—never pushy or demanding—just giving, and settling for what little I gave back.

"Then one day I woke up and something was different. It was such a foreign feeling I had to think for a moment to identify what it was. I finally realized I was happy, and the reason I was happy was Nick. That revelation really freaked me out. It was scary knowing that someone else in my life had the power to hurt me the way Chris had, and I almost decided it wasn't worth the risk. I started avoiding him and acting real cool when I saw him. I even started dating this guy named Teddy something-or-other. Can you imagine. . . ? Teddy!"

"Let me guess. Nick's patience finally ran out."

"Big time!" Amanda said, rolling her eyes at the memory. "It was a Thursday afternoon, and Michelle and I were sitting with a bunch of other kids talking in one of the college courtyards. I looked up and saw Nick coming straight at me with this look on his face that said, 'You can run and you can hide . . . but it ain't gonna do you any good!' I remember watching him with my heart beating in my throat, and suddenly everyone around me just got up and backed off, leaving him a clear path. I honestly didn't know if he was going to hit me or what, but it didn't matter. I was frozen to the spot.

"When he finally reached me, he grabbed me by the arms and pulled me to my feet. 'I have only one thing to say to you, Amanda,' he said, looking like he could break my neck. Then he kissed me, right there in front of everybody. And I kissed him back. And when we'd finished kissing, everyone clapped, just like in the movies."

"And the frog became a prince?" Laura asked, delighted with the story.

"Before my very eyes," Amanda replied, a soft expression on her face. "And they lived happily ever after . . . or at least they're trying to," she added with a sigh.

"So I guess that means you won't be letting Mr. Davies know you're here."

"I don't think he would care if he knew," Amanda said with conviction. "But more importantly, *I* don't want to care. I love Nick. He and the girls are everything to me. And just because he turns back into a frog every once in a while is no reason to start looking up old boyfriends."

Laura nodded in understanding, then added thoughtfully, "Still, you must be curious. Wouldn't you like to know why he never called or wrote?"

A strange expression came into Amanda's eyes, and it looked as though she was trying to decide whether to tell Laura something. Finally she just smiled a sad little smile and said, "Knowing the answer to a riddle doesn't always give you peace of mind. Sometimes I think it's better not to know. Besides, look at us all today. Chris has his career. I have Nick and the girls. I think it all worked out for the best, don't you?"

Laura smiled in agreement. But she couldn't help feeling there was more to this story than Amanda had told her.

Fifteen

*I*t was a few minutes after midnight when the two women wearily walked through the deserted lobby to an elevator and pushed the button for the sixth floor. They were both exhausted, talked out, and ready for bed. The door had nearly closed when they heard a shout, and a hand shot in front of the door, causing it to rebound. A young man flashed them a smile, then yelled at his companions to hurry up. Two more men followed, one obviously helping the other to walk. The stench of alcohol filled the elevator, and it was clear they had all been drinking. But the youngest of the three was quite drunk.

Amanda immediately recognized the long-haired musicians as part of Chris's band, and she turned away, not wanting to talk. But she could feel the youngest man's eyes on her, practically undressing her in the elevator. She glanced at him, distaste written all over her face, but he immediately took her look as encouragement.

"Hey, pretty lady, do you know who I am?" he slurred, leaning unsteadily in her direction. "I'm Keith Rogers. This here's Sam Waters and that's the great Bayley Reese." He waved grandly in the others' direction, nearly losing his balance. "We're part of Out Cry! and tomorrow night we'll be playing Carnegie Hall," he announced, impressed with himself. The other two men nodded, obviously uncomfortable with their associate's behavior.

"I'm happy for you," Amanda replied in an icy voice that was lost on the inebriated young man.

"Listen," he said, moving in even closer, "there's a party at the penthouse tonight. If you wanna come, I'll introduce you to Christopher Davies."

He pronounced the name with great reverence, and Amanda was

sure it had been an "Open Sesame" for him many times in the past. "You can get his autograph and *everything*, honey." He said "everything" with a leering grin, leaning close enough to Amanda for her to be almost overcome by the smell of liquor on his breath.

Pulling away in disgust, Amanda said through gritted teeth, "We've met!" just as the elevator door opened, allowing her to escape and flee down the hallway to their room.

The whole thing had happened in the short time it took for the elevator to travel from the first floor to the sixth, and Laura stood shaking and outraged, barely able to believe what she had witnessed. There was no way she was leaving that elevator without giving the three men a piece of her mind.

"That was the most offensive display I have ever witnessed," she raged, blocking the door from closing. "Just who do you think you are? Why, if your boss knew how you just treated someone who used to mean a great deal to him, you'd all be out of a job! You're a disgrace, that's what you are!"

Laura stormed down the hall toward their room, still shaking and reciting to herself all the things she wished she'd thought to say. She was almost to the room when a hand reached out and stopped her. She turned to see that Bayley Reese, the oldest of the three men, had followed her, looking very contrite.

"Now what do you want?" she snapped, at the end of her rope.

"Please," he said with a conciliatory smile. "I just want to apologize and make sure the young lady's okay. You're absolutely right. Keith was rude and totally out of line. . . . No, really," he continued, seeing the skeptical look in her eyes. "If Sam and I hadn't been a little over the line ourselves, we would have stopped him."

"Well . . ." Laura said, softening but not quite convinced.

"I want you to know that this incident will be dealt with," he continued earnestly. "Keith is the newest member of the group. He's only been with us for about a year, and while he's a good bass player, he's young and hasn't handled the pressure very well. Being on the road all the time and having women throwing themselves at you and telling you how wonderful you are can be heady stuff.

"Actually," he went on to confide, "Chris has already decided to replace him after this tour ends. He is real careful about the kind of people he surrounds himself with, and he won't put up with this kind of stuff. I just wanted you to know that."

Laura relaxed as she listened to the man's heartfelt apology. He was a good-looking guy in his mid-thirties, with shoulder-length hair pulled back in a low ponytail. His clothes were expensive but casual, and there was a nice down-to-earth quality about him. If the other band members were like this one, Laura could easily believe that the young hooligan who had accosted Amanda didn't fit in.

"I appreciate your taking the trouble to follow me, and I accept your apology. I know Amanda will, too, when I tell her," Laura said, turning to walk on.

"Wait," he said sharply. "I need to ask you a question, if you don't mind."

Laura turned back with a tired nod.

"What did you mean when you said your friend had once meant something to my boss?"

"What?" Laura asked, suddenly alarmed and trying to remember what she had said.

"You said that 'my boss' once knew her. I assume you were referring to Christopher Davies."

"I didn't mean anything, really. I was angry and just said the first thing that came into my head. Look, it's late and I'm tired. Thank you again and good night."

"Well, would it be all right if the band sent her some flowers . . . to say we're sorry?"

Laura gave him a doubtful look.

"It's the least we can do."

"That would be very nice," Laura finally agreed.

"Great! What's your friend's name? Did you say Amanda?"

"Yes, Amanda Kelly. *Mrs.* Nicholas Kelly."

The man's expression froze. "Amanda Rose," he whispered softly. "I thought so."

"How did you know?" Laura asked, too stunned to deny it.

"I've seen her picture often enough. Of course, it's an old photo, but she hasn't changed all that much."

Laura felt her heart start to beat faster. "Now it's my turn to ask a question. How did you ever see a picture of Amanda?"

"Chris has a picture of her. When I first met him he had lots of pictures of her—and of them together. I finally got him to get rid of them. They used to just bring him down. But I guess he couldn't let go completely. He doesn't know I know, but he kept one of her standing on this cliff overlooking the ocean. The wind is blowing her hair, and she's looking back at him with this smile on her face. She was real pretty. She's even prettier now," he added, thinking out loud. "Anyway, he has that picture in a gold frame locked in this little leather box. He never goes anywhere without it. I bet it's in his suitcase right now."

Laura listened to Bayley talk as though she were in a dream. She knew she was hearing his words, but they simply didn't compute. Why would Christopher Davies have Amanda's picture after all these years? Why would he keep a reminder of someone he'd walked away from and no longer cared about?

Bayley shook his head as though his confusion was as great as hers. "She really did a number on him, didn't she? I mean, she looks so nice. It's hard to believe she would dump someone like that. Between losing her and his dad dying, Chris almost didn't make it."

Laura felt as though she had entered the Twilight Zone. Her head whirled with all she had learned that day, and she was getting a sick feeling in the pit of her stomach. "Mr. Reese," she started to say.

"Please call me Bayley. This conversation has lasted longer than my first marriage," he smiled, teasing.

"Yes, well . . . I'm afraid I'm feeling a bit at a loss. Are you telling me that Chris Davies told you Amanda broke off their relationship?"

"Yeah, cut him off cold after she went off to college."

"Bayley," Laura said slowly, struggling to make sense of the situation, "I'm afraid there's been a terrible misunderstanding."

For the next few minutes Laura did most of the talking, while Bayley alternately shook his head in amazement and nodded in agreement. Finally the two conspirators shook hands and parted.

"Where in heaven's name have you been?" Amanda demanded the moment Laura entered the room. She had already put on her nightgown and was standing at the bathroom sink cleansing her face when she heard the door open. "I was about to call out the National Guard. I was afraid those creeps in the elevator had carried you off to the penthouse and were having their way with you!"

Laura smiled at the ludicrous thought as she sat on the bed to slip off her shoes and rub her tired feet. "No, I'm quite all right, dear, thank you. Although one of the young men did follow me off the elevator."

"Really? Why?" Amanda asked, patting her face dry.

"He said he wanted to apologize and make sure you were okay. Seemed like a nice enough guy. His name is Bayley Reese. He's the drummer."

"Yes, I know. I met him once a long time ago in Santa Barbara. He played with a band that Chris really liked. I wasn't surprised when I read they had linked up to form Out Cry!" Amanda was dabbing on face cream as she spoke.

"He recognized you," Laura said carefully, trying to ease into the conversation.

"What? That's impossible!" Amanda replied, coming to stand in the doorway with a worried look on her face. "I only saw him for a few minutes and we never actually talked. How could he remember something that insignificant from twelve years ago?"

"He didn't. He recognized you from your picture. It seems that Christopher Davies has carried it with him all these years . . . and that's not all." Laura patted the bed next to her. "Come sit down, Amanda. What I'm about to tell you is going to come as a shock."

Amanda ignored her invitation, crossing instead to the window where she parted the curtains and stared unseeing out the window.

Laura took a deep breath and went on. "Bayley told me that Chris believes *you* put an end to the relationship and that it is a wound that still troubles him to this day."

Amanda's head sank into her hands, and Laura could barely hear her whisper, "Dear God, I thought he would just forget. . . . Why didn't he forget?"

"Amanda, did you hear me? Somewhere along the line a terrible mix-up happened."

Amanda looked up at her with tired old eyes and simply said, "I know."

"You know? . . . I don't understand."

Laura looked expectantly at Amanda, but no explanation came. Instead, Amanda busied herself pulling down the covers and getting into bed. It was now well after one in the morning, and the young woman fell between the sheets, curling up on her side like a child to go to sleep.

"Amanda, please explain," Laura pleaded, totally mystified.

"Can't . . . too tired . . . have to sleep . . . so tired." The muffled reply faded out as Amanda closed her eyes and fell instantly asleep.

Laura sat for a moment, trying to digest everything that had happened during the last hour. Every muscle in her body ached and her eyes burned with fatigue. Finally she found the strength to slip her dress off. Then she got under the covers still in her slip. For the first time in thirty years, Laura Stanley went to bed without washing her face or brushing her teeth.

❧   ❧   ❧   ❧

The phone rang early the next morning. Laura reluctantly opened one eye just wide enough to read the clock. Seven-thirty. She turned over, grateful that Amanda had answered it, and closed her eye again to go back to sleep. A few seconds later the previous day's events came flooding back, and she sat up with a start. Amanda was hanging up the phone.

"Was that him?" Laura asked, her heart pounding.

"It was the front desk. They wanted to know if we're checking out on Saturday or Sunday." The reservation had been left open because Laura hadn't been sure exactly when she was going to be able to meet with an important supplier. It turned out she couldn't see him until Saturday afternoon. "I told them Sunday."

Amanda was already dressed, looking refreshed and particularly beautiful in a creamy cashmere sweater and tan wool slacks. Her hair was parted on the side and fell softly to her shoulders, curling slightly under at the ends, and Laura wondered for the umpteenth time how she got it to fall so perfectly. Her makeup was characteristically understated, but her eyes shone with a brightness that turned them jade green and gave away the excitement hidden behind her calm exterior.

Laura sat up, propping pillows behind her. "What are you going to do if he calls?"

"*When* he calls, I'll see him," Amanda answered with simple certainty. "I always knew this day would come. I was just hoping that it would be when we were old, gray, and toothless, surrounded by our many grandchildren, and beyond regrets."

Laura was beginning to squirm with curiosity. "Are you ever going to explain everything to me?" she asked, knowing she sounded like a petulant child.

"I suppose I'll have to. You know what curiosity did to the cat. I certainly wouldn't want to be responsible for your untimely demise!" Amanda laughed, seeing her friend's pleading look.

But before she could go on, the phone rang again. Amanda picked up the receiver. Laura watched her face as she heard the voice on the other end. She saw the bright flush come to her cheeks as she said, "Hello, Chris." Then she turned away and lowered her voice. A few seconds later she hung up.

"Well?" Laura asked, uncertain whether he had told her to get lost or asked to see her.

"He wants me to come up to his suite."

"And are you going?" Laura asked, suddenly afraid she might have opened a Pandora's box.

Amanda just nodded and walked into the bathroom to check her makeup one more time. Then she picked up her purse and walked out the door without another word.

Sixteen

*A*ll the way up in the elevator Amanda tried to imagine what she would say, but everything she thought of sounded trite and contrived. By the time the doors opened she had decided there *were* no words, and she was close to chickening out. Her finger was on the down button when one of the doors off of the foyer opened and Bayley Reese stepped out.

"Mrs. Kelly," he greeted her respectfully. "I'm Bayley Reese. We met, unfortunately, last night."

"Yes, I remember. How's your friend's head this morning?"

"He's in the agonizing pain he so justly deserves," Bayley informed her with mock seriousness. "I wanted to apologize once again, although if it hadn't happened, I never would have recognized you. Life is funny sometimes, isn't it?"

"You don't mind if I reserve my judgment on just how funny this is, do you?" Amanda said, glancing at the open doorway nervously.

Bayley smiled understandingly. "He's waiting for you on the terrace. Come on, I'll show you."

He led Amanda through the open door into a world that she had only visited in movies and books. The living room was opulent in every way, the furnishings exquisite French reproductions upholstered in delicate cerulean blue tapestry. A massive fireplace took up one whole wall, the mantel hand carved and adorned with a pair of priceless antique vases. A large gilt-framed mirror hung over it, reflecting a sparkling crystal chandelier and the baby grand piano that sat in the opposite corner.

Normally Amanda would have been completely taken with her surroundings, but now she barely took note, her eyes locking on the

French doors that opened onto the private patio.

Bayley pointed toward the doors. Seeing her hesitate, he confided, "Don't let him fool you. He's as nervous as you are. Maybe even more so."

She smiled at him gratefully and took a shaky breath. Then she walked across the room, her legs stiff as tree trunks, heavy and unbending. She saw him as soon as she reached the doors, standing at the railing looking out over the city. Her stomach lurched as long-forgotten feelings flooded her senses, and for a moment she stood with her hand frozen on the door handle, unable to move.

She just looked, letting her eyes drink in the sight of him without having to feel self-conscious or careful. Long legs, trim waist, broad shoulders . . . all as she remembered. Only the gold Rolex that glinted on his wrist and the expensive Italian knit sweater that topped his faded blue jeans jarred the illusion that nothing had changed.

She watched him shift his weight slightly in his well-worn leather sneakers as he rolled his shoulders to relax the muscles that habitually knotted across his back, and she smiled at the familiar movement. He ran his fingers through his hair and his chest expanded as he took a couple of deep cleansing breaths in an attempt to slow the heart that was hammering against his rib cage, despite his determination to stay calm. She knew all this as surely as she knew her own thoughts, and it occurred to her as she unconsciously played with her wedding ring that she had no business reading him this easily.

She opened the doors carefully, trying for some silly reason to be quiet. Inside she knew she was hoping to postpone the moment when he would turn and look at her. That first look would say it all. His eyes would tell her of his pain and unforgiveness . . . those eyes that had never looked at her with anything but humor, tenderness, and love. And she knew she wouldn't be able to stand it . . . with that one look he would tear out a piece of her heart and she would never be the same. Maybe that was why she couldn't find the right words . . . because it would all be said with a look.

Oh, God, please help me, she prayed silently as she stepped out onto the terrace and closed the door behind her.

❧   ❧   ❧   ❧

Chris hadn't known what to think when Bayley walked in last

night and told him she was here. The strange thing was, he hadn't been surprised. For weeks he had felt a restlessness in his spirit—a kind of churning expectancy that told him something was coming. And he'd dreamed about her a couple of times during the last month. It had surprised him, for truthfully he had stopped dreaming about her years ago. His life was full of other things . . . other people, other stresses.

But a few weeks ago she had invaded his sleep, bringing back memories he had fought long and hard to bury. When she'd popped up a second time about a week later, he had taken drastic steps, taking a bottle of scotch and a nubile young thing named Tiffany to bed with him for the next few nights. The combination had done the trick, and he hadn't thought of her again until Bayley had come with his extraordinary news last night.

"Well, Keith did it again!" Bayley had announced, plopping down with weary disgust in one of the two wing-backed chairs in front of the fireplace.

Chris barely spared him a glance in reply. He was seated at the piano, sheets of music spread in front of him and littering the floor at his feet. His brow was furrowed in concentration and frustration as he tried to rework a song that had come to him in the night. This was his way of unwinding the cords of tension that wound around his insides like creeping vines of fear before a big concert.

The rest of the band and crew were next door anesthetizing their nerves with loud music and the "poison" of their choice. A few years ago he would have been right there with them, enjoying the calming effects of a strong drink and a pretty girl. But lately the drill had gotten old and tiresome. Worse yet, it made *him* feel old and tired and ready for a change. That's why tomorrow night was so important.

For nearly eight years, Out Cry! had stayed on top. They had firmly established themselves as the musical icons of their generation, and they had done it by making sure that what they did never got old or predictable. Just when everyone thought they had a handle on what their music was all about, Chris would turn a corner, reinventing himself and his sound, to the delighted surprise of both his audience and his critics.

Tomorrow would be another metamorphosis as the band would step out of its accustomed venue and into a whole new setting. The last time they had played New York City, they had filled Madison

Square Garden, nearly blowing the roof off the grand arena with a record-setting crowd of screaming young fans who clapped and danced their way through the three-hour set, rarely making use of the seats they had paid top dollar to sit in. But tomorrow night they would play Carnegie Hall, backed by a full symphony orchestra before a sellout crowd of tuxedos and designer gowns. The first half of the evening they would do a number of old favorites, keeping the energy and spirit of the music high and the amplifiers appropriately low. Then, in the second half, Chris would come out without the band, sit at the piano or with his guitar, and, with the help of one of the world's greatest symphony orchestras, once again reinvent himself. It was a risk, one that many of his counselors had warned could backfire, and his nerves were taut as violin strings. The last thing he needed right now was Keith Rogers acting up and adding to the tension.

"We gonna read about it in the papers tomorrow?" Chris asked, picking up a pencil and angrily erasing the last three notes he had just written in. Then he threw down the pencil and rubbed his eyes, ready to call it quits.

"No, but as far as I'm concerned, he just hammered the last nail in the coffin. I don't think you should even wait until the end of the tour. I heard Matt Sizemore is available, and if we call him right away, he can be ready to rock 'n' roll by the time we hit Cincinnati."

"Geez, I hate this!" Chris spit out.

Bayley knew exactly what Chris was feeling. Keith was a talented musician, almost brilliant when he gave himself to it. That was why they had taken a chance on him, even when they were warned that he wasn't exactly stable.

But Keith had been trouble ever since he had joined the group at the beginning of this last tour. While he usually managed to stay in sync on stage, he marched to the beat of a different drum the minute he stepped off—drinking too much, playing too hard, and often embarrassing the group with outrageous pranks both on stage and off. Last month he'd been arrested for soliciting a prostitute who turned out to be an undercover cop. That had been the last straw. Chris had given him an ultimatum. Either get his act together or get out. Keith had tearfully repented and promised to be good. Now Bayley was saying he had broken that promise. The mere thought of the confrontation he had ahead of him gave Chris a pounding headache, and he stood up and walked to the bar to get some aspirin.

"I'll deal with it as soon as we're through here. Think he'll be all right for tomorrow night?"

"Oh, you know Keith. He'll be absolutely saintly for the next few days, praying that the ax don't fall. Just don't back down this time," Bayley warned, remembering Chris had said the same thing last time. "He's not getting any better, and one day he could do some serious damage. I don't want us to get caught in the fallout when it happens. Besides," Bayley paused, wanting to drop the bomb gently. "I don't think you'll be inclined to forgive and forget when I tell you what happened.

"He practically attacked a lady in the elevator tonight. If we hadn't been there, I honestly think he would have been all over her." Bayley watched Chris's eyes grow dark with anger and disgust. "'Course, I can't say I blame him. She was a real looker. I could hardly take my eyes off her myself. Then a funny thing happened. The longer I looked, the more familiar she seemed. I couldn't shake it that I'd seen her before."

Bayley got up and helped himself to a Coke, taking a long drink before going on. Chris moved to the window, preparing himself for the worst. Obviously this woman was someone important if Bayley recognized her. Chris stood rigidly waiting for the punch line, but he was totally unprepared for Bayley's next words.

"It was Amanda Rose."

He felt the room begin to tilt as the words reverberated in the air around him. "You're sure?" he asked, more because it seemed the logical response than that he needed confirmation. He already knew it was true.

"I'm sure," Bayley replied, watching Chris carefully to gauge his response. "She was with an older woman—a nice lady named Laura—and she told me her name. Amanda Kelly. That's right, isn't it? The newspaper clipping your friend sent you said she married a guy named Kelly, right?"

"Go on," Chris said, not bothering to answer.

"Well, Keith, as I said, had made a real jerk of himself, and it was obvious that Amanda was upset, so I followed them off the elevator and caught up with her friend. I told her we would send some flowers to apologize, and she said to send them to Amanda Kelly. Mrs. Nicholas Kelly."

Bayley had been prepared for an explosion, some sign of surprise or anger, even tears. But he had a hard time interpreting the deathly calm with which Chris was taking the news. Only the muscle working in his jaw revealed any emotion as he stood like a statue staring out at the lights of Manhattan.

"So what are you going to do?" Bayley finally asked, unable to stand the suspense.

"Send her a dozen roses and an apology. Isn't that what you said we'd do?" The voice was tight and brittle, belying the attempt at indifference. Still he didn't move.

"I think you ought to see her," Bayley kept his voice low and soothing, as though he were speaking to a skittish horse he didn't want to spook.

"Why?" The word came out flat and tired.

"Because you *need* some answers. You need to know why, so you can lay the past to rest once and for all and . . . and get on with your life."

"Get on with my life? Get on with my life?!" The words built to a roar as Chris whipped around, pinning his friend with a look of icy rage. "You act as though all I've done the past twelve years is lie in bed and feel sorry for myself—like I've done nothing! Accomplished nothing! Good grief, man, look at me! I'm Christopher Davies!"

Chris began to pace, his movements fueled by a mounting anger. "Get on with my life," he repeated, shaking his head in disgust. "Just how much farther do I need to go, huh? A roomful of platinum records and Grammys with an Emmy or two thrown in isn't enough for you? Why, I had to build a special room just to hold all the awards and plaques and . . . get on with my life!"

His pacing became more agitated as he wildly waved his arms to take in the grandeur of the room. "Why, if my daddy could see how far I've come, where I live, *how* I live . . . he'd be so proud he'd split clean in two! Just how much does a man have to do to be good enough? When is it enough? When is it ever enough?"

This last was a wail thrown up to heaven as Chris literally raised his fist. "And just who do you think you are to criticize the way I live my life?" Chris suddenly challenged, turning back to the white-faced man who silently stood watching.

Bayley hadn't moved from his place at the bar, but his eyes had been locked on his friend, recording every move as he had delivered his impassioned diatribe. He had never seen Chris get this worked up before, and he knew there was a chance that he was stepping over the line, but the man was the closest thing to a brother he'd ever had. He knew him inside and out and he knew that, ready or not, the time had come for him to speak the truth, regardless of the consequences . . . because he loved him.

Bayley's look didn't waver as he returned Chris's angry stare. "You live it all alone, Chris."

The words came out sharp and clean as a two-edged sword, slicing through Chris's defensive barricade of words like a hot knife through butter. Chris stopped his pacing and gave Bayley a hard glare. Then he sank into the closest chair, suddenly drained and uncertain how to respond. Bayley took a deep breath and continued.

"Who do you share all *this* with?" he asked, gesturing around the room as Chris had. He saw Chris look up and open his mouth to speak. "*I* don't count," he hurriedly cut him off. "And neither do any of the other guys in the band. *Or* your agent. *Or* your secretary. *Or* your business manager! And without us that leaves exactly no one . . . zip . . . nada—that's who."

He finally broke away from the spot where he'd been rooted and crossed to sit opposite Chris's slumped figure.

"The truth is that in all the time I've known you, you've never let anyone of the female persuasion get close enough to really know you. . . . I mean *you*, not 'Christopher Davies, Superstar.' Oh, you charm 'em and flatter 'em, give them that 'little boy lost' grin and they all fall at your feet, sure that they're just what you've always been looking for. And for a short time they are, until the day comes when they realize that they haven't even gotten past the first line of defense, and they begin asking questions and making a few demands.

"'Course, by that time you've already bought the diamond consolation prize and the standard It's-been-great-but letter is in the mail. And then it's on to the next pretty face. Good grief, man, you're thirty-four years old and you've never even 'gone steady' for more than a few weeks!"

"That isn't true. What about Alicia?" Chris hated the fact that he couldn't keep the defensive note out of his voice.

"What you had with Alicia wasn't a marriage. It was a merger, a business deal . . . the world's greatest publicity stunt. 'Christopher Davies, King of Rock, Marries Alicia Bennett, Queen of the Silver Screen!' Not very original but good for a front-page headline going in and at least a week of publicity coming out! Not that it couldn't have been more if you had given it half a chance. That girl really cared about you, pathetic little thing that she was.

"But you just couldn't handle anyone actually needing you. So the minute things got too close for comfort, you pushed her away and called it quits!"

"You're one to talk!" Chris lashed back. "How many Mrs. Reeses have there been? Three? Four?"

"Well, at least I'm not afraid to try. I just figure I'll keep practicing until I get it right." Bayley gave Chris a rueful smile and was rewarded with a slight flicker in return. "Besides," he continued, "it's usually them, not me, who call it quits. I'm all too happy to let them see the 'real me,' and once they get a good look, it's bye-bye, Bayley!"

"Hey, didn't they write a musical about you?" Chris teased, giving his friend a crooked smile that said they were out of the danger zone.

"That was 'Birdie,' schmuck, not Bayley. Back then they didn't write musicals about neurotic, self-destructive musicians who foul up every decent relationship in their lives and end up sitting around writing sad songs about it. You might have something, though," he added after a moment, as though suddenly struck by the brilliance of the idea. "The way things have changed, today we'd probably have a hit!"

The two spent a few minutes throwing out possible song titles for a musical based on Bayley's life—each one crazier and sicker than the last. Their laughter was contagious and cathartic. Finally they lapsed into a relaxed silence.

"So what are you going to do?" Bayley finally asked.

"Go to bed . . . get some sleep," Chris said, rising from the sofa and arching his back to stretch out the stiffened muscles.

"I meant about Amanda."

"I know what you meant. I just don't have an answer. Maybe in the morning." Chris headed for the bedroom. He stopped just short of the door and turned to look back at Bayley. "You're a good friend. Not that I always appreciate your 'Dear Abby' routine, but . . . well . . . thanks."

Bayley watched him disappear behind the bedroom door with a bemused smile. "You're welcome," he answered back softly.

Chris had tossed and turned all night, grinding his teeth until his jaw ached. If his shrink had known he was even considering seeing Amanda again, he would have had him committed! By morning he had made the sensible decision not to see her. It was best for both of them, he told himself.

Ten minutes later he called her room.

Now he was standing on a balcony overlooking the most beautiful part of the most exciting city in the world. He was surrounded by the trappings of his success, and in about twelve hours he would walk onto the stage at Carnegie Hall to the applause of fifteen hundred adoring fans. He had money, fame, everything this world has to offer. Everything, that is, except the one thing that would have given the rest of it meaning. Maybe it was true that you always want what you can't have. Or maybe it was the simple fact that she had been the one to walk away that made her so unforgettable. Maybe he would see her and feel nothing but the nostalgia of a time and place artificially sweetened by time. They would meet and talk with the stilted formality of two people with nothing in common but a distant past, and once they had walked down memory lane, they would have nothing more to say to each other. She would leave and he'd be free. At last.

At least, that was what he told himself as he stiffened at the sound of the doors opening behind him.

Seventeen

*A*manda stood uncertainly for a moment, waiting. She knew he'd heard her, even though he didn't turn around. The traffic noises were distant and muted this high up, and while there was a stiff breeze blowing, it couldn't possibly have drowned out the sound of the doors opening and closing.

Finally she walked over to stand beside him at the rail. The view from up there was breathtaking. Central Park surrounded by towering skyscrapers, their windows gleaming like diamonds in the early morning sun. She let her gaze drop straight down to the street below. The cars looked like tiny miniatures and the people like colorful ants scurrying in all directions. It was a dizzying drop.

"Did you bring the net?" Amanda asked, the familiar words slipping out before she could think to stop them.

Her words stunned him, causing the composure he had put on like armor to slip. He had known exactly what he was going to say, scripting each word and movement as though he were on stage to create the right effect. He had purposely not turned to look at her, letting her know he wasn't anxious or overly excited to see her. He had planned to let her wait, nervous and unsure, before speaking her name with the low, sexy drawl designed to turn her knees to water. Then he would turn and give her a slow, appraising look guaranteed to make her mouth go dry and establish beyond any doubt who was in charge. Then and only then would he let her off the hook.

But she had beaten him to the punch, slipping under his guard as easily as water under a bridge, and he was honestly surprised at the torrent of anger, hurt, and need the sound of her voice unleashed inside him. He felt a rueful smile sting his lips as he turned to look at her just as she raised her head to glance uncertainly in his direction.

Blue eyes clashed with green, brutally honest . . . questioning. She could feel the answering tears coming. It was useless to try to stop them. They welled up like a spring and ran shamelessly down her cheeks. His look never wavered, the accusation clear and icy cold. She had been right. There was no need for words.

Amanda stood helpless as the rush of emotion crashed over them like a tidal wave. She kept her eyes locked on his, needing to let him sear her heart with his pain and anger in some kind of penance. Finally she turned away, breaking the spell and giving them both a chance to regroup.

"It's a beautiful city." She found her voice after several unsuccessful attempts and was relieved that it sounded calm and close to natural.

"Yes, it is," he replied as though they were picking up an interrupted conversation. "Funny, I always thought I'd hate it, all the noise and crowds and boxy, closed-in places. But we hit it off fine, New York and me. Now it's one of my favorite places. Like a piece of good jazz that picks you up and carries you along all breathless and wild and unexpected."

Amanda nodded, understanding perfectly. She found the courage to really look at him for the first time. He looked the same, only more so. The cleft in his chin, the sensual mouth, the slightly crooked nose. All seemed more defined somehow, as though time had gone over them with a darker pencil and a heavier hand. Amanda's eyes swept his face leisurely, taking in every feature, looking for the familiar, noting the changes.

His hair still fell nearly to his shoulders, only now it lay in precisely careless layers, and there were threads of silver woven in with the black. It pleased her that he didn't feel the need to wash them away. There were deeper lines across his forehead, and the laugh lines around his eyes were permanent now, serving only to accent more dramatically his expressive eyes. There was an air about him, the unmistakable aura of money and power and success. And yet she knew if she scratched the surface she'd find a vulnerable, needy boy . . . still searching.

"It really is good to see you, cowboy. I'm glad you called," she said, confident for the first time that she was right to be there.

"Are you really? Frankly, I wasn't sure if you'd even come." He turned to her with a hard look meant to put her on the defensive.

"Yes, you were," she teased, not buying it. "You just weren't sure if you wanted me to."

He opened his mouth to argue but snapped it shut again when Amanda lifted her chin and gave him a grin that let him know she saw right through him. He laughed as he shook his head and threw up his hands in surrender. "Okay, okay! Truce!"

"Excuse me, Chris." Bayley's interruption surprised them both. "Just thought you'd want to know the breakfast is here."

Bayley disappeared as quickly as he had appeared and was nowhere in sight when Amanda and Chris walked back into the living room. The smell of coffee, bacon, and freshly baked croissants filled the room, and Amanda felt her mouth start to water.

"I took the liberty of ordering up some breakfast." Chris motioned toward the table, which was now laden with a feast in covered silver serving dishes. He felt back in control as he watched Amanda's eyes widen in appreciation.

Feeling like a character in a play, Amanda walked over to the table, wondering even as she took the plate Chris offered her how she could possibly eat. But eat she did, and so did he as the feeling of unreality kept growing. This was not happening as she had imagined it would. After the first emotional collision, they had retreated into formality, as if someone had pressed a button and a dividing wall had risen out of the floor, built of polite conversation and careful avoidance. It was as though they had reached a mutual unspoken agreement to ignore the past and all its unresolved questions and play the part of casual old friends.

As the hour passed, Amanda pulled out the pictures of her daughters, making Chris laugh with several anecdotes about the trials and tribulations of being a mom. In return, he entertained her with tales of famous people and a number of road stories. The closest they came to talking about the past was when Chris asked about her grandparents.

"They moved to a retirement complex in Santa Barbara about three years ago," Amanda told him. "Grams suffered a stroke, and though she made a full recovery, they figured it was time to make the move. So they rented out the house and sold the Shoppe. It was hard at first, but they've adjusted pretty well."

"Good people. Please give them my best," he responded.

The morning was going pretty much as Chris had planned. After the first shaky moments on the terrace, he had regained control, finding strength and confidence in the role of the benevolent Superstar. Still, he hadn't been prepared for the impact the sight of her would have on him.

In his dreams she was still a long-legged, fresh-faced girl, the full promise of her beauty not yet fulfilled. He had often comforted himself with the thought that marriage and children had surely taken their toll. He'd seen it often enough . . . the stunning beauty of a seventeen-year-old dried up and burned out by the age of twenty-five. But the woman before him was at her peak, her beauty fully developed yet still fresh and appealing. Even her voice had ripened, awakening feelings inside of him that he had long ago sacrificed on the altar of self-preservation.

Still he had managed to keep things under control, laughing politely at her stories and listening to her talk about her husband and children. It wasn't until she pulled out their pictures that he felt an uneasy tightening in his chest. Two beautiful little girls, amazing composites of the two people who had given them life. Amanda's children . . . not his.

Amanda was beginning to think she had imagined the pain and anger she had read in his eyes out on the balcony. Maybe this whole thing had been blown out of proportion and Chris had gotten over her years ago. Certainly there was no sign that he was still agonizing over the way they had parted, and she nearly blushed with embarrassment thinking of the emotional true confessions she had come prepared to make. Feeling a little foolish and uncomfortable, she began to think about leaving.

"Well . . ." she said when a pause in the conversation had stretched out too long and it was clear they were both trying to think of something to say.

She looked up to find Chris studying her with an intensity that set every nerve in her body on edge. His eyes bore into her . . . honest, hungry, and still searching for an answer he was unwilling to ask for. It was obvious he was battling with himself, and suddenly she realized it had all been an act . . . a well-planned and beautifully executed deception.

"Well," she said again, clearing her throat and looking around the room, suddenly terrified as his look systematically stripped her of all her composure. "I guess I'd better be going."

Chris stood up, picking up their coffee cups as he walked over to the table. "How about one more cup before you go?" he asked, not waiting for an answer before filling her cup and lightening it with cream. "Still use sugar?"

"Please. I've tried to drink it without or use that new sweetener, but it's just not the same."

She heard how thin her voice sounded as she tried to keep up her end of the conversation, but her heart was starting to pound as she watched him move with new deliberateness.

"Well, it's nice to know that some things never change. I mean, life is so uncertain."

The casual tone of the morning was lost as she heard him fight to keep his voice even.

"If there's one thing I've learned, it's that there are no guarantees. No absolutes. Things change. People change. Even the people you love. Sometimes without warning . . . without reason. And the very things you think you can count on, maybe even build your life around, can disappear in a puff of smoke. Just like that. No good-bye. No explanation."

Amanda sat in stunned silence listening to the reproofs and accusations, both spoken and unspoken. He still stood at the table, his back to her, stirring her coffee with slow, methodical movements. When he finally turned to face her, he had lost all pretense of congenial aloofness. Instead his eyes were hard as steel, his expression rigid and set. She tried to think of something to say, but the coldness of his look froze the words in her throat. All she could do was look back, feeling lower than she ever had in her life. The power of speech failed her as she searched helplessly for the words to make it better and found only silence.

Nothing had changed. Their silences had always been more eloquent than their words.

Watching her struggle, Chris found himself enjoying her obvious discomfort. He knew he was breaking every promise he had made to himself not to let her see the power she still had over him. He should say something dismissive and conciliatory and pretend that the pain of the past was forgotten, if not forgiven. But he felt locked in an emotional vise, and it was all he could do to keep from sweeping the table clean of its artificial bounty and smashing the china teacups against the wall!

He could tell by her alarmed expression that she was reading every emotion he was feeling, and yet she put up no defense, waiting quietly for whatever was coming. It was her acceptance of his disdain and her look of answering despair that finally gave him back his control.

Amanda watched him literally rein himself in and decide not to act on the emotions that had suddenly overwhelmed him. He made a pitiful attempt at a smile and shrugged his shoulders, looking just like her brother, Nathan, used to when he had run off at the mouth during his rebellious teen years and was trying to get back into his mother's good graces without actually having to apologize. Still, Chris's eyes had lost any warmth, and it was clear that it was time to put an end to their mutual misery.

"Well," Amanda said again, feeling like a broken record. "Laura is going to wonder what's become of me. I'd better get going." She stood, pausing awkwardly before taking a few steps toward the door. "This has been . . . I mean, it's been great seeing you."

"Yeah, you too. Great. Really great." Chris laughed and shook his head at some inner joke. "I almost said let's keep in touch, but given our past history, that seems sort of ludicrous, don't you think?" His voice was laced with sarcasm and his look was deliberately hard, challenging Amanda to respond.

This was it. This was the chance she'd been waiting for. She opened her mouth to explain but closed it again in defeat. What was the point? Better to leave without opening old wounds. Wiser to walk out the door, away from the past and back to the life she had chosen.

No . . . the life that had been chosen *for* her.

The thought came out of nowhere, bringing unwanted tears to her eyes as she struggled with the old demons. For the first time she realized how foolish she had been. She should never have come. She should never have played so close to the fire. For fire it still was . . . banked and buried, perhaps, but never completely extinguished and still hot enough to burn.

For the past ten years she had lived with and loved a good man worthy of all her devotion and loyalty. She had kept his house and shared his dreams and given birth to his children. And in return he had loved and cherished her, doing his best to be both friend and lover. And for the most part she had been happy. And content. And safe.

But there had been those times in the middle of the night when she would wake up crying, clutching desperately at the fading edges of a dream that would leave her restless and disturbed the rest of the day. And there were the times when one of his songs would come on the radio, catching her in a vulnerable moment of weariness or discontent, and bring back memories that still had the power to rob her of her peace of mind, if only for an afternoon. Or she would be walking down the street and see the back of a head, dark hair blowing in the wind, or the blue of a stranger's eyes. And she would lose her breath for just a moment.

Now she looked across the room and across the years and saw a young man in a black T-shirt standing on a cliff overlooking the sea. She was eighteen again, overwhelmed with feelings of passion and longing and need. And the anger she felt at what they had lost made her feel reckless and rebellious!

She needed to leave. Despite or probably because of what she was feeling, she needed to turn away and walk out the door. Forget rectifying the past. What was the point? It was too late to change things! She turned and started once again for the door. She could feel his eyes on her—angry, accusing, pleading. Her hand was on the doorknob. Two more seconds and she would be out the door.

Eighteen

"My dad died."

The words stopped her cold.

"It looked like he was going to be all right. He was lookin' good, gettin' out of bed, startin' rehabilitation. It wasn't goin' to be easy, but everyone said he was gonna be fine."

The recitation was spoken in a softly accented monotone. "I'd found us a place. Nothing fancy, but clean, close to rehab. . . . He wanted a hamburger, well done with cheese and onions. The doctors would have skinned me alive, but he seemed so good. . . ."

Amanda leaned her head against the door, grinding her forehead into the wood, feeling his pain with him, picturing everything as if she had been there.

"I was only gone about thirty minutes. When I came back he was gone. Just like that. No warning. No good-bye. We buried him up on the hill behind the ranch beside my mother. After Mama died, Daddy had the ground 'sanctified' or somethin' by a priest. Mama would have laughed. She always said that the whole earth was God's creation and He didn't need any man to make it holy, but Daddy wasn't about to take any chances. Not with her."

His voice sounded pathetically young and vulnerable as he added, "I wrote you. I told you all about it. I asked you to come. . . . I needed you to come."

Silence.

Amanda could feel her heart throbbing under her skin. A thin film of sweat covered her forehead. Her hand tightened on the doorknob as she heard him move across the room, pull out the piano bench, and sit down. He began playing softly. She listened, letting the music soothe her while she waited for the courage to speak.

"I never got the letter."

The piano kept playing, and for an instant Amanda thought she had only imagined the words, not spoken them out loud. She turned away from the door and moved to stand behind him.

"Chris? Did you hear me?"

No response.

"I never got your letter. I never got *any* of your letters. If I had, I would have been there. Nothing would have stopped me!" Urgency made her voice rise, but his hands kept moving across the keys, faster now, louder.

"Please, Chris. You've got to hear me!" Amanda was crying as she placed her hand on his shoulder. "For years I thought *you* didn't want *me*. I thought you'd just gone back to your old life and forgotten me! And the pain nearly killed me!"

Then in a small voice she said the words she had never found the courage to say that summer. "I . . . I loved you."

His back went rigid at her words, but his hands stilled and the room echoed with the quiet. He was breathing heavily, his shoulders rising and falling as if he had just run a race. Finally he took a deep, shuddering breath, and Amanda could feel his shoulder relax under her hand.

Suddenly her legs wouldn't hold her. Amanda walked over to the sofa and sat on the edge, feeling nervous and uncertain about the direction the morning had taken. But as Chris turned to face her, she realized there was no turning back. She searched for a way to begin.

"About five years ago my mother had a real scare. They discovered a lump in her breast, and since breast cancer runs in her family, we were all terrified. She had a biopsy that eventually turned out negative, but it took several days for the results to come back, and during that time we were all living on pins and needles."

Chris took a deep breath and looked away, obviously not interested in her mother's story. Just what did this have to do with him?

"Please, Chris. This is hard enough. I've got to tell it my own way. It's important to me that you understand!" Amanda's look was beseeching, and Chris nodded at her to go ahead.

"During those few days of waiting, we were all going through our own private hell, imagining life without my mom, praying constantly for God to spare her. But my mother seemed to find an inner strength and peace. It was the first time I truly understood what it meant to have no fear of death. She knew she was a child of God and that if she died, something far more wonderful waited for her.

"The only thing that seemed to be important to her was to make sure that if she did have to face God soon, she could do so with a pure heart and a clean conscience. So she started making restitution for every 'bad' thing she could remember doing. Like, she went to the local grocery and paid for a box of laundry detergent the checker hadn't charged her for a few weeks before. She even called her brother in Wisconsin to confess that she had been the one to break their mother's antique candlesticks when they were kids, a crime for which *he* had been punished. We all thought it was sort of a funny but endearing way to handle the stress she was under . . . a bit hysterical but harmless.

"Then one morning she called and asked me to come for coffee. . . ."

❧   ❧   ❧   ❧

The minute Amanda walked in and saw her mother's face that fateful day, she knew something was terribly wrong. Her first thought was that the doctor had called and her mother was going to tell her she was dying.

"Oh, Mom. Oh, Lord Jesus!" Amanda immediately threw her arms around her mother's trembling form and held her close. "Tell me, Mom. What is it? Did you hear from the doctor?"

"No! Oh no, darling! I'm sorry," Karen said, realizing what Amanda thought. "I haven't heard anything yet. I'm sorry I scared you." She gave her daughter's worried face a kiss and then led her into the living room.

"I do need to talk to you, though," she went on, motioning her daughter to sit but too agitated to sit herself. "I guess I should have done this long ago, but somehow you always think there's going to be plenty of time . . . to talk . . . to make things right."

Amanda sat on the sofa and watched her mother's strange performance, totally mystified. What could she need to tell her that was so serious?

Her mother stood for a moment staring off into space, lost in a world only she could see. Then she squared her shoulders and walked over to a small desk that stood in front of one of the living room windows. She opened the drawer and removed some papers. Just what they were, Amanda couldn't see. Her mother clutched them to her breast and walked over to the fireplace, where she stood staring at Amanda's high school graduation picture, which stood on the mantel along with a half dozen other family pictures.

"The first thing I need to say is that I love you, Amanda. I love all my children . . . perhaps too much. And sometimes when you love that much you feel, particularly as a parent, that you have the right to . . . interfere . . . in order to protect the ones you love from hurt." Karen's voice broke for a moment, and Amanda immediately stood up.

"Mom, please, whatever it is, it doesn't matter. I love you and if this is going to upset you, just forget it . . . at least for now."

Her mother shook her head and waved at Amanda to sit back down. "I'm all right, sweetheart. I need to do this."

Karen took a deep breath and went on, still talking to her daughter's picture. "When you were little I used to take you to the park. There was a big, old oak tree in the middle of the playground and the older kids would climb it, hanging from the branches like monkeys and daring each other to go higher and higher. You always wanted to climb that tree, and when I thought you were old enough, I would lift you up and help you climb on the lowest branches. But I never let you go very high, and you would get so upset when I made you come down, saying I was treating you like a baby . . . that the other kids got to go higher.

"What you didn't know . . . what I didn't tell you . . . was that a few years before, a little boy had fallen from that tree. Lindsey was just a baby then, and I would bring her there to play in the sandbox. I became friendly with another young mother. She had a little girl Lindsey's age and a boy about six.

"One day we were talking, laughing at something funny the girls had just done, when we heard this terrible scream. We both went running to find her beautiful golden-haired boy lying on the ground. His neck was broken.

"I held that young mother the day of the funeral while she cried. Over and over she kept saying, 'Why didn't I stop him? Why did I let him climb that tree? I knew it was dangerous. Why didn't I just say no?' "

Amanda's eyes filled with sympathetic tears as she heard her mother recount the sad story, and she remembered the day, long ago, when she had run away and climbed that tree. Surely that wasn't what this was all about. Her mother finally turned to face her as she continued.

"The summer you went to Walker's Point and met Chris Davies, I was filled with that same kind of fear. You were so young and inexperienced. I looked at you and I looked at him, and I knew you were in way over your head. It wasn't that I thought he was a bad person. Please believe me, Amanda. I never meant him any harm. I just knew that he wasn't right for you and that if you let your heart get in the way of your common sense, you could really get hurt.

"So I made a decision. I did something I had no business doing. I played God in your life. . . . I had no right. And now I must risk losing your love and respect right at the time I need it most."

At this point Karen walked over to her daughter and handed her a packet of yellowed, dog-eared letters. Three, to be precise, all unopened and wrapped in a red ribbon. "I only hope that one day you'll find it in your heart to forgive me."

Amanda took one look at the handwriting on the top envelope and knew precisely what her mother had done. She stared at the letters in her hand, unable at first to deal with all the contradictory feelings that collided inside her like amusement-park bumper cars. Shock and disbelief ran headlong into sudden clarity. Hurt rammed sideways into joy and a strange sense of relief. Finally, outrage and indignation plowed into them all, bursting into red-hot anger.

"You lied to me?" Amanda looked up at her mother, her face contorted with rage. "All the times I called you—crying, desperate, heartbroken, asking if he'd called or written—you let me think he had forgotten me? How could you do that? How could you let me suffer so?"

She stared again at the letters, remembering the years of pain and desperation. She saw herself back in her college dorm room, lying on her bed, curled like a wounded puppy around her pillow, her face buried in her hands, crying, "Why, God? Why? Why did you bring him into my life if all I would ever have to show for it is this pain? Why aren't I good enough? What did I do wrong? How could I be so stupid?!"

The questions had gone on and on, even after time had dulled the unbearable pain to a nagging ache. Even after Nick had come into her life, the questions didn't go away. It had taken her years to trust her own instincts again, and she had never, up until that moment, stopped thinking of herself as flawed.

Now she looked at her mother, the woman she had always trusted and admired most, and saw a stranger. "Why?" was the only thing she could think to say.

"I panicked," her mother confessed, her face a mask of misery and regret. "I felt like I was watching you climb that tree once again and I knew that tragedy lay ahead. So right or wrong . . . I said no. Once I'd done it, I didn't know how to take it back." Karen walked back to the mantel and picked up a picture of Amanda, Nick, and Kimberly, taken before Casey was born.

"The worst part is that I honestly believe that you and Nick would have found each other eventually. You belong together. He _is_ God's best for you. Now, because of me, you may always wonder."

Amanda just looked at her mother and shook her head. She carefully tucked the letters away in her purse, then stood up and walked to the door. As she reached for the doorknob, she heard her mother call after her.

"Amanda?"

The pain and uncertainty in her mother's voice was enough to make Amanda hesitate, but she couldn't bring herself to look at her. "It's all right, Mama. Just give me some time," she said, walking out the door without looking back.

Nineteen

I drove down to the beach," Amanda said as she continued telling the story to Chris. "It seemed like the right place to read your letters. It was a clear, sunny day, but cool as I remember. I didn't care. I took a blanket and sat on the sand. I read them in order.

"The first one was newsy, telling me about your dad and the hospital and how weird it was to be back in Lubbock. You talked about the apartment you'd found and gave me the address, explaining that you couldn't afford to put in a phone, so we'd have to write for a while. It was so strange to be reading your letters, so fresh and alive and real sounding, knowing I was reading a letter from a ghost . . . a shadow that didn't exist anymore.

"The second letter was about your dad's sudden death. You asked me to come to you. I could barely read it I was crying so hard. My tears kept falling on the paper and smearing the ink. I finally had to stop and just cry and scream into the wind for a while, or my tears would have washed the words right off the page.

"I couldn't finish the third letter . . . not then. It killed me to read you asking me, 'Why don't you write me? What's happening?' and demanding, 'At least have the decency to tell me it's over!' You were so hurt by my silence and so angry!

"I remember I looked out at the water and wondered for the first time in my life if there really was a God. How could He let this happen? All that pain . . . all that disappointment. I felt like screaming at the letters, 'I'm here! Please don't be angry! Don't be hurt and don't hate me!'

"But it was too late. I was reading the words of a boy who no longer existed written to a girl who no longer was. It was all shadows and echoes."

During this long retelling, Amanda had focused fixedly on a spot in the carpet halfway between her feet and Chris's. She hadn't needed to see the look on his face to feel his anger as he heard what her mother had done or to sense his frustration and aching regret as he listened to her talk about reading his letters. Now as the memory of those letters came flooding back, she looked up at him, not bothering to hide the pain she still felt or the tears that came with it.

"Reading those letters was the most wrenching experience of my life. For seven years I had believed that you had walked out of my life and never looked back. I thought you'd gone back to Texas and met an old girlfriend. Or that after giving it more thought, you'd decided that we were too different and you didn't want me after all."

As she was speaking Chris closed his eyes, picturing the face of the eager young girl he had fallen in love with. He saw her dancing at the ocean's edge, walking in the moonlight, looking at him with tears in her eyes the day he'd shown her the heart in the tree. He'd promised her "happily ever after" and given her nothing but heartache.

His own pain was forgotten as he moved to kneel on the floor in front of her. He took her face in his hands, and the two looked at each other with the unabashed joy and wonder of two holocaust survivors who'd just rediscovered each other. The past fell away as he gathered her into his arms and held her while she cried.

Amanda didn't even try to fight what was happening. She needed him too much. This was what she had dreamed of . . . the feel of his arms around her, his breath on her hair. There was warmth and comfort and a sense of healing . . . needful things that pushed every other thought from her mind. He cradled her head against his chest and stroked her hair, gently rocking her.

"Why didn't you contact me when you found out? Didn't you think I had a right to know?" His words were gentle, not accusing.

She laughed, nuzzling his chest with her nose. "I tried. Do you have any idea how hard it is to get a letter to the great Christopher Davies? I mean, I didn't know where you were living. I didn't know anything about you except for what I read in the fan magazines."

"Oh, so you read about me, did you? Keepin' track?" he interrupted, allowing himself the incredible luxury of teasing her.

"Sometimes . . . at the beauty parlor, *trapped* under the hair dryer.

I didn't have anything else to do," she replied drolly, falling back into their easy repartee as easily as he had. "Anyway, I finally called CTI and asked for an address where I could write you. Then I wrote a letter and sealed it in an envelope marked 'Personal, Private, and Important!' I put that in another envelope with a letter explaining that I was an old friend and that I would be very grateful if they would see to it that this very important letter got into your hands personally."

"I never got it."

"I know. Five weeks later I received a personally autographed eight-by-ten glossy signed 'To my good friend, Amanda. Love, Christopher' and a form letter thanking me for my letter."

"Um. And what did you do with the picture?" he asked, rocking back to look at her with an expression that awakened the butterflies sleeping in the pit of her stomach.

"I gave it to the baby-sitter," Amanda replied with a stern behave-yourself look. "My husband would have wanted to know what I was doing with a picture of my old boyfriend, and I wasn't in the mood to talk about it."

"So you never told him about the letters?"

Amanda let out a big sigh. "I couldn't. It would only have hurt him and made him worry. You see, Nick was the one who picked up the pieces. He was sort of the glue that stuck my life back together after I lost you. Of all people, he knew how much you'd meant to me. I was having a hard enough time dealing with my own feelings without having to worry about placating his."

Chris reluctantly released her and stood up, moving to the bar to pour himself a glass of juice. It was just something to do. Amanda's deliberate reference to her husband had doused him with an icy bucket of reality, and he struggled to find his balance between the sudden revelations of the past and the realities of the present.

For twelve years he had lived with the agony of her rejection. Now he knew it had all been a lie, that she had never willingly walked away from him and that her pain had been as great as his. But the fact that they had found each other again held no promise. They were simply being given a chance to finally say good-bye properly. And as he looked across the room at her, he knew he wasn't ready to do that . . . not yet.

"This whole thing is so hard to believe. I mean, I feel like you've returned from the dead or something. Or maybe it's me. . . . Maybe

I've finally returned from the dead." He smiled, letting his eyes just rest on her for a minute.

"I've got an idea," he said, suddenly animated. "Spend the day with me. See what my life is all about."

Amanda's eyes widened in surprise.

"I'm serious. 'A Day in the Life of Christopher Davies.' "

He looked at his watch and was amazed to see that it was nearly noon. The morning had evaporated.

"A reporter for *People* magazine is going to be here at one, and I've got a press conference this afternoon. Then I have to get to the theater for final sound checks. It will be crazy and hectic and more fun than it's been in years if you're with me!" He walked back to the sofa and sat down beside her, grabbing her hands in his. "Then to-night you can come to the concert, you and your friend, and tomorrow we'll run away together . . . just for the day," he added quickly, seeing her look of alarm.

Amanda gently pulled her hands away. The morning had left her drained and confused. Chris was right. The whole thing *was* hard to deal with. At some point during the last couple of hours she had stepped out of herself, entering a world where her most fantastic day-dream had come true. To Amanda, daydreams had always seemed like harmless imaginings, made up of a dozen *what if*'s and *if only*'s that had no power to actually affect one's life. But this dream was all too real, and she looked at Chris, searching for reassurance that when the time came, they would both know when to wake up. He immediately understood her misgivings.

"Look, Amanda, I know that what we had in the past is gone and that your future belongs to someone else. But you and I, we just got cut off without warnin'—without a chance to close it down or say a proper good-bye. Now it's like that God of yours has seen fit to give us a present, like a comma between yesterday and tomorrow. It's a chance to rediscover each other . . . to talk, to remember, and then to lay it to rest. All I'm askin' is that we have a little time!"

Time! The word brought Amanda abruptly back to her senses. "Good grief! What time is it?" she cried, looking around the room for a clock.

"A little before twelve."

"Great! Just great! Laura and I had an eleven o'clock appointment. She's probably worried sick."

"No, she's not. I called her about an hour ago."

Amanda and Chris both jumped at the sound of Bayley's voice coming from the entry hall.

"Sorry I startled you. I let myself in. I thought I'd better check on you two kids. Make sure you were 'playing nice' and everything," he said with a satisfied smirk. Obviously things were going very well indeed from what he'd just overheard. "Anyway, Laura said to tell you that she was going to go ahead without you. Not to worry. She's done this a million times and is sure she can manage. She'll check back with you this afternoon."

"There, you see?" Chris said. "You're free for the afternoon. Come be with me, Amanda. Please."

Amanda looked over at Bayley beaming at them like a proud parent. Then she looked at Chris's eager face, and suddenly all caution was lost in an overwhelming surge of joy and excitement. What could it possibly hurt? They both understood the ground rules and they would stick to them. They were just taking a few hours. After all they had been through, surely there was no harm.

"Okay. I'd love to. Just one thing . . ." Amanda paused, suddenly feeling shy.

"You're safe with me, Amanda Rose. Scout's honor." Chris raised three fingers, then kissed her gently on the forehead.

Amanda closed her eyes and smiled. She could almost swear she heard sea gulls in the distance.

Twenty

$\mathcal{A}$manda went back to her room to leave a note for Laura and freshen up while Chris changed and met with the reporter from *People*.

"It's best if you're not here for that. They're nosy as all get-out and will want to know who you are," Chris had explained as he saw her out. "At the news conference downstairs there will be so many people, no one will single you out. By the way, if anyone does ask, just say you're my cousin or something. They'll lose interest immediately if they think we're related."

"Oh, they'll really believe that one . . . us looking so much alike and everything," Amanda said, rolling her eyes.

"You're my cousin on my father's side from a little town outside of Bakersfield, where you teach school and raise angora kittens for fun and profit," Chris recited without blinking.

"Hmm. That's pretty good." Amanda nodded her head approvingly. "I wouldn't have thought of the angora thing. Gives it that ring of truth. Sounds like you've done this before," she mused, giving him a calculating look that brought him ridiculously close to blushing.

"Only one thing wrong with it," she added smartly as she backed out the door Chris had opened for her and pushed the elevator down button.

"What's that?"

"*Are* there any 'little towns' outside of Bakersfield?"

Chris opened his mouth to reply, then shrugged, conceding the point. He leaned against the doorjamb, watching her, still struggling to believe she was there. Then his expression became all business as he instructed, "Meet me in the lobby at two. It will be better if you don't come off the elevator with me. Fewer questions."

"Still giving orders, I see," Amanda teased, stepping into the waiting elevator.

"Please," Chris added, hoping his rakish smile would hide the sudden panic he felt at the thought she might not come.

Amanda just smiled and nodded as the doors closed.

❧   ❧   ❧   ❧

At two o'clock sharp, Amanda entered the lobby. She had changed into an ankle-length Kelly green skirt that hugged her hips and flared becomingly over the brown kid boots she now wore. The cashmere sweater she had worn that morning was now tucked in and belted in matching leather suede. She had added a gold pin to her sweater and carried her trench coat and wide-brimmed hat. The effect was both elegant and anonymous, and she was immediately swallowed up by the crowd of guests and press that milled around the lobby waiting for Chris to appear.

She felt a strange excitement that all these people were waiting for "her" Chris. But the Christopher Davies that stepped off the elevator a few minutes later was someone Amanda had only seen in pictures and on TV. Although he had simply changed into jeans, boots, an open-collared white shirt, and a black leather jacket, the transition was startling and had far more to do with attitude than attire. What would look ordinary on someone else made a powerfully sexual statement on Chris. It was the way he moved and held his head and the expression in his eyes that charged the room with his presence and made even the most nonchalant onlookers unable to take their eyes off of him.

Amanda felt her heart quicken as his eyes scanned the room, resting on her long enough to let her know he'd seen her before the hotel security spirited him and the other band members along to the small conference room where the majority of press were waiting.

For one heart-stopping moment Amanda was at a loss. Had she misunderstood? Was he expecting her to follow?

Then she felt someone take her arm in a firm grip and begin propelling her through the crowd in their wake. Looking up, she was relieved to find Bayley smiling down at her.

"Chris asked me to look after you until we leave the hotel. Hope you don't mind. I'll get you seated in the conference room, then I'll have to go up with the other guys. At the end of the conference someone will come get you and take you to the limousine. The password is 'Louie,' " he said, raising his eyebrows in an imitation of Groucho Marx. "Isn't this fun?" he added, waving off the security guard as they entered the crowded room and showing Amanda to an empty chair in the back. "Just like playing 'I Spy' when we were kids!"

Amanda laughed and settled back to watch the show. There were reporters from every major newspaper, magazine, and television station. Several TV cameras were set up to capture the interview that would accompany the coverage of tonight's performance. Chris and the band were seated on a platform behind a long table covered with microphones of every size and description. The whole room buzzed with energy and excitement, and Amanda found herself completely mesmerized by the scene.

Finally a young woman dressed in an expensive navy blue suit stepped to the front and called for everyone's attention. The buzz quieted to a drone.

"Ladies and gentlemen of the press, my name is Marcia Hadley, and I am happy to welcome you to this special interview time with Christopher Davies and Out Cry! As I'm sure you can appreciate, our time is limited since the guys have to get over to Carnegie Hall in preparation for tonight's concert. So I ask you to keep your questions brief and to the point. Yes, Mr. Correy," she said, pointing to an eager young man in the second row.

As cameras flashed nonstop around them, the band fielded questions about everything from how they liked New York to how they liked their women. Some of the questions were impertinent and ribald, others serious and probing. The five band members took turns answering, joking with the reporters and one another like a well-rehearsed comedy troupe.

Amanda watched in amazement as they effortlessly answered the same old questions with fresh enthusiasm and avoided the more personal inquiries with diplomacy and humor. These were professionals who had honed their skills with hard work and careful planning. Only Keith Rogers appeared unusually subdued, speaking only when directly addressed and only minimally entering into his fellow band members' easy banter. She also noticed that most of the questions directed at Chris were affectionately respectful and that when he spoke the room became intently quiet.

"So why are you doing a concert at Carnegie Hall?" a voice called out from the back. "I mean, what business does Out Cry! have playing in a symphony hall? You goin' highbrow on us, Christopher?"

The room broke into laughter at the good-natured ribbing, but it was a question they all wanted answered.

"A little culture wouldn't hurt you, Will!" Chris responded, recognizing the voice of the *Rolling Stone* reporter. More laughter followed, then Chris continued.

"In all honesty I don't know how to answer you, except to say that to me music is a living thing. You don't catch it and stuff it in a bottle and say 'This is it!' I have no intention of layin' down my electric guitar for a violin, but I also refuse to have anyone tell me that I can't make music any way I feel like it. That's what life is all about . . . new experiences. Some good, some bad. That's how we grow as people and as artists. So tonight I'm gonna grow a little. And tomorrow you'll all tell me if it was a step forward or backward. But to tell the truth, that doesn't really matter. What matters is taking that step . . . call it a 'step of faith' if you want."

Amanda smiled to herself as she saw Chris glance meaningfully in her direction. She was still caught up in the spell of his words when someone tapped her from behind and motioned her to follow him out. Once outside, the long-haired, slightly blank-faced young man introduced himself.

"Hi, I'm Lou Bradey . . . um, Louie." He grabbed her hand nervously and pumped it twice. "I'm a roadie," he proudly announced, as if that should answer any questions Amanda might have. She had to fight to keep a straight face as he went on to repeat his instructions with laborious care. His speech was unnaturally slow.

"Bayley said to get you to the limo before the party broke up, so . . . this way." He turned abruptly and headed for a side exit. Amanda had to hurry to catch up.

"So, Louie, just what exactly is a 'roadie'?" she asked, trotting along beside him.

The question seemed to stun him and he came to an abrupt stop, taking a moment to compute his answer. Then he carefully replied, "You need it? I get it. You break it? I fix it. You lose it? I find it." He smiled, obviously pleased with himself that he had said it right.

"Sounds like Chris is lucky to have you around."

"Naw, I'm the lucky one!" he said, taking off once again at full speed and forcing Amanda to run to catch up.

Louie introduced Amanda to the liveried limo driver, then took his leave with a self-conscious "Nice to meet you."

The large black man tipped his hat respectfully and opened the door for her. One look at the bulging muscles under his coat and the battle-scarred face told Amanda that he doubled as a bodyguard when necessary. Yet there was a gentleness to his voice and manner that put her immediately at ease.

As she settled back to wait, Amanda took stock of the limo's luxurious interior, which included a well-stocked bar, a small television set and stereo, and polished mahogany paneling. Pretty fancy surroundings for a simple boy from the country who once told her he was strictly a beer-and-pretzel man.

She thought about the eclectic group of people Chris had surrounded himself with. It was obvious that he was demanding and had a discerning eye for talent. But he also had a heart for people, taking in lost puppies like Louie and misfits like Keith Rogers and making them an integral part of the family.

"Sweet, sexy, scary, safe" she had written in her diary the first day she had met him. Twelve years later he was every bit of that and more.

The limo door suddenly opened and Chris catapulted in, slamming the door behind him as if the armies of Pharaoh were after him.

"Take off, Ruby!" he ordered, and they peeled away from the curb like racers in the Indy 500. Then he turned to Amanda.

"Well, fancy meeting you here!" He reached out and touched her hair with a light, tentative stroke, as if needing to see if she was real. The look on his face was more than joyful. It was almost worshipful as he took in every detail of her appearance. "You look beautiful," he said simply.

Amanda felt herself blush, a full body blush that she was sure turned even her toes pink. It had been years since anyone had looked at her like that, and the feeling was both wonderful and disturbing. For one breathlessly terrifying moment she thought he was going to kiss her. He obviously wanted to. But thankfully he seemed to think better of it and settled back in the lush leather seat beside her instead. She let out a relieved breath. This was going to be trickier than she'd thought.

"So what'd you think?" he asked. It took her a second to realize he was talking about the press conference.

"That was some circus!" she replied honestly. "Do you have to run that gauntlet everywhere you go?"

"All part of the job description, although it usually isn't so intense. Everybody's hyped up to see if the great Christopher Davies is gonna fall on his face tonight," Chris said, reaching to open the bar and pour them each a Coke.

"Do my ears deceive me or did you just refer to yourself as the 'great' Christopher Davies? Cowboy, you've definitely got to stop reading your own press clippings!" Amanda laughed, taking the cut-crystal glass he handed her.

"Man, I'm only with the woman a couple of hours and already she's givin' me grief," he moaned in an exaggerated drawl.

"Probably exactly what you need . . . a little grief from a good strong woman to keep that big head of yours from blowing up and carrying you off like one of those Macy's Parade balloons!" Amanda relaxed and started enjoying herself. She'd forgotten how much fun it was to verbally spar with him.

"You're probably right. Problem is, the women I meet these days don't have the gumption to speak their minds the way you do. I'd forgotten what it's like to be with a woman who says what she thinks without worrying if it's what I want to hear or not. I've missed that. It feels real good."

While his voice was still playful, Amanda saw the rueful expression in his eyes, and she realized that for all his fame, fortune, and adoring fans, the "great" Christopher Davies was lonely. Here he was facing one of the biggest challenges of his career, and there was no one to support him. No wife, no kids. . . . She didn't know what it was like to be alone like that, and her heart went out to him.

She leaned toward him and gave him a searching look. "Seriously, are you worried about tonight?"

Chris hesitated before answering, giving her question some thought. "A performer has to worry any time he steps out of the norm and tries to create a new space for himself. Am I afraid it won't be good? No. I like what we're doin'. I believe in it. I may be the only one there who does, but I'm gonna enjoy every minute of it. Whether anyone else does is up to the gods."

Amanda tentatively reached out and placed her hand on his, giving it a reassuring squeeze. Chris turned his hand to take hold of hers and squeezed back, but the introspection had taken him momentarily away to a place Amanda couldn't follow. An old feeling emerged from deep in Amanda's consciousness. She had forgotten how easily she lost him when his music called.

They pulled up in front of Carnegie Hall and were immediately spotted by a number of photographers, cameras ready.

Chris cursed under his breath. "Better put your hat and glasses on. We'll make a run for it, but they're bound to get us on film. Keep your head down and don't stop no matter what they yell at you. Got it?"

Amanda was already pulling her hat on and searching for her dark glasses. "Got it!"

The limo stopped and the two looked anxiously at each other for a moment, waiting for Ruby to open the door. Amanda's heart was beating and her palms were sweating. She felt just like when she was little and she and Lindsey would play hide-and-seek with their father. She would wait, hiding behind a sofa or door for just the right moment when she could slip past Daddy and run to safety. Her mouth would be dry and her whole body would be shaking with nervous energy as she struggled to keep from giggling out loud and revealing her hiding place.

Amanda had the random thought that she had always liked to dabble with danger, and today was no different. She felt a nervous grin spread across her face as she waited for Chris to give the word.

"Ready?" he asked as the driver approached the door. Amanda nodded, her eyes shining, her cheeks ablaze with excitement.

They made a mad dash for the stage entrance, cameras flashing all around. The door magically opened for them just as they reached it and slammed behind them, blocking out the reporters' shouted demands and questions. Amanda and Chris looked at each other and grinned. In her head Amanda could hear a little voice call "Safe!"

The first thing Chris did was get her a backstage pass to pin on her sweater. "Don't take that off. You'll be out on the street before you can say 'Jack Sprat' without it," he warned sternly.

He took her hand and led her farther into the bowels of the grand old theater. The air hummed with activity as people rushed here and there, all looking very important and official. The sights, the sounds . . . even the smells reminded her of being backstage at the Walker's Point theater, only more so!

Chris announced he was going to give her the grand tour, showing her his dressing room, then taking her down the route he would walk to the wings from which he and the band would enter. From there she could see the world-famous stage.

The symphony would fill most of it, wrapping around the back in several rows of evenly spaced chairs. Nested at the center was a set of drums, an electric keyboard, and five sets of microphones strategically placed to highlight each band member. A small army of sound technicians was busy checking and rechecking to make sure everything was just as it should be.

"Come on," Chris said, taking Amanda's hand and pulling her out onto the stage.

At first Amanda was too busy stepping over cords and feeling out of place to appreciate where she was. But then Chris stopped and stood her in front of him right at center stage. He stood behind her, his hands gripping her shoulders.

"Close your eyes," he whispered in her ear. "Hear the rustle of the crowd grow quiet in the dark, waiting just for you. Feel your heart start to pound like a drum beating out the rhythm of your life. Feel the energy starting to build, rising from the soles of your feet and charging every nerve in your body till you're quivering like the string on a bow."

Amanda let his voice carry her away, his words creating a reality free from time and space.

"Now . . . open your eyes."

Amanda looked out at the rows of empty seats but saw them filled with a glittering crowd of people. She experienced the first blinding shock of the spotlight and heard the welcoming thunder of applause as Chris described it, and for one dazzling moment she caught a glimpse of what it must be like to be him.

"Chris, we're gonna need you in about five minutes for sound checks on the acoustical. Then we'll want the rest of the guys out here," a voice rang out of nowhere, shattering the magical moment.

"Gotcha, Maury," Chris called back to the faceless voice. "I'd better get you backstage and alert the others. Besides, I want you to meet the rest of my 'merry men,'" he said, taking her hand once again to lead her back through the tangled maze they'd just navigated.

"Oh, I've met them, and they were merry all right."

"Good grief, in all the excitement of seeing you again, I forgot. I never even apologized for what happened. I am sorry, Amanda. But please don't judge the rest of the guys by Keith. Sam and Bayley and Trevor are the salt of the earth. Keith was a mistake, one I'm goin' to correct before we leave New York. He's probably one of the most talented musicians I've ever worked with, but he's a loose cannon."

They entered the green room to find the other band members grabbing a quick bite from a table laden with platters of sandwiches, fruit, and assorted pastries.

"Gentlemen, and I use the word loosely, I'd like you to meet an old friend of mine," Chris began as the other men turned to look at Amanda with interest. Obviously Bayley had filled them in on what was happening after Chris bolted from the press conference and left them stranded at the hotel. "This is Amanda Kelly. Amanda, this is Sam Waters, Trevor Lee, Keith Rogers, and of course, you know Bayley."

Amanda felt awkward seeing Keith again, but she soon realized that he didn't recognize her as the lady he'd accosted in the elevator. He probably didn't remember anything about last night, and she was glad Chris was going to leave it that way for the time being. He would deal with Keith later, when she wasn't embarrassed by it.

Sam immediately picked up that they were going to ignore their first introduction in the elevator and was quick to give her a smile and a warm handshake. "So you're Amanda Rose. We all knew that it took a great lady to inspire such a great song. It's an honor," he said with a courtly bow, and Amanda immediately labeled him "the troubadour."

"It's right nice to meet you, ma'am," Trevor followed, his soft manner speaking of his Georgia upbringing.

Keith started to give her a cocky smile and say something smart, but a look from both Bayley and Chris killed the words in his mouth, and he simply nodded and said, "How are you?"

A head popped into the doorway announcing that they needed Chris and the others onstage. The band members hastily finished their snack and headed out the door.

"This sounds like a good time for me to make my exit," Amanda said, slipping on her coat and gathering up her purse and hat. "I think I'll go back to the hotel and check in with Laura. Besides, I've never been to a Christopher Davies concert before. I've got to figure out what I'm going to wear!"

"Sure you have," Chris corrected her. "You were at the very first one, and it was quite a night, as I remember it."

"Oh, that's right," Amanda stammered, hoping he didn't see the red creeping up her neck as the memory of that night came back full force. "What I meant was—"

"I know what you meant," Chris interrupted, reaching out to straighten her coat collar. "And whatever you wear, you'll be the most beautiful woman in the place, so don't worry."

Amanda felt the red flood into her cheeks at the compliment, and she gave up trying to look cool and unaffected by the admiring look Chris was giving her.

"*Definitely* time to exit," she announced with a shaky laugh.

"Shall I have Ruby take you back?" Chris asked.

"What, and risk all those photographers again? No, I think I'll go back to being a normal nobody and grab a cab." She started out the door and nearly ran into the harried young man who had called everyone on stage earlier.

"They're waiting, Chris!"

"Coming!" he yelled back. "Well, at least let me send Ruby to pick you and Laura up. It will be a zoo here tonight, and I don't want you to be late. He'll be at the hotel at seven-thirty sharp, so be ready!" Without giving her time to object, Chris gave her a quick kiss on the forehead and was gone.

Twenty-one

*I*t was nearly five-thirty when Amanda let herself into the room to find Laura on the phone.

"Oh, wait, Nick. Here she is. She's just walking in the door."

Laura threw her a look of both censure and relief as she held out the receiver. Her expression said, "Where the heck have you been?" but her voice was light as she announced, "It's Nick, Amanda. It's the *second* time he's called. . . . The beauty parlor did a wonderful job with your hair. It looks great," she added, letting Amanda know that she'd made up a cover story.

Amanda gave her a quizzical look as she took the receiver. "Hi, sweetheart, how are you? How are the girls? Is everything all right?"

Amanda was immediately alarmed by the midday call. She and Nick had talked every other night since she had left. Nick would always wait until after eight in the evening California time so he would catch Amanda getting ready for bed.

"Everything is fine," he quickly reassured her. "I was just thinking about you and needed to hear your voice. I also couldn't wait to tell you the good news." His voice rang with excitement over the phone. "They like my designs! Shea looked at them himself and said with just a couple minor adjustments he thought they were ready to present to the client!"

"But I thought you weren't going to show them the plans for another week! What happened?" Amanda asked, stunned and barely able to assimilate what he was saying.

"I know, but the time schedule got pushed up. Something about the building permits running out. So Shea called me last night and told me to bring them in today. I meant to call you, but I started working and ended up working straight through the night to finish up.

"Amanda, I can't tell you how nervous I was. I really missed having you here. Your mom was real sweet and insisted on praying with me before I went in to work, but all I kept thinking was how hard we've worked and what this could mean to us."

Amanda was struck by the way Nick included her. She loved the way he talked about his own accomplishments as if they belonged to them both.

"At first I didn't think he liked them," Nick continued, talking with the animation of a boy describing his first home run. "He spread them out on that big desk of his and just looked and looked. Then after what seemed like an eternity of silence he finally said, 'Excellent. Clean, functional, and well thought out'—you know, in that clipped British accent of his. I swear, Amanda, it took every ounce of self-control in me to keep from hugging the man!"

The mental image of her wild Irishman throwing his arms around Mortimer Shea's stiffly rotund figure sent Amanda into peals of laughter. "Oh, Nick, I think you should have. I'm sure no one's had their arms around Mortimer for years!"

Nick laughed with her, then went on. "He also said that looking at my work reminded him of some of his own early work 'when I was still willing to take some chances.' Those were his exact words, and I could tell he was excited. He said he wants to talk to me about a couple other projects we have coming up! Honey, I think it's all going to happen . . . everything we've dreamed of and planned for."

"Oh, Nick, I'm so proud of you! I wish I were there to celebrate."

"We'll celebrate as soon as you get home on Sunday. Laura told me you have to stay the extra day to finish up. I was hoping I'd see you tomorrow, and so were the girls. They miss you."

"And I miss them! How's everything going?"

The two talked a few minutes about the girls and then got ready to say good-bye.

"Oh, by the way," Nick threw in at the last second. "I read your old friend is having a big concert in New York. You seen anything about it?"

"Yeah, as a matter of fact . . ." Amanda started, realizing that she had totally forgotten about Chris in the excitement of Nick's good news.

"Whoa, hold it, sweetie. Grace is signaling that Shea is holding on the line for me. I'd better go."

"But, Nick, I need to tell you—"

"Tell me all about it when you get home. I've really got to go. This is important! See you on Sunday."

"But Nick—!" Amanda found herself listening to a dial tone. "This is important, too," she finished in a small, defeated voice.

The joy she had felt a few moments before at Nick's good news dimmed as she battled feelings of resentment and hurt. Amanda knew in her heart that Nick hadn't meant to hurt her. He was excited and didn't realize how insensitive he had just been, cutting her off like that. Still, Amanda couldn't help comparing his thoughtlessness to the way Chris had treated her.

She looked over at Laura and shrugged. "Well, I guess it will keep."

"You should have told him," Laura said, shaking her head in disapproval.

"I tried! You heard me. He had to hang up." Amanda couldn't keep the anger out of her voice.

"So call him back."

"Look, you're making too much out of this," she said, taking a reasonable tone. "Chris and I are just two old friends reminiscing about the past and doing exactly what you and your little co-conspirator thought we should do—healing old wounds and putting the past to rest. I thought that's what you wanted!"

"It was . . . it *is*," Laura said, struggling to put her feelings into words. "It's just that I got so caught up in the romance and mystery of it all, I didn't stop to think how Nick might feel about the two of you seeing each other again. When he called today, I felt so guilty I lied about where you were!"

"Yes, I was surprised by that. But it was probably better that you did," Amanda said thoughtfully. "I mean, this way I can sit down with Nick and explain it all from the beginning. Once he knows the whole story, I know he'll understand why I had to see Chris."

"Speaking of which," Laura said, suddenly reminded, "you promised to explain it all to me when you got back! If I were a cat, I'd be dead by now!"

"Okay, but we'll have to talk while we get ready," Amanda instructed, shaking off the troubled feelings of the past few minutes.

"Chris is sending the limo for us at seven-thirty, and I don't even know what I'm going to wear!"

"The limo, huh?" Laura's eyebrows nearly disappeared into her hairline.

"He just wants to make sure we get there," Amanda laughed. She went on to give Laura an abbreviated version of the story she had shared with Chris. Then Laura demanded to hear every detail of their morning and afternoon together. By the time Amanda finished, Laura was once again completely caught up in the story.

"It sounds just like *Romeo and Juliet*—only nobody died," she said, actually wiping tears from her eyes.

🐦 🐦 🐦 🐦

Ruby escorted Amanda and Laura to the door of the concert hall, making sure that they were safely in and being seated before reluctantly releasing his charge. He may have had some of the wealthiest and most famous people in New York in his limousine, but Mr. Chris had told him that this lady was special and to take real good care of her. Ruby would have fought off an army to protect her after that, and Amanda was touched once again with the gentle way the big man treated her.

Amanda and Laura were shown to a box about midway on the right-hand side. Two other couples were already seated, one couple middle-aged, the other in their twenties. One look told Amanda they were related. The older of the men was the first to acknowledge them, giving Amanda a warm smile and introducing himself.

"You must be Mrs. Kelly. I'm Walter Pembrook, Chris's agent. I was so glad to hear you were in town and would be joining us," the tall, silver-haired gentleman graciously welcomed them, indicating that they should sit in the first two seats. "This is my wife, Lillith, and my daughter, Jamie, and her husband, Bill. This is Chris's cousin and her friend, Mrs. Stanley," he explained to his wife, who was looking Amanda over with undisguised interest. Obviously she would be giving her friends a full report about the mysterious young woman that Christopher Davies had insisted sit with them at the last minute. "From Bakersfield, I believe?" he added, giving Amanda a slight wink that told her he knew the whole story but thought it best if his wife didn't.

"Actually, just *outside* Bakersfield," she replied, sitting quickly to hide her smile.

From their front-row seats in the small box, Amanda and Laura could people watch to their hearts' content. Never before had they seen so many diamonds, furs, and egos concentrated in one place. This was one of the major events of the year, and it was evident that people had come as much to be seen as to see. As the saying goes, everyone who was anyone was there . . . and then some.

When the lights flickered for everyone to take their seats, Amanda felt her stomach suddenly do a back flip.

"I can't believe how nervous I am for him," she whispered in Laura's ear. "You'd think I was going to have to sing!"

"Perish the thought," Laura deadpanned dryly.

Amanda gave her a quick little jab, then grabbed her hand as the lights went down. She closed her eyes and imagined herself on the darkened stage, listening to the crowd quiet, waiting for the blast of light just as Chris had described. She felt her pulse quicken and this core of energy begin to build in her innermost being. It was as if they were connected, as though she was feeling it with him . . . building . . . building . . . until the stage burst into light and the room exploded into music.

To say the evening was "a triumph," "a revelation," "a musical apocalypse," as the critics would proclaim the next day, would be putting it mildly in Amanda's opinion, because for her it was much more. Sitting in that darkened theater watching Chris and the others take the simple process of making music and turn it into an emotional and spiritual experience was almost more than she could bear. Hearing his voice on the radio or watching him on Johnny Carson had not prepared her for the force of his presence on stage, the perfect harmony of voice, image, and personality that took a sound and created a whole world.

In the first half of the evening, Out Cry! proved that they had remained at the top not because of cheap gimmicks or clever marketing but because of the power of their raw talent and showmanship. Stripped of the usual light show and stage theatrics, they presented their music like a fine wine grown richer and fuller with the passage of time, revealing layers and subtleties that had been missed in the popularized renditions.

At intermission Amanda didn't have the strength to rise up out of her chair, even though a trip to the ladies' room would have been greatly appreciated. She was too exhausted from the emotional marathon she had just run, and the race was only half over. The hardest part was still to come.

The second half of the evening began with the symphony playing an artfully arranged medley of Christopher Davies' songs. Amanda was immediately impressed by how complex and classical in nature many of the melodies were.

When Chris walked out on the stage at the end of the symphony's tribute, the audience rose to its feet, paying their own tribute to the man's accomplishments before he played a note. If he went home now, he would be an unqualified winner. He had nothing to prove, no enemies to conquer or mountains to climb. But Amanda saw the fear in the set of his jaw and the rigidness of his body.

"They like my music," he had said to her that day on the beach, as though he couldn't believe it.

"Of course they do," she had answered. "Did you really think they wouldn't?"

"I didn't know. I wasn't sure."

His voice traveled back through time to her, and she knew instinctively how his heart was pounding and his palms were sweating. This was what it was all about for him, pressing that envelope . . . putting himself out there. Seeing just how far he could go before the inevitable rejection.

Oh please, God. Be in his music. It was an odd prayer, but Amanda didn't know what else to ask.

They labeled it a "rock concerto," an innovative coupling of the youth and energy of rock 'n' roll with the agelessness and texture of Beethoven and Bach. Many instruments were used as never before as Chris explored uncharted territories of sound and rhythm. Most of the time he sat at the grand piano they had rolled center stage at intermission, his eyes closed, his hands flying across the keys in a dance of their own. But a couple of times he moved to a stool, picking up his guitar and adding words to flesh out the images the music had already created.

The concerto was simply called "Journey," and Amanda immediately recognized Chris's life. It began with the joy and safety of his childhood and traveled through the wrenching pain of losing his mother. She heard baseball and Lucy B's and their whole summer at

Walker's Point. And she heard his anguish at losing her and the struggle and solace he found in his music. Amanda wondered if he would add to it, now that they had met again. The other band members joined Chris on stage for the final few numbers, creating a finale that brought the audience to its feet long before the program was over. No one could stay seated. The music had grabbed them at such a basic emotional level that they all were caught up in its magical flight.

When it was over the applause was deafening, swelling back up every time it began to die with a demand for more. Of course, the band expected to come back out for an encore, but they made the audience pay for it first, with stinging hands and hoarse cries of "Bravo!" and "More!" When they finally returned to take the stage they were like conquering heroes, presenting themselves to receive the adoration and even worship of the crowd. Even as she joined in, Amanda couldn't help thinking that applause like this must be a heady drug, easy to become addicted to.

The band eventually delivered three encores, and by the time they were finished everyone in the place was thoroughly wrung out. Amanda didn't think she could raise her hands, which had lost any sense of feeling long ago, to clap one more time. Still no one moved to leave, and as if by some unspoken order the crowd grew quiet, waiting.

The stage was nearly dark when a lone figure walked out and sat on a stool in the center of the empty stage. A single spotlight cast a soft, rosy glow around him, creating an illusion of intimacy.

"I hadn't planned on playing this for you this evening, but that's why you come to live concerts, to experience the unexpected."

As if to verify his words, a technician came rushing out of the wings to adjust Chris's mike and add another one to pick up his acoustical guitar. "I want to end the evening with the song that marked the beginning for me. This is for you, Amanda. . . ."

Amanda gasped softly, unable to believe he would single her out in this way.

"For all the Amandas of our lives who give us hope and teach us what love is all about," he added smoothly.

"Nice save," Laura mumbled in Amanda's direction.

Of course she knew what was coming. She steeled herself against the emotional impact, literally locking her knees and clenching her jaw. But at the sound of the first melancholy chords, the floodgates opened and tears streamed down her cheeks, dripping off her chin and creating a pattern of small, dark stains on her blue satin skirt.

The music took her back twelve years to the first time she heard it, and she felt all the wonder of that first revelation of love. She also remembered the first time she had heard it on the radio. Then she had felt robbed and exposed, as if Chris had blown up a picture of her naked and transmitted it to the whole world. Now she knew he was giving it back to her in a spirit of sweet regret and forgiveness. It was a gift of healing meant to restore the beauty of the past—not an invitation for the future—and she received it, embracing the old memories with joy once again. When the song was over Chris lifted his hand, reaching out in a gesture that filled her with an old, sweet longing. Then he simply said, "Good night" and left the stage.

He had been gone several seconds before the audience awakened from the spell the song had cast and started to applaud. But the applause was dazed and almost hesitant. The song had been a benediction to an evening that had touched them all and most filed out in awed silence.

Twenty-two

$\mathcal{A}$manda and Laura sat in the back of the limousine as it wove its way through the streets of the city, content not to speak. The ride gave them both time to meditate on what they had just experienced. Even at nearly midnight the midtown traffic was heavy, thinning as they took a shortcut through Central Park and finally found themselves on West Sixty-seventh Street headed toward Rosselli's. Chris and Bayley would join them there for a late-night supper as soon as they had changed.

Rosselli's was one of hundreds of nondescript little restaurants nestled in the basements of the brownstones that lined the streets of Manhattan's West Side. Amanda and Laura had walked by dozens of them during the past few days, their attention drawn by the blue or green or red awning that usually marked the entrance and the exotic smells wafting up through the vents in the sidewalk. Often they had stopped to peek in and read the menu posted in the window. Most of the places were small, boasting no more than a dozen tables often set with white tablecloths, fresh flowers, and fine china. All looked inviting and cozy and expensive. And most were closed and locked up by midnight on a Friday night, having seen their last customers out an hour earlier.

This was where Rosselli's was different. As Ruby deftly maneuvered the black limousine to the curbside and hurried to open the door for Amanda and Laura, the women were greeted by the sound of music and laughter. Light spilled out across the sidewalk as a great bear of a man rushed up the front steps to greet them.

"Welcome! Welcome to Rosselli's! I am Carlo Rosselli, owner of the best'a Italian restaurant in all of New York!" he announced proudly in a thick Italian accent, patting his enormous girth as if to prove the point. "And you must be Signore Chris's friends, Mrs. Kelly and Mrs. Stanley, sì?" Mr. Rosselli's face broke into a hundred merry wrinkles as he buried Amanda's hand in an effusive handshake, and she couldn't help laughing as she nodded yes.

"It's'a all right, Ruby," he said, giving the driver a friendly but dismissive wave. "I have them now. You don't'a need to worry. I'll take'a good care of them until Signore Chris gets here . . . such'a beautiful ladies. Bèlla, bèlla!" he said, turning to give Laura a look that told her he knew how to appreciate the beauty of a mature woman. Then he motioned with a grand flourish for the two women to proceed with him down the stairs into the warmth of the restaurant.

Mr. Rosselli led his charges through the small but crowded dining room, stopping briefly to greet customers who called him by name and were obviously regulars. Laura and Amanda exchanged smiles, immediately appreciating the old-world charm of their surroundings. About twenty tables had been squeezed into the basement storefront. The walls were the original red brick and were nearly wallpapered with Italian travel posters. The lively sound of concertina music provided appropriate background music, and red-checked tablecloths and Chianti bottles with candles topped the tables, adding to the Italian theme.

The waiters burst out of the swinging kitchen doors with huge trays of steaming pasta, antipasto, and garlic bread balanced high above their heads, maneuvering between the tables like circus performers, always on the verge of catastrophe but far too skilled to ever actually lose control.

Amanda recognized immediately that while a few of the late-night diners were well-dressed theatergoers, most of the young people relaxing with glasses of hardy red wine around the red-checked tables were actors, dancers, and chorus members unwinding after a show. The easy laughter and hum of conversation stopped briefly as heads turned to check out the newcomers but picked up again within seconds as it became clear that no one of importance had arrived.

Amanda scanned the room for an empty table that might give them some privacy, but except for a small table left forlornly alone in a corner bereft of its chairs, she could not figure out where their host meant to put them. Mr. Rosselli led them through a curtain, down a small hall past the rest rooms, to a door marked "Private" in what appeared to be the back wall. Knocking twice, he opened the door slowly.

"Don't want to take a waiter with a tray full of spaghetti by surprise," he explained with a wink. "We don't usually use this door."

The door opened into a dining room about half the size of the one they had just passed through. Here again the walls had been left unplastered, but this time the red brick served as a background for a number of beautifully framed oil paintings, some muted and impressionistic, others bright splashes of color and light. Several large booths upholstered in plush red leather lined the back of the room. Other tables lined the floor-to-ceiling windows that looked out on a private flagstone courtyard. Instead of red-checked tablecloths, these tables were covered with fine white linen, although red-checked napkins were cheerfully arranged like small crowns at each place, and a Chianti bottle layered with multicolored candle wax still provided each table with its candlelight centerpiece. The result was a delightful mix of elegance and Italian homespun.

Six of the ten tables were occupied. As Mr. Rosselli showed them to one of the booths, Amanda casually let her eyes sweep the room. An Academy Award-winning director and his actress wife sat at one of the window tables, holding hands and looking like newlyweds, which, in fact, they were. At another table for four, Amanda recognized an actor who was currently starring in one of the season's biggest Broadway hits. Amanda was sure that if she could go from table to table, she would find a show-business notable at every one. Obviously Carlo Rosselli had been smart enough to create a haven for the rich and famous, a place where they could let down their guard and enjoy a good meal without the prying eyes of their fans and the media.

"Did you see who's sitting over there?" Laura asked out of the side of her mouth, after she and Amanda had scooted into the booth and settled themselves to wait. "My mother would kill me if she knew I was in the same room with Tony Bennett and didn't get her an autograph!"

"She wouldn't get the chance. You'd already be dead. They shoot autograph seekers in places like this," Amanda whispered back, keeping a bright smile on her face. "You see that door over there? Two waiters would discreetly escort you through it out to a back alley, where a man named Lefty would be waiting to drive you on a one-way tour of the East River."

The words were barely out of her mouth when the door marked "Exit" opened and Chris and Bayley strode in. Obviously there was a side alley that allowed Rosselli's more famous patrons to enter without having to march through the main restaurant. Carlo Rosselli appeared out of nowhere to greet them and show them to their table. As they passed through the room there were a few handshakes and congratulatory nods, but the sudden appearance of the mega rock stars created only a minor ripple in this pond where everyone was a big fish.

Amanda felt her heart flutter as Chris approached the table, his eyes immediately locking in on her with undisguised delight. She had expected him to be exhausted after the extraordinary workout she had just witnessed, but both Chris and Bayley were bright-eyed and full of energy, still wired by the music and applause.

"I could eat a horse!" Chris announced, scooting into the booth beside Amanda and giving her a light kiss on the cheek before signaling to the watchful waiter for the menus. He then reached across Amanda to extend his hand to Laura. "It's nice to finally meet you, Mrs. Stanley. I understand that you are partially responsible for bringin' Amanda and me back together. You have my deepest thanks."

Chris smiled directly into Laura's eyes, giving her hand a warm squeeze, and she was embarrassed to feel herself blush like a young girl as she stammered, "Oh please, call me Laura." No wonder Amanda had never been able to forget this guy. From a distance as a performer he was mesmerizing, but up close he was devastating!

The four ordered quickly. As late as it was, Amanda and Laura stuck with spaghetti with marinara sauce and a small house salad. But Chris and Bayley went whole hog, ordering fried calamari, antipasto, the house lasagna, and extra cheese bread. A bottle of champagne was sent over to the table by a well-wisher, but while they popped the cork and toasted Out Cry!'s stunning performance, no one did much more than sip at the wine, not wanting to dull the natural high they all felt.

"Now, really, how was it?" Chris turned in the circular booth in Amanda and Laura's direction, which allowed him to casually rest his arm behind Amanda's shoulders. Amanda could feel the energy still radiating off his skin, and suddenly she was painfully aware of how close he was sitting. He looked down into her eyes and repeated the question. "Was it all right?"

"*More* than all right," Amanda answered, hoping he could read in her eyes all she couldn't say with her words. "It was wonderful. *You* were wonderful . . . and so were you, Bayley," she added, needing to end the moment before it got any more intense.

"Why, thank you, ma'am. I'm glad someone noticed!"

"And what about you, Laura? Did you enjoy the evening?" Chris reluctantly moved his gaze from Amanda to her friend.

At first Laura was rattled to once again be the center of Christopher Davies' attention. But he started asking her questions, probing gently and honestly for in-depth answers as though he sincerely cared what she thought. His relaxed manner put her at ease, and soon they were all talking and laughing like old friends.

"So, Bayley, tell us what Chris is *really* like to work with," Amanda said, sometime between the antipasto and the main course.

"Oh, he's just your typical, run-of-the-mill, ego-maniacal, semi-genius, workaholic superstar. Impossible one minute, even more difficult the next. . . . But we all love him and want to *be* him when we grow up!" Bayley gave Chris a wide grin, saluting him with his wine glass.

"Of course, I've known Chris almost as long as Amanda," he explained for Laura's benefit, "which means I knew him before he was *Christopher Davies*, capital *C*, capital *D*. Back then we were all just struggling to stay alive and play our music one more day before reality caught up with us and we all went home to become shoe salesmen!"

Chris had been listening to his friend's good-natured ribbing with amused tolerance, and now he laughed as the memories came back.

"Man, I'd forgotten about old Henry."

"Who's Henry?" Amanda asked, turning to Chris with a curious smile.

"Henry was this guy we met . . . where was it, Bay? In Tulsa?"

"Someplace like that," Bayley agreed. "He was a marimba player."

"A what?" both women asked in unison.

"A marimba player. You know, it looks like a xylophone, only bigger? Anyway, this guy was really good, and believe it or not he'd been making a living at it for at least twenty years. I mean, he could hold as many as six mallets, three in each hand, and play all kinds of mean jazz without missing a note. Only problem was . . .'' Bayley hesitated, trying to keep from bursting out laughing, "when he got excited and worked up, as he always did—I mean, you can imagine, those mallets pinging, his hands flying, his head bobbing, sweat flying every-where—his nose would run.''

"Pardon me?'' Amanda asked, not sure she had heard correctly.

By now both Bayley and Chris were howling.

"You see,'' Bayley said, taking several deep breaths to gain control, "in his later years he developed this sinus condition, and when he'd really get going, his nose would start running. Only I don't mean just a few drips. I mean a real gusher! Now, half the time old Henry didn't even know it was happening, he was so caught up in his music. And even when he did, he'd be holding these sticks in his hands and he couldn't do anything about it! Soon it would be running down his lip, and every time he'd turn his head, this snot would just fly every-where.''

"Now, we were playing in small clubs at this time in our illustrious career, and the audience was always right on top of us,'' Chris explained, picking up the story. "Every time we'd run into old Henry, the same thing would happen. People would really dig what he was doin' at first. I mean, the man could jam! But eventually some nice lady in the first row would get a good spray of snot across her dress or down her neck, and then someone else, and pretty soon the whole room would be diving for cover!''

"I can see where this might put a damper on the evening,'' Laura agreed with a shudder.

"Anyway, this one night old Henry had finally had enough,'' Bayley cut back in. "He felt his nose beginning to run and stopped dead in the middle of his song. He put down his mallets, dug in his pocket for a handkerchief, and blew his nose—a big honkin' blow, right there on stage. Then he put his handkerchief back in his pocket, turned, and walked off the stage, heading for the door. 'Henry,' I said, 'where are you going?'

" 'I'm goin' home to sell shoes in my daddy's shoe store,' he said. 'I guess I'm just not cut out for this business.' ''

"He just quit like that after twenty years?'' Amanda asked, not sure whether to believe this incredibly silly story.

"Guess we all have our limits, and old Henry'd reached his,'' Bayley said, still laughing. "Anyway, after that it sort of became a standing joke with the band. Whenever things got tough or someone got frustrated, we'd always tell them they could go home and sell shoes."

"Tell me more about those early years," Amanda encouraged. "I mean, it all seemed to happen so easily. One day I turned on the radio and there you were, and the next thing I knew, I couldn't turn around without hearing your music or seeing your picture or reading about you."

"Ah yes. The old 'overnight sensation' trick." Bayley chuckled and gave Chris a look that spoke eloquently of the hardships they had faced.

"Actually, it was a lot easier for me than the rest of the guys. I sort of jumped on just in time to enjoy all the goodies," Chris confessed. "As you know, Amanda, Eagle's Cry was movin' right along, and it was my good fortune to link up with them just before they really hit."

"How did you finally get together?" Amanda asked.

Chris went on to explain that after his father died he had gone back to the ranch. "I needed time to lick my wounds and go a little crazy, I guess."

Amanda knew he was referring to losing her, not his dad, and she felt her stomach clench.

"It was a dark time of the soul. Me and Jack Daniels got to be real good friends, and for a while I wasn't sure I was ever gonna see the light of day again. Then I got a phone call from this guy named Bayley. I remember I was so out of it, I thought he was referring to that Irish whiskey. But he finally managed to make me understand that he wanted to talk about making music."

"You must have been thrilled," Amanda commented.

"On the contrary. The fool hung up on me," Bayley replied. "Said he'd given it up. Planned to stay on his daddy's ranch and raise horseflies or something. Then he hung up on me."

"He's giving you the PG version," Chris interjected.

"Wise man," Amanda countered. "One disgusting story about snot at the dinner table was quite enough."

Bayley continued, giving the interrupters a warning look. "Anyway, I got on a plane and flew out there. I rented a car and drove out to the ranch, which is actually pretty impressive as ranches go."

"And did you find him swilling the hogs?" Laura asked, thoroughly enjoying the Noel Coward-esque dialogue.

"Swilling the hogs?" Chris repeated, arching an eyebrow in disdain.

"Actually, it was hard to tell who was swilling who," Bayley threw back neatly. "He hadn't had a bath in a week, and if I hadn't been so desperate, I probably would have taken one whiff and headed straight back to Los Angeles. But our lead singer had quit, with a little subtle encouragement from the rest of the band, and we were booked for a number of gigs that could actually start paying off for us. I had never forgotten hearing Chris sing up in Santa Barbara, and I knew we could really do something if we put the whole package together. Besides," he added, tongue-in-cheek, "my cousin Vinnie had turned us down, and I couldn't think of anyone else. So I cleaned him up, took him back with me on the plane, and the rest, as they say, is history."

"Sounds like Chris is lucky to have met you," Laura commented.

"Right," Chris snorted. "Tell them what you did to me in San Antonio, and what about the time I saved your bacon in Biloxi?"

This started a riotous retelling of one outrageous story after another, and by the time they were ready to leave both Amanda and Laura were weak from laughing. It was after two when the foursome finally walked out. As late as it was, Mr. Rosselli was there to bid them good night and issue a warm invitation for them to come back and see him anytime.

Ruby was waiting in the alley with the limousine, and the four climbed wearily into the back. Amanda could literally see Laura deflate as she settled into the seat next to her, leaning her head back and closing her eyes.

"Tired?" Amanda asked, gently patting her friend's hand.

"Just resting my eyes" was the sleepy reply. "By the way, Chris, Bayley," the weary voice droned on, "in case I forgot to say it properly, thank you. This entire evening has been remarkable. The concert, the dinner . . . I feel so privileged to have been included."

"The pleasure was all ours," Bayley's equally sleepy voice replied. "All ours . . ." He squirmed in the narrow jump-up seat, trying to get comfortable. Finally he leaned against the cushioned door panel and joined Laura in "resting his eyes."

Amanda smiled across at Chris sitting in the seat facing her. He smiled back. The car was dark and quiet, a safe cocoon traveling effortlessly through the night. They let their eyes rest on each other, barely able to see in the various shades of shadow that enveloped them. Occasionally a streetlamp or passing headlight would invade their space with jarring brightness, causing them to squint or turn away briefly. But they immediately came back, smiling at the fresh shock of recognition.

The limousine pulled to a stop in front of the hotel, and Ruby stepped smartly around to open the door. There were no reporters or fans to worry about at that time of night, and the four took their time leaving the warmth of the car to step out into the chilly night air.

"Thank you, Ruby," Amanda said, reaching out to shake the driver's hand. "You've treated us like royalty, and I'll never forget your kindness."

At first Ruby seemed embarrassed by the compliment. Most rich folks saw what he did as a simple service, bought and paid for, and few took the time to say more than a perfunctory "thank you." Of course, Mr. Chris had been an exception, asking him questions about himself and treating him like a person worth knowing the first time he ever rode in his backseat. After that, Chris always called him directly instead of going through the agency when he was going to be in town, saying he was much more comfortable riding around with a friend than some stranger.

Now Mr. Chris's lady was treating him with that same special respect, and the big man's face broke into a huge grin.

"Thank you, Miss Amanda. Next time you're in town, you just give old Ruby a call," he said, handing her a card with his home number. "If Mr. Chris's not here to take care of you, I will!"

Amanda smiled and took the card, thanking him.

"You be needin' me tomorrow, Mr. Chris?" Ruby asked.

"No thanks, Ruby. Tomorrow's strictly a subway day, but I would like you to plan on taking Mrs. Kelly and Mrs. Stanley to the airport on Sunday."

Amanda started to protest, but the two men overruled her, settling on a time before Ruby said his final good-night.

"That wasn't necessary," Amanda said as they turned to walk into the hotel. Bayley had escorted Laura in as soon as they arrived, and the two were alone for the first time that evening.

Chris stopped and looked down at her, her cheeks flushed from the stinging cold, her eyes still bright with the excitement of the night, despite the late hour, and a sudden melancholy washed over him.

"Please, Amanda, there's so little I can do for you. Let me do something to take care of you."

He reached out and gently brushed a stray strand of hair off her face. The gesture was so sweet and natural, Amanda felt her insides melt, setting off warning bells that had her literally shaking her head to silence them.

They hurried to the elevator, grateful that the lobby was deserted, and Chris pressed the button for Amanda's floor. They rode silently, acutely aware of each other's presence. Amanda stood erect in the center of the elevator, her eyes glued to the changing floor numbers as though fascinated by their progression.

Chris leaned against a side wall, his arms crossed, studying the way the short hair that curled around Amanda's ear had gotten caught in her earring. He wanted to reach out and untangle it. He wanted to run his fingers through the shiny brown silk of her hair and expose the soft white skin of her neck behind that ear. He wanted—

A bell dinged, making them both jump, and the elevator doors opened. Amanda stepped out quickly into the safety of the hall before turning to say good night.

"Well, I honestly don't know how to say thank you. As Laura said, tonight was remarkable. The whole day was remarkable. . . . Certainly an experience for a simple housewife from Sierra Madre." Amanda smiled, searching for the right words. "I'm glad we finally straightened things out."

"Me too." Chris smiled a crooked half smile before changing the subject. "So I'll see you in"—he glanced at his watch—"seven and a half hours. Sleep fast. I'll be at your door at ten sharp!"

Amanda looked hesitant. "Chris, are you sure this is a good idea? I mean, how are you going to go out into the city without being recognized and photographed everywhere you go?"

They both knew she was worried about more than Chris being recognized.

"Leave it to me. It will be fine, I promise." He released the door he'd been holding and pointed a finger. "Ten o'clock. Be ready!"

"*Still* giving orders!" Amanda laughed back as the doors closed.

Twenty-three

*A*manda was up and dressed well before ten. Amazingly she had slept several hours, her exhaustion finally winning over the agony of thoughts and worries that had assailed her the second she had let herself into the room the night before. Laura was already in bed, sleeping like a baby, and Amanda had looked at her with envy. For once her body wasn't going to shut down and let her escape into the sleep of the innocent.

The events of the day had kept replaying themselves. The emotional revelations of the morning, the afternoon at Carnegie Hall, the concert and dinner. What a difference twenty-four hours can make, she had thought as she started methodically cleansing her face.

She had rinsed the makeup away and patted her face dry. Then she had leaned close to the mirror, studying every small line and blemish. Her skin was still good, the pores tight, the texture smooth. But there were light tracings around the edges of her eyes, and the lines around her mouth were definitely deepening. And there was a crease beginning between her eyes from squinting in the sun without her sunglasses. She took mental note not to go outside anymore without them.

No, this was not the face of young Amanda Mitchell, she had sadly admitted to herself. This was the face of Amanda Kelly, a not-so-young matron with a husband and children, who had no business going out on the town with someone like Christopher Davies! She slapped the light switch off in the bathroom and began quietly pacing around the room, too wound up to get into bed.

What exactly was making her feel so guilty? she kept asking herself. She hadn't done anything wrong and she wasn't going to. She was a loving mother and a loyal and faithful wife who had never so much as looked at another man since the day she and Nick married. Yes, she and Nick were going through a hard time, and yes, it was probably not the best time for her to be reliving memories with her old boyfriend, who just happened to be an amazingly sexy rock star. But she wasn't looking for an affair. She loved her husband! And she knew that while he didn't always act like it, Nick loved her. All she wanted was a few hours together with someone who had once meant a great deal to her! That wasn't a crime, was it?

She had glanced over at Laura, worried her restless movements would disturb her, yet half wishing she would wake up. She needed to talk to someone, to have them tell her what to do.

She looked at the clock. It was only midnight at home. She could pick up the phone right now and call Nick. He was probably still up watching Johnny Carson. She could call him and tell him everything that had happened and casually mention that she and Chris were planning to spend a few hours together tomorrow.

She started to imagine the conversation . . . the sound of Nick's voice . . . the way it would turn from warm and loving to coolly questioning at the mention of Chris's name. He'd never understand what she was doing or why. He'd never loved anyone but her. He wouldn't understand her need to recapture what she had lost, if only for a moment, in order to finally let it go.

And she would let it go. Picturing Nick at home propped up in bed, his copper hair slightly mussed, his hand absently stroking the empty pillow where she should be beside him, she felt a sudden ache to be home. To be away and safe from all the disturbing feelings and memories the day had resurrected. Nick and the girls were everything to her. This was a fact, a reality in her life as necessary as eating and breathing.

But tonight she had barely thought of them. This was also a fact . . . one that deeply worried her. It was as if she were two people, the one who had loved Chris with an eagerness and passion that can only be felt by the very young, and the one who had slowly grown in love with a wonderful man, carefully building a life with him.

Her pacing got more frantic. She felt like a cartoon character with a little white-robed angel on one shoulder and a red devil on the other. Each was whispering advice in her ear, arguing for and against, their voices growing louder and more urgent until she had felt like screaming at them to shut up.

She walked over to the nightstand by her bed and absently picked up her Bible.

"In here you'll find all the answers to life's hardest questions," her grandfather had told her when he and Grams had given it to her on her twelfth birthday.

"You mean, God will tell me anything I want to know?" she had asked with wide-eyed wonder.

"Sure will, if you ask Him," he'd replied with certainty. Then he'd added, "Just be sure you really want to know the answer before you ask."

At twelve Amanda had thought that was a silly thing to say. Why would you ask a question if you didn't want to know the answer? Now as she remembered her grandfather's words, Amanda understood perfectly what he had been saying.

She laid the Bible reluctantly back on the nightstand and slipped into bed, resigning herself to another hour of tossing and turning before she finally fell into an exhausted sleep.

When she awoke the next morning the situation seemed far less dramatic. The feelings from the night before had shrunk to manageable proportions, and as Amanda stood in the shower, letting the hot water beat on her back and neck, she felt her anxiousness relax with her knotted muscles.

This was silly. She knew who she was and what she wanted. Spending the day with Chris was just a pleasant detour, an unexpected chance to revisit a time in her life that had been incredibly happy and carefree. She had come to New York to rediscover herself, and in some ways she felt more like herself when she was with Chris than she had in years. This was probably because he represented her youth, with all its hopes and dreams, unencumbered by the harsher realities that came later in life. With Chris she could just be Amanda, free from any demands or expectations. They'd talk and laugh and create a happy ending for what had once been a painful past. Then they'd say goodbye and she would go home. No one would be hurt; nothing would change. And when she explained it all to Nick, he would understand.

At least that's what she told herself.

Amanda was just finishing her makeup when the phone rang. It was Chris, checking to be sure she was up. Amanda knew it was his way of making sure she hadn't changed her mind.

"Up. Showered. Powdered. And if I could decide what to wear, I'd be ready to go," Amanda answered cheerily. She could feel her excitement building at the sound of his voice, and she glanced over at Laura, who was watching her out of one groggy eye, hoping she didn't look as flustered as she felt.

"Well, it looks like we're goin' to have a beautiful day," he informed her enthusiastically, "so jeans and a light sweater should do it. Keep it real simple and don't worry about a coat. I'll bring you a jacket."

Amanda hung up wondering why Chris would bring her a jacket. What was wrong with her own coat?

She heard Laura stretch and groan as she pulled out the jeans buried at the bottom of her drawer. She had thrown them in at the last minute, and now she was glad she had. She pulled on a rust-colored ribbed turtleneck and slipped on her most comfortable walking shoes. She tied a gold, green, and rust scarf around her neck, noting with satisfaction how it brought out all the colors in her eyes, and started to put on her gold hoops. But earrings seemed too fussy and she put them away. She stood back to take a final look in the mirror.

"You look eighteen," Laura commented, giving Amanda a start. She had been so quiet, Amanda thought she had gone back to sleep. Amanda smiled self-consciously, not certain if it was a compliment or a warning.

"Oh! My head!" Laura moaned, struggling to sit up. "I am definitely too old for all this late-night gallivanting around! I don't suppose you called for coffee."

"Actually, I did," Amanda replied, giving her friend a sympathetic look.

"Good. Just pour it straight from the pot down my throat when it gets here. Then maybe I'll be able to get out of this bed in time to make my one o'clock appointment!" Laura gave up the fight and rolled over, snuggling back down.

When the knock came a few minutes later, Amanda fully expected to find the bellboy at the door with coffee. Instead she found a vision from the past. Dressed in baggy jeans, a black T-shirt, tennis shoes, and an old army jacket that she remembered had belonged to his father, Chris stood grinning at her, no longer the image of the mega rock star but the Chris she remembered . . . simple, comfortable, and unpretentious.

Chris knew exactly what she was feeling because he was struggling with the same sense of déjà vu. The slender, jean-clad figure who opened the door was *his* Amanda, yet he had to remind himself that he had no right to take her in his arms and give her a good-morning kiss.

"Good morning, Mrs. Kelly." The use of her married name was not lost on Amanda, and she was grateful that he had remembered the rules and was going to play by them.

"Good morning, Mr. Davies. You're early. I didn't expect you till ten."

"I know, but you said you were nearly ready, and since we only have one day, I wanted to make the most of it." He glanced around her into the still-darkened room. "Laura still recovering?" he asked.

"Laura will be recovering for a week!" Amanda laughed. "I called for coffee to get her jump started, but it's not here yet. We'd better get out of here before the bellboy comes and recognizes you."

"Not much chance of that once I complete my disguise."

Chris proceeded to tuck his signature hair under a baseball cap— Dodgers, of course—and put on a pair of tinted wire-rimmed glasses that made his distinctive baby blues look green. He zipped up his jacket and slightly hunched his shoulders, and suddenly he was Mr. Nobody. Amanda looked at him and wasn't sure *she* would recognize him if she passed him on the street.

As if to prove the point, the bellboy chose that moment to appear, handing Amanda the tray of coffee without giving Chris a second glance. Even when Chris tipped him, the young man barely grunted, eager to move on with the next breakfast tray that promised a bigger tip.

"Here, I brought this for you," Chris said, handing Amanda a well-worn oversized jacket much like his own. "Can't have you blowing my cover by walking around looking like some kind of high-fashion model and drawing everyone's attention. This way we'll blend in with the crowds."

Amanda took the coffee in to Laura and grabbed her purse.

"Have a good time," a muffled voice called after her, "but not *too* good," Laura added into her pillow. Then she remembered to warn, "And don't stay out late! We have to leave for the airport by ten!"

Amanda and Chris walked out of the hotel into a picture-perfect day. It was as though the city knew this was a special day and was showing off for them. The air was still crisp and winter clear, but a bright sun was rapidly taking the bite out of it. By noon they'd have to unzip their coats.

They took off down the street like kids just let out of school for an unexpected holiday. At first Amanda kept looking around nervously, expecting any minute that someone would recognize Chris. But the busy New Yorkers simply brushed past them, taking no notice. Chris was right. They blended in. By the time they'd walked several blocks, she had relaxed.

"Hungry?" he asked.

"Starved!" was her honest reply.

"Good! We just happen to be a block away from bagel heaven. Turn right at the next street."

Amanda could smell the enticing aroma of fresh-baked bread and smoked salmon as they approached the entry to Sol's deli. This was New York at its purest. Noisy, crowded, filled with the clatter of dishes and sharp voices. People pushed their way in and out, grabbing what they needed without apology in a way that would have been considered rude anywhere else but here was proper etiquette.

Chris pushed through the melee, pulling Amanda right behind him. With practiced ease he elbowed his way through, seemingly oblivious to the angry looks and comments being thrown their way. Amanda started to apologize, then gave up, locking her eyes on Chris's back and praying that they would reach safety before the mob turned on them.

Miraculously, there was an open table in the very back. Or maybe it wasn't such a miracle, Amanda amended when a large tray of assorted bagels and cream cheeses suddenly appeared at the table.

"Hey, Sol. Meet my friend, Amanda," Chris said, shaking hands with the deli's owner.

"Nice ta meetcha," the man replied in a gruff voice straight out of the Bronx. "Read about last night in the paper this morning," Sol continued, being deliberately vague in case he was overheard.

"Sounds like you done good, kid."

Amanda heard the pride in Sol's voice and saw the easy familiarity between the two men as they talked. She figured Chris must come here often when he was in town, always in disguise and safely anonymous, known only by the small staff and accepted for himself, not his celebrity.

"I'll bring you some coffee. You want the house blend? Or we got some of that new hazelnut stuff. Mable made me get it," Sol explained with a disgusted shrug. "Said it's the wave of the future . . . all this flavored coffee. Personally, I think she's crazy! I tell her, real coffee drinkers don't want nothing but coffee in their coffee. A little cream, maybe . . . a little sugar. But nobody's gonna go for all this fancy-schmancy stuff! But you know Mable!" He shook his head, looking at Chris as if he'd understand.

"House blend," Chris ordered decisively, taking Sol's side.

"I'll try the hazelnut," Amanda smiled sweetly in defense of poor Mable.

Chris gave her a look across the table as Sol walked away, and the two burst into laughter.

"Yum. These look good," Amanda said, choosing a sesame bagel and spreading on it a thick layer of herbed cream cheese.

Chris watched her take a big bite and laughed. "You're the only woman I know who wouldn't be moaning about all the calories she was eating." He reached over and wiped a glob of cream cheese from her chin, then began devouring an onion bagel with equal gusto.

Amanda looked across the table at him. "I still can't believe I'm here with you! This whole thing is so amazing."

"You can say that again. It's almost enough to make me believe in that divine plan you were always talkin' about."

That was the second time he'd brought God into the conversation. Yesterday he'd said this time was like a gift from God, a comma between the past and the future. Now he was talking about a divine plan. Amanda couldn't help wondering just where Chris stood with God these days. She hadn't thought of it before, but maybe God had some deeper purpose for their "accidental" meeting than even she had realized.

Sol brought the coffee, and as she took a sip, old memories came flooding back. "This reminds me of the first day we met at May's.

Remember? I was so scared and nervous. I didn't have the faintest idea what you were going to say."

He looked back over his cup at her, his blue eyes sparking at the memory and igniting an old fire in the pit of Amanda's stomach. "Oh yeah, I remember."

For the next hour they reminisced, thinking of people they hadn't thought of for years and laughing at memories they had both buried in self-defense long ago, but which they could now safely take out and enjoy in the light of their new understanding.

"Have you ever gone back?" Amanda asked.

"Once . . . about eight years ago," he answered. "It was just after our first record was released. We were up in San Francisco playing a gig and then we were scheduled to play in Santa Barbara."

"Not at the Seventh Wave!" Amanda squealed.

"Yup. Actually got paid and everything," he smiled back. "Anyway, Sam and I were driving down, and since I was sort of on a sentimental journey anyway, I had him pull off at Walker's Point. It was winter and the place was practically deserted. But it was a pretty day and we walked on the beach a bit."

Wondering if he'd gone to "their" beach, Amanda started to ask, "Did you go—?"

"No," he cut her off. "I couldn't bring myself to do that, but we did climb on the rocks. Tried to see that blowhole you'd told me about."

"That only happens during a big winter storm," Amanda explained.

Chris nodded and continued. "We went by the theater and it was closed, of course, but May's was open. In fact, your friend was there. You know, the daughter."

"Nancy?" Amanda said, truly surprised. "But I thought she was in school . . . going to be a doctor or something."

"Well, it seems she had to put that on hold. Her mother got sick and she had to come help out. Anyway, it all looked the same." He took a deep breath, remembering the pain he had felt sitting there and seeing Sam across the table instead of Amanda. Then he added, "I went by your grandparents' place, too."

"Really? They didn't tell me."

"I just walked by. I didn't go to the door or anything. Thought about it. I would have liked to have seen your grandfather. He was a great old guy. I always enjoyed talkin' to him. We had some interesting discussions when I'd come help him in his shop."

"You did, did you? And just what did you two talk about? Not me, I hope," Amanda teased flirtatiously.

"Believe it or not, Amanda Rose, I did occasionally have other things on my mind besides you."

Amanda grimaced at him and he grimaced back. Then he took a big gulp of coffee, nearly spitting it out. "Cold." He put the cup down and signaled the waiter for a fresh cup. He fell silent as the coffee was poured, and Amanda figured he'd decided not to say any more. So she was surprised when he continued.

"Actually, we talked a lot about God. Your granddaddy had a way of talkin' about things that kept it simple and down-to-earth. I never felt he was preachin' or talkin' down to me. He was like you, talkin' about Jesus like a personal friend and makin' Him sound like someone I might like to know. Not all religious and stuff, but real. It got so I felt easy asking him questions, and the answers he gave seemed to make sense. Toward the end of the summer, I was thinkin' real hard about things . . . things I hadn't thought of since I was a little boy. I guess that's what made me start thinkin' that you and I might have a chance. . . ."

His voice trailed off, and Amanda realized there were tears in her eyes. "You never told me that. I wish you'd told me."

"If wishes were ponies," he answered with a sad shrug. "Anyway, things are what they are. And the only thing I'm certain of is that we have a whole day to be together, and I don't want to waste another minute of it lookin' back and feelin' sad!" Chris slapped the table and gave her a brilliant smile.

"Sounds good to me," Amanda readily agreed. "So what's the plan?"

"This is it. You and me together, doin' whatever we feel like. So . . . what do you feel like?"

Amanda thought some and then gave Chris a triumphant smile. "I know exactly what I'd like to do."

Forty-five minutes later they were standing at the railing of a ferry traversing the sparkling waters of the Hudson. The skyline of New York stood brilliantly outlined against the winter blue sky, and white clouds were reflected across the shiny surfaces of the glass skyscrapers. The wind was bracing but manageable as the two breathed in the fresh air and let the sun warm their faces.

"I've always dreamed of doing this," Amanda confided. "It's just like in the movies."

Chris watched her out of the corner of his eye. Her expression was completely guileless, her mouth curved in a small smile of contentment. She looked young and innocent and very beautiful, and he remembered the way he'd felt the first day he saw her. The irresistible attraction and hunger—and the undeniable danger. He'd known right away she'd have the power to destroy him. He'd seen it clear as day, and he'd had the good sense to walk away. The problem was, he hadn't been able to keep himself from looking back. And he'd been looking back ever since.

Amanda tried not to think about the way he was looking at her, concentrating instead on the magnificent view before her. How often they had played this game in the past . . . him watching her, his smoldering look daring her to meet his gaze; her primly acting unaware, as though her own heart wasn't pounding with the same need. It was a game he'd always won and she had been happy to lose, as his arms would come around her to claim his prize.

But things had been different then. They'd both been young and free to explore wherever those feelings might take them. Now Amanda's life was set on a different course, a course that demanded that she keep her eyes glued to the Manhattan skyline. She took a deep, calming breath and brought up the one subject certain to keep things in perspective.

"I'm sorry my girls aren't here to see this. But then, they're so young, they probably wouldn't appreciate it. I remember my folks took Lindsey and me to see the Grand Canyon when I was about Casey's age. It was supposed to be this wonderful educational experience, but when we finally got there, all we wanted to do was run around and climb the rocks. Finally they made us stop running and really look at the magnificence of God's creation. But looking down over the edge after all that running made me feel dizzy, and the next thing I knew I was throwing up all over my new white Keds! For years that's all I ever remembered about the Grand Canyon, that it made me throw up on my new shoes!"

Amanda looked at Chris, expecting some kind of wise-cracking response. But she found he had joined her in her study of the approaching skyline. His expression was distant and dreamy, and she instinctively knew that he was imagining what their children might have been like. She determined not to bring up her family again.

"Laura would have loved this," she offered brightly, once again trying to divert his train of thought into neutral channels. "We talked about riding out to the Statue of Liberty, but the weather wasn't nice enough. Today couldn't be more beautiful."

As if to prove her wrong, a gust of cold wind suddenly hit them, knocking Chris's hat off and sending them scurrying in a panic to retrieve it. It landed at the feet of an overweight woman sitting on one of the benches behind them. The woman was bundled up in a heavy coat and a thick knit scarf. Bending to pick up the hat was no little chore and she grunted and groaned, nearly unable to reach it. Amanda and Chris reached her just as she triumphantly sat back up, hat in hand.

"Thank you, ma'am. Appreciate it," Chris said, reaching greedily for his hat.

His long dark hair was whipping around his collar, and Amanda glanced nervously at the half dozen other brave souls who had traded the warmth of inside for the pleasure of being out in the fresh air. Her heart was pounding, fearing that at any second he'd be recognized.

The woman started to hand it back and then stopped, giving Chris a long, hard look. Her eyes narrowed, as if she was trying to decide if she was seeing what she thought she was seeing.

Chris smiled his most ingratiating smile and reached out farther. "Ma'am? My hat?"

The woman kept staring, still holding tight to the hat.

Amanda's palms started to sweat. If Chris were recognized and word got out, they would be trapped on the boat with no way off. Pictures would be taken and people would want to know who the woman was with him. Her whole life flashed before her eyes as she envisioned the newspaper headlines. "Christopher Davies Caught in Shipboard Romance With Married Mother of Two!" She closed her eyes and started praying.

Finally she heard Chris say "Thank you." She opened her eyes to see the woman give Chris a nod as he hastily slipped his hat back on. Her expression never changed, but as they turned away Amanda could have sworn the woman winked. She didn't turn fast enough to see if Chris winked back.

Twenty-four

W hatever gave you the crazy idea that you could go out in public and not be recognized? I mean, you're practically a national treasure!''

Chris and Amanda were sitting on an isolated bench in Central
Park, and Amanda was still fighting to regain her composure. After
the hat incident, she was sure she saw several people giving them second looks, and they had hurried off the boat and jumped into a cab
the minute the ferry docked.

Chris had brought her to his favorite spot in the park. In the summer the isolated little knoll was nearly hidden by the trees, but today
the bare branches gave them a spectacular view of the park and the
ice rink beyond. The sunny day had brought out the joggers and
strollers, and nearly every open area was filled with groups of people
playing frisbee or tag football.

"Marilyn Monroe."

"What?" Amanda asked.

"You asked me what gave me the idea. I got it from a story I once
read about Marilyn Monroe. See, she came to New York to study with
Lee Strasburg. She was already a big star, but I guess she didn't feel
like much of an actress. While she was here, a friend came to visit. He
was the one who wrote the story."

Amanda turned to look at Chris, her nervousness lost in her sudden interest.

"She suggested they do some sight-seeing. He couldn't figure out
how she could go out without being mobbed. But when he picked
her up, he understood. She was wearing an old baggy coat and had a
scarf on her head. She wore no makeup, and in her dark glasses she

was unrecognizable. See, Marilyn Monroe was an image more than a person, and people see what they expect to see.

"The same is true of Christopher Davies," he went on. "If you think about it, you never see him in public wearing anything other than tight jeans, an open-collar shirt, cowboy boots, and a black jacket. I do that on purpose. Anytime I don't want him with me, I just take off the image and put on my old clothes. If I couldn't do that, I'd go crazy."

Chris smiled at her, and Amanda understood for the first time why he referred to himself so often in the third person. It wasn't an affectation. It was a wonderfully healthy way of reminding himself that he wasn't the image.

"Is this your way of saying that I'm not really out with 'Christopher Davies, Superstar'?" Amanda pouted, feigning disappointment.

Chris laughed. "Yup. You're just goin' to have to settle for me . . . plain and simple. Actually," he added, "Marilyn's friend felt disappointed, too. He'd sort of looked forward to being able to show off a little with a famous movie star and I guess she knew it, 'cause he wrote that halfway through the day she turned to him and said, 'Would you like to see Marilyn?' She turned her back, whipped off her scarf and glasses, put on some lipstick, and took off her coat. When she turned around, she was 'Marilyn Monroe.' They were surrounded within minutes!"

"Well, you can just leave the glasses on, thank you. And the hat!" Amanda gave the visor of his cap a playful tug. "I don't want any curious mob of onlookers spoiling this day. I'm having too much fun!" She put her elbow on her knee and rested her chin in her hand, her head turned to study him. "I used to accuse Stacy of being a split personality, but I've never known anyone who actually had two separate identities. Who do you like being most? Chris or Christopher?"

"Hmm. Hard question. Of course, life is more relaxing and a lot less complicated like this. I need to be treated like a regular guy every once in a while. Go in a bar, kick back a few . . ."

"I think I've heard this speech before," Amanda commented, remembering the speech he'd given her at the bar in Walker's Point.

"Right. Well, we'll move on, then," Chris said, clearing his throat self-consciously and giving her a sheepish grin before continuing.

"I've worked long and hard to make 'Christopher' who he is today," he said thoughtfully, "and there's a lot of things I admire about him. He works hard and never takes his success for granted. He's got a lot of confidence, but I think he has a realistic grip on his failings and limitations. He treats people fairly and doesn't take advantage . . . well, no more than one might expect," he amended, trying to be totally honest. "And he gets to do what he loves best, which is something few people can say."

Chris stopped to gather his thoughts.

"But I have to say that he's gotten to be a bit of a strain lately," he finally continued, letting out a deep sigh. "For all the perks, life on the road is hard. Movin' all the time—settin' up, tearin' down. Goin' out on that stage and giving one hundred and ten percent night after night. Knowin' you've got to do more than just go through the motions, because if you ever start doin' that, someone else will come along with *real* heart and *real* soul and push you right off!"

Amanda listened, fascinated. This was a side to Chris that she had never seen . . . probably because she'd known him before all the fame and success, when it had all been nothing more than a dream. She put her hand on his arm and he covered it with his own, unconsciously stroking her fingers the way he used to.

"There are times when I think it's not worth it. I mean, it's getting harder and harder to keep the priorities straight. It's like we forget that the music is what it's all about because so many other things crowd in. Sometimes the schedule gets so hectic, I wake up in the morning and don't even know where I am. And the people all start lookin' alike. I stand up there on that stage and open my mouth and I don't even recognize what's comin' out. I look around and there's nothing there. It just doesn't mean anything, you know?"

He took another deep breath, and his eyes seemed to search the park looking for an answer . . . an answer Amanda knew he wouldn't find until he started looking up.

"And I feel like I want to run away, to just be still and quiet and . . ."

"Listen?" she finished for him.

She felt his hand tighten around hers as they exchanged a smile of understanding. She picked up his hand and pulled his arm around her shoulders, needing to be close to him . . . needing to comfort and encourage. How was it possible? How could they understand each other so well after all these years?

They sat for a long time, watching the shadows grow, sharing the silence.

"Why didn't you ever get married?" It had taken her until nearly five o'clock, but Amanda had finally found the courage to ask him the question.

They had walked down to the skating rink and were watching the few late-afternoon diehards. Earlier in the day the ice had been covered with brightly dressed skaters, and later that evening the crowds would come again. But it was nearly dinnertime, and it appeared that the only ones left were either wobbly kneed novices or semiprofessionals, eager to show off their jumps and spins on the nearly deserted ice.

"I was married once," he replied defensively. "To Alicia Bennet," he added, seeing her blank look.

Amanda rolled her eyes. "Oh, right. I'd forgotten. The thirty-day wonder!"

" 'Scuse me? We were married for three hundred and seventy-two days, I'll have you know!" Chris corrected.

"That isn't a marriage. It's a long date!" Amanda replied, struggling to keep a straight face. "Seriously, I hate to think of you living your life all alone. I mean, what does all the success and money mean if you don't have someone to share it with?"

"You and Bayley been exchangin' notes?" Chris protested, obviously unwilling to get into a serious discussion of his love life. "Next thing I know, you'll be saying you have a girlfriend you want me to meet!" he teased.

"Well, I do have one nice single friend," Amanda joked back, following his lead. "Her name's Bernice, but we all call her Beanie for the cute little hats she always wears. She's got a great personality and a pretty smile . . . well, it will be pretty, once the braces come off. And she's already lost nearly forty pounds on Weight Watchers! They say the second forty will come off in a snap!"

Chris had been slowly backing Amanda around the rink railing, his look warning her to quit or pay the consequences. They were kids again, oblivious of where they were or who was watching. In order to see her better in the fading light, Chris had unconsciously removed his glasses, and his blue eyes danced dangerously as he closed the gap.

Amanda squealed as he grabbed for her, turning to run. But hands like a vise closed around her middle and snapped her back to him. They were laughing and wrestling, completely unaware of the group of teenagers who had sat down behind them to change into their skates. The kids thought it was cool to see two grown-ups having so much fun, and they all stopped what they were doing to watch.

In a desperate move to extricate herself, Amanda swung around, accidentally knocking Chris's hat off. He made a grab for the hat, momentarily releasing her, and she sprinted away.

"Oh no, you don't!" he called after her.

"Look! It's Christopher Davies," a young voice cried out.

Chris looked up with dismay, grabbed his hat, and took off running. Amanda could hear him gaining on her, and she stopped, winded, to let him catch up. But instead of stopping when he reached her, he kept right on going, grabbing her hand and pulling her along with him.

"What. . . ?" Amanda managed to get out, barely able to keep up.

"Look behind us," Chris yelled, slowing slightly so she could glance back over her shoulder, then picking up speed again.

A dozen or so girls and boys had joined the chase, yelling out Chris's name, and their number was growing as others recognized their idol.

Amanda thought her lungs would burst if they didn't stop soon, but just as she thought she was going to collapse, they reached the street. With amazing wind reserves Chris put his fingers in his mouth and let out an earsplitting whistle. Amanda watched in amazement as a taxi cut across three lanes of traffic and screeched to a stop before them. They jumped in and slammed the door just as the kids reached the sidewalk.

"I think I saw that scene in a movie once," Amanda wheezed when she was finally able to speak again.

The cabbie dropped them in the middle of Greenwich Village. The sun was gone and the twilight was fading fast. The streetlights came on as they walked. Amanda turned up her collar against the biting wind that had come back to remind them it was the middle of winter.

Chris had suggested they eat early and avoid the crowds, and

Amanda had readily agreed, realizing that they hadn't eaten anything since the bagels. Now Chris grabbed her hand to pull her across the street as they headed for the welcoming glow of a Moroccan restaurant. Amanda was content to let him keep it when they reached the other side.

Because it was still so early, the small restaurant was nearly empty when they entered. Wonderfully exotic smells greeted them, making their stomachs growl and their mouths water. Chris pointed to the back where a number of curtained booths stood waiting. The hostess hesitated, explaining that the booths were all reserved for later parties, but Chris took off his hat and gave her one of his knee-melting smiles.

A few minutes later they were seated, studying the menu and sipping hot tea, which had been ceremoniously poured into their cups like a waterfall from three feet up in the air. Amanda let Chris order and soon the table was laden with bowls of couscous and Tajines, a Moroccan curried lamb stew named for the earthenware pot it's traditionally cooked in.

"We eat with our fingers right out of the bowls," he explained when she commented there were no plates or silverware. "It's okay," he reassured, seeing her hesitation. "This is one time when you can be as messy and disgusting as you like. That's why they put curtains around the booths . . . so no one else has to look at you!"

He dipped his hand into the bowl of couscous and stuffed it into his mouth. "Umm, good," he commented, chewing happily.

Amanda watched him take a few more bites, then reached out tentatively as though expecting to have her hand slapped. She picked up a small amount and placed it carefully in her mouth. Umm, it was good! Her next bite was bigger and less self-conscious.

Eating the lamb was trickier. No matter how careful she tried to be, the juices dripped across the table and ran down her hand and chin. By the third or fourth bite, she gave up worrying and entered into the spirit of things, laughing as Chris tried to feed her and stuffing a piece of lamb in his mouth in return. The whole thing felt wild and decadent, like a scene out of *Tom Jones*.

"I can just see my girls here," she laughed, wiping her face for the umpteenth time. "Casey would love it! In five minutes she'd be covered from head to toe, happy as a clam. But Kimmy would barely be able to eat, her sense of orderliness thoroughly offended."

Realizing she had broken her unspoken promise not to bring up her family, Amanda fell silent. But Chris leaned back and gave her a long, searching look.

"Tell me about them. Tell me about your life. You've seen what mine is like. But I know nothing of yours."

Amanda felt her stomach tighten. All day she had deliberately avoided talking about her family. They just didn't seem to have a place in this fantasy she and Chris were living. Today was about revisiting the past and healing old wounds, and the last thing she wanted to do was hurt Chris again with thoughtless stories about her happy life as the wife of another man.

"It's all right," he said, reading her thoughts. "I really want to know. Tell me what it's like to be you."

"What it's like to be me," Amanda repeated, trying to get comfortable with the subject.

She started with a quick description of where they lived and of Nick's job. She felt awkward talking about Nick, afraid Chris would sense that the past couple of years had been a struggle. She only wanted Chris to know that she had married a truly wonderful man, who loved her and took good care of her, for in reality that was the truth.

Her voice relaxed and became warmly animated when she began talking about her two daughters. She talked about Kimberly's sweet, gentle nature that all too often left her defenseless against her younger sister's overbearing personality, but which also gave her great compassion and a remarkable intuitiveness about people.

"We were walking down Colorado Boulevard in Pasadena one afternoon," she related as an example. "It was late and growing dark, and I always get nervous when Nick isn't with us because of the panhandlers that have claimed that part of town for their own. We were almost to the car when Kimmy just stopped and wouldn't budge. She had seen a man curled up in a doorway, sleeping. He was dirty and smelly, and he had a cup set out for loose change.

" 'Why is that man lying on the sidewalk, Mommy?' she whispered.

" 'That's where he sleeps,' I said. I was really uncomfortable and wanted to move on before she woke him up. But she wouldn't be moved.

" 'Why doesn't he go home to sleep?' she asked me, unable to make sense of what she was seeing.

"I explained that something must have happened . . . I didn't know what . . . and now he was living on the streets. Kimberly just couldn't accept it.

" 'Doesn't he have a family? Maybe he just got lost and his family is looking for him. I think we should wake him up and ask him if he's lost.'

"She started to walk over to him, totally without fear, and I literally had to grab her.

" 'Kimmy,' I said, 'we don't know who this man is. Please, honey, let's just get to the car.'

"She looked at me with her big blue eyes and said, 'I know who he is, Mommy. He's a lost sheep, waiting for the shepherd to find him.'

"The Bible story about the little sheep that wandered away from the flock and the shepherd who left the ninety-nine to go find it has always been one of Kim's favorites," Amanda explained. "I can't tell you how ashamed I felt at that moment. Here I was the one who supposedly was teaching my daughter about God's love, but she was the one living it out. I gave her some money and told her to just put it in his cup. But she walked right up to him instead and crouched down, patting his shoulder.

" 'Here's some money so you can go home,' she said.

"The man sat up a little, and she put the money in his hand. He looked at her like she was an angel. I guess he'd been awake all along and heard everything she'd said.

" 'God bless you,' he said.

"She just beamed at him and then she came back, took my hand, and we walked to the car. I glanced back at the man and he was still watching us . . . crying like a baby."

"Sounds like you have a pretty incredible girl there," Chris said, visibly moved.

"Yes, I do. And Casey's just as incredible, in her own way." She soon had Chris laughing at her younger daughter's unpredictable antics, telling him about the time she'd gathered up all the neighbors' pets and dressed them in costumes, then sold tickets to the neighborhood kids to come see her circus in the backyard. "It wasn't until I started getting panicked calls from pet owners asking if I'd seen their cat or dog that I realized what Casey had done.

" 'I was only borrowing them, Mommy. I was going to put them back!' she told me, amazed at all the fuss."

"Sounds like you've got one who will save the world and one who'll turn it upside down!" Chris observed.

"Oh, I'm sure that God has great plans for both their lives. After all, there's more than one way to move a mountain. Kimberly's the rain, patiently wearing it away, and Casey's a stick of dynamite, blasting it to kingdom come! Both will get the job done," Amanda laughed.

They fell silent while the table was cleared and sipped one last cup of tea while they waited for the check.

"You know, I asked you to tell me about *you*, and all you've done for the past twenty minutes is talk about other people," Chris chided gently.

The observation made Amanda think. "I guess that's because that's how I define myself . . . by my family. I'm Nick's wife and Casey and Kimberly's mother. There hasn't been much time to be anything else for the past eight years."

"And is that enough?" he asked, picking up on her slightly mournful tone.

"Yes," she answered slowly, "and no. I mean, I can't imagine not being married to Nick or having the girls in my life. They're definitely the best part of it! But I will admit that for a while there I felt like I was giving so much of myself away, I was in danger of disappearing altogether. Thank God I met Laura and she offered me the job at the store. It gave me a chance to dust off those creative parts of me that have been lying dormant since I was a young girl and helped me discover who I am apart from the demands and needs of my family.

"You know, I'm actually very good at what I do," she confided, as though he might find that hard to believe. "Laura says I have a good eye for detail and an imaginative flair! She actually talked to me about a partnership—sometime in the future, when the girls are older."

"That doesn't surprise me at all," Chris said honestly. "I still remember those bears you arranged and the displays you did for your grandparents. You never seemed to realize how clever they were, but I did, and so did everyone who saw them. You have a real talent, Amanda, and it would be a crime not to use it."

The force of Chris's conviction as he spoke startled Amanda. He was saying that *he* admired *her*. That he saw something special and worthwhile in her that made her a valuable human being in her own right. His words of praise made her flush with pleasure.

"And what does Nick think of you going into partnership with Laura?"

Amanda felt her pleasure turn to embarrassment. "I haven't told him about it. He's been so busy and distracted lately, it didn't seem like the right time. Besides, he's just gotten used to the idea of me working part time. It was hard for him when I told him I wanted to go to work. I think he saw it as a criticism . . . my way of saying he wasn't providing well enough or that I wasn't happy just being his wife. And that wasn't it at all! I just needed something for me. Can you understand that?"

Amanda felt suddenly uncomfortable, as though she'd said too much and been too transparent. She didn't want to talk about any of Nick's shortcomings with Chris. It seemed disloyal, like she was betraying her husband by allowing Chris to see him or their relationship as anything other than perfect.

"Of course I can and so will Nick. From everything you've told me, it sounds like he's a great guy, and I'm sure he'll come around as soon as he sees how much it means to you. He's just struggling with that old 'man thing,' you know? I mean, every man wants to feel that his woman depends on him. It dates back to when Egor would go out and hit dinner over the head with his club while Egette stayed behind and swept out the cave. It's all part of this giant delusion we have that you need us 'cause we're smarter and stronger. By the way, you want to arm wrestle?"

He put his arm on the table and flexed his muscles a few times, making Amanda laugh.

"No? You sure?"

Amanda knew exactly what he was doing. He'd inadvertently led her into a sticky topic, and now he was leading her out again. "Come on, chicken! I bet I take you two out of three!"

"Okay, cowboy, you're on." Amanda set her elbow on the table and made a great show of grabbing his hand just so. They were just set to begin when she added, "But if I win, I don't want to hear any whining about how tired and weak your arm was from all that guitar playing last night!"

Chris relaxed a second to answer, and Amanda pushed with all her might, sending his arm crashing to the table.

Amanda was laughing and whooping up her victory while Chris loudly accused her of cheating, when the curtains whipped open and a stern-faced waiter presented them with the check. The two culprits froze, looking out to see that the restaurant had filled while they ate and every head was turned in their direction.

Chris slipped on his hat and glasses, but it was a pointless exercise. It was obvious by the looks and whispers that he'd been recognized. He threw down a wad of bills and they walked meekly out the door, holding their breath until they were able to escape the curious eyes that followed them.

Twenty-five

*I*t wasn't hard to lose themselves in the throng of Saturday-night revelers who crowded the streets of the Village to enjoy the comparatively mild temperatures and wild night life. A few hardy street performers dotted the scene, creating a carnival atmosphere. Chris and Amanda wandered hand in hand, taking in the sights and sounds, invisible in their upturned collars and nondescript dress.

They passed a guitarist doing a bad imitation of Bob Dylan, a trio of folk singers who sounded more like Peter, Paul and Mary than Peter, Paul and Mary, and a saxophonist who had Chris wildly writing notes on the back of his hand when he couldn't find any paper.

There were a half dozen white-faced Marcel Marceau wanna-bes mingling among the crowds, climbing out of invisible boxes and presenting pretty girls with imaginary flowers.

"They're probably on a field trip with the Acme School of Mime," Amanda commented, laughing out loud at one young man's ridiculous attempt to free his shoe from a nonexistent gob of gum on the sidewalk.

The sounds of music and voices and laughter drifted out of open doorways, and the sidewalks were mottled with light and shadow, creating contrasts that were almost artificial in their perfection. Amanda was once again overwhelmed with a sense of unreality and déjà vu. It was like being caught in a remake of an old movie, the characters and setting all familiar yet strangely different. There was something so comfortable about feeling her hand safely tucked in his, matching her steps to his . . . knowing that conversation was not necessary in order to know what the other was thinking.

Memories of their late-night walks through Walker's Point came flooding back, and along with them came old feelings. She'd forgotten what that first surprising rush of physical attraction had felt like. It was like the first big plunge on a roller coaster, when your stomach leaps into your throat and your heart forgets to beat, just for that one instant. After that, the sensation is never quite as pure and intense. After that, you know what to expect and the knowing changes things, giving you time to anticipate and prepare.

Amanda felt Chris tighten his grip as his thumb began gently caressing the palm of her hand and her pulse leapt in response. It was as if he were reading her mind, remembering with her, feeling everything she was feeling. Suddenly the simple, innocent act of holding his hand became unbearably intimate, and Amanda found herself wondering nervously for the first time that day just how they were going to bring this fantasy to a close.

Her thoughts were abruptly interrupted when she and Chris turned a corner and nearly bumped into a couple standing at the end of a long queue of people inching their way into a small theater. The marquee read, "Once More, With Rhythm! An American Musical Revue."

"I've heard about this!" Amanda exclaimed as she and Chris made their way to the front.

Large blowups of reviews declaring it a "Smash Hit" and "The Hottest Ticket Off-Broadway" were proudly displayed on either side of the entry.

"Would you like to go?"

"I'd love to, but . . ." Amanda pointed to the "Sold Out" sign in the box-office window. "The tickets are sold out weeks in advance."

"Well, you never know. Maybe somebody won't show up."

Amanda watched nervously as Chris walked over to the "Will Call" window. The lady was busy filling out paper work and didn't even look up until Chris tapped on the window. She gave him a disapproving frown, obviously unhappy about being interrupted.

"We're sold out!" she informed him. "Try next Tuesday. Tuesdays are slow."

As she was speaking Chris had straightened his shoulders and lifted his head, extending his neck like a turtle coming out of its shell. He then looked the woman in the eye and gave her a smile. "I think you might have something if you look again, ma'am," he said in his most pleasing Texan drawl.

For just a moment the woman looked as though she might faint as her eyes grew huge in recognition. But to her credit, she quickly pulled herself together, acting unimpressed as she fumbled to find the envelope with "Davies" written on it and dispassionately handed him the tickets. She kept her voice level as she quietly told him to step around to a side door just beyond the ticket booth. Only the slight tremor of her hand as she withdrew it gave her away.

The minute Chris and Amanda walked away from the booth, they grinned at each other as they heard the unflappable ticket lady lose her cool, almost screaming into the phone, "Ma! You'll never guess who I just talked to!"

They were led to their seats just as the house lights blinked to announce that the show was about to begin.

"Wow! Am I impressed!" Amanda whispered, settling into her seat in the third row, center section. "I can't believe we got in. I mean, she just saw you and suddenly there were tickets! Does that happen everywhere you go? I mean, I never realized the privileges you got for being—"

"A national treasure?" Chris finished, teasing her with her own words. "Well, I'd love to say it's all because I'm so famous and wonderful, but the truth is, we got in more because of you than me."

Amanda looked at him, thoroughly confused.

"Seems you've got a friend in high places," he said, handing her the program with an anticipative grin. "Open it to the center page."

The center of the program was a full-color picture of the cast during the grand finale. There were sixteen in all. The girls were all dressed in flowing, glittering gowns, and each was paired with a partner in a silk hat and tails. In the center, down on one knee, his hat at a cocky angle, his arms spread wide in a final "ta-da!" was the star and choreographer of the show.

"Ben!" Amanda looked at Chris with complete astonishment and delight. "I don't believe this! Did you know? Well, of course you knew. Silly question! You had this planned all along, didn't you? This is totally unbelievable!" Amanda's words spilled over each other as she alternated between hitting him and hugging him. "Why didn't you tell me?"

"I wanted to surprise you," Chris laughed, marveling at how little she had changed. She was still as joyously uninhibited as a little child when she wasn't carefully censoring her feelings and measuring her reactions, as she had been doing all day.

"Well, you certainly succeeded!" she bubbled, her excitement blocking out any concern she might have felt at the curious looks she was drawing. "Did you talk to Ben? Are we going to be able to see him?"

"Yes, ma'am. He wants us to come backstage after the show."

"But how did you arrange this? And when? Everything's been so last minute! And—"

"Shhh," Chris put a finger to his lips as the house lights began to dim. "I'll explain everything afterward. The show's startin'."

For the next two and a half hours Chris and Amanda were carried away on a magic carpet of music and dance. The songs had been carefully selected to represent the best of over thirty years of Broadway and film musicals. Each number had been brilliantly interpreted to give it a fresh, updated look without losing the original sentiment that had made it a hit to begin with. The result was a joyous celebration of the timelessness of good music . . . like taking a priceless diamond and putting it in a new setting.

And there in the middle of it all was Ben! In one number he reminded Amanda of Fred Astaire, all grace and fluid movement. In another he demonstrated the energy and style of a young Gene Kelly. And toward the end of the evening he came out dressed as the scarecrow in *The Wizard of Oz*, his arms and legs appearing jointless and rubbery in a tribute to Ray Bolger.

Amanda and Chris clapped and hooted along with the enthusiastic audience, and by the end of the evening, it was obvious why the show was such a hit. While there may not have been any deep message or profound punch line, there wasn't one person who walked out of the theater without a smile on his face or a song on his lips.

The theater was pretty well empty before Chris and Amanda attempted to leave. As they got up a head popped out from between the stage curtains and a familiar grin hollered, "Hey, you two! Get your sorry behinds back here!"

Chris and Amanda rushed over to the side door and up the stairs leading backstage. Ben was waiting at the top. He grabbed Amanda up in a huge twirling hug before setting her back on her feet and turning to give Chris a back-thumping bear hug.

"It's good to see you, guy. How long has it been? Two, three years?"

"'Bout two and a half," Chris replied. "The last time was when we were here to play the Garden and you were doin' that show with Carol Channing."

"Well, this is just unbelievable," Ben said, turning his attention back to Amanda. "Boy, you sure grew up gorgeous!"

"How can you tell?" Amanda laughed, pushing her hair back and realizing she hadn't even bothered to freshen her lipstick all day.

"I just can't believe you two are here," Ben continued, looking back and forth at his two old friends. "You know, it's like one of those dreams you have—that you'll make it *really* big and that one night you'll walk out on stage and the people who knew you 'when' will be sitting out in the audience, and you get to impress the socks off of them! You *were* impressed, weren't you?" he abruptly paused to ask, suddenly looking panicked.

"Incredibly! Completely! It's amazing! Wonderful!" his two friends rushed to reassure him, stepping all over each other's words.

"Good!" he responded, visibly relieved. "Just let me get this makeup off, and we'll get out of here and celebrate!"

Half an hour later the threesome was comfortably settled in Ben's one-bedroom loft just two blocks from the theater. They had decided this was the best place for them to relax and talk.

"And besides, I make the best cappuccino in town," he had reassured them.

Now they sipped the strong brew and nibbled on shortbread cookies as they talked.

"The first thing I have to know is how you two ended up here together. I couldn't believe my ears when Chris called up out of the blue and said he needed tickets for tonight so he could bring an old friend."

"Yeah, and the jerk wasn't goin' to get 'em for me, either, until I told him who the old friend was!" Chris sputtered through a mouthful of cookie.

"Hey, you may be the 'King of Rock' and I may have 'the fleetest feet to dance across a Broadway stage in years'—I quote *Variety*—and

I may love you like a brother, but if there ain't no seats, there ain't no seats! What can I tell ya?"

"So how did you get us seats?" Amanda asked.

"Fortunately some friends of mine had bought tickets two months ago . . . it's their anniversary. So I called them and asked if they would mind coming another night."

"You made your friends give up their tickets on their anniversary? I don't believe this. I feel so guilty!" Amanda wailed, looking at Chris as though it were all his fault.

"Don't worry about it," Ben consoled. "I got them front-row center seats for *A Chorus Line* instead, and they can come to this show another time. They actually ended up way ahead!"

"Really?" Amanda perked up, looking greatly relieved.

"Really," Ben asserted, giving Chris a look behind Amanda's back that said he was lying through his teeth. "So come on, tell me how you two got together again. You are still married, aren't you?" Ben asked Amanda, the thought suddenly hitting him.

"Oh, you bet," Amanda replied a bit too gaily. "And before the night's over you're going to look at pictures of my kids and listen to at least a couple of my proud parent stories!" Amanda warned.

"And fine stories they are, too," Chris interjected. "I've been listening to them all evening and haven't died of boredom yet!"

Amanda threw a pillow at him. "To answer your question, it was an amazing series of ridiculous coincidences."

She and Chris went on to relate the events of the past forty-eight hours, passing the narrative back and forth like the baton in a relay race. Ben watched in fascination as the two of them fell into a natural rhythm, finishing each other's sentences, laughing at each other's jokes long before he understood the punch line . . . their hands constantly reaching out in an unconscious dance of light touches and strokes. Although Chris sat at one end of the sofa and Amanda at the other, the space between them seemed nonexistent, and Ben realized with a concerned start that the electricity between them was as great as ever.

When it came time to tell Ben about how Amanda's mother had intercepted the letters, the air around them nearly pulsated with emotion.

"Well, that certainly clears up the mystery, doesn't it?" Ben said, shaking his head in disbelief. "I remember when Chris and I first got back in contact about five years ago and he told me what happened, I couldn't believe it. It just didn't sound like you, Amanda. You were too much of a person to do something like that, even back then. I suggested that he get back in touch and ask you about it, but he told me you were married and that the whole thing didn't matter anymore. Then he picked up a full glass of Jim Beam and drained it in one gulp. It seemed prudent to drop the subject."

"How did you know I was married?" Amanda asked Chris, suddenly curious. "I didn't send you a wedding invitation, although I would have if I'd known how to reach you. Believing what I believed at the time, I would have loved to let you know that I had found someone else and was moving ahead with my life. Now I'm grateful God didn't let that happen. You would have taken it as such a slap! It makes me cringe to think about it," Amanda said, grabbing up a pillow and squeezing it to her chest as she imagined the pain she would have caused him.

"Yeah, that was sure nice of God, lookin' out for my feelings like that."

The bitterness in Chris's voice made Amanda's heart sink. This was the first time he'd expressed any anger toward God for what had happened, and she realized it was inevitable that the revelations of the past two days would bring many of his old hurts and anger to the surface.

It had been an unintentional slip, and Chris regretted it the second he saw Amanda's pained look. He and the "Old Man Upstairs" had been heading for a showdown for nearly as long as he could remember, and the events of the past forty-eight hours had only intensified the sense of inevitability. But now was not the time nor the place. He and Amanda had only a few more short hours before he was going to have to let her go, and he wasn't going to let anything rob him of the pure joy of her presence.

"It was Ana and Mack," he picked up, answering Amanda's question. "I'd kept in touch with them, not wantin' to burn any bridges until I was sure that the singing career was going to work out."

"Sure yet?" Ben interrupted to ask.

"Nope. I still send them a Christmas card every year . . . just in case."

"Me too," Ben concurred.

Amanda smiled at the ludicrous thought of either Chris or Ben ending up back at Walker's Point after all their success, but one look at their faces told her they were only half joking. It was then that the insecurity they constantly lived with really hit home.

"Anyway," Chris continued, "Ana mentioned that they'd gone to the wedding, and she even sent me a newspaper clipping. She was always passing on bits of information about the people I'd worked with that summer. That's how I got back in contact with Ben. He was traveling with a touring company performing *The Music Man*, and we both ended up in Denver at the same time."

The three spent some time reminiscing about the summer that had brought them all together, one memory triggering another.

"From Walker's Point to Broadway! You've certainly come a long way!" Amanda finally commented to Ben, looking around the high-ceilinged apartment.

Ben had furnished it with an eclectic mix of Swedish modern furniture and old show-business memorabilia. Old movie posters and playbills shared the walls with framed pictures from the different shows he had done. Amanda spied one from *Oklahoma!* and walked over to take a closer look. There were all the wonderful people who had shared that summer with them, frozen in time.

"Look at you, Ben! I'd forgotten how incredibly skinny you were," Amanda laughed. "And Stacy . . ." She reached out to touch the beautiful, smiling girl in the picture. "I wonder where she is. We lost touch shortly after Nick and I were married."

"She's married and living somewhere in Georgia," Ben answered.

"You've kept in touch all these years?" Amanda asked, surprised. She had never thought that Stacy and Ben were that close. While she and Chris had looked as though they might be heading toward a long-term commitment, Ben and Stacy had always kept their relationship light, treating it like the summer romance it was.

"More by accident than by intent," Ben admitted. "I tried L.A. for a couple of years, and we kept running into each other at auditions and such. Actually worked together a time or two in the early seventies. Then Stacy got that sitcom, and it looked like things were going to really take off for her."

"I know. I was so proud and happy for her. Then suddenly it was off the air and she just disappeared. I always wondered what happened. I even tried to reach her once through her parents. But they had moved and I just didn't know how to find her. Do you know what happened?"

"Only bits and pieces. I know she married a real scumbag. He was the one who was managing her when the TV show came up, and from what I heard, he pretty much ruined her, both professionally and personally. There were rumors of drugs and other trash. I don't really know any details. It was too bad. She had real talent and she could have done something."

Amanda's eyes filled with tears as she took another look at her friend's smiling face. "I wish I had known," she whispered hoarsely. "I would have been there for her."

Ben came up behind her, looking over her head at the picture, his hands resting comfortingly on her shoulders. "I know you would have. You and Stacy really loved each other. But what you have to know is God turned it around for her, and the last I heard she was married to a good man and making a new life for herself. Like you always used to tell us . . . God has a plan."

Amanda looked up to give Ben a surprised look, and he gave her shoulders a confirming squeeze.

"Don't look so surprised," he chuckled softly close to her ear. "Even a stubborn old hoofer like me can finally come to his senses and realize he doesn't make the rules."

Uncertain what to say, Amanda smiled back. Her head was full of questions, but glancing over at Chris and seeing his sudden discomfort, she knew this was not the time or place to get into a deep spiritual discussion.

She moved on to look at other pictures, with Ben closely shadowing her. The wall was a time line of Ben's career from Walker's Point to the present. Some shows were immediately identifiable, like *The Music Man* and *My Fair Lady*, and others he had to name for her, explaining that they either opened and closed the same night or had run a few months, then fizzled out. In all, Amanda counted nearly thirty shows, and as the years progressed she recognized more and more faces as Ben began working with one Broadway legend after another.

Then she came to a collection of personal photos. There was Ben standing awkwardly between a tall, gaunt gentleman with a stern, martyred look on his face and a small, buxom woman wearing a proud but self-conscious smile . . . obviously Ben's parents, taken after the opening of one of his shows. It was apparent from the expression on his face that Ben's father had never gotten over his disappointment in his son's choice of careers, and the look in Ben's eyes clearly showed the pain and rejection he felt at letting his dad down.

There was a candid shot of Ben and his sister, Amy, playing with her two little boys, and several pictures with friends. But it wasn't until she saw a picture of Ben with his arm possessively around a pretty girl with long brown hair and startling blue eyes that her interest was piqued. Amanda was just about to ask about her when Chris glanced at his watch and let out a yelp.

"Whoa, baby! It's nearly two. I need to make a couple quick phone calls. I promised my agent I'd phone him around ten. He flew back to California today, and he's probably pacing by the phone wondering what happened to me."

"Use the phone in my bedroom," Ben offered.

"Great. Then we're goin' to have to get going."

Amanda helped Ben collect the cups and carry them into the small efficiency kitchen. She couldn't help noticing the gourmet herbs and spices crowded on the counter.

"Don't tell me you cook!" she said, giving Ben a gentle jab.

"I'm learning. Robin's teaching me," he responded, running water in the sink to quickly wash the few dishes.

"And just who is Robin, and why is this the first I'm hearing about her?" Amanda asked, picking up a towel to dry.

"Well, if you and Chris had stopped talking long enough to sneeze, I would have said, 'I'm getting married' instead of 'gesundheit.' As it is, I'm glad we have these few minutes alone so I can tell you about her."

"You're getting married?" Amanda squealed. "When? And who is this remarkably lucky girl?"

"The wedding is in June, and I'm the lucky one, believe me. You know how people talk about someone turning their life upside down? Well, I'd done a great job of doing that all by myself. Robin came along and turned it right side up again." Ben's voice grew husky with emotion as he spoke her name, and the glow of love softened his features, making him look twenty again.

"How did you meet her?" Amanda asked, totally enthralled.

"She's a 'gypsy,' like me . . . a dancer who travels from one show to another," he explained in response to her quizzical look. "She was working in *Hello, Dolly!* with me, and I noticed her the first day of rehearsal. I mean, you couldn't help but notice her . . . legs up to here, a waist your hands can encircle, hair that falls like a dark brown cape nearly to her waist. Well, you saw her picture. I wanted her the first time I saw her, and at that time I was used to getting what I wanted."

"But not this time?" Amanda asked, liking this girl already.

"It was like slamming my face against an invisible plate-glass window. The way *looked* clear. She was friendly and lots of fun to talk to at work, but every time I asked her out or tried to make a move, she froze me out—in a nice way, of course. Which was what was so frustrating! I could sense that she liked me, but something was getting in the way. She became this incredible challenge. I mean, nothing like this had ever happened to me. Oh, I'd been shut down before, but I never cared enough to worry about it. Now that's all I did . . . think about her, look forward to seeing her at the theater, and try to figure out why she kept me at arm's length.

"Finally I just came right out and asked her what the problem was. Instead of answering, she came back with another question. She asked me what the most important thing in my life was. I told her I guessed it was my career. Then she asked me what would happen if I fell off the stage tomorrow and damaged my leg so badly I couldn't ever dance again? What would give my life meaning then? I didn't have an answer for her. She told me to think about it and that she'd meet me for coffee the next day to talk about it.

"All that night I couldn't get her question out of my mind. I tried to imagine my life without dancing and I realized I'd have nothing . . . *be* nothing . . . if I couldn't dance. It was a terrifying thought."

Ben finished rinsing the last cup and handed it to Amanda to dry. Then he turned and leaned comfortably against the sink before he continued.

"We started meeting every few days for coffee or a quick bite and we'd talk. At first I did most of the talking and she'd just ask questions and listen. There was something so calm and centered about her. I felt like I could say anything and she never got rattled or argumentative or defensive.

"Then a funny thing started to happen. The more I talked, the more I realized I didn't have a clue half the time what I was talking about. I tried to answer the questions she asked, and she never made me feel like my answers were wrong, but the more I heard myself, the more empty and dissatisfied I became with the sound of my own voice.

"That's when I started asking her some questions, and her answers were easy and direct, right out of the Bible. Of course, by then I knew that was where she was coming from. She talked about God so easily, like He was someone she knew and talked to daily. But somehow, hearing her talk about God's love and forgiveness didn't make me bristle and turn off as it always had before. Instead, I found I wanted to hear . . . and then I felt desperate to hear. It was like waking up after a long sleep with this huge, gnawing hunger, only the more I ate, the hungrier I got."

"And are you still hungry?" Amanda asked.

"Ravenous!" he declared with an infectious grin. "But a year and two months ago I gave up trying to feed myself. I stopped fighting and arguing and simply decided to believe. It was the scariest moment of my life.

"I know this is hard for you to understand coming from your background, but people like Chris and me find the whole concept of God incredibly threatening. I mean, we spend our whole lives fighting to convince ourselves and other people that we have something special to offer. Control is essential! And we need to make sure that people only see what we want them to see so we can protect the dream and the image. The greatest asset we have is our belief in our own strength and ability, and vulnerability is a liability we can't afford.

"Then God comes along and says, 'Give it up. Lay it down. Become like a little child and let me be in control.' And there's a part of us that wants that desperately, a part that's tired and uncertain and desperate to believe there's something beyond our own strength. But we're afraid that the minute we let our guard down and dare to believe, someone will jump out from behind the curtain and yell, 'April Fool's, you sucker!' And we'll be left feeling foolish and weak, and perhaps worst of all, truly hopeless."

"I wish you could say all this to Chris. It's exactly what he needs to hear," Amanda said, thrilled by Ben's story.

"I will . . . someday . . . when the time is right. Chris isn't ready yet. He's still too certain of himself. The one thing I've learned is that you can't give a person an answer before they ask the question. God says 'Seek and you will find,' and Chris is a seeker, even though he doesn't realize it yet. One day he'll wake up hungry, and when that day comes, look out!"

Amanda felt Chris come up behind her. "Ben's getting married!" she announced, looking at him to see how much he had heard. But all she saw was honest surprise.

"Hey, man, that's great! Congratulations!" Chris said, shaking Ben's hand.

"Her name's Robin, and Ben's been telling me how they met," she explained, linking one arm through Chris's and the other through Ben's to steer the two men back into the living room. "You'll have to ask him sometime. It's quite a story!"

"I'd love to hear. Maybe we can get together for lunch one day before I leave," Chris said, holding Amanda's jacket for her as she slipped it on.

"Just let me know when you're hungry and we'll do it!" Ben responded, giving Amanda a slight wink.

Twenty-six

*A*manda and Chris walked out of Ben's building to find Ruby waiting with the limousine and a sleepy smile. Obviously he had been one of Chris's quick calls.

"It's impossible to find a taxi at this time of night," Chris defended when Amanda scolded him for making Ruby come out so late.

The two climbed into the backseat and curled up together like bears ready to hibernate for the winter. Their bodies ached with physical and emotional exhaustion. After all, they had been going nonstop for over forty-eight hours with only snatches of restless sleep, and exhaustion threatened to suck them down a sinkhole of sweet oblivion.

It was in this blurred, dreamlike state that Amanda found herself safely snuggling against Chris's chest, his arms holding her protectively, the sound of his heartbeat as reassuring and relaxing as a lullaby. She closed her eyes and rode to the hotel drifting on a cloud of semi-consciousness.

For Chris the ride was agony. His eyes burned and his lids felt weighted with lead. His muscles cramped, screaming for the release of sleep. Yet he would not waste one minute of this precious time. For the next twenty minutes he could let his guard down and stop pretending that having her so close didn't drive him crazy!

He was free to look at her, to breathe in the fragrance of her skin and hair, to feel the sculpture of bone and muscle and flesh that made up the remarkable woman he held in his arms. Even through the multiple layers of clothes and padding he could feel her softness, and the answering need in his body and soul told him what up to now he had been unwilling to admit, even to himself. He still loved her. Not her memory or some dreamlike fantasy of the girl she had been, but the woman she had become, here and now. And he had to figure out what he was going to do about it.

By the time the limo pulled up in front of the Plaza, Chris was no closer to an answer. A wave of panic washed over him as he realized the moment of good-bye was upon them. His eyes traced her profile, the gentle slope of her forehead, the curve of her cheekbone, her lips, relaxed and slightly parted in sleep as though waiting to be kissed, and he suddenly knew he wasn't going to let her go without a fight! He hadn't voluntarily forfeited his place in her life. And she hadn't decided she didn't want him. Someone else had robbed them of their chance together, and he was simply not going to watch her walk out of his life without letting her know how he felt!

Ruby pulled the limo to a smooth stop at the curb and got out to open the door. Chris leaned over to plant a gentle kiss on her brow. He let his lips linger just a moment before reluctantly drawing back.

"We're here, baby girl. Time to wake up."

She stirred in his arms, nestling closer to him as though reluctant to leave her place of warmth and comfort. For a moment his arms tightened around her, and he wondered what would happen if he told Ruby to get back in the car and just keep driving.

"Amanda Rose."

The familiar voice drew Amanda back from the sweet place her dreams had taken her. She had been back on the beach at Walker's Point, lying in the sun with Chris beside her, and seeing his face smiling down at her now, she was momentarily lost in the depths between dreams and reality. Smiling back, it seemed natural to raise her head to gently press her lips to his.

Her action stunned him. He knew she wasn't completely awake and that he was taking advantage, but the feel of her mouth on his was like a match set to gasoline, consuming any self-control or rational thought in an explosion of need and passion. His mouth claimed hers as the feel and taste of her sent shock waves of familiar longing through his body and his arms became steel vises, crushing her to him with such force he could feel her ribs crunch, causing him to loosen his hold for fear of hurting her.

But she seemed oblivious of any pain as her arms went around his neck and she joined in his urgent search for closeness. Her lips began an exploration of his face, kissing his cheeks and chin and eyes, filling him with an unspeakable joy as once again she was completely his.

He knew the exact moment when she came to her senses . . . the second when reality hit and she realized the inappropriateness of her actions. The unguarded moment had opened the door to feelings she had never intended to acknowledge, much less express, and he felt the sudden rigidness in her body as she struggled to put the brakes on.

He stroked her hair, combing through the silky coolness several times before gently pulling her head back to look into her eyes. He searched for signs of anger or accusation, but all he found was a mirror of his own longing and uncertainty mixed with surprise and a certain amount of embarrassment.

"Amanda, I'm sorry—" he started, but she put her fingers to his lips and hushed him. She didn't want or need an apology. What had just happened had taken them both by surprise and she had to take equal responsibility.

If she was going to be totally honest with herself, she had to admit that when she agreed to take this walk down memory lane, she knew it would awaken old feelings. She had deliberately ignored all the warning signs and tuned out the still small voice that had warned her against putting herself in this place of temptation and danger. Now looking up at Chris it was clear that she was in way over her head. Her hand skimmed down the side of his face in a gesture both achingly sad and supremely gentle, and her eyes became pools of light as tears welled to run silently down her cheeks.

At that moment it was everything he could do to keep from grabbing her to him and pouring out his love for her. He wanted to tell her how empty and meaningless his life was without her and that what they had was worth fighting for. But even as the words rose in his throat, he swallowed them. In his world it would all be so easy. When two people felt the way he and Amanda did, nothing else mattered. The elusive search for happiness was all-consuming, and other concerns and considerations were easily pushed aside in the name of love.

But this was Amanda, and suddenly it was a new world with new rules. It was a world that included a husband and children and a life he had no part of. It was a world where love was synonymous with commitment and fidelity, and where breaking the rules even for one night was simply not allowed.

He could read the battle in her eyes, and he knew he dared not push or interfere. If she stayed with him, the consequences would be unavoidable and the price would be dear. It had to be her own choice, made with a clear head and a certain heart. They were both fully awake now. No more dreams. No more pretend. The "comma" was over. It was time to deal with reality.

Sometime during this unexpected outburst Ruby had opened the door, only to close it again the second his disbelieving eyes told him he was intruding. As he turned to wait a discreet distance away, he shook his head in amazement. Ever since he had met Miss Amanda it had been evident to him that there was something special between her and Mr. Chris. But he had also known that the lady was married, and up till now the two had behaved with the utmost integrity, obviously determined to keep their relationship above reproach. He couldn't help but wonder just what had happened to destroy that resolve in the few seconds it had taken him to get out of the car and open the door.

When the door finally opened, Ruby moved hesitantly to stand at attention. Amanda and Chris stepped out of the car looking dazed and distracted. Still, Amanda stopped to give him a smile and thank him again for coming out so late to get them. As he watched them walk arm in arm up the steps, he couldn't decide if they looked more like lovers or like mourners at a funeral, holding on to each other for strength and comfort. And he couldn't help feeling sad. Anyway you looked at it, this one was going to be a heartbreaker.

Chris and Amanda entered the elevator and stood looking at the buttons. Suddenly, deciding which button to push was of momentous importance. Amanda felt Chris looking at her, the muscle working in his jaw the only sign of his extreme nervousness. He wasn't going to pressure her. The decision had to be hers.

There wasn't any sense in denying it. God knew she was tempted. The world she had tasted these last two days was full of excitement and glamour and a level of romance that she thought only existed in books. Chris had made her feel beautiful and clever and interesting, and the fact that after all these years this famous, powerful man still wanted her was immeasurably seductive.

The two stood in the elevator, immobilized by indecision. Amanda felt her heart skip a beat as a wave of nervous nausea hit her stomach. What was she doing here? How had things gotten so far out of control? This wasn't her, standing in this elevator at two in the morning on the edge of being unfaithful to her husband. This was someone she didn't know or understand, and a desperate cry for help rose in her spirit.

Oh, God, help me! she silently prayed.

The words had hardly formed in her mind when she heard a voice call out, "Hold, please!" A young couple joined them in the elevator. Their weariness was written all over their faces. The husband was carrying a little girl about three. She was dead weight in his arms, her head resting on his shoulder, sound asleep.

"Thanks. That's the first thing that's gone right all day," the young man smiled gratefully. He went on to briefly explain that they had driven out to Long Island to see relatives and their rental car had conked out on the way back. They'd had a terrible time getting back to the hotel.

But Amanda barely heard what he was saying. Her eyes were fixed on the angelic profile resting on his shoulder. The child had strawberry blond hair and cheeks flushed pink by the winter wind. Kimberly's cheeks had always chapped like that in the winter, her skin was so fair. The child's face was pressed against her daddy's shoulder, pushing the rosebud mouth to the side and slightly apart, and a small trail of drool ran down her father's coat.

Amanda was suddenly transported to another night, long ago. She and Nick had taken Kimberly to Disneyland for the first time on her second birthday, and she was thoroughly worn out. They had taken the tram to the parking lot, but the car was still a good walk away. By the time they reached the car, Kim was fast asleep, her Mickey Mouse ears nestled on her daddy's shoulder. As Nick went to put her in the backseat, she tightened her grip and whimpered.

"Do you mind driving, honey?" he had asked, settling in the passenger seat with Kimberly on his lap.

During the hour-drive home Amanda had kept looking over at her two exhausted sweethearts . . . Nick patting Kimberly's back reassuringly even as his head lolled back and his eyes fluttered shut, and Kim contentedly sucking her thumb, safe in her daddy's arms. By the time they got home, Nick's shirt had been soaked with spittle, but he had just laughed, saying it was good to know that he still had the power to make women drool.

That was the night they decided they wanted another child. It was one of many nights when Amanda fell asleep feeling like the luckiest woman in the world.

The memory was so sharp and real, it nearly took Amanda's breath away. She closed her eyes, feeling dizzy and disoriented. When she opened them again the young family was exiting the elevator. She watched them walk wearily down the hall until the doors closed, then she turned to look at Chris. Her expression was calm, her eyes clear and certain, and even before she spoke, Chris knew what she was going to say.

"Do you remember that you once told me how hard it was for you to decide if you wanted to be a baseball player or a musician?"

"I remember."

"You said you really loved baseball, but life demanded that you make a choice. And when it came right down to it, you could live without baseball, but music was who you were. Do you remember?"

Chris just nodded.

Amanda looked at him, giving him a sad little smile. "I love baseball. I think I always will."

She paused, letting her words take root as she reached out to gently brush an imaginary piece of lint from his shoulder. Then she continued with unshakable conviction.

"But Nick and the girls are *my* symphony. They're the music God's given to me, and without them, I'm nothing."

Chris didn't have to ask if she was sure. The rightness of her words rang in his own heart. He understood now why his hope had been tinged with a confusing pang of regret. He would have gained her body but lost the essence of who she was . . . the only person besides his mother who had ever stood for righteousness in his life. He reached out and pressed the button for the sixth floor.

They walked to Amanda's door without touching or talking. Their demeanor was strangely calm and unemotional, like two people who had narrowly missed a great catastrophe and now were trying to regain their composure.

"Well . . ." Amanda smiled up at Chris, wanting desperately to say the right thing and feeling totally at a loss. "These last few days have been . . ." Her voice trailed off as words failed her.

"Yeah, they have," Chris agreed, watching her bite her lower lip and wishing that the sight of the familiar habit didn't twist his insides into a pretzel. "This isn't the way it's suppose to end, you know," he said, attempting to mask his pain with a boyish grin. "Everyone who's ever seen a movie knows the story goes, 'Boy meets girl. Boy loses girl. Boy *gets* girl.' Nowhere is it written that boy loses girl again!"

Amanda smiled at the old cliché. "I suppose that all depends on who the boy is and who the girl is and who's writing the script."

"Something else I have to thank the Big Guy for, huh?" Chris's tone was teasing, but Amanda knew that behind the flippancy was real hurt.

"Chris, you can't keep blaming God for every painful or unhappy thing that happens in your life, while at the same time refusing to give Him credit for all the good! I mean, look at you! You possess one of the greatest musical talents this generation has ever seen. People all over the world hear your music and find something wonderful or encouraging in it. It doesn't matter what language they speak or how different their lives are. Your music touches them! And last night at Carnegie Hall I felt the power of the gift God has given you . . . to you and no one else! Do you have any idea how blessed you are?"

"You make it sound like everything was handed to me on a silver platter!" Chris fought back. "You don't have any idea how hard I've worked for this 'gift,' as you call it, or what it has cost me!"

Amanda reached out to put her hand on his arm. "The gift was free," she said. "God's gifts always are. It's when we try to do it all on our own that the gift becomes a burden."

She could feel his arm stiffen, and she knew he didn't want to hear what she had to say, but something inside welled up and would not be silenced.

"I don't fully understand why God brought us back together this way. It really hurts to be standing here with you, saying good-bye, knowing that our lives are going in separate directions and that I may never see you again. But I know one thing, and that is that God loves you, Christopher Brian Davies. And He's been trying to make you know that for a long time! Don't you see? God didn't 'blink' when your mother died. He was there all the time, waiting for you to let Him comfort you and help you through the pain. *You* were the one who turned away. And when things didn't work out for us, it wasn't some kind of punishment. God simply loved us both too much to let us ruin our lives. We were too different to be happy together."

"I don't believe that," Chris replied, pulling away and refusing to look her in the eye.

"Yes, you do . . . deep down. Why do you think you never tried to get in contact with me? You were back in L.A. within a few months and you knew where I was. You could have come to the school and found me, but you didn't. You didn't because deep down inside you were relieved. With me out of your life, you didn't have to face your demons. You could go on nursing your hurt and your anger and find one more thing to blame God for."

Her words stung him, like needles of truth pricking his soul. He shook his head and tried to hide how deeply affected he was with a cocky smile. "There you go again, giving me grief with that sassy mouth of yours."

"I don't want to give you grief," Amanda said, equally stunned. The words had just poured out, without thought or conscious effort, and Amanda was horrified by her own boldness. "I want . . . I mean, I just wanted . . ." Her voice broke with emotion and Chris took her in his arms one last time.

"I know. I know what you wanted," he whispered, strangely touched. "And I heard what you were saying. I'll think about it. I promise."

Chris let her go and the two stood looking at each other, letting the silence grow and fill up the space between them. There was nothing left to say. Finally he took her face gently in his hands and kissed her on the forehead.

"Good-bye, Amanda Rose," he said and turned abruptly away.

Amanda watched as he walked down the hall to the elevators. The doors opened as soon as he touched the button, and Amanda waited expectantly for him to turn and raise his hand one last time. But he disappeared into the elevator without breaking stride, the doors closing behind him. This time he would not look back.

Chris smiled in spite of himself when he walked into his suite and found Bayley waiting up for him. It was obvious by his sleepy expression that his friend had been struggling not to fall asleep, and now he stood up awkwardly, searching Chris's face with undisguised curiosity.

"What happened? Are you all right?" he asked, stifling a yawn.

"First you're 'Dear Abby' and now you're my mother. Haven't you got anything better to do than baby-sit me?" Chris said, touched but also irritated to see Bayley's concerned face. He simply wasn't up to playing "Twenty Questions" right now.

He took a tired breath and walked over to the bar.

"To answer your question, nothing happened. We walked, we talked, we straightened things out, and we said good-bye. And tomorrow she's going home to her husband and kids, where she belongs."

He picked up an unopened bottle of Jack Daniels, broke the seal, and poured himself a stiff drink.

"You can wipe that hangdog expression off your face, Bay. I'm just fine. And I'll be even better after Mr. Daniels, here, has a chance to do his thing."

He took a deep swallow, his shoulders shuddering as the whiskey stung its way down his throat.

"By the way." Chris turned and gave Bayley a shrewd look. "Didn't it occur to you that you could have found yourself in an embarrassin' situation, waiting here like this? After all, two's company. Three's a crowd." Chris raised the glass to his lips, his blue eyes challenging Bayley over the rim.

"Actually, it never even crossed my mind," Bayley replied honestly. "Amanda is a class act, all the way. She's special. Different. There's no way she's gonna play that kind of game . . . not even with you."

"Oh, is that a fact?" Chris replied, his already bruised ego taking another lick. He drained the glass and turned for a refill. "And I suppose you could tell all this about her the first time you met her?"

"No. But you could. At least that's what you've always told me. And I know you. There had to be something very special about this lady for you to love her all these years. And for you to be willing now to let her go."

"Yeah, well, I didn't exactly let her go. I never really had a chance. Wasn't in 'The Plan,' you know."

Chris fell into a thoughtful silence, a faraway expression on his face. Bayley began to think that he'd forgotten he was there. Then Chris spoke again, his voice ragged with exhaustion.

"I'm tired, Bay . . . bone tired. . . . tired down to my soul. Sometimes I think my entire life has been one big wrestlin' match, only somehow things got messed up and I got put in the heavyweight division when I've never been anything more than a welterweight. Underweight and overmatched, that's me. But I've never figured out how to say 'uncle.'"

Bayley watched with growing alarm as Chris tried to take another drink. But the liquid choked him, making his throat burn and his eyes water. He put the glass down and hung his head, grabbing the bar for support.

"Come on, buddy. I'll help you to bed." Bayley came up behind Chris and started to put his arm around him for support. Chris seemed oblivious at first. Then he turned to look at his friend. The expression on his face was so anguished it froze Bayley to the spot. Bay's sudden panic made Chris realize how transparent he was being. He closed his eyes, leaning heavily on Bayley's shoulder, and when he opened them again, he had regained control.

"It's all right, Bayley. I can make it. You get on to bed yourself. You look like—" He was about to use a familiar expletive, but something stopped him.

"Like what?" Bayley challenged with a good-humored grimace.

"Like a good friend who needs about a week's sleep," Chris finished, giving Bayley's shoulder a squeeze as he headed toward the bedroom.

Bayley watched him shuffle slowly across the room, moving as though every muscle in his body ached. When Chris safely reached the door, Bayley turned to leave, stopping to twist the top back on the Jack Daniels bottle and put Chris's glass in the sink for the maid to wash in the morning. He turned off all the lights but one and was headed for the door when the sound of a low, anguished moan made him turn back.

He was at the bedroom door in a few quick strides, but something kept him from bursting in. Instead he felt compelled to open the door quietly, peeking in through a small crack. What he saw broke his heart.

Chris was kneeling by the side of his bed, his head buried in his hands, sobbing. Between sobs he spit out incoherent words and phrases, most of which made no sense to Bayley, and for one frightening moment he was afraid his friend had lost his mind. Then one word broke through and Bayley suddenly understood. Christopher Davies was finally saying "uncle."

Twenty-seven

*F*or Amanda the ride to the airport the next morning passed in blurred silence. She was too exhausted to notice the curious looks Laura kept giving her or the concerned glances Ruby kept taking in the rearview mirror. All she knew was that she could hardly wait to get back to Nick, to feel his arms around her, and know she was home, safe and sound.

Amanda slept the sleep of the dead all the way home, and by the time she stepped off the airplane she was wide awake and surprisingly refreshed. Laura had a hard time keeping up with her as she hurried through the terminal, eager to get their luggage and head toward home.

Home! The word rang with new meaning as she thought of Nick and the girls waiting for her. There was so much she wanted to tell Nick. So many things she needed to say. She had left home a week ago feeling restless and dissatisfied with her life. She had wanted to "rediscover" a part of herself she thought she had lost, and she had been very sure it could only be found somewhere new and exciting. But like Dorothy in *The Wizard of Oz*, she now realized that everything she was looking for had been at home all along. She had simply needed God to give her new eyes to see it.

Now as they rode in the limousine toward Sierra Madre, even the smog-tinged air of Los Angeles smelled sweet. And when she saw the mountains of home in the distance, she could barely contain her excitement. She remembered the scripture that had crossed her mind as she had driven away from those mountains a week before and the curious sense of loss she had felt as the limousine had turned and left them behind. Now she understood why. It was so simple. Her home was at the foot of those mountains. Her husband, her children . . . her whole world.

She could feel her excitement building with every passing mile, and when they finally turned down her street, she was on the edge of her seat, poised to jump out the second they pulled to a stop.

It was nearly six in the evening, and the winter sun had set behind the mountains an hour ago. All the lights were on in the house, casting a welcoming glow out of every window, and Amanda was filled with special pride and affection for the home she and Nick had created.

Before she was even out of the car, the front door flew open and she heard the ecstatic cries of the girls as they raced down the walk.

"Mommy! Mommy's home! Daddy! Grammy! Come quick!" She had barely found her footing before she was nearly knocked over by the impact of two little bodies throwing themselves into her arms. The three struggled to hug and kiss and talk all at the same time. Finally Amanda pulled away long enough to poke her head back in the door and speak to Laura.

"It's still early. Would you like to come in? I'm sure Mom has dinner waiting. Nick could take you home later," Amanda offered, knowing there was nobody waiting to welcome Laura home.

But Laura shook her head. "*I* didn't sleep from coast to coast! All I want right now is a hot bath and my own bed! But thanks for the invitation. I'll take a rain check, all right?"

"Anytime," Amanda answered sincerely. "Thank you, Laura," she said, reaching in to give her friend's hand a squeeze. "This trip has meant more than you know. Someday I'll tell you just how much!"

"I think I can guess," Laura said, squeezing back. "Go on, now, and enjoy your family," she said, laughing as the girls, whose patience had been stretched to the max, started pulling on their mother's skirt and demanding she come in and see their surprise.

Amanda allowed herself to be pulled and pushed up the walk to the front porch. She expected to find Nick and her mother waiting to welcome her, but only her mother stood at the top of the steps, watching the happy scene with a misty smile.

"Hello, darling. Welcome home," Karen Mitchell said, greeting her daughter with a warm hug. "How was the trip? Everything go well?"

"Everything went great!" Amanda replied, linking arms with her mother to walk into the house. As she stepped through the door, she was immediately ordered to shut her eyes as each girl took a hand and led her into the living room. Colorful streamers hung from the door-ways and a homemade banner across the fireplace read, "Welcome home, Mommy!"

"Oh, girls, this is wonderful!" Amanda cried, crouching down to give more hugs.

"Daddy helped us," Kimberly told Amanda, happy to be held. But Casey wriggled away, pirouetting around the room with proud glee.

"And just where is Daddy?" Amanda said, looking around for her missing husband.

"Right behind you."

Amanda smiled and whirled around at the sound of his voice. Nick was standing in the archway between the dining room and the living room, where he had enjoyed a ringside seat for the girls' surprise. His smile told her how happy he was to see her, but his eyes held an un-certainty, as though he wasn't sure she felt the same. Now he moved to give Amanda a hug.

"Welcome home," he said, brushing her lips with a light kiss. Amanda responded by wrapping her arms around his neck and pulling him close, giving him a long, deep kiss that left no question about how glad she was to see him. The girls hooted and clapped their hands, filled with the special joy and embarrassment children feel when they see their parents act like lovers.

When the kiss ended, Nick pulled back and gave Amanda a look she couldn't quite interpret. But before she had a chance to even think about it, the moment was broken as the girls surrounded their parents in a group hug.

Back to his old self, Nick picked up Casey and "flew" her into the dining room, announcing in his best Irish brogue, "Soup's on, me dearies, and we'd better be eatin' it before the little people do!"

The table was set for a celebration with their fine china and crystal. The smell of Grammy's roast filled the air with a mouth-watering blend of onions, garlic, and spices. Hungry, everyone sat quickly, reaching out to join hands as Kimberly prayed to thank God for the good food and for bringing Mommy home safely.

The conversation around the table was animated as the girls took turns telling Amanda about their week and asking questions about New York. They demanded to hear every detail of their mother's adventures, and Amanda relished their enthusiasm. She told them about the man who took their picture, then asked for an autograph. The girls doubled over with laughter at the thought that anyone would mistake their mother for a celebrity.

She told them about eating at the Tavern on the Green and riding the elevator to the top of the Empire State Building. "I looked, Mom, but Cary Grant wasn't there," she said, giving Nick a wink he didn't return.

She described the colorful skaters at Rockefeller Center and the huge theater billboards on Times Square. She even talked about riding the ferry on the Hudson River and eating with her fingers at a Moroccan restaurant. She just didn't mention who she was with at the time. This was something she intended to tell Nick when they were alone.

As she talked, Amanda became increasingly aware that something was wrong. Even though Nick appeared to be listening with rapt attention, Amanda had the distinct impression his mind was somewhere else. He never asked a question or made a comment unless one of the girls prompted him. Then he would turn on an unnaturally bright smile and answer with forced levity. The rest of the time he seemed faraway, lost in a world of his own. He had the look of someone who had just experienced a small death, and as they finished dinner, Amanda began to suspect what was wrong.

She looked over at her mother with a questioning look and was rewarded with a worried nod of understanding. Karen had noticed Nick's strange mood earlier that day and had wondered what was wrong.

"Girls, why don't you help Grammy clear the table so Mommy and Daddy can have some time together. They haven't even had a chance to say hello with all your jabbering."

The girls began dutifully helping Karen as their parents excused themselves and walked the narrow hall to their bedroom. Again Nick didn't speak or reach out to touch her, and Amanda's sense of foreboding grew.

Amanda entered her bedroom and felt an immediate rush of joy. Her mother had seen to every little detail, arranging the throw pillows on the bed with an artist's eye and placing an arrangement of yellow roses in a blue vase on the small lace-covered vanity. The air was still lightly scented with lemon from the furniture polish Karen had used to give every surface a healthy glow, and a cheerful fire burned in the fireplace. It was the perfect setting for a romantic reunion.

Since she hadn't even had time to take her shoes off before dinner, Amanda sank on the bed with a grateful sigh.

"It is so good to be home," she said, kicking her shoes off and starting to unbutton her blouse. "It seems like I've been gone a month instead of a week. I really missed you," she added, realizing as she spoke how true the words were.

Nick walked over to the fireplace and started to poke at the logs. It was as if he hadn't heard her. It was apparent something was eating at him and he was struggling to find a way to tell her.

Amanda could think of only one thing that would make him feel so low. She slipped off the bed and walked up behind him in her bare feet. He obviously didn't hear her because he literally jumped when he felt her arms come around his waist.

Amanda leaned her head against his back and said in her most comforting voice, "You lost the job, didn't you?" She felt him stiffen at her words and rushed on. "Honey, I am so sorry. But it's going to be all right. You'll see. You're a brilliant architect, and if Mortimer Shea doesn't have the sense to see it . . ."

Nick gently extricated himself and turned to look at her with a weary expression. There was no joy or reassurance in his voice as he corrected her. "I didn't lose the job. The client loved my plans and they'll be starting construction right away."

"Then I don't understand. Obviously something is wrong. What is it?" Amanda asked, completely stumped.

She watched as Nick silently walked over to his nightstand. He picked up a section of newspaper and turned to offer it to her. She approached him slowly, taking the newspaper out of his hand, but she didn't have to look to know what was in it. Suddenly everything became horrifically clear. He knew about Chris!

Amanda had known exactly how she was going to tell Nick. First she would give him Chris's letters, explaining what her mother had done. She would be honest about the anger and confusion she had felt and confess the doubts she had struggled with from time to time.

It would be pointless to be anything but completely honest. Nick knew her too well and would immediately know if she was holding back.

But he would also know she was telling the truth when she told him that she had never regretted marrying him. And that seeing Chris again had only confirmed what her spirit already knew. *He* was God's best for her life, in every possible way.

With that settled between them, she would then go on to tell him about meeting Chris again and the time they had spent together. She planned to be honest about the things she had felt. She would probably even tell him that for a moment she had been tempted. But she would finish by saying that the love she felt for him and their children had easily overcome her momentary wavering, and she had come home newly committed to their love and their life together.

In her head it had all played so easily. Nick was one of the most reasonable and trusting people she knew, and she had been sure that when he knew the whole story, he would understand and forgive her for any lack of judgment she may have shown.

But all her careful planning had just been blown to smithereens. The paper was folded back to show a picture of Christopher Davies and his "Mystery Lady" ducking into Carnegie Hall the day of the concert. The woman with him was unrecognizable, her face completely obscured by her hat and sunglasses. But Nick had recognized the slim figure immediately. He had been with Amanda when she bought the coat the year before in Carmel, and the hat had been one of her favorite "disguises" for years.

Amanda stared at the picture. She had forgotten all about the photographers who had surrounded them that day. And it had *never* occurred to her that a picture of Christopher Davies with some nameless woman would make it into the papers on the other side of the country. There wasn't even an accompanying article. Just the picture with a short subtitle stating that the elusive bachelor had been sighted in the company of a "Mystery Lady" on several occasions immediately following his triumphant concert at Carnegie Hall. Now her marriage was on the line because it had been a slow news day and some idiot at the newspaper had needed to fill the space!

"Nick, I am so sorry you found out this way! I can imagine how you feel. But you have to know that absolutely *nothing* happened!"

Amanda said, unconsciously crushing the paper into a ball and dropping it on the floor.

"If nothing happened, why didn't you tell me you were seeing him?" Nick asked in a carefully modulated voice. "Why didn't you mention him when we talked on the phone or at the table earlier? Certainly he was one of the 'interesting things' that happened. I kept waiting for you to bring it up . . . to say, 'You'll never believe who I ran into!' "

"I guess I felt it was something I needed to tell you in private," Amanda said quietly. "I didn't want to just drop some bomb at the dinner table in front of the kids and not be able to tell the whole story."

"Oh, so there's *more* I don't know?" Nick asked, his voice growing dangerously soft as his eyes narrowed in suspicion. "What? Have you been seeing this guy all along? Is that it? Did you two have this planned? Is that why you just *had* to get away and take this trip to New York? To be with him?"

The last words were like a slap across the face, and Amanda nearly staggered back from the blow. Anger and jealousy had transformed Nick into a stranger, for only a stranger could think her capable of such treachery and deceit. And the ugliness of what Nick was suggesting was more than Amanda could fathom.

As she looked across the few feet that separated them, she felt like she was experiencing one of those crazy special effects in the movies, when something close suddenly zooms back and appears at a great distance. And she knew if she reached out to touch him, her arms wouldn't be long enough. She only hoped the truth would be.

"I haven't seen or talked to Chris Davies since before I met you," she started, fighting to speak slowly and clearly. "I guess I knew he was going to be in New York for the concert, but I honestly didn't know the exact dates, and it never occurred to me I would see him.

"I'll admit I needed to get away for a while," Amanda continued, searching for just the right words. "And when Laura invited me to go with her, I saw it as an opportunity to put some distance between us for a few days and get a new perspective. And I did, Nick," she said, moving a step closer in an attempt to bridge the gap. "The time in New York really helped me see how blessed I am to have you and Kimberly and Casey!"

Amanda stopped to assess if her words were having any effect, but

Nick just gave her a cold look that told her so far he was unimpressed. Her husband had never had reason to doubt her faithfulness before, and she hadn't known he was even capable of this kind of anger and rigidness. Fear suddenly made it hard to breathe normally, and she had to sit back down on the edge of the bed before continuing.

"I had completely forgotten about Chris being in New York until the day he stepped out of a limousine in front of our hotel. Even then I didn't intend to contact him, and I wouldn't have if a crazy set of coincidences hadn't brought us together. Nothing was planned! And I repeat, *nothing* bad happened!"

"And *I* repeat, if nothing happened, why didn't you tell me?" Nick challenged, his Irish temper finally reaching the boiling point. "If everything was so innocent, why did you hide it from me?"

"I wasn't hiding anything!" Amanda whipped back, frustrated by the fact that he wasn't listening and beginning to lose her patience. "I *tried* to tell you the last time we talked on the phone, but *you* didn't have the time to listen, if you remember!"

"So why didn't you call me back? If I'm not mistaken, telephones work twenty-four hours a day. Don't you think it would have been worth dropping the extra dime to let your husband know that you were running all over New York with your old boyfriend?" Nick's voice dripped with sarcasm, and he had given up any attempt to keep his voice down.

"I was *not* 'running all over town' with my old boyfriend!" Amanda rasped back in an angry whisper. "I was spending time with an old friend and letting God heal old wounds so we could both get on with our lives," she continued. "And I would appreciate it if you would keep your voice down before our children hear you!"

At that, both Nick and Amanda looked toward the door. Neither of them had bothered to close it when they entered, but it was now firmly shut, proof that their fear of being overheard had been justified. Not that it would be the first time Kim and Casey had ever heard their parents fight. During the past year or so, Amanda and Nick had often found themselves in shouting matches, their frustration with the harried circumstances of their lives building up a head of steam that demanded to be released.

But this argument was different. It was not the product of being overworked or underappreciated. It had not been sparked by a thoughtless word or a broken promise to take the family to the beach on Saturday. It was born out the most basic sense of betrayal and hurt, and an answering need to be understood and trusted. This argument was about the very fabric that made up their relationship, a fabric that was already frayed around the edges and now was threatening to unravel altogether.

Nick moved to sit in the high-backed chair by the window. He covered his face with his hands, the picture of dejection. His head was swimming and his stomach felt as though he'd just done a dozen barrel rolls. Everything about the last twenty-four hours was unreal. Nothing made sense anymore. And the worst part was that during all the madness he'd discovered some terrible truths about himself.

He had known from the first time he met her that Amanda would be a "high maintenance" lady and that he was the one who had been created to take that maintenance on. In the beginning she was so broken from her relationship with Davies that he could do no more than comfort and soothe. Back then he had rated success by the number of times he got her to smile or laugh or how long he kept the haunted look out of her eyes. It was a long, tedious process of recovery, and while he sometimes worried that she'd never get over the guy, he never lost patience or even considered giving up.

The day Amanda became his wife, Nick had known all the waiting and sacrifice had been worth it. And in the nearly ten years since then, he had never doubted either the rightness of their relationship or their commitment to each other. But he realized now their relationship had never really been put to the test. Never once in all those years had Amanda given him reason to doubt her love and devotion. And now at the first sign of serious trouble, he was falling apart.

He had seen the picture purely by accident. He and Shea had gone back to the office yesterday to finish up some paper work after making a presentation to their client. His secretary, Grace, had agreed to meet them, and she was reading the newspaper at her desk when they walked in.

Nick had gone directly to his desk and begun taking out the necessary papers when he heard Grace say something about Christopher Davies. His ears automatically perked up, a Pavlovian response he had never gotten over.

"What about Christopher Davies?" he had asked casually.

"Oh, nothing. His picture's in the paper with some amazingly lucky woman, that's all. Seems the man of my dreams may be in love with another woman!" she had said, throwing the paper down in mock despair.

Nick couldn't explain why his mouth suddenly went dry or why his hand was shaking when he handed Grace the contracts to be typed. And he would never know why he felt compelled to walk across the room and pick up the paper after Grace had busied herself at the typewriter. All he knew was that the moment his eyes fell on the page his world turned upside down.

He had raced into the bathroom and vomited for the first time since he was nine years old—when he and Terry Pond had had a contest to see who could eat the most hot dogs. The difference was that then he had felt infinitely better once his stomach had been emptied of the twenty-two hot dogs he had stuffed down. But this time there was no way to vomit up the pain, hurt, and fear that sickened his soul.

Waiting for Amanda to come home had been an agony of imagined scenarios, each one worse than the other. No matter how hard he prayed for God to take away the images, every time he closed his eyes the figures in the paper came to life. He kept telling himself he was a fool to worry. He knew Amanda loved him and she would never betray his trust. But then, why hadn't she told him about Chris? Why was she sneaking around, hiding her face so as not to be recognized? If everything was innocent, why was she acting so guilty?

By the time Amanda walked through the door, Nick wasn't sure he was going to be able to look at her without exploding. That was why he chose to wait inside, hiding out of sight so he could look for any telltale differences in the way she looked or acted. But the woman who walked through the door had been his Amanda, loving and laughing and acting completely happy to be home. His heart had lurched at the sight of her, and when she turned and smiled at him, he had been flooded with relief and joy. Maybe everything was all right, and he was overreacting.

Then she had thrown her arms around him and kissed him with a desperation that had sent suspicion rippling through his mind once again, and he had spent the rest of the dinner watching her and waiting. If she mentioned being with Davies right up front, it would go a long way toward dispelling his fears about what had happened between the two of them. Yet by the end of the meal she had talked about everything else but him, and he could feel the anger and out-rage he had put on hold roiling back up to the surface. That anger had finally boiled over when he saw the look on Amanda's face as he handed her the newspaper. The bitter accusations had literally burst from his lips, surprising even him with their vehemence. He had heard others talk about being so angry they didn't know what they were saying, but this was the first time he had ever been that out of control.

Now he was sitting in the silent aftermath, his angry words hang-ing in the air like gun smoke, impossible to take back or erase. And he knew as he slowly dragged his hands away from his face to look at Amanda that their relationship would never be the same.

Amanda looked back at him, sharing his feeling of shell shock. The room that had represented such beauty and promise a few short min-utes before now felt ravaged, and a kind of numbing paralysis crept through her body, draining her of any will to fight or defend herself. What was the point? If Nick really believed she had been unfaithful simply because of a picture in the newspaper, there was nothing left to fight for!

After all, her thoughts raced on, she hadn't really done anything wrong. And after ten years of loving him and being there for him and putting her own needs and feelings second so he could have his dream . . . well, if he didn't know what kind of woman she was . . .

But you didn't tell him about the letters.

The thought came out of nowhere and gave Amanda pause. That's true, she conceded. She never had told him about the letters, but that was for his sake more than her own. She hadn't wanted to worry him or awaken old insecurities. And that was exactly why she had decided not to tell him over the phone about seeing Chris.

But Laura warned you that you should tell him.

Again the challenging thought invaded her mind, bringing back Laura's words of caution. Even her dear, overly romantic friend could see she was headed for trouble and had tried to warn her. And then the night she had struggled over whether or not to see Chris again came back in vivid detail. Something had told her to pick up the phone and call her husband, but she had refused to listen, and now she was facing the consequences.

Amanda felt an uncomfortable stirring deep in her spirit. Perhaps she wasn't guilty of being unfaithful, but there is more than one way to betray a person's trust. As she looked over at her husband's anguished face and saw the pain she had caused him, something broke inside her. Suddenly she was willing to do anything to take that pain away.

Standing up from the bed and walking across the floor to humble herself at her husband's feet was the most agonizing thing Amanda had ever done. She knelt down in front of him and looked up into eyes made of emerald ice. He wasn't going to make this easy for her, and she had to fight the urge to stand up and walk out the door, defeated before she began. But running away wasn't going to solve anything, and Amanda finally understood that while Nick had been wrong to jump to conclusions, she was the one who had put him on the ledge in the first place. Now it was up to her to start the healing process.

"I need to apologize to you," she began haltingly. "I can't say that it doesn't hurt to know you think I would destroy what we have for a meaningless fling, but I realize now I have to take responsibility for giving you any reason to doubt me in the first place. 'Be sure your sins will find you out,' my grandfather used to say. I guess I should have listened."

Amanda tried to smile, but she could feel the tears just behind her eyes and she had to fight to keep her voice strong and steady. "But if you're going to forgive me, forgive me for the many stupid sins I really committed—like being afraid to be honest with you and thinking I could safely step out of my life for a few days without doing any damage. And wanting to be eighteen again! I am guilty of all these things and more that God is still helping me understand.

"But the one thing I am not guilty of is being unfaithful to you. Was I tempted? Yes. But only for a moment and then only because I had truly forgotten who I was. As soon as I came to myself, I knew what I wanted and what was important. You and the girls and our life together! That's what I came home to tell you. That's what I need you to believe, because . . . ." Amanda searched for words as the tears started to flow. "Because you are the music of my life, the thing that makes my life worth living. I don't know what I'd do without you!"

By the time she had finished, the ice had melted and tears were freely streaming down Nick's face, also. He reached out a tentative hand and traced a tear down her cheek, and Amanda was sure he was going to take her in his arms and tell her it was going to be all right. But instead his hand dropped back into his lap, as though the effort to hold it up was just too much for him, and he turned his head to look out the window.

The streetlights were on and a cold mist was beginning to shroud everything in a wintry haze. He watched fascinated as familiar trees and bushes took on ominous shapes in the changing shadows and gathering fog. By midnight it would be impossible to see from the house to the street.

Finally Nick gave out a deep sigh and motioned that he wanted to stand. He helped Amanda up, studying her ring hand for a moment before reluctantly letting it go. Then he walked over to the fireplace, bracing himself with one hand against the mantel, as though he didn't have the strength to stand on his own. He stared into the flames a long moment before he began to speak.

"I've loved you, Amanda Rose Kelly, since the first time I saw you," he started, in a voice raw with emotion. "And I know these past few years have been difficult for you. Looking back, I realize that I let myself get too caught up in trying to make something of myself. But see, that's the way I thought I was supposed to love you . . . by making a good life for you and our children. I never thought you would hate me for it!"

"Nick, I don't hate you!" Amanda immediately protested. "I love you!"

Nick nodded sadly. "Yeah, you love me so much you needed to run away from me, to 'step out of your life,' as you put it, and see if there wasn't something better somewhere else."

"Sweetheart, don't do this to yourself," Amanda pleaded. "I wasn't running away from you. I was running away from *me*! Don't you see? The only problem is, you can't ever get away from yourself. Everywhere I went—" Amanda gave a little shrug—"there I was. And there *you* were . . . and the girls . . . because you're a part of me. The best part. And when I finally realized how foolish I was being, all I wanted to do was come home . . . to you."

Nick gave her a long, searching look. She could see how badly he wanted to believe her, but there was something still holding him back. He took a deep breath and pushed away from the mantel.

"I love you, Amanda, and I am more grateful than you'll ever know that you came home. I can't imagine my life without you."

Nick's voice broke, and he had to pause for a moment before he was able to go on.

"But I'm more confused than I've ever been in my life. I don't know who we are anymore, and I'm going to need some time to figure this whole mess out . . . to do some praying and soul-searching of my own."

He started toward the bed as he announced, "I'm going to sleep in my office tonight. We'll talk some more tomorrow."

Amanda nodded and watched as he grabbed a pillow and the comforter off the bed. He had reached the door when he stopped. Without turning he said, "I just need to ask you one more thing."

Amanda felt her pulse quicken.

"Did he kiss you? Did you hold his hand? Did you let him . . . hold you?" he asked, his voice breaking slightly at the end.

Amanda felt like a knife was cutting through her heart. It would be so easy to say no. He'd never know if she were telling the truth, and she'd never know if he really believed her. But at least it would be over.

Even as she thought it, Amanda knew she had to tell him the truth.

"Yes," she answered in a small voice.

Nick looked back at her, his eyes pools of sorrow. "Then how can you say you weren't unfaithful?"

As he walked out the door, Amanda sank to her knees, the enormity of what she'd done finally sinking in. In her heart she knew that God would help them through this, and when they came out on the other side, they would be stronger and better for it.

But for the first time she realized just how close she had come to losing it all.

Twenty-eight

Walker's Point, 1990

*T*he old house had welcomed her back with open arms, its familiar creaks and groans expressing delight as her feet hit the floorboards and bounded up the stairs. She had arrived two weeks ago, her energy bringing the rooms to immediate life as she whipped off the dust covers, flung open the windows, and began the tedious task of dusting, scrubbing, and polishing. Not a cobweb escaped her eagle eye and not an inch of wood went unpolished as the house awoke from its long winter's nap to glory once again in the summer sun.

For Amanda, opening up the old house every summer was a labor of love. Three years ago, when her grandmother passed away only two short months after her grandfather's home-going, Amanda had been overwhelmed to find out that the house in Walker's Point had been left to her. At first she had felt awkward. After all, rightfully it should have gone to her dad. But both of her parents had reassured her they were happy for her to have the house.

"In some ways, it's always belonged to you more than the rest of us," Warren Mitchell had commented. "Every summer you were the one who couldn't wait to get to the beach, helping your grandparents in the store, and even skipping your senior trip to be there. Besides, the rest of us can still come visit, can't we?" he had asked.

"You bet! Anytime!" Amanda had responded, throwing her arms around her dad to give him a big hug.

A few weeks later Amanda and Nick had driven up to Walker's Point to check out the house. It had been rented out on and off since her grandparents' move to Santa Barbara, and it was obvious that the house had suffered at the hands of strangers. At first Amanda felt sick at the run-down condition. But Nick only saw the possibilities, and they had spent much of that summer working on the house together and bringing it back to its former glory.

That was the summer Amanda had first thought about buying back the Shoppe and running it as a summer extension of Treasures of the Sierra Madre, where she was now a full partner. The current owners had moved back to New England, finding it difficult to make a profit on the seasonal business, and a dusty "For Sale" sign had been in the window for months.

By the end of the summer, the house was well on its way to recovery, and Amanda had closed a deal to buy back the Shoppe at a real bargain.

The following summer she and the girls reopened the Shoppe with a grand flourish. Everyone was happy to see a Mitchell back behind the counter, and once again local artists brought their unique offerings to Amanda to sell. She augmented these with carefully chosen gift items and the usual assortment of cards and souvenirs.

Gone were her grandfather's lovingly restored antiques, but with her buying power from Treasures, she was able to offer quality reproductions at reasonable prices. What she didn't sell she took back to Sierra Madre with her at the end of the summer. The result was a nice little profit the very first year!

Nick had come up on the weekends that first summer, usually driving up on Friday and staying until Tuesday morning. As a senior partner at Morris and Shea, he had the freedom to set his own schedule, and he had set up a studio in the attic where he'd work while Amanda and the girls were at the store.

But when the store closed at six, Nick would always be waiting to walk his girls home or catch a bite to eat. The evenings were family time, and as those who worked under him could attest, Nick Kelly was a man who had his priorities straight. God first. Family second. Work third. It was a lesson he had learned the hard way and one he never intended to forget!

Now Amanda lay in the bed of her youth, remembering how perfect that summer had been. Kimberly and Casey had actually been excited about spending the summer in Walker's Point and helping in the Shoppe. At sixteen and fourteen, they hadn't quite reached the I-don't-want-to-be-with-my-parents stage, and they had both proven to be helpful in the business.

Kimberly had inherited Amanda's artistic eye and came up with some wonderful display ideas, although her gifts ran more toward sketching and painting. And by the end of the summer several of her charcoal sketches had been displayed and sold.

Casey, on the other hand, was the marketing and sales expert in the family. Unsuspecting tourists would come in for a postcard and leave with an armful of gifts they had never intended to buy, until Casey got her hands on them.

"You simply have to help people understand how much they want something," she had explained to Kim when her older sister had asked her for her secret to success.

Amanda had even learned to wallpaper that summer! Looking now at the roses that once again bloomed on the walls of her old bedroom, she still felt pleased with herself. It was a Laura Ashley pattern, and she had pasted each strip with her own two hands, painstakingly matching each leaf and bud. It had taken her nearly a month, and she had had to reorder paper twice, but she had done it! Nick and the girls had loved to come in and tease her, saying she had more paste on her shirt than on the paper and if she wasn't careful, they'd be scraping her off the walls!

She chuckled softly at the memory, almost expecting Nick to pop his head in the door with a cup of coffee in one hand and the morning paper in the other. But nothing stirred to break the morning silence.

Amanda sighed, feeling the old, familiar ache and giving herself permission to feel the sadness one more time.

It was the November after "the summer of the wallpaper," as the girls called the summer they'd opened the Shoppe. Amanda and Laura had been working overtime at Treasures. The approaching holidays always brought a flurry of new customers as people spruced up their homes for Thanksgiving and Christmas, and Amanda was too tired to even think about cooking. Since both of the girls were gone for the evening, she called Nick and asked him to pick up Chinese on his way home from work.

"No problem," he had replied. "Mongolian beef and sweet 'n' sour okay?" he had asked, a needless exercise, since that was all they ever ordered.

"Is there any other kind?" Amanda had laughed back.

They agreed to meet at home by eight o'clock. Amanda finished up what she was doing, said good night to Laura, and walked in her front door by seven-forty-five. She quickly changed out of her work clothes and hurried to set out the dishes. She was really hungry, and the thought of the tangy sweet 'n' sour had her stomach doing flips.

Nick finally drove in at eight-fifteen.

"Sorry I'm late," he announced, giving Amanda a kiss and setting the bag of white containers on the counter as he passed through the kitchen on his way to the bedroom. "Start dishing it up, honey. I'm just going to get out of these duds and take a couple of aspirin. I've got a headache that just won't quit!"

Amanda opened the steaming containers and started filling their plates with neat piles of rice, beef, and pork. She poured them both big cups of tea from the pot she had brewed while waiting for Nick to get home, then set everything on the kitchen table. After a few minutes, when Nick hadn't come to join her, Amanda called to him, but there was no reply. She started to feel irritated. Why had he told her to dish it up if he wasn't coming right back?

She got up and started down the hall to their room. The bedroom door was open slightly, casting a thin wedge of light across the carpet and onto the wall.

"Nick?" Amanda called. "Are you coming, sweetheart? The food's getting cold." She reached the door and pushed it open. "What in the world are you doing?" she asked, walking into the room.

Nick was lying on the bed, still in his shirt and tie, one shoe on and one shoe off, sound asleep. Amanda almost turned around and tiptoed out. If he was this tired, she'd just let him sleep!

It was the shoe that stopped her. It bothered her that he had only removed one, so she went to take the other one off and cover him with a blanket. As she picked up his foot, she immediately sensed something was wrong. Her eyes went to his face, so relaxed and peaceful . . . too peaceful. All the lines of tension were erased and he looked young again.

She put her hand on his chest, waiting to feel the gentle rise and fall of his breathing. Then she began to shake him, softly at first, then with greater and greater urgency as she called out his name.

When she realized he wasn't going to wake up, she raced to the phone to dial 9–1–1. Her hand was shaking so violently it took several tries before she managed to hit the right numbers. But her voice was surprisingly calm as she gave the operator her address.

It wasn't until she called her father and heard his familiar voice that she lost control. Her hysterical sobbing made it hard for him to understand what she was saying, but no words were necessary for him to know that she needed him.

"Stay right there, baby. Mom and I are on our way!"

She put the phone down and turned back reluctantly toward the bed. The physical reality of death had always frightened her, and a part of her wanted to rush out of the room, away from the lifeless body. But that was Nick lying there . . . her Nick . . . and suddenly she didn't want him to be alone.

She walked back to the bed and took him in her arms, rocking him gently and telling him how much she loved him, until the paramedics arrived and said it was time to let him go.

The memory brought tears to her eyes, but she quickly shook them off. It had been a year and a half since Nick had gone to be with the Lord, and Amanda had done a good job of grieving and moving on.

It was being back in the old house, surrounded by so many happy and tender memories that made her so emotional. Everyone who had ever meant anything to her had been in this house. Grandpa, Grams, her parents . . . Lindsey, Nate, and Stacy. And of course, the two men she had loved. All had been here. Their voices still echoed in the walls.

Amanda got up and slipped on her robe. It was only nine o'clock on this bright Sunday morning. She would pour herself a cup of coffee and sit out on the back porch for a while. Church didn't start until eleven, and she still had time before she had to get ready. Then she would spend the afternoon walking on the beach.

The Shoppe remained closed on Sundays. It was one of the rules she and Nick had established years ago. Sundays were for the Lord and the family. It was a rule she intended to stick to, even though it would be weeks before either Kim or Casey came to join her.

She followed her nose down the stairs and into the kitchen, grateful for coffeepots with timers. She filled her mug and added a touch of milk and a pinch of sweetener. She had finally managed to join the rest of the modern world and switch to Sweet 'n Low.

The morning sun was unusually bright, promising an early beginning to a hot summer season. The garden was as chaotic as ever, having taken its own course since the years when her grandmother had so lovingly kept it in line. But Amanda liked it this way. As long as the weeds were still outnumbered by the flowers, she was happy.

She closed her eyes and let the sun warm her face. Early morning was the only time she exposed her face to the damaging rays. Now that she was forty, the sun was no longer her friend, and she was careful to wear sunscreen and shade her face. But that was the only concession she was willing to make. She still looked forward to lazy days lying in the sun, and as soon as the Shoppe was up and running and she'd trained her part-time help, she would schedule "serious beach time" for herself.

She smiled as she remembered how Stacy used to use that expression. Her thoughts made a natural progression from wondering how her friend was doing to memories of the last summer they had spent together. Frozen moments in time flickered through her mind like flash cards, and she found herself thinking about Chris for the first time in many years.

"Penny for your thoughts."

Amanda felt her smile broaden at the remembered words. It was amazing how real a memory could become when the setting was just right. She could swear she'd actually heard his voice!

Reluctantly she opened her eyes. The birds and the bees and the butterflies were still her only company. For a brief, absurd moment she was disappointed. Then she stood up, shook off the memories, and went back into the house. If she didn't get dressed soon, she'd be late for church.

Amanda took one last glance in the mirror to check her hair and makeup before racing down the stairs to look for her car keys. Somehow, even with all the time she had given herself, she was running late, and now she wouldn't have the time to walk the ten blocks to the white-steepled church.

The keys weren't on the key ring, where she was sure she had left them. Nor were they on the hall table or in the dish on the sink. Ten minutes later, she still hadn't found them.

"One of the first things I'm going to ask you, Lord, when I get to heaven is where do all the missing keys and socks go?" Amanda lamented, certain that the keys had grown legs and walked away.

Conceding defeat, she decided to walk, even though she would barely get there in time for the sermon. She picked up her Bible and hurried out the front door, using the spare key hidden in a flower pot to lock it. She returned the key and started down the walk.

He was standing at the gate as though he was waiting for her.

"Good thing I'm a trustworthy sort," he teased, giving her his familiar cocky smile. "Now that I know where you hide your key, that is."

Twenty-nine

Amanda couldn't believe her eyes. She blinked several times to make sure she wasn't just imagining Chris standing at the gate, but every time she opened her eyes, he was still there. She walked down the walk, feeling her heart start to pound as she kept telling herself this was impossible. He simply couldn't be here!

"What in the world are you doing here?" she asked, her amazement written all over her face. "I can't believe this! I was just thinking about you this morning, and here you are!" she said as she reached the gate and stopped to look at him.

"You were thinkin' about me?" he immediately picked up, looking pleased.

"About you and Stacy and Ben and that whole incredible summer!" Amanda stammered, excitement running her words together. "I was sitting out on the back porch, and I thought I heard your voice, clear as day. But of course, you weren't there. And now I come out of my house and here you are! I mean . . ." Amanda took a deep breath to slow herself down. "What are you doing here?"

"I wanted to see you," he answered simply.

"But how did you know I was here?"

"Your mother told me," Chris said, enjoying the surprised look on her face.

"*My* mother? Karen Lorraine Mitchell told you where to find me? Next you'll be telling me Elvis is alive and there really is a Santa Claus!" she said, shaking her head in disbelief.

"Actually, your mom and I had a nice long talk. She's not half bad, when you get to know her."

Amanda couldn't help raising an eyebrow at that one.

"No, really," Chris laughed. "She's a great lady, and after we talked awhile, she volunteered that you were up here for the summer. I didn't even have to ask her. I guess she felt she owed me one," he added, letting Amanda know they had talked about the letters.

They both fell silent, taking a moment to just look at each other. Then Chris realized he was keeping her.

"I'm sorry. You were on your way to church, weren't you? And now I've made you late."

"You didn't make me late," Amanda corrected. "It was those silly keys!"

"What?" he asked, thinking he hadn't heard right.

"Never mind. Why don't you come in while I change, and then we can really talk."

Amanda went upstairs while Chris went into the kitchen and made fresh coffee. While he waited for her, he roamed around the familiar rooms, surprised at how comfortable he felt. He studied the family pictures on the mantel. There was one of Nick taken shortly before he died. His arm was around Amanda, and they were both laughing at something off-camera. Nick looked like a man who knew how to live life well, and Chris found himself wishing he had had a chance to know him.

The pictures of Kimberly and Casey really threw him. Both of the girls were knockouts but in entirely different ways. Casey, who was now sixteen by his calculations, was a mischievous pixie, her red hair and brilliant green eyes promising to give you a run for your money. And Chris was sure that with her feminine curves and pretty face, many young men would be taking her up on the challenge.

But it was Kim who took his breath away. Except for her strawberry blond hair, she *was* Amanda at eighteen, from the dreamy expression in her eyes to the slight pout of her lips. He could tell she was tall and graceful like her mother, and he would have bet a million dollars that when she spoke, she even sounded like her.

By the time Amanda came back down, Nick had finished his reconnaissance and was waiting on the back porch with two mugs of coffee. She sat down on the swing next to him and took hers gratefully, taking a big swallow.

"Ugh, sugar," she said, grimacing before she could stop herself.

"Did I fix it wrong?" Chris asked, worried. "Milk and two sugars, right?"

Amanda started to tell him she no longer took sugar, then relaxed and took another sip instead.

"It's absolutely perfect," she said, smiling at him.

The two sat enjoying the morning, feeling no need to talk until they had something to say. Amanda's eyes kept retracing his features. At forty-four he was still trim and gorgeous. In fact, he had changed remarkably little since the last time she'd seen him. And yet there was something different about him, something about the expression in his eyes or the set of his mouth. Amanda couldn't quite put her finger on it.

"You cut your hair!" they both exclaimed at the exact same time, pointing at each other's shortened do's. They burst out laughing at the unexpected duet, and Amanda self-consciously ran her fingers through her new wedge cut.

The girls had talked her into trying it six months ago, about the same time she had climbed out of her bed of mourning and decided to live again. Casey had said it made her look younger, and Kimberly had insisted Nick would have liked it, both strong recommendations. Amanda had felt very confident about the change until this moment.

"You don't like it?" she now asked Chris, trying to hide how much his opinion mattered.

"No, I don't, as a matter of fact," he said, looking seriously miffed. "It makes you look about twenty . . . a breathtakingly beautiful twenty . . . and you know how I feel about datin' younger women!"

Amanda looked nonplussed for a moment, then laughed, blushing at the compliment.

"And what about you?" she countered, referring to his new shorter style. The hair barely touched his collar in the back, and the top and sides were neatly trimmed. It still wasn't Wall Street, but it was a far cry from the wild look of his rocker days.

"Well, we've all got to grow up sometime. You can't just keep on thinkin' you can go on forever."

"Some try," Amanda said, thinking he was talking about his declining career. "Look at Rod Stewart and the Rolling Stones."

"I rest my case," he said dryly, making Amanda giggle again.

They talked for hours, touching on all the important areas of their lives. Amanda was telling Chris about her girls when he asked why they weren't there with her.

"Well, Casey's in summer school. She's determined to graduate from high school early, so for the last two summers she's been taking college classes to get ahead. Looks like she's going to do it, too," Amanda beamed, her pride evident. "When classes are over she'll come here for the rest of the summer. And Kim will come for a few weeks when she gets back from her senior trip. She and four other girls are touring the British Isles."

"Hard to believe she's the same age you were when I met you," Chris commented. "Where did the time go?"

"It goes fast when you're raising kids," Amanda agreed. "Life goes fast."

Chris knew she was thinking about Nick. He reached out to touch her hand.

"I was terribly sorry when I heard about Nick. I wish I had been here for you, but I was in Europe at the time and didn't find out until after I got back. By then it had been six months, and it seemed a little late to send condolences. Can you tell me what happened?"

"It was a stroke. Very quick. Very unexpected. He was in perfect health, strong and active. He just came home one day, lay down on our bed, and went to sleep . . . as simple as that."

Amanda felt her lower lip begin to tremble, and she immediately sucked it in and began to chew. She had just relived those terrible moments earlier this morning, and the memory was very fresh.

Chris put a comforting arm around her and commented, "He was so young."

"He'd just turned forty. I'd given him a birthday party, and friends came from all over the country. People really loved Nick, and that night he got to see how much. I'll always be grateful for that."

"And are you doin' all right?" Chris asked.

"It was hard at first. I guess I felt like God blinked." She looked at Chris, knowing she didn't have to say any more for him to understand her enormous hurt and sense of loss. "But I'm past that now," she went on with a brave smile. "Now I just miss him."

They sat for a few moments in comfortable silence, then Chris slapped his leg. "Listen, I'm starvin'. How about we go to May's for a bite?"

"It isn't May's anymore," Amanda said, breaking the news gently. She remembered how devastated she had been when she'd arrived three summers ago and seen the new name on the restaurant. "Now it's the Village Cafe. But it's still good, and food sounds great!"

❧ ❧ ❧ ❧

After their late lunch, Chris and Amanda walked around town. Amanda took him by the Shoppe and proudly showed him its new updated appearance.

"It looks like you're really goin' for it," Chris commented, seeing her sign offering decorator services and the expanded line of linens and bath items.

"My dream is to live here year-round someday. But I have to figure out a way to make this place profitable twelve months a year to do it."

They walked by the theater, now shuttered and dark. It had been closed for more than five years, and it was sad to see its once bright facade falling into disrepair.

"Do you know what happened to Mack and Ana?" Chris asked, staring bleakly at the empty marquee. "We quit exchanging Christmas cards years ago."

"They retired after their twenty-fifth season. They'd done every decent musical at least twice and they were ready for a change! So they sold it to some young fool who tried to produce 'meaningful' original plays, half of which weren't fit for children and most of which left the audience coming out of the theater trying to figure out what they'd just seen! Still, he lasted two or three seasons . . . longer than any of us thought he would! Since then, nobody's wanted to bother with the old girl."

When they hit the beach they both stopped to appreciate the spectacular view. The sun was beginning its downward trek, and the water sparkled in its slanted rays. The sand was just beginning to get that pearly glow, and the air was like a rich dessert, full of the many smells of the sea.

As they stood there, Amanda could no longer hold back her curiosity. "Why'd you really come here, Chris? Why did you want to see me now?"

Chris looked over at her. She was looking out to sea. The afternoon breeze blew her hair back off of her forehead, revealing her distinctive profile. He could see the light crow's-feet at the corner of her eye and the deepened crease at the side of her mouth. Her neck was no longer smooth, and there was a looseness to the skin under her chin he'd never seen before. He saw all the changes, the signs of her passage from young to middle-aged, and he thought she'd never looked more beautiful.

"I guess I was hoping it might be baseball season."

A slow smile spread over Amanda's face, even as a painful pang hit her heart. She turned to look at him. Of course he would think this was the way it should go. Now that she was free, there was no reason they couldn't at least explore the possibilities.

But the reality was that what had made their relationship impossible twenty years ago still hadn't changed. Much as her pounding heart told her she still cared for him, she understood today better than ever how important it was to share her life with someone who shared her faith.

Without their common faith and desire to live their lives obediently before God, she and Nick would never have made it through the painful days that followed New York. There were times, as they struggled to deal with the real issues that threatened to destroy their marriage, when their love for God had been the only thing keeping them together—for surely they had felt none for each other!

But God had been faithful! It took over a year for them to slowly climb back up onto solid emotional ground, but when they did, they discovered a new depth of love and friendship and respect for each other that had made the last six years of their marriage happier and more fulfilling than Amanda ever dreamed it could be. Looking at Chris now, Amanda felt the old familiar tugs. For some unfathomable reason, she had a love for this man that seemed destined never to be realized, because no matter how much she cared for him, she could never consider a serious relationship with someone who didn't have a serious relationship with her Lord.

Chris saw the pained look in her eyes and knew she was trying to find a way to let him down gently. He grabbed her hand and said, "Before you say anything, walk with me." It wasn't a request, it was an order, and as Amanda felt herself being pulled toward the rocks, she smiled, happy to put off the inevitable as long as possible.

When they reached the foot of the cliffs leading to their beach, Amanda pulled back.

"I haven't climbed these rocks in years," she protested. "The last time I tried was with Casey, and I nearly didn't make it!"

Chris had already jumped up to the first level, and now he turned to offer her a hand up. "You're safe with me, Amanda Rose. I won't let you fall."

She smiled as old memories came flooding back, and Amanda took his hand, suddenly feeling young again.

They made the climb with amazing ease, reaching the spot where they had met without a problem. They stopped to look down. There was the beach, its half-moon of white sand as deserted and pristine as ever, still guarded by the bony fingers of rock and coral.

"It never changes, does it?" Amanda said. "Time passes, we grow older, our lives take all kinds of twists and turns. But every time I come back, there it is, exactly the same."

"But it has changed," Chris responded. "It's changin' right now, even as we watch. It's just you have to look real close and know what you're lookin' for to see it."

Amanda looked at him, her curiosity piqued. He was trying to tell her something, but she didn't have the faintest idea what.

"Come on. Let's sit for a few minutes. I hear this is the best place to catch a sunset."

Amanda let Chris lift her up on the ledge, but before he joined her, she was surprised to see him reach behind some rocks and pull out a guitar.

"Now, I know you didn't leave that here the last time we were here together!" she laughed.

"No, ma'am," he replied sheepishly. "I left it up here this morning, before I went to your house. Thought maybe it would come in handy . . . if I could get you here," he said, showing his uncertainty for the first time.

Amanda couldn't help feeling flattered, and she gave his arm a squeeze. "One thing's for sure, Chris Davies. You know how to make a woman feel special. So what are you going to play for me?"

Chris began strumming the guitar softly.

"I've been working on my concerto again," he explained. "After Carnegie Hall I put it away for a while. Didn't feel like I had anything more to say, you know? But life goes on and things happen. Big things. Important things. And I finally felt I had something worthwhile to add to it. Sort of a new ending, if you will. And since you've been a very important part of this journey I call my life, I wanted you to be the first to hear it and tell me what you think."

Amanda listened with rapt attention as Chris began playing in earnest. The melody immediately captured her, lifting her spirit on wings of sweet joy and hope. It was different than anything Chris had ever written before. There was a spiritual quality that touched her soul as well as her spirit, and she found herself weeping, not with sorrow, but with joy.

Then Chris started to sing. The melody was still his own, but the words were as old as time.

Amazing grace, how sweet the sound,
That saved a wretch like me!
I once was lost, but now am found,
Was blind, but now I see.

When the last chord had faded out, Amanda could do nothing but look at him, tears of joy streaming down her face. She felt frozen as she watched him set the guitar back down. When he turned to look at her, she understood why she had thought he looked different earlier that day. His eyes had a new brightness and his mouth was relaxed, ready to smile. Gone was the tortured, angry look of the fighter he had been. Christopher Brian Davies had finally made his peace with God and in the process had discovered what it really meant to be loved.

"Well, what do you think?" he asked, feeling like his whole life was hanging in the balance.

"I think we have a lot of talking to do," she smiled back, her tears still flowing freely. "And I think we have all the time in the world to do it!"

He ran his finger down her cheek, aching to take her in his arms and never let go. But he knew she was right. They would take it slow and easy and let God have His way. Amanda had been right all along. God did have a plan, and Chris felt confident that *this* time he was part of it!

As if reading each other's minds, the two settled back against the rocks to watch the sunset. The sun blazed its way toward the water like an orange banner declaring God's faithfulness, and the waves crashed in celebration on the rocks below. Sea gulls danced and